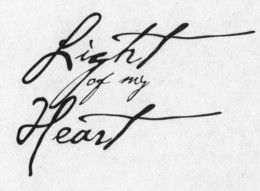

Light
of my
Heart

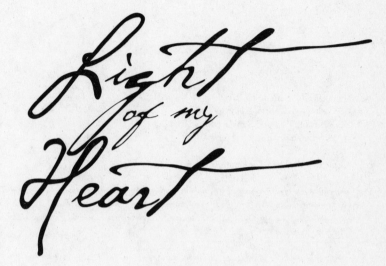

Ginny Aiken

Fleming H. Revell
A Division of Baker Book House Co
Grand Rapids, Michigan 49516

Published by Fleming H. Revell
a division of Baker Book House Company
P.O. Box 6287, Grand Rapids, MI 49516-6287
www.bakerbooks.com

Printed in the United States of America

Library of Congress Cataloging-in-Publication Data
Aiken, Ginny.
    Light of my heart / Ginny Aiken.
        p.   cm. — (Silver Hills trilogy)
    ISBN 0-8007-5874-9
    1. Women physicians—Fiction. 2. Newspaper publishing—Fiction. 3. Colorado—Fiction. 4. Orphans—Fiction. I. Title.
    PS3551.I339L54 2004
    813'.54—dc22   2003018409

Scripture is taken from the King James Version of the Bible.

Verily I say unto you, Inasmuch as ye have done it unto one of the least of these my brethren, ye have done it unto me.

Matthew 25:40

Prologue

The creaking floorboards on the front porch announced a corpulent visitor.

"Dr. Morgan! Dr. Morgan, lass. Come quick!"

Letitia Morgan opened the door and found Mrs. MacDoughal, Mr. and Mrs. Arnold Forrest's cook, huffing steamy gasps into the late November air.

The matron patted her chest as she tried to catch her breath. "Lassie, it's bad, it is. Mrs. Forrest and her unborn bairn dinna fare well."

Letty flung a wool cape over her shoulders, hefted her medical bag, and turned off the lamps. "Let's not waste time. I'm ready."

At the Forrest home, Mrs. MacDoughal puffed up the front steps. "Mrs. Andrews," she called just inside the door. "Dr. Morgan is here." To Letty she whispered, "Mrs. Andrews is Mrs. Forrest's eldest sister, she is."

Heavy footsteps descended the stairs. "What is *that* woman doing in my house?" bellowed Mr. Forrest. "I said to fetch a midwife, and a midwife I shall have!"

Dear Lord Jesus, please, not another one. His wife and child could die. They needed her. Tipping her chin, Letty said, "Mr. Forrest, your cook tells me your wife is struggling. I'm a doctor. Please let me help."

If anything, Letty's plea brought more red into the man's florid features. "Doctor? Bah! No self-respecting woman calls herself a doctor or plays at being a man. Get out. My wife doesn't need you. I won't have you corrupting my family."

"Will you let your wife labor until she bleeds to death, taking the baby to the grave with her? Set your opinions aside, sir. I can help."

Mr. Forrest turned and began ascending the stairs.

Desperation stung Letty. "For their sake, *do* something. Call another physician—a man if you oppose a woman doctor. Don't let your pride endanger Mrs. Forrest."

He spun around and glared. "Young lady, my wife wouldn't want a man to see her in childbirth. We do not tolerate such immorality." With a wave, he again dismissed her, then said to Mrs. MacDoughal, "Call the midwife."

"Aye, sir." The cook nodded but also clasped Letty's shoulder.

With tears in her eyes, Letty left the Forrest home. Perhaps the midwife would turn the child in time to save its life. Perhaps she would wash her hands before touching Mrs. Forrest. Perhaps she would stanch the flow of blood soon enough.

Perhaps.

Letty shivered all the way home. She wondered whether to blame her tremors on the frigid Philadelphia winter or on her fear for Mrs. Forrest and the unborn child. For the past six months, making the most of her modest inheritance, she had struggled to make her clinic succeed. Her only patients were street urchins, children of immigrant families with resources even more meager than hers. The end of her funds lay right around the corner.

A lone carriage sped down the street, heading west toward the sun as the mauve light of dusk faded into sad, frosty gray.

A lamplighter, finished with his nightly duty, ambled down the opposite sidewalk.

With another shiver, Letty ran up her snow-dusted front steps and stumbled over a bundle of humanity seeking refuge on her porch. Another child in need.

"Doc . . . Dr. Morgan . . ."

The boy was so weak Letty realized she would have to carry him inside. Praying none of his wounds was serious, she wrestled the key into the lock and picked him up.

As she settled her patient on the examining table, she murmured words of comfort. She made sure the boy wouldn't thrash himself off the slender platform, then went around the room and lit the kerosene lamps.

When she returned to her patient's side, she couldn't hold back a gasp of horror. The boy's battered features made it hard to see much beyond swollen eyelids, bloodied nose, and cut lips. The way he hugged his ribs suggested fractures.

Letty cleansed the wounds with a Calendula Mother Tincture lotion. Mercifully, the child lost consciousness as she bound his ribs.

Later she faced facts. She couldn't keep him here. Since her office took up most of her home, she could only offer shelter for a short time. Still, her conscience wouldn't let her send him back to the life that had brought him to the clinic in the first place. What should she do with him?

Letty watched over her patient through the long night, changing his dressings and dosing him with the proper remedies to hasten healing. The morning brought no improvement, but since she had no other demand on her time, she focused on the poor mite.

That night, he woke up for brief moments, and she took the opportunity to feed him a bit of rich broth before he slept again. The pattern continued for yet another day, and finally, that next evening, the youngster stayed awake long enough for her to glean details of his accident.

"What happened?" she asked.

Young Patrick O'Toole's angular chin tipped up with pride. "T'weren't nothing wrong, it weren't."

"I didn't think you'd done anything wrong," she murmured, smoothing the black, glossy curls from his forehead. "I just want to know how you were hurt."

Sky blue eyes studied her. He shrugged. "I work for my keep," he said. "I . . . help the fine gents wi' the horses they leave on the streets while they do fancy business, I do. Someone's got to watch 'em, don't'cha think?"

She nodded, her stomach knotting at the picture the lad drew. She didn't comment, however, letting him tell his tale.

"This red devil of a beast got the best of me, he did," Patrick continued. "I was arrangin' for a job wi' his owner, and the demon spooked. Took 'is partner wi' him, prancin' and rearin' and knockin' me down. Lost me pennies, too, I did."

Letty shuddered. He'd actually come through the event in surprisingly good shape. A ten-year-old boy's frame was no match for a horse's hooves.

Her determination strengthened. Patrick O'Toole's days on the streets of Philadelphia had ended. She would make sure of that.

After much coaxing, he agreed to speak with a deaconess from Letty's church. After Sunday's service, she brought the grand-motherly woman to the clinic and made the introductions.

"Mrs. Woolsey is especially fond of smart, enterprising young men," she said, noting with satisfaction the compassion on the older woman's face.

"I most certainly am," the deaconess said, "and I've an empty room at home that needs an occupant."

Patrick narrowed his eyes but didn't speak.

"And Mr. Woolsey's stables are in a shambles," the older

woman added. "We would be much obliged if you'd agree to work for us as soon as you're well enough."

Patrick gaped. "You . . . you really mean that?"

Mrs. Woolsey laid a gentle hand on his shoulder. "I most certainly do. We miss our son now that he has a family of his own, and that perfectly good room needs a growing lad." A sage smile curved her lips. "I'm also known as a fair cook, and you look as though you might appreciate my efforts. Chocolate cakes are my specialty."

A look of longing warmed the blue eyes, but the pride Letty had earlier noted tipped Patrick's chin. "I'm a man of my word, I am," he said, "an' I'm hopin' you are, too. I won't be takin' no charity, I won't, so that stable job had best be real."

Letty averted her face to conceal her smile.

"The Lord Jesus is my constant witness," Mrs. Woolsey replied. "I won't dishonor Him with untruths. We need your help and want your company. We've a great deal of love to share. Please come home with me."

At her plea, tears welled in Patrick's eyes and his bravado melted. The gentle lady took one final look at the child and gathered him into her plump embrace.

Letty thanked the Lord for the excellent resolution to her patient's dilemma, but her own dilemma didn't show signs of resolving anytime soon. She still had no patients.

Despite that lack, Letty clung to the feelings of goodwill the unfolding holiday season ushered in. At least she did until the creaking of her front steps and the huffing on the porch broadcast Mrs. MacDoughal's return four days after Letty's failed visit to the Forrest home.

Swathed in black bombazine, the cook wore a veiled hat on her graying copper curls. Through the fine black net, Letty saw swollen and tear-washed eyes. The worst had happened.

"Both?"

"Aye, lass, both."

Around the knot in her throat, Letty said, "I'll only be a moment." As she changed into proper clothing, tears of rage scalded her eyes, but she dismissed them as futile and hurried back to Mrs. McDoughal. "Shall we go?"

❦

Heavyhearted, Letty entered the Forrest home. She doffed her cape and handed it to the maid by the door. In the stifling, flower-scented parlor, she waited her turn to express sympathy. "I'm so sorry, Mrs. Andrews," she murmured to the sister, then turned to the widower. As she extended her hand, the outrage on his face froze her in place.

"You!" he roared. "How dare you set foot in my home? I sent you packing once already, and I still don't hold with your notions. A woman is a woman. If God had meant women to doctor, he would have made them men."

Letty cringed at the venom in his voice. She tried offering condolences, but he raged on.

"Indecent, a woman doctoring. What's wrong, spinster? Can't find a man to make you a proper lady? Mrs. Forrest was a lady. You should try being more like her."

Letty bit her tongue. The man who had turned Mrs. Forrest into such a "proper lady" had probably hastened her death. Turning away, she caught sight of two tots with red-rimmed eyes, huddled in the corner of a navy velvet settee. Had their father been less obstinate, they might have been spared their loss.

Knowing she could do no more, Letty left. That night, the faces of the Forrest children haunted her sleep.

Then came morning. Another quiet morning that stretched into another quiet afternoon. Some might have taken the inactivity in stride, others might have quit, but Letty couldn't do either. She refused to give up, even faced with her dismal situation, even when her optimism threatened to wilt.

"Since I'm not likely to have any patients today," she muttered, noting how talking to herself had become a habit, "perhaps I can help at the college."

Wearing her cape against the bitter winds and snow, Letty left a message on the door. Not that she expected any patients.

A few blocks later, she shed her glum thoughts and ascended the steps to the massive wooden doors of the brick bastion that was the Homeopathic Medical College of Philadelphia. Inside, she hung her cape to drip rivulets on the damp floor. She hoped that she would find someone in the office, that someone somewhere might put her training to good use, but when she opened the door, she found the room deserted. At the desk, however, partly covering an open volume of Hahnemann's *Materia Medica Pura,* was a letter addressed to the college. Unable to squelch her curiosity, Letty tilted her head until she could read the missive.

```
Gentlemen,

It is with great urgency that I entreat you
to notify your graduates and associates of
our situation. Hartville, Colorado, has
seen inordinate growth since the Heart of
Silver Mine began to produce. Due to the
boom, we need a physician, preferably a woman
experienced in the care of ladies and children
as well as in general medical practice. We
must avoid further loss of life.

Please inform qualified candidates that yours
truly will locate a home and office, and will
endeavor to ease the move to our town. I await
your prompt response, as our need is dire.

Sincerely,

Eric K. Wagner, Esq.
```

Letty could hardly believe her eyes. She darted a guilty glance down the hall. Finding it empty, she allowed temptation the upper hand. She folded Mr. Wagner's letter into a tiny square and tucked it into her skirt pocket. Donning her cape, she left the medical college at a near run.

Hartville, Colorado, had found its doctor.

1

Letty extracted the pilfered and by now much-read letter from the satchel at her feet. Each time she looked at the creased page, a pang of guilt crossed her conscience. Each time it did, she lay the burden at the foot of the cross, having sought the Lord's forgiveness even as she'd taken the missive. Mr. Wagner *had* requested a qualified physician experienced with women and children, and he was getting just that.

The memory of Arnold Forrest's disdain led Letty to believe that only a perceptive man would understand a woman's medical needs. A man who would seek a woman's doctor from halfway across the country had probably married a wise, strong woman. Letty looked forward to befriending the fortunate lady.

She sighed. Resignation was necessary in her case, but hardly enjoyable. Yes, she was a spinster, twenty-five years old and a doctor at that, so her prospects for marriage were few indeed. Most of the time she could suppress any traces of longing, but this endless train ride provided ample opportunity to ponder most any subject.

Even Mrs. Agatha Tilford's conversation occupied only a fragment of Letty's attention. Having regaled her with Hartville gossip ever since Pittsburgh, the lady caught naps only occasionally. Letty welcomed each rare respite.

She couldn't wait for her first glimpse of the town, especially since they were close now. Leaving Philadelphia had been easier than she had expected. Her dismal situation at the clinic had offered strong inducement. And she had no family left since Mother's death a year ago and few acquaintances to bid farewell.

Besides, most of the Morgan family's friends had agreed with Mother about Letty's chosen profession. Scraps of past conversations came to mind.

"Your actions set you beyond what society deems proper, Letitia."

"But, Mother, I want to heal the hurting and care for those who suffer."

"Think of my suffering, Letitia. I cannot hold my head up among our friends. My daughter, training to become a doctor. A real lady would never do something so unfeminine."

Staring at the motion-blurred landscape through her window, Letty tried to block the image of a dear face, but nothing stopped the memories or the residual sadness. Marcus Roberts.

Dear Marcus. It would have been lovely had their budding feelings grown to full bloom, but Mother's dismissive wave the day Letty confided Marcus's interest still cut deeply.

"A gentleman in Mr. Roberts's position would never consider you for marriage," she'd said. "Had you excelled in womanly arts instead of pursuing your father's profession, then perhaps you might aspire to that honor. He can't possibly be serious."

Letty's eyes stung, and as usual, she fought the tears. This was the last time she would let herself think of Marcus and what might have been. He belonged in the past, in Philadelphia with his bride of four months. Her future lay in Hartville, Colorado.

She focused on that future. Each turn of the train's wheels soothed her pain as she saw the nation out her window. After a while, she closed her eyes, letting her mind go blank. When she reopened them, it was to peer out with equal measures of excitement and trepidation. Mountains reached toward heaven, covered in a blanket of white. The sun, burning sharply in a blue, blue sky, caught the lacy patterns of mounded snowflakes and turned them into prisms. Tiny rainbows seemed to hover wherever her eyes roamed.

If she had to relinquish her dreams of a man, a home, and children to fill her arms, at least she would do so where winter looked appealing. The landscape outside replaced her memories of Philadelphia's dingy street slush, and Letty knew she would forever picture winter as this pristine scene on the way into Hartville.

She soon caught sight of a cabin up ahead. The sturdy structure perched proudly on the foothill, a plume of smoke announcing that welcome and warmth would be found inside.

A short span beyond that first house, Letty saw another. Then another. Clusters of buildings soon peppered the snowy valley.

The blast of the train whistle announced their approach to Hartville. A ripple of anticipation and a wobble of wariness worked their way up Letty's spine. She reached for her satchel, not to reclaim the letter, but to embark upon her new life. A life she hoped would be eased by Mr. Wagner's assistance. And she mustn't forget his wife. That lady could provide mountains of information and support. Letty hoped she had accompanied Mr. Wagner to the station.

The train whistle shrieked again, and the wheels grabbed the track. The braking train pulled against her, dragging her deeper into the lumpy upholstery. As they slowed, her compartment rolled closer to the station platform.

Two men stood there. *Pity,* she thought, *Mrs. Wagner hasn't come. We will have to meet another day.*

One of the two men appeared quite old, round-shouldered and slender. She'd heard enough about Mr. Tilford from his wife to identify him at first glance, and to know she preferred to avoid meeting him today.

The train chugged in slower now, and Letty got her first clear look at the other man. Since he held his black hat, his wavy hair caught the sun and shone gold. His eyes, deep and dark, matched the shade of her favorite chocolate bonbons, while a blade of a nose ridged his face above a well-trimmed mustache. His square jaw suggested an uncompromising nature. Surely this wasn't Mr. Wagner. This man was far younger than she'd envisioned her sponsor.

"Oh, honestly," she muttered under her breath. "It doesn't matter whether that man is or isn't Mr. Wagner. What does matter is finding your luggage and starting your new life." Firming her shoulders, satchel in hand, she joined Mrs. Tilford in the aisle.

༄

Eric waited on the platform, numbed by the drone of Hubert Tilford's advice. The man expounded on every topic known to mankind. Unfortunately for his listeners, he knew almost nothing about nearly everything. Well, that wasn't quite right, either. Tilford displayed true genius in the sawmill business. At the moment, however, Eric lacked the patience to learn the merits of sawdust, much less to listen to directives on how he should run his newspaper.

He had to locate the new doctor. It was ironic that he had finally lured a physician, a woman yet, to practice medicine in his town too late to do him any good.

The past two years had blunted his pain. He had turned regret and failure into action; he had found a lady doctor for Hartville. Still, no number of good deeds could atone for his sins.

Eric didn't have time for bitter memories just then. He had to find Dr. Letitia Morgan, homeopathic physician. Because of the daunting title, Eric expected a middle-aged spinster, large enough, tough enough, and experienced enough to handle any eventuality. He pictured her with steel-gray hair coiled in a tight knot, spectacles riding the bridge of a pragmatic nose, a severe black suit encasing her stout body.

Hartville needed a most competent woman. Someone who would scare everyone back to health.

The train ground to a stop. Passengers left the cars. The conductor barked instructions to a pair of burly youths who began unloading luggage. Two black leather trunks labeled with the doctor's name and Eric's address thudded onto the platform at his feet. Two trunks—not much for a person setting up medical practice. Surely a physician needed supplies, a certain quantity of the medications she might prescribe. Could those two unremarkable cases hold it all?

Then he had his answer. Box upon crate joined the trunks in rapid succession, filling the platform. Mr. Tilford edged closer as the cargo threatened his presence on the structure. When the mountain grew no more, Eric counted thirteen pieces.

As he looked for the woman responsible for the abundance of baggage, Mrs. Tilford stepped down from the train. A tiny woman in a gray woolen ulster followed. Beneath a trim, gray hat, brown curls bounced on her forehead.

Then she looked up.

Her dove-gray gaze met his and reached deep. He stared—he couldn't help himself. A random thought came to him: *This woman is strong enough to heal all that ails Hartville.*

Pity medicine can't heal your tattered heart, his conscience taunted.

Eric spat a German word for which his mother had once scrubbed his mouth with soap, scolding him in the family's native tongue. He then rammed his hat on his head. Perhaps it would keep his thoughts from straying.

The train whistled again, startling the gray-eyed lady as it pulled out. He approached and extended his hand. "Dr. Morgan?"

She tilted her head. "Mr. Wagner?"

"At your service." A shiver sped through Eric when their hands touched. Taken aback, he turned to preserve his dignity.

A fleeting notion crossed his mind. What if one of her many cases hid a cure for festering guilt?

"Dummkopf," he muttered under his breath, falling back on German as he occasionally did. Anyone could see she was too clean, too innocent, to be acquainted with the darkness he knew. He hadn't expected a woman so young. Although the diminutive Dr. Morgan was no classic beauty, she had round, shining eyes, an uptilted nose, and a smile—goodness, what a gentle smile.

Clearing his throat, Eric fought to restore normalcy to a day that had veered far from normal. "I had no idea a homeopathic physician needed so much paraphernalia. What's in the boxes?"

"Most people are familiar with our preference for infinitesimal dosage and think I need only medicated pellets. But for my practice I need textbooks, a microscope, tongs, tweezers, knives, scissors, and linens. Since I had it all at my clinic in Philadelphia, I brought it along. I'm ready for patients." Her words came in a lilting rush, punctuated by nods.

He smiled. "I hope you'll be pleased with the arrangements we've made for you. The house is small, but it has enough room to turn the parlor and dining room into a clinic."

"Why, that's precisely what I had in Philadelphia. It worked well. I made myself a sleeping area in the kitchen and kept everything close at hand. I'm certain this will be lovely."

Her verve and optimism were contagious. "There's a bedroom upstairs," he added. "You won't need to sleep in the kitchen like an orphaned kitten."

He'd hoped his words would bring on another smile, but instead, her lips formed an "oh!"

He gestured toward her belongings. "We can't fit your boxes in my carriage, but we'll take the trunks now. The rest can be delivered later."

He spoke with the porters and let them know his plans. Then he said, "Let's get you home. After your long trip, you must be ready for a rest."

Letty shook her head. The curling brown wisps of hair danced again. "I can't wait to be on my way, but I'm so happy to be here, I doubt I could lie down and rest right now."

Her vibrancy enticed Eric to smile again, but a warning rang through his thoughts. Drawing himself to his full height, he remembered the glare his late father had used to convey displeasure. He hoped he could carry it off. "You need the rest. Hartville can't afford a worn-out physician."

Reading the success of his efforts in her surprise, Eric led the way to the carriage. The sooner he got her to her new home, the sooner he could turn her over to the ladies of Silver Creek Church. With that in mind, he helped the doctor into his rig.

❦

Using Mr. Wagner's hand for balance, Letty climbed into the rig and smoothed the heavy folds of her ulster on the leather seat. Although he'd smiled a few times, those smiles hadn't altered the shadows in his eyes, and she had the impression Mr. Wagner didn't smile often. When he did, sorrow underscored the smile. What a pity, so young yet so sad.

Once she'd settled, Mr. Wagner climbed up, sat, and snapped the reins. The horses obeyed, and they left the station. As the sights along the street registered, dismay edged out her excitement. A blush scalded her face, and she screwed her eyes shut.

"Not your preferred part of town, is it, Dr. Morgan?"

Mortified, Letty risked another peek. She had never been this close to a saloon, but the noisy establishments she saw could be nothing else. Amid the saloons, other lairs sported signs that read "Billiards," with the rare "Barber," "Baths," and "Laundry" scattered in for good measure. One read, "Bessie's Barn." Letty knew what that one housed.

"No, Mr. Wagner. I'm more comfortable around libraries, schools, and churches. It seems a shame that visitors on their way into town from the station must see this."

A frown creased his forehead. "Quite true, and it's worse since the Heart of Silver Mine's production grew so fast last year." With a flick of the reins, the matching mares picked up their pace. "You should appreciate the location of your home. It's on a quiet street with Silver Creek Church at the corner."

Although Mr. Wagner hadn't laughed or even smiled, Letty discerned a touch of taunt in his words. Oh, dear. What if he frequented those places?

Studying him through downcast lashes, she tried to learn his feelings toward their seedy surroundings, but his expression remained oddly blank.

He turned and caught her staring. "Even though it's none of your concern, Dr. Morgan, I don't patronize this street. Each time I've come this way, it's been to meet a train or to cover a story for my newspaper." His jaw tightened and his voice hardened. "I oppose saloons, gambling, and womanizing just as you seem to."

Feeling relieved though foolish, Letty gathered her dignity and entertained a vague curiosity about Mr. Wagner's sudden vehemence. Then she cautioned herself against indulging that troublesome part of her nature.

"It really is none of my concern," she murmured.

"I recently started a series of editorials urging the town to rid itself of this blight," he added.

"I see."

Letty breathed more easily once they turned onto a wide street lined with official-looking structures. "Main Street?"

"And flourishing."

She had expected pride in his town's growth, but instead she heard disapproval in his voice. As he concentrated on guiding the horses down the busy thoroughfare, she studied him again. In the short time she'd known him, she'd seen sadness, concern, and humor in his dark eyes. She preferred the humor. It made him look approachable and easy to talk to. She hoped he was both, since she knew no one else in town.

He startled her when he spoke again. "Since last year, new-comers have overrun the town. Not all are welcome. You may as well hear it from me now, since you'll certainly hear it from the town gossips later. I don't think Hartville can handle going from five thousand citizens to somewhere close to fifteen thousand in less than a year. Despite the numbers, this is a small town at heart."

Letty considered her companion's words. Everywhere she looked, she saw new construction. The clip-clop of the horses' hooves played counterpoint to the hammering of carpenter's nails on a mansion partway down Main Street. The workman wore so many layers that Letty wondered how he could move his arms well enough to pound nails. She pointed him out to Mr. Wagner.

"That home belongs to our illustrious banker. Came into town last summer, and as a result of our productive mine, he turns a healthy profit."

Letty chuckled. "I can't see that as my fate. I don't expect to get rich delivering babies, treating childhood illnesses, or patching up miners injured at work."

His whiskers lifted in a wry smile. "You're right. You'll probably be paid in kind. Chickens, vegetables, eggs, milk."

"Since I'm not fond of hunger, I'll welcome my patients' generosity."

"Not that you'll need much," he countered, humor in his voice. "You're a tiny thing. Barely more than a girl."

Letty sobered. "Not at all. I'm a doctor and have seen more suffering than anyone should."

A measuring look came her way. "It looks as if Hartville's fortunes have improved," he finally said. "Welcome to town."

"Thank you . . . I think."

"It was a compliment."

"Then thank you again." Just as she was about to inquire after Mrs. Wagner, her mind went blank when a child darted in front of the carriage.

"Stop!" she cried, reaching for the reins. The memory of another child, in another town, catapulted to life. *Not again. Heavenly Father, help!*

Mr. Wagner fought to stop his horses, crying out in German. Somehow, he missed trampling the boy, who stood frozen to the spot.

Letty rushed from the carriage. "Are you hurt?" she asked, probing a reed-thin body through layers of too-large clothes. "Why did you run into the street? It's very, very dangerous."

The boy wiped his nose with a drooping coat sleeve. He cocked his battered bowler, revealing bright blue eyes. Those eyes sized her up in no time.

"'M all right," he answered, dusting himself off. "Didn't mean no harm, ma'am. 'M sorry."

"Why, I never thought you did, dear, but something made you run out in the street. What was it? Were you frightened?"

The scamp played with his frayed tie, then tucked the slice of silk inside his waistband. He wiped the toe of first one and then the other old but clean black boot on his trouser legs.

Crooking a finger under his sharp chin, Letty tilted his face toward hers. "What's your name?"

He scuffed his toes in the street dirt but didn't speak.

Mr. Wagner's roar startled Letty and the boy. "Steven Patterson, what were you thinking? You ran out in front of my horses. Mighty foolish thing to do, young man."

Letty cringed at the booming voice. She also noticed the furtive look Steven cast over his shoulder. When she matched it, she saw nothing out of the ordinary.

Then the boy sighed. And grinned. Fisting the lapels of his chopped-down-to-size tweed coat, Steven rocked back on his heels, much like a boastful businessman or a pompous politician. Lifting his chin, he shot a cocky grin at Mr. Wagner, but the effect was ruined when his bowler, worn to a shabby shine, tipped down over his eyes.

With a thumb poking out from a trimmed-down leather glove, Steven shoved the hat out of his way. "Sorry, Mr. Wagner. Won't hap'n agin, sir. Gotta git goin' now." Two fingers tapped the hat brim. "G'bye!"

"Wait!" Letty cried.

Steven darted up the street.

Turning to the man at her side, she asked, "Who *is* that child? Why is he running in the streets? Where are his folks?"

Mr. Wagner cupped Letty's elbow, and the warmth of his fingers winnowed up her arm. Startled, she glanced at him. The surprise on his attractive face unsettled her even more. He turned and tugged her toward the carriage.

Letty allowed Mr. Wagner to lead her, but she pondered the change she'd seen come over her companion. Had he felt that same strange sensation, too? Oh, dear. And he a married man . . . *The boy, Letty, the boy.*

"You haven't answered, Mr. Wagner. Who is responsible for that defenseless mite?"

To her amazement, he laughed. "My dear Dr. Morgan, Steven is as defenseless as a rattler, and he's older than he looks. True, he needs taking in hand, discipline is lacking, and an education would work wonders, but he's a Patterson, and there's nothing we can do."

"What does his name have to do with anything? Does Hartville hold his family against him? I hope I haven't moved to a sanctimonious town." Crossing her arms over her chest, Letty glared at her companion. "Tell me more about Steven."

Discomfort, or so she hoped, colored Mr. Wagner's cheeks. "Hartville has its share of hypocrites," he admitted, "but no more than other towns. Steven Patterson lacks adequate parents. Horace, never devoted, quit pretending to care the day his wife died. He now finds comfort in a bottle. Steven fends for himself."

At first, Letty felt iced with horror, but by the end of his account, anger again heated her face. "Why doesn't someone else help the child? What about missionary boxes? Surely you can find a coat to fit the boy. And that decrepit derby . . . Don't the sons of other families cast off warm hats or caps?"

"Of course. We've all tried, but Horace returns the gifts. The ladies often feed the boy, but that's about all they can do."

Letty made a noise uncomfortably similar to an undignified snort. But it was a bit late to worry about how dignified she sounded. She had behaved abominably—quarreling, for goodness' sake—ever since meeting this man.

Concentrating on the fingers working a loose thread on her ulster, Letty gathered the courage to ask another question. "Will anyone object if I try to help?"

"No, but if you take on the Pattersons, you'll take on more than you've bargained for. I wish you well. Others have failed."

Urged on by a touch of mischief, Letty smiled. "I have it on good authority that I'm distressingly determined. A most unattractive tendency, I'm afraid."

Mr. Wagner smiled. Letty counted that smile as a victory.

"I'm learning just how determined Hartville's lady doctor really is," he said. "I don't find determination unattractive, although it can be daunting."

"You hardly look daunted."

"I'm a newspaperman. You must know how brash we are. We can handle anything."

"I look forward to watching you."

Wearing a shadow of a smile, he pulled on the reins, and the horses stopped before a black-shuttered white frame house. As Letty gazed in wonder at the home that, by all indications, Mr. Wagner intended for her use, an unseen person opened the door in welcome.

Letty placed a hand on Mr. Wagner's forearm. "Is this my new clinic . . . my house?"

Mr. Wagner looked down from his superior height. "Of course. Shall we go in? The women from the church have fixed it up for you. They can't wait to meet you."

Letty folded her hands on her lap to keep from clapping with enthusiasm as she admired the place. She breathed a prayer of thanksgiving for the Lord's splendid provision and seconds later clambered out of the carriage and went up the walk. With a final lingering glance at the exterior, she stepped inside.

She was home. No one had to tell her. The scent of fresh baked bread and roasted meat wafted it to her nose. The roaring fire in the grate boasted it to her eyes. The warm clasp of plump hands imprinted it into her own.

"Welcome to Hartville, dear. I'm Adele Stone, Pastor Stone's wife. I'm so happy to finally meet you."

For once, Letty found herself speechless. She looked from face to kind face, and tears sprang to her eyes. Oh, dear. She mustn't cry. What would they think of a weepy doctor?

She returned the squeeze with a watery smile. "You can't imagine how happy I am to be here, and to be greeted like this. . . . Why, it's better than a dream come true. It's the answer to my prayers."

The five ladies smiled among themselves, each one nodding approval. Then chatter broke out.

"I'm Miranda Carlson, but please call me Randy," offered a redhead with green eyes.

"I'm Miss Emmaline Whitehall," said a thin, gray-haired lady with spectacles on her long nose.

So went the round of introductions and lively conversation. Soon Letty noticed a conspicuous absence and could no longer contain her curiosity. Turning to Mr. Wagner, who watched from the side, a smile curving his mustache, she asked, "And where is your wife? I've so looked forward to making her acquaintance."

All eyes locked on Mr. Wagner, who, head bowed, stood still as a statue, pale as marble. Letty couldn't even hear the sound of breathing. She wondered what social sin she had committed.

Finally, he lifted his head, his look so bleak it pierced to the marrow of her bones.

"My wife is dead, Dr. Morgan."

2

When the echo of the slammed door faded into silence, Letty took a shuddering breath and tried to dispel her dismay. She could scarcely believe what had happened.

After she'd ripped open his wound, Eric had obviously had no thought but to flee and tend to his pain. Unfortunately, she still had to deal with the women and the ache she felt at her uncalculated cruelty.

Then she realized that in the space of one pain-filled moment he had become Eric to her.

"Come along, sweetheart," said Mrs. Stone, laying an arm around Letty's shoulders. "Don't fret over Eric. You had no way of knowing, and as much as he has helped, why, it was only natural to expect his wife to welcome you to town."

"But—"

"No," Mrs. Stone said. "Listen to me. I know him well—have known him since our families came out West a long time ago. He holds on to trouble much longer than he should. He still blames himself for Martina's death. Foolishly, of course, but no one has been able to talk sense to him."

"What happened?"

"Let's take this heavy thing off," Mrs. Stone suggested with a tug on Letty's ulster. "It was tragic. They had so looked forward to the birth, but from the start, Martina had trouble. The child was large, like Eric, and breech. She labored for two days, refusing to see a doctor—a man. She wanted a midwife."

Letty gasped. Just like Mrs. Forrest. Only this time, the woman had denied herself the benefit of a physician. No wonder Eric wanted a woman doctor for the town.

"How long ago did it happen?"

Silence.

Letty persisted. "Was it recent?"

"Two years ago."

Strange. Two years seemed long enough for him to come to grips with the deaths. Since his wife had died in childbirth, Letty saw no reason for him to blame himself. But, as she well knew, everyone grieved in different, private ways. Perhaps Eric was the sort who loved so fiercely that pain pierced him deeper than it did others.

"I still feel awful," she said. "I have a tendency to blurt out whatever comes to mind before thinking it through." She managed a weak smile. "I'm awful at keeping secrets, too."

Randy caught Letty's attention with a wink. "You're probably an abysmal liar as well. Hartville's fortunate to have you."

Letty smiled her thanks, glad for the help in easing the awkwardness. If everything else went as well as these women's reception, then life in Hartville would indeed be a dream come true.

Randy waited for Letty to follow the others into the kitchen. "I didn't want them to overhear, Dr. Morgan. I think I'm expecting, and I'd be proud to be your patient."

Letty experienced a pang of envy and another of joy. "Oh, Randy, that's wonderful. How do you feel? Any nausea in the morning? What about dizziness? No strange bleeding, I hope."

"I feel absurdly well. Sleepy all the time, but I have none of the complaints my friends warned me about." She laughed. "In fact, Dr. Morgan, I scarcely feel pregnant."

Letty reached for Randy's hand. "There's one thing you must do if you're going to be my patient. I'm hoping we can become friends as well, and I refuse to feel I must scrub my hands before we talk. Please call me Letty."

Randy smiled, and the two new friends joined the others.

The women insisted on guiding Letty through the minuscule house, pointing out the touches they'd added. Mrs. Richards had donated the worn but comfortable settees arranged against two parlor walls. Mrs. Crowley had provided the six oak chairs lining the third wall. The brown braided rug had once graced the parsonage.

The kindness of these strangers brought a knot to Letty's throat, and she could scarcely respond to their questions. No one had ever shown such interest in her before.

The rest of the house displayed more of their generosity. An oak table took up most of the space in the kitchen, its scarred top telling the tale of many meals. Mismatched chairs nestled at its four sides.

Randy insisted on showing Letty the bedroom before sitting down to a cup of tea. While her new friend chattered about every item in the room, Letty took note of the pitched ceiling and the quilt in white and rose-flowered squares.

Finally, as the hours sped by, the ladies left one by one. The irrepressible Randy was the last to depart. Letty was thrilled to find a friend. She'd always had too few of those.

She had grown up the only child in a family of reserved adults. Her father, a physician who had served with the Union forces during the War between the States, had been a solemn, studious man, consumed by his calling well after his service to the Union cause ended. Her mother had always supported his devotion to his profession, leaving Letty's care to servants.

How she came away from that home with her optimism intact

Letty would never know, but that attribute had always served her well. Particularly as a woman determined to breach the masculine stronghold of medicine.

After extinguishing the lamps, she went up the stairs to the bedroom in the eaves. When she was partway there, a sound out front made her stop. Thinking it might be one of the ladies returning for a forgotten item, Letty hastened to open the door. In the hazy gray and crimson of the wintry sunset, she found a child dragging a hamper down the porch steps—a little girl, her braids more unraveled than not.

"You!" Letty called out. "What are you up to?"

Bending to her task with redoubled intent, the scamp cast a look over her shoulder. She seemed determined to steal what an anonymous donor had evidently intended for Letty's use.

Oblivious to the cold, she ran after the urchin. "Where do you think you're going with that, missy?"

Letty caught the sprite around the waist of a too-large, plum-colored wool wrapper. The child struggled for freedom, but Letty hung on to a handful of the black flounces that trailed behind the girl. She tried to reach the basket, redolent of roast chicken, but found her hands full with the little bandit.

The basket fell to the snow. Letty's captive took one look at her face, then unleashed all her fury upon her. Biting, scratching, kicking, and howling, the imp refused to surrender to an adult's greater power. Eventually, she had no choice. Letty was larger, though not by much.

Letty scooped up her adversary and carried her into the house. She would retrieve the basket after extracting some answers.

She plopped her unwilling guest onto a kitchen chair. "Who, pray tell, are you, and what were you doing in my yard—alone—at this hour of the evening?"

As she uttered the words, she recognized a similarity between this situation and Steven Patterson's unsupervised presence on the streets of Hartville. Upon closer examination, she even found a resemblance between this little fiend and Steven. The girl's attire was peculiar, with an adult's straw boater perched on her head.

The girl didn't answer.

"You're a Patterson, aren't you?"

That got a reaction. Letty's guest raised her head. The red silk rose poking up from the crown of the boater bobbled, rolled its way past moth-eaten black fur on the collar of the wrap, and tumbled to the floor. The hat slid back on the girl's head, revealing her most telling features. Bright blue eyes widened, and a pointed chin dropped in astonishment. "How'd ya know?"

Despite the seriousness of the matter, Letty stifled a smile. "I've met your brother, Steven. You look alike."

The girl frowned at the comparison.

"Tell me," Letty continued, "why were you taking my basket?"

The girl stared at her boots. Small though they were, the heels and the many hooks running up the inner leg declared them a woman's castoffs. Letty didn't know whether to laugh or groan at the child's attempt at mature attire.

The chin lifted. "Why's it matter?"

Letty tried again. "Where were you taking it?"

From what Eric had revealed about the Pattersons, Letty knew the girl needed the food. She also knew that confession was good for the soul, especially that of a young poacher.

She waited for the answer. Then waited longer still.

"Well, if'n it's all the same to you, I'd rather not tell."

"Well, if it's all the same to you, you will tell, or you won't be going home."

The starch melted out of the urchin. She began to look around. Fingers fidgeted and uneasy "umms" betrayed fear.

All at once, the child leapt to her feet. "I gotta go. Now. You c'n keep yore ol' basket. We don' need yore food."

As the girl ran for the door, Letty regretted her clumsy efforts. She had wanted to help but had only scared the child. "You haven't told me your name," she called. "I'd like to know."

The girl stopped, hand on the doorknob. After a moment, she faced Letty, who realized her measure was again being taken. She prayed she wouldn't be found wanting.

"It's Amelia. Amelia Louise Patterson."

Letty resumed breathing. "Well, then, I would like to give the contents of the basket to my new friend, Amelia."

Blue eyes opened wider.

"But only the contents." Letty prayed she was doing the right thing. "Someone left that basket to welcome me to town. I'd like to thank them, so I want the basket back. Will you return it? Tomorrow?"

Again the blue eyes assessed her. "I'll bring it back."

"Very well, Amelia. I'll expect you tomorrow. We can find the owner and thank her for all she shared. Enjoy what's in the hamper."

Amelia turned to the door. "We'll try."

Letty wondered why the girl had answered that way, but she dared not probe, lest Amelia back out of her promise to return. Letty intended to turn tomorrow's visit into the next of many steps toward the rehabilitation of the Patterson children.

"Isn't the basket too heavy?" she asked. "Perhaps I can help you take it home."

Amelia smashed her hat tighter on her head and yanked the door ajar. "No! I c'n do it. Sure'n I c'n, Dr. Miss. I c'n do it." She ran outside. "Thank ye, Dr. Miss."

The thin child grabbed the hamper and resumed her trek, the train of the once-fine wrap trailing behind her. Letty wondered how far Amelia would have to drag the feast she'd just inherited.

With her gaze on the girl, Letty vowed to become an expert on the Patterson children. She would start by questioning a certain newspaperman who'd neglected to mention that more than one Patterson child needed her attention. She would do so tomorrow before Amelia returned.

The night, quiet and deep, sped by. Letty was accustomed to vehicles clattering down the streets of Philadelphia, so Hartville's peace came as a welcome surprise. She slept better than she had since . . . She couldn't remember when she'd rested so well.

In the sunlit winter morning, her thoughts soon turned to her planned meeting with Eric. She'd heard concern under his anger at Steven the day before. She wagered he'd lost his temper because the boy's recklessness had endangered him. Somehow, she would win Eric's cooperation in her efforts on behalf of the Pattersons. Those two deserved better, and she was just the woman to make sure they got it.

She sat up in her nest of covers and thanked God for the welcoming committee who'd provided them as well as the wooden steps beside the tall bed. As short as she was, she greatly appreciated their presence. She stepped down and stretched.

Her satchel offered a choice between a gray woolen skirt and one of charcoal serge. She pulled out the wool skirt and a white cotton shirtwaist.

Shortly after breakfast, she set off for the center of town. Humming, she studied her surroundings as she went along. By the time she reached Main Street, she was sure she remembered enough landmarks to return home without getting lost, especially since at the corner stood Silver Creek Church, solid as a belfry-topped rock of ages. Its glass windows sparkled like diamonds in the sunlight. Venturing a guess at which direction might take her to the newspaper, she turned right.

In front of the sheriff's office, she stopped a stout man carrying a walking stick to ask directions to the Hartville Day. While the man spoke, she only half listened. She'd never before seen a cane with its handle carved into a cow's head, and she couldn't stop staring.

Soon she reached Eric's workplace. Pieces of newsprint were

nailed to the wall of the plain storefront, and Letty drew near to read them. Most dealt with the town's silver business, but as she reached for the doorknob, one particular item caught her attention.

EAST CRAWFORD STREET BORDELLOS
Prurient Pastime of the Prominent

Letty scanned the column, bottom lip between her teeth. Eric had launched an attack against the houses of ill repute. His editorial urged the city to appropriate and close them, then jail the women who plied the sinful trade. His plan, he wrote, would eliminate temptation for men who felt the need to stray. Although she couldn't see what good a newspaper article would do, she certainly hoped he succeeded.

Peering through the dusty window, she saw Eric leaning over a desk where another man worked on a typewriting machine. The man's dexterity and the speed of his fingers intrigued Letty.

She grabbed the brass handle, threw open the door, and flew into the office. "Oh, Eric, that's marvelous. How can his fingers move so fast? Could he teach me?"

Eric turned, and Letty felt the intensity of his gaze to the tips of her toes. How could the man affect her so strongly with nothing more than a look? She blushed and studied the drawstring of her reticule, fiddling with it until she dropped the bag.

Bending to retrieve her purse, Letty scolded herself. She was a doctor, for goodness' sake, not a flighty miss to be flustered by a man's stare. She had come for answers about the Patterson children, to gain Eri—Mr. Wagner's—help with those two scamps . . . and to apologize for her blunder of the previous day.

Squaring her shoulders, Letty met his gaze. "I'm sorry. Please forgive me for bursting in. I can be terribly impulsive when something catches my fancy, and this gentleman's work is fascinating."

When Eric remained silent, she plunged ahead. "I would also like a moment with you. In private."

He lifted an eyebrow. Clearly, yesterday's thoughtless question remained a fresh memory. She added, "It's important."

A long-fingered hand rose to Eric's mustache and smoothed the brown hairs. This troubled widower attracted her in a most puzzling way. An impermissible way.

She reminded herself that a woman who dared practice a man's career couldn't yield to such an attraction, since attraction could grow into something deeper. She remembered Marcus. Another ill-fated infatuation might devastate her. Letty promised to keep a tighter grip on her imagination and asked God's help in the doing.

"Follow me," Eric said warily.

She set aside her foolishness and tried to relax but caught herself studying the golden hair that waved over the back of his head. Her gaze strayed to his back, and she noticed the impressive breadth of shoulders encased in navy serge. Following the line of his jacket, she admired the fine formation of his torso. Eric could have posed for any of the drawings in her textbooks. He embodied the ideal healthy male.

When he paused at a door in the hallway, she nearly ran into his back. He gestured for her to precede him into the room, and ducking her head to hide burning cheeks, she did just that.

"Please excuse the disorder," he said as he closed the door. "I rarely let people in my office. When I get involved in an investigation, I often forget to clean up after myself. At least, I do until I have to find something in the mess."

Letty smiled, certain he had no idea he'd given her an intriguing glimpse into his nature. "The clutter doesn't bother me, Mr. Wagner. I came to apologize for my insensitive question yesterday. Do forgive me. I meant no harm, and I am sorry for the pain I caused you."

Eric stiffened. Letty continued regardless. "Please accept my condolences as well."

He closed his eyes momentarily, then cleared his throat. "It's understandable. You had no way of knowing what happened. Apology and condolences accepted." With obvious effort he smiled. "Was there something else you needed? Perhaps something with the house? Or did you just want typewriting lessons?"

Pleased by the return of even strained humor to his voice, she said, "I'd love to learn to use the machine, but I've no need for one. A physician doesn't heal with clacking keys and printed pages."

"True, but they're interesting anyway." He gestured to a machine nearly buried by masses of paper on his desk. "Our work here at the office has become much easier since I bought them."

Instead of sitting in the worn leather wing chair across from Eric's desk, Letty followed him for a closer look at the contraption. "May I?"

"Certainly," he mumbled, shoving pages out of her way.

Letty fought a laugh. The tips of Eric's ears glowed redder than apples in the fall. What an endearing trait in such a controlled man.

"Here, let me help," she offered, putting papers into stacks and rescuing pencils and dried pens from where they'd landed.

"Yes, well, I do apologize, Dr. Morgan. There's no excuse for making you work in my office. The least I can do is teach you to operate the typewriter."

"Would you really? It's not necessary, but I'm so curious about the machine . . . Oh, thank you. I will accept your offer."

Eric smiled. Letty counted another victory.

"It'll be my pleasure," he said. "Why don't you sit here and test it? You insert the paper around this cylinder and turn it until it comes out the front."

As Eric leaned closer, she caught the scents of ink and bay rum and the warm, musky fragrance of a healthy man.

As he continued speaking, she lost track of his lesson. How

embarrassing. She had to stop acting like a spinster and start acting like a doctor.

". . . just like so."

As he spoke, Letty glanced at his long, strong fingers poised over the silvery keys. Somehow his arms had come around her without her noticing. Oh, dear. How should she handle this?

She decided to brazen it out. Mimicking the curve of his fingers, she positioned hers over his. "Like this?"

Eric slid his hands out from under hers and took hold of her wrists. He brought her fingers down onto the keys.

"Like so," he said, his voice oddly rough.

Before Letty could ponder the change in timbre, a man called out his name. Hurried footsteps followed, there was a second yell, and then someone pounded on the office door.

Eric's touch lingered on Letty's wrists for a heartbeat before he released her. "What do you need, Michael?"

A tall man in denim trousers and a chambray shirt entered the room. "You said you wanted to know when Slosh was at it again."

Eric groaned, took a black wool coat from a rack in the corner, and stuffed his arms in the sleeves. As he pulled leather gloves from his coat pocket, he asked, "At Otto's?"

Michael shook his head. "On the street outside Otto's."

With a "wait here" for Letty, Eric ran after Michael. A stream of German words—curses, by the sound of it—trailed behind.

Letty fought her curiosity, but moments later she followed. She didn't try to catch up with Eric's long stride but made sure she kept him in sight. She dodged between two carriages, barely missed being hit, and for her efforts, got splattered with mud and melted snow. When Eric turned a corner, she saw they'd reached East Crawford Street. Dismayed to find herself in the seedy area again but dying of curiosity, she threw decorum to the wind and ran after the newspaperman, darting between heaps of snow and patches of ice.

Before long, she spotted the reason for the alarm. In front of what looked like a saloon, three men were slugging each other near senseless. Eric stood to one side, evidently hoping to end the fracas without being sucked in.

Onlookers watched with avid interest, none showing any inclination to stop the tussle. Eric had yet to do anything to end the fight.

Indignant, she ran up and yanked him around by the arm. "Watching the show, Mr. Wagner? Please get in there and do something before someone is injured."

"How do you want me to stop three skunk-drunk men?"

"I don't know. I've never been in a fistfight. You're a man. You should know what to do."

"Yes, I'm a man, but it doesn't necessarily follow that I engage in drunken brawls, as you just insinuated."

"I did no such thing."

"You certainly did."

"Well, I'm sorry."

"So am I."

Letty snorted. "This is getting us nowhere. Why are you picking a fight with me when there's a perfectly good one in progress? One you really should stop, Mr. Wagner."

"My name is Eric," he said, unbuttoning his coat, "and I'm sick of you calling me Mr. Wagner."

The intense quality of his voice stunned Letty. She gasped.

A second later she snapped her mouth shut. She swallowed, blinked, then noticed the spark of mischief in his eyes. What an absurd time for him to tear down his wall of reserve.

She smiled weakly. "Of course, Eric."

"Furthermore," he said as he folded his coat, "that lofty name Letitia might have suited your parents, but it doesn't suit you. You aren't some bookish schoolmarm. You're like a bird, quick and cheerful."

Eric's words left Letty dumbfounded. He tugged off a glove.

"I know," he said with a look at the battling trio, "I'll call you Tish."

Astonished, she shook her head. "No, it's Letty. Please."

"Fine. I'll get used to Letty." Off came the other glove. "From now on, that's who you are." He thrust his outerwear at her and strode away.

She clutched the items. His subtle essence again teased her nostrils, and she rubbed her cheek against the coat's scratchy wool.

Eric approached the three ne'er-do-wells. Then he grabbed one by the scruff of his neck, dragged him to a watering trough, and sent him crashing through the ice.

3

She was nothing like what he'd expected.

Eric shook his head and laughed, remembering the image he'd formed of the homeopathic physician before meeting her. Letty Morgan was anything but a tough, professional battle-ax. Compassionate and optimistic, she would probably accomplish great things.

What she lacked in height, she more than made up for in gumption. She'd certainly challenged him at the fight, commanding him to intervene for the sake of three strangers. To his amazement, he'd done it.

All because of one look from her silver eyes.

When Martina died, grief had consumed him, and he'd vowed to avoid emotional entanglements. Although the Patterson children's situation concerned him, he'd kept the rascals from stealing his heart while still providing for their basic needs.

Then an eastern bird flew into town. A small bird who was building herself a nest among the Patterson children, at the church, and in the thoughts of a certain Eric K. Wagner. That went contrary to his plans.

His newspaper and Hartville's future had to suffice. He couldn't afford to let that vivacious bird nest in his heart. It would devastate him if one day the bird fell never to rise again. Losing anyone else would rob him of what remained of his heart.

He'd have to keep her at arm's length, even while helping her set up the clinic at the house on Willow Lane. There he had enough to keep him busy, enough to help him avoid her eyes and cheerful smile.

He checked his pocket watch for the eighth time that day. He lifted the fat, orange tabby from his lap, stood, set her on the overstuffed chair, and rubbed her silky orange head. "I'll be back later, Marmie. Another lady needs me just now."

As he picked cat hairs from his old, comfortable jeans, he smiled, picturing Letty's reaction when she saw him dressed this way. No suits for him here at the ranch; he had too much to do. Work helped him feel alive, something he'd needed since Martina died.

The simmering ache that always threatened to boil over rushed to the fore, but unwilling to spoil a day he'd waited for, Eric set the pain aside and remembered Letty's interest in the Patterson children. He'd give her a hand with those scalawags as soon as he had her clinic running. The two of them should be able to improve the Patterson children's lives without getting drawn in too deeply.

He walked the two miles to Willow Lane, enjoying the un-expected thaw that came with the last days of February. The snow gave way in spots to patches of mud, and everywhere the scent of earth—life itself—invited him to join the new world. The sky wore cottony clouds, and the sun bathed everything in golden light.

For the first time in two years, Eric felt glad to be alive, and when he arrived at Letty's house, her welcoming smile increased his contentment.

"Please come in," she said. "I began to open boxes, but I'm not strong enough to move them around. I'll warn you, Mr. Wagner, I intend to put your height and strength to good use today."

"I thought we agreed to stop the Mr. Wagner nonsense."

Rose tinted her cheeks. She clasped her hands behind her back, evidently to conceal her nervousness. "We did," she said. "But it will take time to get used to it."

He conceded with a nod. "Where would you like to start?"

"Follow me." She led him to the former dining room. "I was assured the examining table I shipped from Philadelphia would arrive by tomorrow at the latest, so it's probably best to prepare this room first. How are you at making shelves?"

"Shelves? What for?"

The doctor pointed to a crate filled with amber-glass jars of pellets.

"Of course. Your remedies." Eric removed his coat and gloves and dropped them out of the way in a heap. He gathered hammer, nails, saw, and a board Letty had found in the shed out back and then went to work on the shelves. Once he'd cut the wood, he called her to his side.

At her quizzical look, he explained. "I have to measure you, since it only makes sense to build the shelves to your height. Touch the wall at a convenient spot."

"Thank you, Eric. That's most considerate. My lack of height has occasionally inconvenienced others. Lower shelves will be a luxury."

He wondered whom she had inconvenienced just by being small, but he didn't ask, fearing that if he did, he'd be asking for more than just the answer to a question—he'd be asking her to share bits of herself. That could lead to caring, and he couldn't afford to care again.

So Eric pounded nails in the wall, making braces strong enough to support Letty's shelves, low enough to ensure her self-sufficiency. After a time, the urge to know her better overcame his prudence. "Why did you decide to leave Philadelphia?"

Uncertainty played over her face. Then she squared her shoulders. "The prejudice against women doctors made it impossible for me to make a success of my clinic," she said. "I tried for six months, but aside from a handful of poor street urchins, I had no patients. I'd worked too hard and studied too long to give up on my calling. Your letter came as a blessing. Not only was I running low on funds, but also a tragedy occurred days before."

She paused, and Eric looked away from the brace he'd cut. Letty turned away, then said softly, "A patient's sister called me to a birthing. Although Mrs. Forrest was clearly in trouble, her husband wouldn't let me treat her because I'm a woman. He accused me of corrupting women's attitudes. She died, as did the child."

Her story brought his worst memories to life, memories he fought to control—to no avail. He again saw Martina lying in a pool of blood. And baby Karl—

Nein.

He fought to keep that memory from surfacing, but the image of a white face grew clearer. He could still feel Martina's fingers on his cheek as she told him she hoped he would remarry soon.

Moving as if in a vat of molasses, Eric edged toward the window.

A gentle voice called to him from far away.

A hand covered his. The warmth of her fingers began to melt the darkness around him. Moments later, a sliver of light broke through.

Eric shuddered and ran his free hand over his eyes. Good heavens, it still hurt. How long would this pain last?

One by one, he cast off layers of guilt, grief, and loneliness, each made easier by the unexpected strength of that small hand. "I'm sorry," he murmured. "I don't usually lose control."

He'd let her see too much. It shouldn't have happened. He couldn't let her care for him. He couldn't let himself care for her. Now he recognized the trap he'd set for himself when he'd offered her friendship. Even for friendship one needed to invest emotion, and that price was too high.

The best thing would be to leave, but Eric didn't have it in him to hurt her. Letty had given him silent comfort when he'd needed it. So he settled for treating her like the businesswoman she was. No more, no less.

He retrieved his hand and took up the hammer again, but the silence grew uncomfortable, and Eric knew he had to diffuse the tension. "Why homeopathy and not allopathy?" he asked. "Why would you choose to provide what some consider outmoded treatments?"

Letty straightened as if bitten by a rattler. "I happen to agree with Dr. Hahnemann, homeopathy's 'discoverer.' A doctor must treat the patient, not the disease. Our remedies stimulate the patient's natural powers of healing, while allopaths use harsh treatments to battle the disease itself. Large quantities of harmful substances aren't necessary. An infinitesimal dose of the right remedy will stir the body to heal itself."

He'd known he would get a response, but he hadn't bargained for a lecture on the principles of homeopathy. Before Eric could change topics, Letty began pacing, her cheeks bright with enthusiasm, energetic hand gestures punctuating her discourse.

"We treat symptoms, since they reflect the body's general condition. By studying those symptoms, we identify the remedy that most closely causes the same reaction in a healthy body and then prescribe its minimal dose. Although we don't understand why, a greater dilution of a substance is more efficacious."

Eric stared trouble in the face. Any minute now, obscure medical terminology would start flying around the room. How could he stop the flow of knowledge?

Business. He had, after all, decided to keep their acquaintance on that level. "How do you plan to reach patients in outlying areas?"

Her pacing stopped. "I'll need a horse and buggy, won't I? Do you know where I might buy them at a fair price?"

He remembered her saying she was close to the end of her

resources. "No need. The community needs a physician. I'll arrange for a horse and buggy."

Her eyes narrowed to scalpel-sharp silver slits. Eric braced himself for another dose of the good doctor's pride.

"I'm hardly as naïve as you think," she said. "I have wondered just who is providing my lovely home. I'm aware that church members donated many items, but the house itself must belong to someone. I still don't know my landlord's name."

Eric stared at a spot on the wall above Letty's head. "Ah . . . I own the house. It sat empty for a number of months, and surely you'll agree it's better to use it as a clinic."

With a lift of her chin, she said, "Then you have two options. You can either name a monthly rent, or you can sell it to me."

"But—"

"Two choices. I will not be a kept woman. Under any humanitarian guise."

Eric's cheeks burned, and he conceded defeat. He named a modest sum, close to the value of the property yet low enough not to empty her coffers.

When she nodded, he smiled. "I'll have the necessary documents prepared by my lawyer."

"It's for the best. Now, about the horse and buggy—"

"I'll provide them."

"I must again decline your offer. I pay my own way."

"Of all the obstinate women! Very well, Dr. Morgan, I'll take you to buy a horse, but I have a perfectly good buggy going to waste in my barn. You'll take it and use it to benefit the people of Hartville with no further argument."

"I'd much rather not."

Turning from the maddening woman, Eric cursed the overblown sense of responsibility that had compelled him to find a lady doctor. He'd never expected this much trouble.

When they returned to their individual tasks, uneasy silence again settled around them. Still, they continued to work, and the clinic came closer to reality.

⚘

At noon Letty offered Eric a bowl of soup. One taste and he decided he'd been wise to stay. "Delicious!" He helped himself to a slice of crusty bread. "I'm afraid you've spoiled me for my uninspired cooking."

"Oh, it's not much," she said, smiling. "Just vegetable soup with barley and beef. The guild ladies are most generous."

"Stands to reason. They were quite vocal about our need for a woman doctor. I have it on good authority that they're pleased with our choice."

Letty's hands burst into motion. She broke off a piece of bread, reached for the butter dish, and applied a liberal coating. Her spoon fell to the floor.

This wasn't the first time a compliment had flustered the good doctor. Eric suspected her discomfort came from their scarcity. "Prepare yourself for more praise," he said. "That's all I hear from everyone who meets you."

Her silver eyes sparkled. "Slosh speaks well of me?"

Eric laughed. "More like curses. He insists he was winning and you killed his hopes for victory."

"Pshaw! The nerve of the man. They were beating him to mush. Why, I even saw to his wounds. The ingratitude of a sodden mind!"

Eric tried to keep from laughing, but her eyes flashed, her cheeks blazed, her lips pouted then spewed indignant words.

"Do you mock me, Mr. Wagner?"

"Hardly, Dr. Morgan. I suspect this is the beginning of a safer Hartville. If you fight for our health as doggedly as you challenged me to stop a brawl—"

"I'm sworn to protect human life. I live and work by certain principles. Don't you?"

Eric remembered learning such things as a child. Pity his teacher never learned them first.

"Yes," he said, anger's sudden fire sparking in his gut. "My late . . . father always said evil can't flourish in the light. A newspaper's mission is to enlighten the public on matters that affect it."

"I'm glad we have something in common."

When she smiled, Eric forced away his grim memory. He had to keep a tighter grip on his emotions.

❦

After their meal, Letty waved aside his offer to help neaten the kitchen, and he returned to the examining room. Surveying the morning's work, he saw she'd already filled some shelves with linens.

She resumed work over yet another box of medical supplies. Eric's gaze strayed to her petite though shapely form more often than it should have. Dismayed by his thoughts, he wielded the hammer with greater force than needed. He spewed German as the hammer crushed his thumb.

"What happened?" Letty rushed to his side. She chuckled in sympathy as she examined his throbbing thumb, then returned to her crate, withdrew a remedy jar, and with a silver spoon scooped out a trio of pellets. "Take these. Arnica works better than waving your hand."

Although he saw no further humor on her face, the sparkle in Letty's silver eyes gave Eric the distinct impression that she enjoyed his discomfort. He tucked the remedy under his tongue to let the pellets dissolve.

Favoring his smashed thumb, he dismantled two empty crates, stacked the wooden slats for later disposal, and tried to avoid all thought of Letty. Being so close made his efforts futile.

A timely knock at the front door distracted Letty. When she ushered in a young woman carrying an infant, Eric welcomed the opportunity to observe her with a patient.

"Let me hold the baby," Letty said. Eric noted her poignant expression, heard her soft crooning. In the examining room, she offered the mother a seat on an unopened crate. "What's wrong?"

The young woman shot Eric a panicked look. "Well, I . . ."

Letty sent him a mute appeal. When he didn't budge, she stood, the baby nestled in the crook of her arm, and hurried to his side.

"Can't you see this is a sensitive situation?" she whispered. "My patient needs her privacy."

With a glance at the mother, she continued in a louder voice. "I need a pillow and a woolen coverlet from the room upstairs. Please fetch them for me, Mr. Wagner."

Reluctantly he followed her orders. At the top of the stairs, he found a tidy room, fragrant with the scent of violets. A quilt in white and rose covered a sturdy oak bed, and plump pillows hid the headboard. Comfort beckoned him inside.

Rose-colored slippers peeped from beneath a white bed skirt, and a matching nightdress lay across the foot of the bed, ready for the woman who wore it. He saw the woolen coverlet under the nightdress.

He reached for the blanket but stopped, his hand only inches away. In order to pick it up, he would have to touch Letty's nightgown. The intimacy of that action held him back.

The baby cried downstairs.

She needed the coverlet. He had to touch that bit of cloth, and he did. So sheer that it felt like mist against his fingers, the nightdress bore the scent of violets, the sweetness of Letty. She'd slept in this garment the night before. Unable to resist, Eric brought the fabric to his face and took a deeper breath.

"Mr. Wagner," she called, "we need the blanket."

He cleared his throat. "I'm on my way."

Partway down the stairs, he heard Letty's patient speak again. "He wasn't nursing proper, Dr. Morgan, and the breast turned sore and red. Now it hurts something fierce, worse when he sucks."

"Belladonna pellets should take care of the mastitis," Letty answered. "Continue to nurse him and apply heat to the sore spot."

Eric didn't dare enter unannounced. The women would be mortified if they knew he'd overheard their discussion. He purposely stumbled, and the clatter of his boot against the step led to silence.

Then, "Did you find what I need?"

Going to her side, he said, "Yes, Dr. Morgan. Here you are." He dropped the pillow and coverlet on a crate. To make sure Letty's patient didn't get the wrong idea about his presence in the house, he added, "Since it's late and I'm not done building your shelves, I will head on home and come back to finish them later this week. Remember, I'm still your landlord until the sale of the house is complete. Don't hesitate to let me know if you need anything else. Good evening."

Looking confused, Letty nodded. "Oh," she said, as he opened the door, "before you leave, would you be so kind as to look at Mrs. Miller's buggy? She had a problem with a wheel."

He nodded. "On my way."

❦

After Mrs. Miller left, Letty resumed unpacking. What an odd day. At times she'd sensed Eric's interest in her. At others, it had seemed as if he'd built a rock-hard wall between them. She wondered if he would ever overcome the loss of his wife and son.

And that wasn't all. A grim expression had killed Eric's humor at the mention of his father. Her curiosity, of course, had immediately leapt to life, but it had gone unappeased, since she had no right to pry into such matters.

She would never forget his kindness. He'd tried to make everything right for her, and his generosity encompassed others, too. After he'd examined Mrs. Miller's buggy and determined that repairs would take at least two days, he'd driven mother and child back home.

She couldn't help liking the complicated, fascinating, irritating man she was coming to know. Although at times he appeared too serious and one could nearly touch his pain, at other times a sense of humor came into play.

When she realized where her thoughts had gone, she frowned. "Enough of that, Letitia Morgan. You have too much work to do."

Returning to her boxes, she suspected it was perhaps the idle mind rather than idle hands that provided the devil his playground. She stacked jar after remedy jar on her new shelves. Then she folded linens. When the sun set and the room grew dark, she lit several lamps so as to continue working.

Some time later, Letty pressed her fists into her lumbar region and flexed her spine. A knock startled her. Dusting off her hands on her skirt, she went through the former parlor to open the door.

A disheveled Eric stood there.

She gestured him inside. "What did you do to yourself?"

The mischief in his face brought heat to Letty's cheeks, and she backed into the room. He followed, a smile curving his mustache. He wore the same clothes he had earlier that day, but the hat now sported a crust of mud, and the coat's wool had ripped. Despite the scrape on his right cheekbone and the swelling around his left eye, Eric remained the most handsome man she'd ever seen.

She stumbled.

His smile widened. "I was on my way back to let you know I took care of your patient, and I found Slosh trading punches again. With our earlier conversation fresh in my mind, I let my convictions spur me to action. And Slosh says he doesn't need you doctoring his wounds this time."

"You stopped another brawl!" Letty didn't know whether to scold or hug him. She knew which she preferred, but it was highly improper. Instead, she led the way to the examining room. "At this rate, you'll run through my stock of Arnica in no time."

He laughed. The sound swept up and down her spine. She turned and scooped pellets from the jar. Two tiny white balls fell from the spoon onto the shelf, then bounced to her feet. She blushed again.

"I didn't come for doctoring," he said. "I wanted you to know that before I took Mrs. Miller and the baby home, I fetched her mother. They needed the help."

Letty tried to hide her surprise. How had he known she would worry about her patient?

He was handsome, intelligent, caring, and brave—although in need of occasional prodding. As she gazed into his eyes, her admiration turned to appreciation and something more.

His expression changed. His eyes glowed like the flames from the lamps, and the intensity scared her. She tried to back away but found herself pinned against a shelf. His gaze burned into hers, and she trembled.

She knew she should avoid what was coming but found she couldn't move. Ever so slowly, Eric lifted his hand and, with the back of two fingers, caressed her cheek. A current ran through her.

He trailed his fingers to her chin, cupped her jaw in his rough, warm hand, and lifted her face. Then he smiled, a smile so sad it nearly broke her heart.

"I like you, Letitia Morgan. I like you too much."

4

"Eric Karl Wagner, *du bist ein dummes Huhn!*"

The face in the shaving mirror reflected his disgust. If he weren't careful, not only would he continue to behave like a chicken, but he'd grow feathers and start clucking, too. He should avoid her, and yet here he was, at two o'clock in the afternoon, sprucing up to meet Dr. Letitia Morgan.

During the past two weeks, he'd done everything possible to forget the lovely bird that had alighted in town. But the more he tried to dodge thoughts of Letty, the more tenacious they grew.

Her violet scent spoke of gentle femininity, and her sweet smile charmed its recipient. Dr. Morgan was a lovely woman indeed.

And he was fool enough to seek out the confounded woman again.

He'd offered to help her with the typewriter, and he doubted the determined doctor would forget his offer. That being the case, he'd decided to get the ordeal over and done with as soon as possible. Then he could concentrate on avoiding her altogether.

Ignoring Marmie's persistent purring, Eric dusted off the marmalade cat hairs clinging to his trouser legs. He rubbed her head, collected his bowler from the table by the front door, and went out into the crisp, winter afternoon. He hitched the chestnut mares to his black rig, then headed into town. Reasons to turn back filled his mind. So did visions of Letty.

He tethered the buggy at the post outside the doctor's home. After straightening his black coat, he strode up to the door and knocked.

He wondered if he'd find her with patients. When he received no response, he knocked again and waited. Perhaps she'd gone on a call. Then the door flew open.

"Sorry!" Letty called out, rushing back down the hall and into the kitchen. "Do come in. Please. I'll be with you shortly."

Eric entered, puzzled. What was she doing?

In the interest of good manners, he took a seat in one of the mismatched chairs in the parlor. But to his dismay, she didn't return. Instead, he heard running footsteps, barely audible mutters, strange striking sounds, and odd rustles.

"Ouch!" she cried. "Oh, no. No, sir. This time you won't get away."

Was she treating some particularly resistant patient? Surely not. Letty would never speak in that tone to anyone in need of medical assistance. Eric had seen her with Steven, Slosh, and Mrs. Miller, and she'd always been respectful, concerned, solicitous.

"Come back here, you . . . you scalawag, or I'll . . . I'll . . . oh, I don't know what I'll do!"

Eric stood. He was intrigued—no, he was plain curious. Who was she chasing in the kitchen? Blast manners and all that. He had to take a look.

As he hurried down the hall, a loud thump made him speed even more. At the door to the kitchen, he came to a halt. The goings-on made Eric laugh. Sieve in hand, Letty was trying to scoop up a yellow chick. Quick as she was, the baby bird managed to be just that much quicker.

As he approached the hunter and her prey, he heard a chorus

of peeps from a crate near the cookstove. There he counted four more balls of yellow down. "Why would you want five chicks, Dr. Morgan?"

"Eric!" She straightened and fussed with her hair and her skirt. Her cheeks turned a bright pink. A brown curl caressed her ear, and a longer one dangled a hairpin across her shoulder.

Fists on her hips, Letty turned. "Can't you see I'm trying to catch that imp? I won't abide him soiling my kitchen floor."

Eric stifled another chuckle, knowing she wouldn't abide his mirth right then, either. "No," he said, "I should say not. No self-respecting physician would tolerate a soiled kitchen floor."

"Oh, dear," she murmured. "My reckless mouth triumphs once again. Mother despaired of ever making me a lady, so I stopped trying and became a doctor—" she grimaced "—and a spinster, as she so often predicted I would."

The logic in the comment escaped Eric, but he read pain on her face. "Here," he said, doffing his coat. "What if I help you corner your scalawag?"

She swatted at the hairpin swirling over her shoulder and aimed sparkling eyes at him. "Well," she responded, "it would be the gentlemanly thing to do."

Eric almost hugged her. Instead, he swooped to the floor and presented her with her disobedient fowl. Instead of looking pleased, Letty seemed further irritated.

"And why couldn't I achieve similar results?" she asked.

A smile tried to appear, but Eric forbade it. "The talent must come from growing up on a ranch."

A delighted smile replaced her pique. "A real ranch?"

This time he couldn't stop the laughter. "As real as horse manure, chicken feed, and cattle."

Letty reached for the bird Eric still held in his hand. Bringing the small, warm body to her cheek, she rubbed her skin against the ball of fluff. "Mmmm," she murmured. "How lovely. A ranch, that is. Not manure. You understand."

"Yes, I understand. Any time you wish, you're welcome to visit and get your fill."

"Do you really mean that?"

"Of course. I wouldn't offer otherwise."

She cocked her head in that birdlike way of hers. "I wonder . . ."

"No."

"No?"

"Absolutely not."

"And why not?"

"Because I want nothing to do with mothering five orphan chickens. Do I look like a hen?"

As Eric stared at her, waiting for an answer, Letty turned her gaze from the peeping bird in her hands to the man before her. It flitted from the fringe of his mustache, to the breadth of his wide shoulders, to the narrow waist and long legs. It was his strength that most impressed her, strength he couldn't have developed behind a typewriter.

On her way back to Eric's face, Letty noticed his bemusement. Heat filled her face and she looked at the chick.

Cheek against the living scrap in her hands, her thoughts registered nothing but the memory of Eric caressing that cheek. A hint of wonder, a touch of admiration, a bit of longing had filled his gaze when he'd told her he liked her.

He was no hen.

Hoping to disguise her discomfiture, Letty said, "Did you . . ."

When her voice faltered, she shook her head, and a hairpin flew across the room to land at his feet. Clearing her throat, she tried again. "Do you need medical attention?"

Eric's gaze followed the path of the hairpin back to her. Letty felt warm all the way to her toes. "No," he said, bending. "I feel so well I've decided to enjoy the sunny afternoon. I came to invite you to test our Western Rapid typewriter at the office." He returned her errant pin.

"Why . . . certainly." Excitement shimmied up Letty's spine. First his glowing gaze had warmed her, and now his offer to spend an afternoon of leisure together flattered her. Especially since he'd seen her at her most unladylike worst. "I would love to come. How do those machines work?"

Eric laughed. "That's what I'm about to show you."

"Indeed. Now, if you wouldn't mind waiting a moment, I'll be right back."

Letty nestled the chick in her hands amid the others in the box, then spun and, with gray skirt swirling at her ankles, flew up the stairs.

❦

The interior of Eric's buggy bore the fragrance of luxury. The tang of leather upholstery blended with the odor of the lemon oil that gave a shine to the wood trim. As Eric maneuvered the team, Letty sank deeper into her seat and gazed out the round window.

In the late winter sunlight, Main Street teemed with activity. Hartville's residents bustled down the wooden sidewalks, and friends greeted each other. Letty relished the sight, glad to have relegated Philadelphia to the past.

"I've seen you at church the last few Sundays," Eric commented after a bit.

"Why, yes. Pastor Stone's messages are a blessing. Very uplifting."

Eric looked at Letty in surprise. He couldn't even call up the Scripture texts upon which those sermons had been based. The curve of a slender white neck and the coffee-colored curls that escaped the bounds of the coronet she'd fashioned from her braided hair had unduly distracted him.

"Pastor Stone always offers . . . inspiration and . . . uh . . . comfort to the congregation."

Letty nodded. A brown wisp slid free of a section of plait and bounced by her ear. Eric longed to smooth the lock back into place, to again touch the velvet softness of her skin.

". . . and very conscious of his community's needs, don't you think?"

Letty's words dragged Eric's wayward attention back to the conversation. "Most good pastors are," he said, then scrambled for a new topic. "Speaking of the community, how are you settling into Hartville?"

"Quite well, I'd say. I'm not terribly busy with patients at the moment, but I have been to supper at a number of homes and am invited to church socials, ladies' guild programs, and a soirée the new literary society has planned."

Eric arched a brow. "Not so busy as to exhaust our very necessary doctor, are you?"

Her eyes flashed. "I never shirk my duty to my patients, Mr. Wagner."

Eric smiled. She was delightful, and he was a fool, opening himself to her charm. The danger lay in Letty's vivacity; it had brought the first ray of light to pierce the shadows around him.

He heard her soft voice and assumed she continued to expound on her commitment to her patients. He remembered why spending time with her carried such great risk.

". . . right, Mr. Wagner?"

Since he had no idea what she'd asked, Eric took a different tack. "Back to Mr. Wagner? I thought you'd decided my name wasn't so difficult after all. Try it again; you'll see how easy Eric is."

He pulled up before the *Hartville Day*'s office. "We're here," he announced, keeping his attention on the horses.

The sudden distance Eric had again put between them bewildered Letty. "Indeed we are."

He'd urged her to call him Eric, but his demeanor had clearly changed. Why? She'd thought, after the gentle touch to her cheek the other night, certainly after today's invitation, that they shared a mutual attraction. Had she mistaken the meaning of friendly actions? She didn't think so. A woman could tell the difference between a caress and casual contact.

A terrible thought occurred to her. Did he fear becoming the object of the spinster doctor's admiration?

Then she remembered his warm gaze as he watched her with the chick. She sighed her exasperation. Eric Wagner was a puzzling man.

Marshaling her pride, she stepped down from the buggy and left her taciturn companion behind. She wasn't about to let his odd mood rob her of the chance to test the typewriting machine. She'd just be more careful in the future and control her response to Eric Wagner.

❧

As Letty followed Eric into the newspaper's office, the memory of the first lesson sprang to his mind. The awareness he'd felt when he held Letty's fingers was something he would rather forget but couldn't. He remembered the softness of her small, warm hands, and the time he touched her cheek—

"Well, Mr. Wagner, you offered and I'm ready to be taught."

"I . . . that is . . ." What was he supposed to do? He *had* offered to teach her. He couldn't just back out because he was attracted to her. "Yes, I did offer. Twice."

"Precisely. I expect you to teach me."

"Then teach you I shall." Even if the lessons posed ever-increasing danger for him.

Which it did.

When the second lesson came and went with Eric taking only scant pleasure in Letty's proximity, he thought he'd gained control over his unfortunate response to her. The next one, however, since she'd just washed her hair, distracted him even more. Each time he leaned over the still-damp crown of curls, he'd had to fight the urge to bury his face in the glossy mass.

Even when he stayed away from her, Eric's interest in the doctor continued to grow. He admired Letty. He liked her, as he'd told her once before, a bit too much. He respected her talent, the way she treated her patients, and when they both were in the same room, his senses came to life and his awareness shot up sky high.

But he had to stem his interest in her. Had Martina died differently, then he would have been free to pursue the attraction, but he was responsible for his wife's death. His guilt stripped him of the right to become attached to a woman as worthy as Letitia Morgan. Letty battled disease and death, devoting herself to saving lives. She'd surely reject a man who'd failed to fight for his wife's life.

With a bittersweet pang, he remembered their wedding day. Before God and man, he'd vowed to protect Martina. She'd wanted nothing more than to love him and to raise their family.

He thought back to the time when they ordered the parlor sofa. His wife had set aside her taste in furnishings to purchase the long, unwieldy piece that accommodated his size.

But when she'd really needed his strength, he'd let love make him weak, and he watched her die. Her and baby Karl.

No woman deserved that. Especially not Letty.

Still, he'd offered the absurd typewriting lessons. He'd gone so far as to lend her his typewriter, and even set it on her kitchen table. His instincts understood nothing of his failings, so he had to continue to fight for control. He was coming to dread each lesson.

From his arrival at Letty's home for this most recent lesson, Eric found himself in dire straits. Letty's enthusiasm was running high, and her excitement was contagious.

"Oh, Eric!" she exclaimed. "I've been so looking forward to today's lesson. I'm making progress. Here, let me show you."

She took his hand and tugged him along behind her. Heat

swirled up his arm and pooled in his heart. A hint of violets enfolded him.

Try as she might, he couldn't pay attention to the machine, much less the lesson. A coil of brown hair had come loose, and it tempted him to help it on its way down.

Then Letty locked together a handful of keys. "Ohhh! Could you help me, please? I can't pry them apart."

"Sure. I'll show you how to separate the keys." Knowing himself doomed, Eric took Letty's hands in his. The warmth of her strong, capable fingers penetrated his skin and worked through him, just as before. This time, however, he was bent over with his head close to hers. The loosened strands curled close to his lips, and he yielded to temptation. He brushed his mouth across her hair.

Eric nearly groaned at the softness. He nuzzled the curl again, relishing the gossamer contact. He grew clumsy, and his fingers tangled with hers. Letty froze.

Of course she was surprised. He called himself all kinds of fool. He'd been cold, overbearing even, the last few times they'd met. Now here he was playing with her hair. She had to think him crazed at best. But she didn't pull away.

Knowing he shouldn't but unable to stop, Eric pressed his face into the flower-scented coronet.

Then he felt her grip on his hands. He slipped his thumb to the inside of her wrist and drew small circles over her pounding pulse. Her breath caught; his came to a ragged halt. Time stopped.

❦

With Eric's warmth enveloping her, Letty was stunned by the feelings rushing through her. His touch sent heat like that of a lamp into her veins, shocking her with its intensity. She'd never experienced anything so wonderful.

She froze.

"Mr. Wagner! Mr. Wagner, please come help!" someone called.

Letty's heart had never pumped so strongly, its pounding pulse still beating somewhere beyond her consciousness. Then she realized the knocking came from the front door.

"Please, Mr. Wagner, Ford at your office tol' me to fetch you 'cause Pa's at it again," a child called from just outside the door.

Eric wasted no time. He grabbed his coat and gloves from the chair where he'd left them, then ran to the door and opened it.

Letty followed, tossing her cape over her shoulders. The sight that greeted her shouldn't have surprised her, but somehow it did.

A girl, perhaps ten years of age, ran to Eric, the infant on her narrow hip hampering her movements. "Please, Mr. Wagner. Pa's down by Otto's. Some woman's screamin' at 'im to pay what she says he owes 'er. She says he don' own the cow so the milk ain't free. But we ain't had no milk in days."

Eric spouted German, then reverted to English. "Caroline, go inside with Dr. Morgan. I'll take care of your father."

From her spot in the doorway, Letty got a good look at the two children. The girl's brown coat, quite worn, was at least two, perhaps three, sizes too large, yet its long sleeves protected her hands from the icy weather. A pair of sturdy boys' boots poked out from under the tattered hem.

The baby on her hip also sported strange attire. A swaddling blanket parted to reveal a nightgown made from what looked like an old quilt. A peaked face peered out, and long, thin fingers clutched at the girl's shoulder.

"Take care of them, Letty," Eric said. "I'll be back soon."

The girl took a step toward Eric. "But—"

"No, Caroline. It's too cold out here for you and Willy, and you don't belong where your father is."

Eric didn't bother with his buggy but instead loped toward Main Street.

After a quick, challenging look at Letty, Caroline followed.

Letty threw decorum to the wind and raced after them. Reaching the girl, Letty grabbed a thin arm and turned the child around. Four identical bright blue eyes met her gaze, the same bright blue eyes she saw each time a child met with trouble in this town—the blue eyes she'd expected.

Caroline yanked free of Letty's grasp and ran after Eric again, but Letty had reached her limit. Determination fueling her pursuit, she caught the girl's shoulders to bring her to a standstill.

Blue eyes glared. "What d'ya want, lady? My pa's in trouble an' I gotta help Mr. Wagner. Lemme go!"

The agony on the half-matured features almost made Letty relent. Then the infant cried, and Letty's backbone firmed with renewed purpose. "Very well," she said. "Go, if you must, but give that baby to me. If, as you say, there's trouble, you can't do a thing with him on your hip, nor can it do him any good to be present."

The girl's eyes widened. Evidently, she accepted Letty's logic, but her attachment to the baby kept her from surrendering him even for a brief time. The waif's wail grew louder.

Caroline nuzzled the blanketed bundle. "Hush, Willy. 'S all right. Sis is here." Her efforts achieved no success, and she frowned. She then peered in the direction Eric had taken. She squared her narrow shoulders and thrust her brother at Letty.

"Here, miss," she said, "take care of 'im. I'll be right back." She thrust the featherweight parcel into Letty's arms and resumed the chase.

Letty held Willy by her heart, aghast at what she saw. The Pattersons' mother had died about nine months earlier, but at nearly twelve months old the boy weighed no more than twelve pounds and had yet to cut a tooth. As if that weren't enough, she could see every bone in his tiny fist.

"This is too much, Eric Wagner. I've found two more Patterson children in shameful conditions. You and I need to have a serious talk, and soon, sir. Very soon."

First, though, she had to warm the child. She tucked him in under her cape and close to her heart. Tears flooded her eyes when his little hands took fistfuls of her blouse and he lay his cheek against her breast.

Heartsore, Letty followed her charge's older sister, soon reaching East Crawford Street. She saw what had caused Caroline's alarm. Up ahead, just outside a seedy saloon, a harsh-looking blonde stood over the prone figure of a man.

What was wrong with Hartville's men? First, that disreputable Slosh fought at the drunken drop of a hat. Now it seemed the Patterson children's only parent indulged in carnal vices, shirking his duty as father and provider.

Letty drew nearer, the blonde screamed insults at her victim, and Eric stood to one side, trying to mediate the argument. Dread crept over her. It grew a hundredfold when the swinging doors of the establishment behind the screamer parted and three more women joined her. Letty stopped a few feet away from Eric.

She couldn't help but notice the women's scandalous short skirts, their flesh-filled necklines, the garish paint on their faces. Tinny music spewed into the night from behind batwing doors.

She pounced on Eric. "I demand an explanation."

Vexation filled his face. "I told you to stay with Caroline and Willy. Besides, what sort of explanation do you want?"

"Why . . . I . . ." For a moment Letty was speechless. Then her outrage took over. "For goodness' sake, Eric Wagner, this is a bordello!"

5

Despite the deepening evening, Letty saw red on Eric's chiseled cheeks.

"Ah . . . yes," he answered. "And?"

"And there are children here, Mr. Wagner."

"Had you stayed home with them, as I told you to do, they wouldn't be here. Don't you agree, Dr. Morgan?"

"Oh, no. You can't shift the burden of guilt on me. Caroline said she came because her father was in trouble. The responsibility lies with him."

The sodden lump at the feet of the "soiled dove" rose onto his elbows, hampered by the abundance of spirits he'd consumed. After three tries, he hoisted himself to a half-sitting position and peered at Letty.

"Hey!" he called. " 'S the little lady doctor. You wanna have some fun?"

The unpleasant, familiar voice sent Letty's anger beyond its normal bounds. She rounded on Eric. "Slosh! Slosh is Horace Patterson?"

Eric examined his shoes. He raised his head and studied the street lamp at the corner. Finally, with a glare at the drunk on the road, he nodded.

Before Letty could voice her outrage, a commotion at Bessie's Barn caught her attention. A fat, ruddy-faced miner stomped out, dragging along another blonde woman.

She fought, but slender as she was, she got nowhere. "Missy," the miner proclaimed, "for what I'se jist paid, youse can come wid me anywhere I wants."

"P—please," the young woman cried. "Don't make me go—owww!"

With a furious yank, the man hauled her to the middle of the street. "I paid," he repeated, "so's to do what I wants."

She cleared her pale mane from her face, and the lamplight profiled her features. Letty gasped in horror. The girl wasn't much older than Caroline Patterson.

Letty charged the bully. "How dare you? Have you no shame? Can't you see she's just a little girl?"

When he showed no sign of doing the right thing, Letty grew further incensed. "Let her go! Your intentions are immoral, filthy, debauched—sinful. Let her go, you . . . you big—"

A large hand clamped over her lips. A second hand clasped her waist, careful of the baby she held within her cape. Her captor dragged her back, and her urge to fight increased. She tried to bite the muffling hand, with no success. She kicked, hoping to connect with the legs braced against hers, and had no better luck. Twisting and turning, still conscious of her precious charge, Letty refused to accept defeat.

The cluster of women at the bordello door sang out their objection.

One then asked, "Who's she?"

"Humph," another answered. "Her'n her fine clothes ain't no better'n us."

"Uh-huh," the third concurred. "An' look how cozy the do-good newspaperman is with her."

Letty's face burned at their speculations. Especially in light of the intense moment she and Eric had shared in her kitchen before Caroline showed up.

Behind her Eric stopped. His hand left her mouth and his arm slipped from her waist, but he stayed close. Letty felt safe and protected, if mortified.

His breath warmed her earlobe. "See why I told you to stay back with the children? You don't belong among riffraff."

Letty paid only partial attention to Eric's words. Her focus flew between her awareness of his proximity and the scene before her. The young woman, still fighting her "client," silently beseeched Letty for help, her hazel eyes filled with fear.

Letty's size and the baby in her arms rendered her helpless. In desperation, the blonde raised her knee and aimed for the man's groin.

He blocked her attempt with a beefy thigh. A bestial roar poured from his mouth. "I knows better'n that. Hey, Bessie, we's got us a bill to settle."

As he twisted to protect himself, his grip on the girl's slender arm loosened enough for her to wrest herself free. Intent on escape, she didn't see Slosh's foot and tripped, landing on his prone body. After a scant pause, she resumed her fight for freedom.

Letty noticed the gash over the girl's eyebrow. Her golden curls drooped forward, and her head, seemingly too heavy for her slender neck, followed.

"Here," Letty said to Caroline. "Take your brother. She's hurt. I must see to her."

Letty ran to the girl and cautiously turned her head to better gauge the wound. It was deep and would require suturing. The girl's general appearance and her unfocused gaze told Letty her new patient had sustained a concussion.

"C'mon back, Daisy," said a woman at the brothel door. "Let's git you fixed up again. Night's jist startin'."

"Yeah," urged another. "Suggs already paid. You c'n git yourself another fella an' make out real nice."

A chorus of yesses followed.

Letty looked around and saw that Daisy's "customer" had indeed left, but she could hardly believe the women expected the girl to return to "work" in her current condition.

"No," she said, smoothing Daisy's brow. The street fell silent. "She's hurt. I'm taking her home."

Slosh's rude "hic!" broke the uneasy hush. "I'd sure 'nuff like to take 'er home wid me."

Letty's anger rose again, but before she could act, Eric swooped, grabbed a handful of filthy shirt, and shook Slosh. Letty took Daisy in her arms. She was dismayed by the girl's slenderness.

She struggled to her feet, her movements unwieldy. Eric dropped Slosh and rushed to her side.

He reached for Daisy. "What are you doing? You can't take her with you. If their comments shamed you, imagine what the respectable folks in town will say once they learn you took a tart home."

"I don't give one fig what they say. I care what God thinks. If I don't tend to this child as I've been trained to do, I'll be rejecting His call to serve His children. I won't reject my Lord."

She turned to Caroline. "You come with me, too, dear. Let's hurry home. It's late, and it's getting colder."

The painted women returned to their place of business, muttering among themselves. Two men who'd watched from the entry to a billiard hall went back inside. Slosh sang out a ditty interrupted by belches and hiccups.

"Hey, Ca'line," he suddenly called, "don' leave yore ol' Pa here like this. Gi' us a hand."

Letty urged Caroline to help her get Daisy and Willy to her house. Eric's hand fell on her shoulder. "I can carry Daisy."

Slosh renewed his serenade.

"Your offer's tempting," Letty said to Eric, "but I can manage. Please see to Slosh. He can't stay all night in the middle of the road."

Indecision played on Eric's face, and then he shrugged. "Have it your way, but as soon as I'm done with him, I'll come help."

Letty studied him with shrewd calculation. "Yes, Eric, do come after you're done with Slosh. I'll have the children settled, and we can have a long-overdue conversation. Don't think for a second you can escape this moment of truth."

A sheepish smile lifted the brown fringe over his mouth. "I guess I'm about to get a dose of Dr. Morgan's doctoring."

"I daresay you are. I need to treat your tendency to evade pertinent issues."

"Then I'd better hurry with Slosh. I wouldn't want to evade the pertinent chat."

"Indeed, Mr. Wagner."

"Indeed, Dr. Morgan."

❦

After Letty settled Caroline and Willy in her bed, she returned to Daisy, whose forehead now sported a row of stitches.

Letty woke her to check the dilation of her pupils. "How do you feel?"

Daisy groaned. Her unusual yellow-hazel eyes rolled and then fixed on Letty.

"Can you handle a cup of tea?" Letty asked.

"Sounds good." Daisy tried to sit.

Letty caught her. "Not so fast, young lady. That's too much moving for your head. I'll bring the tea and help you sit."

She hurried to fetch the beverage, her heart aching for the child in Daisy, a child forced to grow up inappropriately and too soon. Daisy should still be studying her lessons, embroidering to fill a hope chest, dreaming of a first suitor, not meeting the basest needs of the basest of men.

Letty sighed. What could she do?

As she helped the girl with the tea, Letty chatted, trying to draw her out. Daisy soon told her how no one took her in after her parents died. Bessie, Slosh's enterprising friend, had offered shelter and the means to earn her keep. Scared, not knowing where else to turn, Daisy accepted the older woman's offer.

Sobs wracked the girl's thin shoulders. Something had to be done. This child could not—would not—return to the brothel.

Daisy soon slept. Letty's thoughts churned up possibilities. She discarded most, since the viable ones required help and folks who'd have to be contacted, whose cooperation had to be obtained.

Mid-deliberations, someone knocked. Expecting Eric, Letty went to let him in, but it wasn't him after all. Bessie stood in the shadows cast by the lamp at Letty's left. "How is she, Doc?"

"She's hurt, but she'll be fine if she gets enough rest. She can't go back . . . go back to—"

"No, Doc," Bessie cut in with a smirk. "She cain't go back to *work.*"

Letty blushed. "Yes, Bessie," she said. "I hate and object to the sin-filled life you lead. As for Daisy, she can stay here to recover—"

"Nah. I'll take 'er with me. I got an extra bed these days, an' she can rest there. I'll keep an eye out for 'er."

Letty wanted to argue, but she saw Bessie's determined jaw and her disdain. She surrendered with grace.

Still concerned, however, she offered detailed instructions. "Please keep her from rising too rapidly. Daisy's concussed, and her head can't handle abrupt changes in position. If she has any problems, do send for me. I want to help her—"

"Ya've helped enough already," Bessie said, eyes narrowed. "I'll take care of 'er now. How much I owes ya?"

Letty met Bessie's gaze. "Not a penny. I did this—"

"Yeah, yeah. Outta the kindness of yer heart. I knows yer kind. A harlot's money's not good enough for ya."

"I *never* said or thought that. I never would, either. I just want to help an injured child, that's all."

Bessie stared. After a moment she lifted a shoulder, dislodging her pea-green shawl. A generous portion of white flesh bulged at the neckline of her blue and black lace dress. The exposure embarrassed Letty, yet it bothered Bessie not one bit.

"Mebbe," Bessie said, "mebbe not. A gentleman friend brung me in 'is carriage. I'll take Daisy home with us."

"Very well." Letty counted pellets into two small envelopes, sealed and labeled them, and gave them to Bessie. "Here. Arnica's for shock, and she'll need it for a while yet. The other one, Ruta Graveolens, is for bruised bones. Make sure she takes it tomorrow."

"How much I owes ya?" Bessie asked again.

"Nothing. Nothing at all."

With another careless shrug, Bessie took the remedies, slipped them into a green silk reticule, and then shook the sleeping Daisy. The girl's eyes fluttered open, widening with what looked to Letty like fear. Daisy bit her lower lip.

"G'bye, Doc," Bessie said, leading Daisy away.

The urge to stop the woman knotted Letty's middle, but any effort would be futile. Her concern for the injured child grew. With nerves stretched to violin-string tension, she neatened the clinic as she sought the Lord in prayer.

Capping the Arnica made her think of Eric. The memory of the intense moment that evening rushed to her mind. Her hands grew clammy. How had she let herself wind up in such a risqué position?

She blushed and acknowledged that her curiosity, that vexing urge to learn, to know more, had again joined forces with her other bête noire, her impulsiveness.

The remedy jar cap slipped from her fingers. Glancing down to where it landed, Letty noted it hadn't shattered.

But *she* was on the verge of shattering. She had never experienced sensations such as those Eric evoked. They surpassed her wildest imaginations, especially since she'd surrendered all dreams of a loving spouse and children, a family. She'd focused instead on developing her God-given gift to heal, and on becoming self-sufficient and needing no one but herself and the heavenly Father.

Men saw her as less than the womanly ideal they sought for wife and mother, and she never pretended to look like anything other than what she was—a doctor. Then she met Eric Wagner. Could this man be interested in her? *Her?*

She puzzled over Eric's intensity after so many days of aloof behavior. Why had he come so close, looked at her with such fervor? Inexperienced she was; ignorant she wasn't. Something had burned in Eric's gaze. It had singed her. She didn't understand why it had happened. Especially since every time they'd met after the first typewriting lesson, he'd been distant and polite, even off-putting, his manner cool.

The man who'd tangled hands with her was anything but cool. That man cared and shared her interest. Today that interest had blazed to attraction. The most intriguing man Letty knew was interested in her.

Perhaps she *was* womanly enough to attract a man.

Perhaps God had heard her girlish prayers. Eric was alone. Although he obviously still grieved the loss of his wife, maybe his interest revealed his readiness to seek another love. Dare she aspire to that? Would Eric want a woman doctor?

Perhaps. In any case, those were matters best left where they belonged: in God's hands.

Letty dozed awhile until a knock came at her door. The sight of Eric reminded her of her earlier thoughts, and she blushed, incapable of even the briefest greeting. She hastened to the kitchen. The chair she pulled out scraped against the floor, and she collapsed in it.

Dear Lord, what did I set myself up for?

As Eric followed Letty to the kitchen, dreading their "pertinent chat," a chick peeped from the comfort of its box.

Letty's cheeks showed a hint of rose, and Eric feared her discomfiture matched his now that they found themselves alone in her kitchen again. The troublesome typewriter sat at the far end of the table. The memory it evoked was almost enough to send him back out for a dose of wintry air.

He needed to clear his thoughts, to chill his attraction to the doctor. He had to prevent a similar episode in the future.

Hoping to forget, wondering if he could, Eric brought up the other matter he would have rather avoided. "I took Slosh home. Amelia and Steven were preparing a meal. I made certain Slosh had a cup of coffee and some bread."

Without looking away from her knotted hands, Letty's head bobbed up and down.

Her awkwardness confirmed Eric's earlier fear. Clearly, Letty was uncomfortable with the memory of that moment. Why shouldn't she be? Why would a lovely, capable young woman like Letty need, or want, the attentions of an older widower? Particularly one who bore guilt in his wife's death. Any number of younger men would be more suitable.

Those were sparks in her gaze, the undisciplined part of his mind taunted. *And she didn't run away.*

True, Letty hadn't rejected him. At first, she'd seemed stunned, but then her gaze had gone warm and caring. Dare he hope?

Nein. He had no right. He had to stifle his interest in this beautiful woman, and he would start now. "I must take the children home, Letitia."

At the sound of her full name, she looked up. Silver eyes broadcast her unspoken question. Eric shook his head. He didn't want to discuss it. "Caroline is needed at home."

She stood. "I thought my na—" She stopped, squared her

shoulders, stood, and faced him. "I'll be brief. I voiced my wish to help the Patterson children when I first came to town. It was your duty at that time to tell me the family had more children than Steven and Amelia. I could have sent food for Caroline and baby Willy."

"I could have said something," he said, "but that family is more than you should tackle while you establish your medical practice and settle into town."

Her silver gaze forgave him nothing. "I'll thank you to note that I can decide for myself what I will and will not undertake. You, Eric Wagner, presume too much."

He received Letty's words as an indictment on his earlier transgression, a more grievous offense than withholding information about the Pattersons. And yet he couldn't bring himself to discuss the incident.

"Please forgive my presumption," he said. "It won't happen again." *Either sin,* he added silently.

As her lashes fluttered down, her features took on an odd expression. When she looked up again, her eyes showed no silver sparks.

Could her gaze have meant what Eric thought it meant? Was it perhaps hope his words had killed? No, he could ill afford such thoughts.

$\tilde{\epsilon}$

Eric's promise killed Letty's budding hope. As far as she could tell, the conversation had been held on two separate levels. She hadn't missed Eric's more personal meaning. He wanted nothing of the spinster doctor.

On the other level, she had one more matter to address. "At the very least, you should have told me Slosh's name. For someone who puts such stock in seeking and sharing truth, you're quite adept at skirting it."

Eric's cheeks showed shame, or perhaps anger.

"I *do* believe in the truth," he said. "I'm only guilty of poor judgment. I sought to ease your move to Hartville. As I said, I regret my presumption."

"I heard you the first time, and your meaning came through loud and clear. Tell me, has anyone in town spared a thought as to the fate of the children while Slosh carouses with women of loose virtue?"

"Yes. Everyone has, but the children do have a parent. Unworthy though he may be, Slosh *is* their father. As to his carousing with prostitutes, you can only do yourself and your practice immeasurable damage by consorting with them yourself."

Letty felt as though he'd slapped her face. "Do you only report happy, decent, and uplifting news? Or do you also report seamier events?"

"Of course I report all news. There is, though, a difference between us. I'm a newspaperman, and I report good and bad news to inform the public of events around them. You, Dr. Morgan, deal with the more delicate members of our town. You were brought here especially for our ladies and children. It's bad enough that Hartville's sudden fortune has helped propagate blight that was previously not so strong or pervasive. We don't need our lady doctor patching up and returning to the street women who pander to men's vices."

Letty fought her rising temper. "How dare you insinuate I intended to return that girl to her horrid circumstances? I only want to heal her wounds and help her find healing for her soul as well. A decent, moral, godly life for her is my goal."

"And how do you propose to do that? All she knows is selling—"

"There, Eric, is the problem. All she knows is prostitution. Why? Because her parents died and she became destitute. No one reached out but Bessie." Letty paused. After careful thought, she met Eric's gaze. "Don't you wonder what might have been her lot had one of Hartville's leading families taken her in?"

Eric grimaced. "You may be right. Perhaps we can prevent what happened to Daisy from happening in the future, but you can't salvage her."

"You would just give up on that child? Without trying? Have you never heard of redemption?"

"We'd be further along if we cleaned up East Crawford Street. The saloons and bars that thrive since the Heart of Silver Mine hit the mother lode are what attract harlots, gamblers, and other undesirables."

"I see," Letty answered. "You advocate 'out of sight, out of mind.' Is that what you want to do with murderers? Just chase them out of town so they can kill elsewhere?"

Eric's eyes widened, than narrowed. He opened his mouth, then closed it again. He shook his head. "I advocate jail, away from innocent people, the innocent people I brought you here to treat."

"Just because you had a part in bringing me here doesn't mean you have a right to control my actions."

He didn't respond to her assertion. The silence grew strained. She'd made her point, but the ugliness of the situation kept Letty from feeling any satisfaction in that minor victory.

A true victory lay in the future, if God so willed. She prayed.

Eric dreaded Letty's reaction when she remembered he'd been working not only to shut down the brothels, but also to have the fallen women run out of town or jailed.

Letty, with her soft heart and eternal optimism, couldn't imagine such sordidness. She'd never watched the downfall of a man caught between the twin vices of alcohol and bought flesh. She'd never seen a family lose their home because the father patronized saloons, billiard halls, and bordellos. Too often, wages meant to buy animal feed, planting seed, clothing, and food went to the well-heeled vice mongers. She had never seen it happen.

But Eric had. One man too many.

How was he going to tell her Slosh began his journey down that path a long time ago?

He wasn't. Eric saw no way to tell Letty how rapacious life could be. She thought that with food and friendship she could make all things right for the Patterson children. For all he knew, she might even entertain the notion of rehabilitating Slosh.

Letty was an innocent, whereas he, besides having lost all he treasured, had been exposed to the worst humanity had to offer. A son could never forget the destruction of a father, the ravaging of a family.

"I'm a doctor and have seen more suffering than anyone should." Her words made him stop and think. But no, her wholesome air belied those words, and he remained certain she had no understanding of the situation.

With a futile gesture, Eric turned to leave. "We're at an impasse. If you want a healthy medical practice, I suggest you avoid the women of East Crawford Street. Few husbands will want their wives treated by a physician who consorts with the likes of them."

"No need to repeat your narrow opinion, Mr. Wagner, and perhaps we should avoid that subject after all. In any case, I'm interested in the four Pattersons, and I'm going to help them."

On his way to fetch the children, Eric paused. Four? She had said *four*. He rolled back his head and laughed.

"What? What is so humorous, Mr. Wagner?"

"You," he blurted out, then realized his mistake. "Not you, your assumption."

"What are you saying?"

"The Pattersons, Letty. There aren't four Patterson children."

"Why, of course there are. There's Caroline, Steven, Amelia, and Willy."

Eric nodded, trying to stop laughing. "Yes, there are those. What I'm saying is that there aren't just four, there are five Patterson children."

"Five?"

"Yes, five."

"But, I've never seen—"

"You probably never will."

Letty started to ask what he'd meant, but he put on his hat, started toward the stairs, then paused again.

"Suzannah hasn't left the house since her mother died."

❦

Suzannah, Suzannah, Suzannah. In the silence after Eric's departure from the room, the name beat through Letty's thoughts like the refrain of a heartbreaking song.

A child, sitting in a house for months. A town that let her stay in the care of a debauched drunk.

Letty ached to rail at Eric's seemingly heartless attitude, but after his shocking announcement, he strode to her room, returned holding Willy to his chest, and led Caroline to his rig. He gave Letty no chance to voice her fears.

She feared that Slosh, to indulge his vices, would beggar the children, and Caroline—serious, responsible Caroline—might see no choice but to follow in Daisy's footsteps—encouraged by Bessie, no doubt.

That could never happen. She wouldn't let it happen. The hideous thought hurt so much, she knew she had to do something. And soon.

But what, Lord Jesus? What should I do?

The Lord kept His peace. No verse came to Letty's help, no prompting in her spirit, not even an idea.

"Nothing tonight," she conceded and prepared for sleep, sleep that never came. Vivid visions filled her night, some pleasant, others not pleasant at all.

The memory of Eric's brief caress seemed seared into her mind. Try as she might, she couldn't banish her bittersweet longing for more of that tender touch.

When she feared she'd lose her sanity, she grasped at other thoughts, but the image of the Patterson children still swirled in her head. Their faces alternated with that of Daisy—Daisy at the door of the brothel, Daisy fighting the drunk, Daisy, who Caroline, or Amelia, or even the unknown Suzannah could one day be.

"And just who is trying to heal poor, lost Suzannah?" Letty asked. No one.

That was about to change. She sat up in bed, her blankets mounded at her waist in the pooling moonlight. Warm blankets, a cozy home, plenty of food, medicine when needed. Who better to provide such essentials for the Patterson children than Letty herself?

Mind made up, she gave up on sleep and began planning in earnest.

Surely this was why God had brought her to Hartville.

6

The sickly sweet scent of blood filled the room. Painful moans and whimpers left Eric desperate, helpless.

"She can't take much more, Mr. Wagner," said the midwife.

"No," he argued, never taking his gaze from Martina's colorless features. He held her icy, still fingers. "There must be something you can do."

The midwife's wise, black eyes stared back at him. "You must fetch Dr.——"

Movement whispered against fabric as Martina shook her matted gold curls. "No doctor. . . ."

Her voice faded, Eric noted the involuntary tensing of her abdomen, and the midwife helped Martina's nearly lifeless body push. "Maybe this time."

Martina strove.

The midwife pushed.

Eric prayed.

"Go on, dear heart," the woman urged. "Just like so." She slipped around to the foot of the bed, and Eric saw hope brighten her eyes.

Then she sobbed.

Eric followed her tear-filled gaze and caught his first glimpse of his son. The infant's immobile face was a mottled dark blue. Dead.

"Nooo!"

Eric's cry pierced the night, waking him as his chest heaved with familiar agony. Since they hadn't haunted him in three or four months, he'd hoped the nightmares had gone for good. But, no, the guilt would follow him forever.

He had to stay away from Letty.

❦

"Eric! Where are you?"

Eric dropped the newspaper. After last night's nightmares, his reporter's yell cranked the pounding in his head to a violent beat. "In here, Ford. What's gotten into you?"

Shoving round spectacles up his nose, the reporter barged into the office. Eric shook his head and smiled at Fordham Giller's boyish energy. As usual, the young man's nose wore a smudge of ink and the knot in his tie had long ago resigned its position.

"Happened again," Ford said. "This time to the Cramers. You know, the old folks just outside town with flowers in front of their barn."

Eric's anger propelled him from the chair. They'd been investigating a series of shady land deals for some time now. "I just reread that last story I wrote. The Cramers, huh?"

Ford's spectacles dipped to the tip of his nose. "And the Swartleys paid them, but only a fraction of the land's value."

"We'll never get them for theft. I must keep missing something, a mistake they've made that I haven't noticed." Eric stood and came out from behind his desk. He rammed his right fist in his pocket and ran thumb and index finger of his left hand over his mustache. "They can't be perfect. No one is."

"Only Jesus," Ford added, tugging down his rolled-up shirtsleeves. He'd dropped his jacket on the floor, and his hat, caved in on one side, sat on the chair across from Eric's desk. "So where did they slip?"

As Ford started to sit, Eric hollered, "Look out! Your hat."

The reporter glared at the offending headgear, picked it up, smashed a fist into the squashed side, and slapped the sorry thing against his thigh. "Anyway," he said, "do you want me to keep watching them?"

"It can't hurt. I'll keep asking questions, too."

Ford rolled up his notebook, tucked his hat under one arm, and swooped to pick up his jacket. "On my way."

"Be careful. The Swartleys will likely turn dangerous when thwarted, and our investigation threatens their pockets."

Ford bobbed his head. Despite his careless appearance, not much got by the reporter. Eric valued him as an employee and knew that between the two of them, they'd get what they needed to nail the Swartleys.

Egbert and Jephthah Swartley were another "boon" brought on by Hartville's sudden prosperity. Since their arrival, they'd bought a number of outlying claims for a pittance and planned to mine the properties. The swindled folk who subsequently tried to find jobs in town soon learned that the few dollars the canny brothers had paid them were all they had. Housing in town had become pricey.

When Eric had asked Douglas Carlson to draft documents to sell Letty the house on Willow, the lawyer grilled him on his reasons for selling so low. When Douglas learned who Eric's buyer was, he plastered on a silly grin and nodded sagely.

He only wanted to help her. What was wrong with that? Not a thing, and he'd continue to help her no matter how angry the independent dove grew. Although, when riled, Letty resembled a woodpecker more than a dove. She hammered away with relentless intensity at whatever bothered her.

He smiled. Dr. Letitia Morgan hid fire under her professional surface, and Eric had been so cold since Martina's death, frozen inside his cage of guilt. He had no right to want any woman, certainly not Letty. Love made him weak when he should have been strong.

Eric had always loved Martina. Their families were among the first to move to Hartville and had known each other well. Friendship first drew Martina and Eric together and then, with the passage of time, blossomed into love.

Marriage had seemed as natural as drawing breath. Their friendship had underpinned the affection that then built a strong marital bond. They'd talked for hours, preferring each other's company to anyone else's. Martina's ethereal beauty had mesmerized Eric, a fascination to which he'd happily surrendered.

When he loved, he loved deeply. Too deeply. Love for Martina had blinded him that fateful day. He'd yielded when he should have stood firm and saved two lives.

He couldn't care again as much as he had for his wife, certainly not for Letty. He already responded to her but had to stifle that response. If he'd been weak for Martina, he didn't doubt he would be for Letty as well.

His weakness had caused Martina's death.

He couldn't—wouldn't—expose Letty to his love.

❦

When Letty rose the next day, her resolve to help the Pattersons lent her actions a new sense of purpose. Not only was she in Hartville to improve the town's health, but she now had a more personal mission. God had brought her to rescue cast-off children. Especially since she'd never be blessed with any of her own.

The looking glass over the washstand reflected her sadness. To dispel thoughts of Eric and their confrontation last night, she cupped her hands in the chilly water and splashed her face again and again. Teeth chattering, cheeks tingling, Letty studied her likeness. Yes, she was a doctor. She'd made her choice, and she was proud of it.

She donned a gray flannel skirt and white shirtwaist with navy stripes, braided her hair, and coiled it into her customary coronet. Patting stray curls, she smiled. She looked efficient, just as she wanted.

The rose and white room brimmed with fanciful dreams, but downstairs she had patients to see. Many patients. One after the other, keeping her busy all morning long.

When the stream of patients dried up, Letty pulled out her heart-shaped pocket watch. Noontime had arrived. She lunched on fresh bread, good cheese, and a tangy apple.

Her chicks' escalating peeps reminded her she had to find them a permanent home. As she bit into the fruit, a knock came at her back door. Surprised, since her patients used the clinic entrance out front, she hastened to answer.

Randy Carlson's hair caught the sunlight beneath her bonnet and shone like polished copper. "Hello, Letty."

"What a pleasure to see you, Randy. Please, come in."

"I wanted to visit sooner," she said, draping her wrap over a chair, "but I decided to give you time to settle in."

Yet another person making a choice for her based on an imagined need.

"You're always welcome here, and I haven't been so busy I couldn't spare time to chat."

Randy's eyes clouded. "Oh, dear. I hope you weren't lonely. It must be unsettling to move as far as you did."

"I can't say I've been lonely, but I do welcome a friend."

"And here I am." The redhead settled into the chair, smug delight on her freckled face. "Oh, before I forget. I feel fine, even though the smell of supper cooking makes me ill. Why is that? I always heard the sickness came in the morning."

"Not necessarily. As the day goes by, you get tired, and some women feel worse in the evening when they're worn out."

"That makes sense. Tell me, what have you been doing? Besides doctoring, that is."

Letty laughed. Randy's effervescence was contagious. "I've befriended the Patterson rapscallions."

A frown shadowed Randy's face. "It's so sad. Their mother died not long ago, and Horace, never the best of fathers, stopped trying."

"So I've heard. Tell me, Randy, why has no one done anything for them?"

"Oh, but, Letty, we've tried. Pastor and Mrs. Stone even offered to keep them so that Horace could work regularly. He refused."

"That's not what I meant. Why are they dressed so oddly? And why are they loose in the streets? Won't anyone spare the time to care for them?"

"How can we spend time with them? We can't even catch them. And the ladies' guild did give them a trunk of clothes."

"A trunk?" Visions of the games such unsupervised bounty must have inspired danced in Letty's head. "So no one helped them choose proper clothing. It's no wonder they look ready for a masquerade. Don't you think that loving them, advising them, teaching them would help? The Lord does call us to feed the hungry and dress the poor."

"Yes," Randy answered. "But they ran wild even while their mother lived. She and Horace weren't the best of parents."

Letty digested the information and deemed it time to change the subject. "You'll be the best of mothers, right?"

Randy beamed her pleasure. "I'll sure try, even though I am a mite scared."

Letty stood, crossed the room, and placed a hand on Randy's shoulder. "That's a normal part of expecting. You're facing something new, and the unfamiliar brings anxiety with the excitement."

"Is that how you felt about coming to Hartville?"

"Precisely how I felt in Philadelphia."

"And now that you're here?"

Remembering the past few weeks, Letty chuckled. "I'm not sure how I feel now that I'm here. Except that I know this is where God wants me."

"Wonderful!"

Letty wondered at her friend's glee but couldn't fathom its meaning.

Randy went on, oblivious to Letty's confusion. "This leads to my second reason for coming today. The ladies' guild is holding a dinner social on Friday evening. We'd love to have you come."

"Is it potluck? Shall I bring a dish?"

"Absolutely not. The guild members take turns cooking throughout the year. Just bring yourself."

"Then I'll look forward to Friday evening."

"These parties are quite lovely," Randy went on, her eyes sparkling. "We often play charades."

"Delightful! I love charades."

Grinning, Randy slipped on her dark blue wrap, looped the matching shawl over her red curls, and hugged Letty farewell.

"Until Friday, then," Letty said.

"Friday," answered Randy.

After the expectant mother whisked out of her home, Letty found herself at loose ends. No more patients came for treatment, and her house needed no further care. Even her chickens were content to peck at some corn a patient had brought in payment.

She sat at the scarred kitchen table, chin in hand, and scanned the room. An uneasy feeling lodged in her middle, brought on by the memory of her aimless existence in Philadelphia. A kaleidoscope of scenes spun through her mind.

The emptiness of her clinic and the silence that filled it, broken only by the weeping of the urchins who occasionally sought her help. And before the clinic, her life had only had room for studies and caring for Mother, who'd never been an easy sort. From earliest childhood, Letty knew she should be seen only when sent for. Mercifully, those times were few, as Mother loved running Father's home, keeping it as calm and pleasant as the busy physician wished. Letty had known peace while Father's needs occupied Mother.

After his death, Mother had directed her compulsion to organize and oversee toward Letty. Days became portions of turbulence, sliced apart only by the time spent at the medical college. Upon Letty's return home each evening, Mother had done her best to disrupt any length of concentrated study.

"Why can you not be like other young women? All our friends' daughters are busy with either wedding preparations or caring for young ones. Why must you pursue such an inappropriate interest?"

"Because, like Father, I'm called to heal."

Mother never understood. She'd often bemoaned the men who wouldn't choose Letty for a wife and all the chances she'd miss to become a pillar of Philadelphia society. Not even on her deathbed did Mother cease her efforts to persuade Letty to abandon her wish to practice medicine.

During the barren months when Letty had had virtually no patients, Mother's voice had often echoed in her mind and made her wonder if Mother might have been right. Then she'd found the trampled boy. If ever she'd questioned her urge to care for those who hurt, all doubts vanished that night. A child had led her to the truth.

Then Steven Patterson narrowly escaped the same fate. Letty smiled. One had to admire the wit of the boy, of all the Pattersons. They were managing on wits alone.

A flurry of feathers from the box near the cookstove drew her attention. The picnic basket Amelia had tried to pilfer sat nearby, filled with potatoes and onions from the Millers' farm.

Letty held her breath, pleased at the thought that came to her. She flew around the kitchen, gathering treasures for the Pattersons. Potatoes, onions, a loaf of fresh bread, apples, cabbage, a dozen eggs, and a dressed chicken went into the large hamper. This time, she had no intention of waiting for Amelia to appear.

This time Letty was going for Suzannah.

In her gray wool cape, and with a thick charcoal scarf around her head, Letty hefted the basket onto her right arm. She went out and turned the small clinic sign from OPEN to CLOSED. With a lilt in her step, she crossed the slushy street, then used the walk that led to the Silver Creek Church manse.

After a brief consultation with Mrs. Stone, she got directions to the Patterson home.

"It's not a nice place," the pastor's wife warned.

"That's why I'm on my way there. Five of God's babies live in that awful place."

When she'd traveled the three-quarters of a mile Mrs. Stone had instructed, Letty saw what she feared was the Patterson place. The dilapidated structure reminded her of a smile turned upside down, its corners bowed under the weight of neglect. Whitewash had long ago peeled off from the walls, and the railing drooped around the porch in stops and starts.

The scrawniest dog she'd ever seen howled at her, and only then did she notice the familiar black buggy, its team of mares tied to a spindly tree. Her foolish heart picked up its rhythm a beat or two.

An irritating thought crossed her mind. Last night Eric had said the Pattersons were more than one person could handle. Had he made another decision as to what she ought to undertake? Had he decided to take them on to keep her from shouldering the burden he considered too great for her?

She'd chosen her career over a more conventional life, and she'd taught herself to cope with anything that came her way—on her own. If Eric insisted on making choices for her, she'd soon give him a newsworthy headline: There is little Letitia Morgan can't do.

Before she reached the rickety front steps, the door opened and Eric stepped onto the porch. Letty's breath caught when she saw the gleam of sunlight in his hair. The man was far too handsome for her own good. *Oh, honestly, Letty.* After yesterday, she had no reason to harbor such foolish thoughts.

Peering into the shadows beyond the doorway, she saw Caroline with Willy at her hip. When Eric turned to leave, he spotted Letty.

She waved. "Caroline, I brought a basket of food. Amelia hasn't been by for a few days, and I had some items you might enjoy."

She started up the steps, holding the basket out to the girl, but Eric blocked her way. "If it isn't the ministering angel of Hartville, Colorado."

"Th—thank ye, Dr. Miss," Caroline said when Eric handed her the hamper.

"You're most welcome, dear." Letty smiled. Then, loath to leave without accomplishing her purpose, she asked, "Is everyone well?"

Caroline nodded and hitched the baby higher.

"Good-bye, Caroline," Eric said, heading down the steps again. "Allow me to offer you a ride back to town, Dr. Morgan."

Letty pulled out of his reach before he took her elbow. She feared she wouldn't have been able to stop a recurrence of yesterday's heat had she allowed the contact.

A scowl marred Eric's features, broadcasting his displeasure at her evasion. It suited her quite well if he thought her rude. At least he wouldn't think her a desperate spinster.

She squared her shoulders. "I came for a walk, Mr. Wagner, and I will continue my walk."

The normal curve of his mustache flattened as he clamped his lips. To her surprise, he said nothing more.

She waved to the children who filled the doorway, irritated that Eric had thwarted her plan to find Suzannah, and then she marched away from the attractive man grinding his teeth in obvious annoyance.

"Good day, Mr. Wagner."

❦

Eric fumed all the way home. Would that woman ever listen to reason? He'd tried to warn her, but had she listened?

Not at all. First, there was that business with the "soiled dove," and now she'd denied herself in favor of feeding the Patterson brood.

He'd been seeing to the children's needs since their mother died. Quietly, without fanfare. Then Dr. Letitia Morgan flew into town and began ruffling to rights every wrong she found. The doctor seemed compelled to heal every wound society bore. She was stubborn, too. Irritated, he tugged on the reins, urging the horses on.

At home, he tore off his overcoat and flung it onto the table in the entry. Marmie's welcoming meows went unattended, as did her habit of weaving in and out between his legs. Inevitably, he stepped on a paw, and her yowl spoke of injured sensibilities as well as a sore foot.

"Sorry," he muttered, conceding he was a sorry sight indeed. Letty was wreaking havoc in his life, and, fool that he was, he wished he had the right to let her turn it inside out.

But he couldn't pursue the attraction between them; a door in his house served as a reminder, a door he hadn't opened in two years. The door hid the memory of his most poignant wishes, his most tender dreams. The door belonged to the room that would have been his son's.

Baby Karl.

Eric had failed his son before the child even drew breath, before he knew the sweetness of light, of life.

He had to stifle the feelings between Letty and him; they couldn't take root and grow. Weak as he was, he had to find the strength to fight his soul-deep need for love.

※

Letty couldn't wait for the church social. She hoped the evening would offer the opportunity to make new friends who might fill her time and thoughts. Maybe then she'd stop think-ing of Eric.

Late Friday afternoon, she took a watered-silk dress in rosy plum from her trunk. She'd taken great care packing it; it scarcely needed a touch with the iron.

Spreading the garment across her bed, she remembered Mother insisting she have the dress made. Letty rarely indulged in frivolous luxuries, and although her serviceable skirts and shirtwaists suited her most of the time, tonight was a special occasion. Letty reveled in the beauty of plum silk and cream brocade.

She bathed in the large enameled tub in the lean-to off the kitchen. After the soak in violet-scented water, she dried off and donned her only corset. Though she abhorred the contraption, Letty had enough vanity to want the smallest waist possible for her beautiful gown—even if it did take contortions to lace up the corset.

She faced the looking glass over the washstand to do her hair. She piled the curls in a soft arrangement on the crown of her head, golden strands catching the lamplight and sparkling among the deeper brown. The rich plum of her dress set off her fair skin and reflected rose onto her cheeks. Behind her, the softer pinks and whites in the room offered her a perfect background.

Tonight, in this beautiful dress, Letty's plain, gray eyes looked almost silver. Yes, indeed, the spinster doctor looked anything but dowdy tonight. Letty refused to acknowledge the reason for her excitement. As she flung her cape over her shoulders, she picked up a pretty beaded reticule.

She went straight to the fellowship hall at the church and hung her cape on the hall tree by the door. Happy chatter drew her inside.

The noise and bustle momentarily stunned her. Large lamps illuminated the room, and ladies in colorful clothes flitted like butterflies. In contrast, dark jackets lent the men a stark elegance. Clusters of folks leaned close to carry on conversations, and the perfume of food enticed a grumble from Letty's neglected belly.

"Letty!" Randy's soprano soared over the chatter. Her friend's copper-colored hair reflected the light of the lamps. Oblivious to the people milling about, she cut a path to Letty. "You're finally here!"

Letty laughed. "Finally, Randy? I'm not even late."

Randy waved the comment aside. "I'm just so very happy to see you looking so lovely. That color is marvelous. You look more regal than England's Queen Victoria."

Letty glanced down. "My dress is nice, but I'm too small to manage regal."

Tugging her friend along, Randy waded through the sea of people. "I've heard say Her Majesty is tiny, just like you, and I think you should always wear that shade. It makes your skin glow."

Letty blushed. "Perhaps what you see is the lamplight on my skin."

Then Randy stopped. Letty plowed into her back. She peeked around her friend and gasped.

Eric.

"Well, now," Randy said, "we can get another opinion. Don't you agree, Eric, that our doctor looks lovely tonight?"

Letty fought to keep from melting into a puddle of mortification. Eric, in a coffee-colored suit, stood before them, more handsome than ever. His jacket set off the crisp white of his shirt, a precisely knotted brown silk tie kept the shirt's high collar closed, and in the lamplight his hair gleamed like old gold in contrast to his dark eyes—eyes fixed on her.

Letty's cheeks blazed, and she studied her hands.

The moment lengthened. The hubbub faded. When Eric didn't respond, Letty wondered if Randy's question had offended him. Had he perhaps walked off? She looked up and wished she hadn't.

She caught his gaze.

Letty's middle fluttered. Heat wove through her veins. Then a titter to her right broke the spell.

She glanced at Randy, embarrassed by her lack of control. The expression on the redhead's face made Letty again wish she'd kept her gaze fixed on the floor. Randy smiled gleefully at Eric and then at Letty, an almost parental pride on her features. Letty wanted to run back home.

"Well?" Randy asked again. "Isn't Letty lovely?"

❦

Eric hadn't realized he'd been staring at Letty, but dressed like this she was a revelation. Her wholesome prettiness had appealed to him from the first. Tonight, though, her simple freshness had given way to stunning femininity.

She'd piled her dark hair high on her head, and her cheeks echoed the rose of her gown. He closed his eyes and shook his head in an effort to dispel the effect of her beauty. When he looked at her again, her gray eyes gleamed like silver, and he feared he might drown in their molten depths.

"Without a doubt, you're an exquisite sight," he finally said.

She looked away. "Thank you."

"Well," Randy chimed in. "Douglas seems to be looking for me. Enjoy yourselves!"

She dashed away, mischief in her green eyes.

Just wait until I catch up with Douglas Carlson, Eric thought. *I'll give the lawyer an earful about his wife's latest prank.*

Letty took a step away, and without thought, he caught her hand. "Please don't go. It is a pleasure to see you tonight. You look lovely."

Letty nodded but avoided his gaze. Again without thought,

Eric reached out and lifted her chin with his other hand. She blushed a deeper shade.

"Randy's tactics can irritate," he added, hoping for a response. Unable to stop himself, he caressed the velvet curve of Letty's jaw. She trembled, and he couldn't help but think how different she seemed tonight. Letty was an intriguing mix of contrasts—medical practicality mixed with elegant femininity.

"Please don't let it bother you. The compliments were sincere, Randy's and mine. Especially mine."

Letty's gaze skittered up and at last met his. Eric enjoyed the shy delight he read there. Why did she affect him so strongly?

"Thank you," she murmured.

Eric decided right then that he didn't care why she affected him. He just knew she did and wished he had the right to pursue his interest. But he didn't, and he had to put an end to it. Intending to release her, his fingers skimmed her jaw one more time.

Again she shimmered, but this time a responding tremor shook him. He tightened his hold on her hand, cursing his weakness.

"There you are, my dears," said Mrs. Stone. "My husband is ready for the blessing. Come, I'll show you to your table."

Eric released her hand as if it were a hot cinder. His fingers felt scorched, singed.

Letty dropped her reticule. Thankful for something to do, he retrieved it. She took the purse, making sure they didn't touch again.

Eric followed the women, refusing to let the appeal of Hartville's new doctor capture him again. So focused was he on walking that he never noticed when Letty stopped. He bumped into her and instinctively wrapped his arms around her. The inadvertent embrace called forth the hunger he'd worked so hard to deny—comfort, companionship, love. No matter how

95

hard he fought his need, Eric still longed for love again. One that would last.

Letty groaned.

His voice cracked. "Did I hurt you?"

"No." She pointed toward Mrs. Stone.

Their voices mingled. "Oh, no!"

7

Mrs. Stone stood proudly in front of a table set for two. Round tables large enough for six or eight were the norm elsewhere, and Eric winced at the blatant matchmaking.

He squeezed Letty's shoulders. "There's little we can do but humor her. It would be worse to say anything."

"I—" She paused and straightened her back, obviously calling on a reserve of dignity. "I agree, and I apologize for the unfortunate situation. You likely had plans of your own. Please understand, this was not my doing."

"Letty, look at me. There's no question whose idea this is."

"Thank you, Eric. I'll try to make the evening as painless as possible."

With a polite murmur for Mrs. Stone, Eric pulled out Letty's chair. As he sat across from her, he sought her silver gaze. When she faced him, he said, "You're not about to dose me with some insufferable remedy. We're about to share a delightful meal. I, for one, anticipate a pleasant evening."

She responded with a wry smile. "I've thanked and apologized a lot tonight. I'm not usually so awkward."

"I know. You normally control every situation. It's interesting to watch you when someone else is in control."

"You are reprehensible, Mr. Wagner."

"Perhaps, Dr. Morgan."

"Most assuredly, sir."

"Perhaps."

Despite the inauspicious start, the evening went well. They enjoyed the tender roast, the well-seasoned vegetables, and the rich, sweet pie. As they savored fragrant cups of coffee, they noticed that other tables had been cleared away. People had broken off into groups, and Eric soon led Letty to a cluster of couples that included the Carlsons.

Randy bounded up. Eric thought her the least likely expectant mother, but Douglas had confided their news, and he had no reason to disbelieve his friend.

Randy shot Letty a sly glance. "I know. Why don't we play charades? Letty said she loves the game."

Letty groaned, suspecting more meddling.

"Oh, yes!" chimed a young lady, who winked at Randy.

Randy's lips widened into a broad smile. "How about works of literature?"

A murmur of approval circled the group as a few others joined to play. Soon everyone had written a title on a slip of paper. One by one, the ladies made their choices. Letty was left for last.

When Randy held out the basket with the last slip of paper, Letty had good reason to mistrust the mischief in her friend's eye. "You're up to no good," she whispered. "Again. Don't think I won't demand retribution."

Randy giggled. "I'm sure you will, but first I'll have my way."

"That's my fear."

As Letty unfolded her slip, Eric leaned close. "What are you afraid of?"

Letty handed him the paper. "This."

He frowned. "I have to speak to Douglas about his wife."

"Not tonight."

"True. Right now we can only hope for the best."

Letty pointed at the title. "So how do you propose we perform *Romeo and Juliet*? Star-crossed lovers, no less."

Eric's jaw tightened, a muscle twitched, and Letty wondered what bothered him more, the embarrassing situation or the memory of his own star-crossed, lost love.

"They do expect us to play," she added.

And they did, to the enjoyment of those present. With cheeks scorching, Letty stood, and Eric knelt at her feet, emulating the balcony scene. Silence flooded the room. Wishing herself anywhere on earth but in this crowded hall, the object of everyone's scrutiny, Letty tried to gaze at anything but the man at her feet.

She took Eric's hand, and the touch of skin against skin sent the now-familiar tingle up her arm. He, too, gazed at her, unrelenting, his eyes demanding her attention.

Silence enveloped the large hall. The atmosphere mellowed, grew richer, like the nap of velvet. Letty's pulse beat a foreign rhythm; her lonely heart took solace in Eric's nearness. How she wished this were real, that Eric truly longed for her, but they were playing a game; only a fool would believe a charade.

Sadness made Letty close her eyes. The silence changed. She tugged at her hand when the other players pretended not to guess, but Eric tightened his grip, making her face him again.

"Let's just do the death scene and be done with it," he muttered, his jaw more blunt than she'd yet seen it.

All Letty wanted was to reach the safety of her pink and white bedroom. The best remedy for her ruffled nerves was the comfort of thick blankets and her well-used Bible, but she had to see this through. Then she'd seek sanctuary. "All right."

When he stood, she again glanced around the room. They'd attracted quite a crowd. Eric dragged two chairs into the circle around them, clattering through the expectant silence. He sat and then gestured for her to take the seat at his side. She arranged her plum silk skirt and looked to him for further guidance.

To her dismay, he moved his chair closer, his solid arm against hers. He pointed to his shoulder, indicating she should place her head there.

"No," she argued in a whisper.

"Let's just finish."

She peered at their audience. Mrs. Stone's beaming smile made the decision for her. "Oh, go ahead."

Eric pantomimed the taking of the poison.

Letty pretended to stab a dagger into her heart.

He flopped back in the chair, simulating death.

She held her breath and placed her cheek on Eric's wool-covered shoulder. The impropriety distressed her even more.

She held the position for a second, long enough to feel Eric's strength. His warmth seeped into her cheek, the spice of bay rum filled her senses, and longing stole into her heart.

Whispers rippled through the silence.

"What a lovely couple they make," someone murmured.

Enough. She'd provided more than her share of entertainment. She stood.

"Romeo and Juliet," called Randy. Her contrite expression said she knew she'd gone too far.

"It's late," said Letty. "Especially for a doctor with patients to see in the morning."

Polite assent circled the group. She bid all a goodnight and headed for the doors.

"Letty! Please wait." Bustling to her side, the pastor's wife cut off her exit.

"Yes, Mrs. Stone. How may I help you?"

"No, no, dear. *I* wish to help *you.* It's cold outside and very dark. You mustn't walk home alone. Who knows what might happen, what with all those saloons, billiard halls, and *other* establishments on East Crawford. One can't be too cautious."

"But that's all at the far end of town—"

Ignoring Letty's words and manacling her wrist, Mrs. Stone dragged her back to the circle of chairs. "Eric," she called, and Letty wished to die. "You do have your carriage this evening, right? Please see Dr. Morgan home."

Eric looked taken aback. Letty cringed. What could he be thinking? She lived only a two-minute stroll away from the church.

After a curt nod for the pastor's wife, he said, "My pleasure."

"It's not necessary," Letty objected.

Neither Eric nor Mrs. Stone paid her the least attention.

She marched toward the doors, retrieved her cape, and put it on. "You could have refused," she told Eric through clenched teeth.

"Of course," he answered, a similar tang to his words. "Then I would have had to explain to Mrs. Stone and the whole congregation why I refused to see a lady home. The lady with whom I'd just acted out that stupid charade."

In the ensuing silence, they walked to Letty's house, neither willing to risk the intimacy of Eric's rig. The temperature had dropped since the afternoon, and patches of ice lurked everywhere. Letty kept her gaze on the ground, afraid of what she might see in his face. Pristine snow glistened in the moonlight, sparkling more than the stars in the jet sky.

"Letty?"

"Yes," she said, then her feet hit ice and flew out from under her. She wasn't surprised—her world had tilted so far off balance that evening. The surprise came when strong arms caught her before she hit the ground.

The moon, full and round and pouring silver over the earth, glazed them with its luster, while elsewhere shadows shrouded corners in mystery. Silence swelled around them.

"Letty." Eric whispered this time.

She met his gaze, and her last scrap of sanity vanished. He touched her lips with his and spun her into a world she'd never known existed.

Without taking his lips from hers, Eric cupped her face and threaded his fingers into her hair. Letty's pins slipped out.

The kiss went on, and on, and on.

Slowly, gently, he released her. Her eyes fluttered open. He reached for her hands and lowered them to her sides.

"Sorry," he said, his voice a rough croak. "Go home. You're almost there."

His abrupt withdrawal hurt. Letty stood in the frigid night, unable to speak, unable to move. He walked away.

She heard his low, heartfelt curse.

❦

In the days after the disastrous church social, Letty was so busy she had no time to think of Eric, much less remember their kiss.

One unusually quiet morning found her wondering what to do with her maturing chicks. Each time she entered the kitchen, the birds chased after her, pecking at the hem of her skirt. Too often they landed nips on her ankles.

"More's the pity I can't see you in my roaster as dinner," she muttered, "no matter how unruly you are."

As she stared at the fortunate fowl, a pounding at the door startled her. Glad for the distraction, she went to respond.

"Mrs. Stone! Are you hurt? Ill? Is the pastor well?"

"I'm fine, dear. It's Elsa Richards who needs your help. The baby's not coming as quickly as it should. We must hurry."

Letty grabbed her bag and her ulster. "Let's be on our way."

Outside, Mrs. Stone hoisted her rotund body into the carriage and sat next to her husband. Letty wedged herself into the remaining space.

"You have no vehicle yet, do you, Dr. Morgan?" the pastor asked once the horse had resumed its pace.

"No, my savings are nearly depleted. And please, I'm Letty."

Mrs. Stone weighed in. "I understood Eric had an unused buggy and was buying you a horse."

"I'm afraid that's unacceptable."

Pastor Stone cast her a shrewd look.

Mrs. Stone frowned. "Pray tell, why?"

"A single woman has no business accepting valuable gifts from a gentleman."

"Bosh, my dear," Mrs. Stone countered, patting Letty's hand. "No one could see it as a gift. Eric just wants to provide for our new doctor's needs."

Letty found no guile in the pastor's wife. "Perhaps you would see no impropriety," she said, "but others would. What good would I be to the town then?"

Mrs. Stone weighed the thought. "I understand your wish to remain above reproach, but think, dear. What would you have done today if we hadn't been on our way to the Richards's farm? Elsa's labor began yesterday, and Peter says the baby is breech."

Letty remembered Eric's warning when she treated Daisy. He'd said her actions on Daisy's behalf could cost her patients, and he'd urged her to guard her reputation. In her opinion the two situations were different. She could control the spread of gossip about her and Eric and no one would be hurt in the process, but if she refused to treat someone because others objected to the life he or she led, that patient could die. Letty couldn't take that risk.

But her refusal of Eric's generosity could endanger innocent lives, too. "You're right, Mrs. Stone. I put my own concerns before my patients' needs. I'm sorry."

The older woman patted Letty's hand. "Don't fret. This is easily fixed. You only need to accept Eric's offer."

Letty struggled with the thought of taking so much from the man who'd kissed her and then walked away. Perhaps she could find a decent horse—not a fancy one, just a sound animal—whose price her depleted account might cover, especially if her patients kept paying her with food.

Then Letty noticed her friend's pleased expression. She wondered how much of that pleasure came from Mrs. Stone's matchmaking bent.

⌘

Hours later Letty waved the Richards children farewell and climbed into the Stones' rig. She sank back, remembering Elsa's joy at the sight of her new son.

Pastor Stone got the horse going. "A precious feeling, no?"

"Incomparable."

"You're an able physician, young lady. The Lord has blessed Hartville with your presence."

"Thank you, sir."

The trip home was serene, each of the vehicle's occupants busy with his or her own thoughts, Letty's on the new arrival.

Once home, Letty knew she had to face Eric again. If only he didn't own the buggy she'd twice been offered. If only she had the means to obtain transportation without his help. She could utter "if onlys" forever and nothing would change. She needed a horse and buggy, and Eric could give her both.

She ran upstairs, poured cold water into her washbowl, and splashed her face. She unraveled her braid, brushed out the dark locks, plaited them, and anchored the coiled rope to her crown once again. She hoped she looked efficient and professional, nothing like the soft woman Eric kissed the other night. She was a physician, not an aging debutante.

Although the day was warm for her ulster, she put it back on, hoping to look sturdier. "Honestly, Letitia," she chided herself, "you really must stop indulging in such silliness. There's no room for spinsterish conduct in the life of a doctor. You're the one with the problem. Eric has probably forgotten the absurd incident."

Hoping to escape her uncomfortable thoughts, she concentrated on the beauty of the early spring day as she walked up

Willow Lane. Although the air bore a nip, a great deal of snow had melted and the rich scent of soil filled the air.

"Good afternoon, Dr. Morgan," called the widow who lived next to the manse.

"Hello, Mrs. Whitley. How's your newest granddaughter?"

"Beautiful. Just beautiful!"

"I'm so glad. Enjoy her."

"And you enjoy the lovely day."

Letty nodded.

As she continued down Main Street, she realized the citizens of Hartville knew she'd saved the Richards baby. They all sang her praises, lifting her mood.

At the door to Mueller's Bakery, Elsa's mother pressed a bag of caraway-studded rye bread into her hands. "Thank you, and the Lord bless you," the woman said.

By the time Letty reached the Hartville Day, she only felt relief. She didn't know how to handle the outpouring of gratitude. As she opened the door, she saw a new crop of articles on the wall outside. She wondered if Eric had further denounced the bordellos, and debated taking the time to read the editorials. The sight of Randy's mother bearing down on her convinced her to do her reading some other time.

Inside, a familiar, disturbing baritone greeted her. "It's today's heroine, Dr. Morgan herself."

Letty tried but found no sarcasm or scorn in his tone, only admiration.

The ulster had been a wasted effort, an uncomfortable, hot, wasted effort. And she still had to ask him a favor. She squared her shoulders. "I need to speak to you, Mr. Wagner. In private."

His expression clouded. Letty suspected he regretted their intimacy in the wintry moonlight. Perhaps she could reassure him such an episode wouldn't happen again.

"Follow me."

As they stepped into the office, Letty prayed for strength. "About—"

"How—"

Both stopped, each offering the other the opportunity to speak. Eric insisted Letty go first.

She started again. "About the other night—"

"No. That's best forgotten."

Cocking her head to the side, Letty studied the color on his cheeks. An odd . . . *something* flickered in his eyes. Could it be pain?

Of course not. He didn't want to discuss what had embarrassed him. Besides, why would an eligible widower feel pain at the thought of kissing a spinster doctor?

"Very well," she said. Perhaps his way was best. "That wasn't the main reason for my visit."

Eric's shoulders relaxed visibly. "What is the other reason?"

Unwilling to face him, she opened her reticule and withdrew a handkerchief. She twisted the linen square without mercy as she related her trip to the Richards's farm. "And so," she summed up, "I've come to realize that you were quite correct. I need transportation, and I'm ready to accept your offer of the unused buggy."

A smile lifted his mustache. Eric Wagner was absolutely reprehensible. He looked quite pleased at her discomfiture and positively wallowed in smugness.

He picked up the coat on the back of his chair. "Shall we, Dr. Morgan?"

"Right now?"

"Why waste time?"

Letty prayed for strength. "Indeed, Mr. Wagner."

☙

Later, Eric's insistence on buying her a horse shattered the truce. "I said I would buy you the horse."

"I remember quite clearly what you said, and I also remember how I responded. *I* will buy my horse. *You* will lend me your unused buggy."

Eric fumed. The stubborn, contrary woman could make him forget his manners, proper behavior, and maybe even his principles faster than anyone he knew. Why did she continue to refuse his help? He threw down the gauntlet. "We shall see, Dr. Morgan."

They went to acquire her transportation in silence. After a bit, Eric's jaw hurt from biting down for so long. He should have been used to it by now; he'd been doing it since the church social. Since then, it had also become impossible for him to concentrate. Nothing he'd written made much sense, nor did any of it carry the conviction for which his editorials were known.

At the most awkward moments he would remember their kiss under a too-bright moon, and he would long for another taste of joy. But that kiss had been a foray into insanity, so he'd avoided her, hoping to prevent a recurrence.

This time she'd sought his help, and help her he would. He *would* buy her the horse, he *would* give her the buggy, and she'd absolutely need additional help if she chose to fight further over the issue. Not that he understood why it mattered so much.

Exaggerated politeness accompanied them as they approached the nearby ranch. So many "pleases," "thank yous," and "excuse mes" were exchanged that Eric wondered if he'd ever put his manners to use again without thinking of Letty.

At the ranch, Letty objected to each horse he suggested as she mentally calculated the cost.

"There," she finally said, pointing.

"For goodness' sake, Letitia Morgan. You'll be the death of me yet. That poor nag has no life left. She's earned the right to rest in her old age. You can't buy her and put her back to work."

The thrust of Letty's chin said otherwise, and Eric scrambled for a better solution. He consulted his fellow rancher, Albert

Schwartz, who eventually barked out a laugh. "That's fine, Eric, mighty, mighty fine."

Eric escorted Letty back to the buggy and had her wait for him there. He grinned in response to her leery expression and followed Albert to gather their purchase and affix it to the rear of the rig.

On the way to his spread, he ducked all her questions. At the barn, he handed the reins to Andy Dobbins, his ranch manager. After instructing the man to cool down the animals, Eric reached for Letty's hand to help her exit the rig, cursing his need to touch her again. He craved the warmth of the fingers he laced through his almost as much as her moonlight-sweetened lips.

Letty's sturdy boots had scarcely touched the damp earth when she yanked her hand back and rammed both fists on her hips.

"Eric Wagner, what is the meaning of that?" She glared at the two horses tied to the back of the carriage.

"I went to buy a horse," he said, "and you went to buy a horse. Two horses were bought. Both are yours, Prince as well as that broken-down nag."

Letty's jaw sagged. She looked at the horses and then back at him. "But—I . . . that is, I can't—"

"It's too late. The animals are yours. Come." He again took her hand, this time to make sure she'd follow. "Let me show you the buggy so we can have you home before night falls."

As they headed for the barn, his unsettled feelings gave him pause. He'd won the skirmish over the horses, but feared he was losing the war against his emotions. Still in the battle, he led her into the vast structure.

The dusty buggy leaned against a wall in the far corner of the building. To their near left, a mound of hay exuded its earthy fragrance. Mewling came from within the dried, golden grasses.

Letty went in search of the kittens. Eric watched, his heart full of longing for the woman who'd stormed his town and his farm and laid siege on his heart.

Patting the hay with gentle hands, Letty looked for the babies she'd heard. She crooned to the mama cat and extended a slender finger to the little ones. Marmie, no longer fat but orange as ever, puffed up at first, ready to defend her brood, but resumed washing her offspring when she saw that Letty posed no threat. Only then did Letty scoop up one of the kittens.

"Look, Eric," she whispered.

Eric looked, but not at the kitten. His gaze traced the curve of her slender neck. The touching vulnerability of the translucent skin and the curling wisps of hair lured him closer.

He placed his hands on her shoulders. When she leaned toward the felines, the burnished glisten of sunset seeping through the loft window caught on hair that glowed mink brown with russet highlights. Dust motes danced in the muted shards of light, but Eric's attention remained on Letty.

The kitten in her hand gave another cry, and she brought it to her cheek in the same loving way Eric had seen her cradle the chick in her kitchen. He shook his head at the sudden flare of uncomfortable emotion. How low could a man stoop? Jealous of a newborn cat.

Letty bent toward the mama, and Eric felt the play of shoulders beneath his hands. Her warmth seeped through his fingers, reaching deep despite the chill of the oncoming night. He had been cold for a very long time.

He leaned closer; still he couldn't resist. He filled his senses with the fragrance of violets, a scent that had come to mean only one thing: Letitia.

8

Eric knelt and brought Letty back against his chest. She laid her head on his shoulder, and he murmured approval. With a new mother's care, Marmie caught one of her babies in her mouth and went in search of greater privacy.

Letty let the pleasure of Eric's embrace seep through her, bringing to life the memory of their shared kiss. She didn't dare move. If she so much as breathed, Eric might pull away as he had before.

Hope and anticipation filled her; melting wonder threatened her strength. She turned and saw a glow in his dark eyes. She could scarcely believe that she, Letitia Morgan, had lit the spark that burned in him.

He then kissed her lips.

Forgotten for the moment were all worries about propriety, about arguments, about the reasons why this moment shouldn't happen. In the soft shadows of evening, Letty only felt.

A cow lowed off to their right. A horse snuffled to their left. The hay prickled her skin through the fabric of her blouse where the coat had swung aside. Where her skirt rode up her ankles, the cold evening air seeped through her cotton stockings, shocking her sensitized skin.

She wished—

"Heidi," hollered Andy, "you stubborn goat. Come here!"

Eric went still. For a moment he didn't move, didn't draw breath. His eyes, though open, seemed unseeing. Then he stood and wiped his face. His gaze touched on Letty, and the pain in his eyes stole her breath.

She reached out a tentative hand. "Eric . . ."

He shook his head and turned, giving her the opportunity to compose herself. But composure and his back were the last things Letty wanted from him right then. Twice he'd kissed her to distraction and then doused his ardor, leaving her with questions enough to fill a book.

"Eric, please talk to me."

His voice rasped in the silent barn. "There's nothing to say."

"Nonsense," she countered. "Why do you kiss me then pull away like this? Your actions leave me questioning my sanity. I need to know why you've toyed with me."

He stiffened. "I haven't toyed with you. It would be better if I had."

She touched his forearm. "I don't see how playing with my emotions would be good at all. Please, Eric, I need an explanation."

He slipped from her grasp and began to pace, pausing long enough to kick a bundle of hay. "You're right. You do deserve an explanation. I just don't know if I can give it to you. I may still lack the courage."

"I don't think you lack courage. A man who can turn his feelings on and off as you do is strong enough to conquer anything."

"Always the optimist, aren't you?"

"I look for potential. It makes life worth living."

He shut his eyes, clamped his jaw, clenched his fists at his sides. "You've reached the crux of the matter. My life is hardly worth living. I'm no better than a murderer."

Letty gasped. "I don't believe you. You're too harsh on yourself. Why do you think that?"

"If anything, I'm too lenient."

As Letty studied him in apparent disbelief, Eric shook his head and tried to find the words to recount his guilt. The deepening dusk bolstered him. He didn't feel man enough to confess in the light of day.

"Martina died," he said, his voice ragged. He wished he could erase the past. He wished what he'd said sufficed, but it didn't. There was more. "Our son died, too, and I let it happen. Compared to someone who battles death daily, I'm the worst kind of man."

"You haven't said anything to condemn you yet."

He cursed her need to strip him of his protection, to have him bare his shame before her. "Of course I have. I'm responsible for the deaths of my wife and son. What more do you want me to say?"

"I want you to tell me exactly what happened and why you've assumed the blame. For goodness' sake, Eric. Hartville's champion of principle, the man who challenges evil and seeks the truth, isn't one who'd stand by and let a woman and child die."

He would have given anything to keep silent and bask in the light of Letty's faith, but that was too cowardly, even for him. He had to confront his failings once and for all.

"That *is* what I did," he said, his voice thick. "Martina labored for two days, bleeding badly. The midwife did all she could but finally told us we needed a doctor."

Eric paused. He relived the horrible moments that still haunted his dreams.

"My wife refused to have a man in our bedroom, much less let him examine her body. She wanted a woman, and the midwife did all she could. I couldn't sway Martina, and since speaking tired her, I let her have her way. She even said her death was God's will, but how could it be His will? Why would He want them dead?

"It wasn't God's will. I didn't have the courage to fight her, and God let me fail."

Eric's torment overwhelmed Letty, bringing tears to her eyes. His pain became hers, and she would have borne it if she could have released him from its grip.

Moisture coursed down the cheeks of the man she loved. Yes, she loved him. She loved Eric Wagner despite the pain piercing them, the pain both would surely still face.

Letty pressed him. "Why do you call yourself a coward?"

"Because I was scared, afraid to fight her any longer. I should have brought the doctor whether she agreed or not, but because I loved her, because I'd always honored her wishes, I gave in. I might as well have killed her with my hands. Love made me weak, and that love killed my wife and son."

Letty reached up and, with a gentle touch, cupped his cheek. "You aren't to blame for Martina's death. You respected her wishes when she made a choice. God gave us all that right. Your only crime was to love her, perhaps too much, perhaps too well. There's nothing to condemn in what you did."

He pushed her aside. "I should have fetched the doctor. I could have saved their lives."

"You can keep living like this, plagued by the 'I should haves,' but 'I should have' won't bring either of them back."

A strangled sound escaped Eric's throat.

Letty took the step that separated them, placing her hand on his jaw, feeling him shake. "Yet you're very much alive, aren't you?"

Had her hand not held his face, she wouldn't have known he nodded. "I envy your wife," she said. "I would rather have the love you gave her than all the medical training in the world. Life is terribly empty when one is alone."

She waited, wondering what Eric thought of her confession. The moment stretched on.

Then he said, "I know loneliness."

"Don't condemn yourself to that, then. I doubt Martina would have wanted loneliness for you."

Eric fastened his gaze on hers. "How did you know that?"

Because I love you, too, and I want only your happiness. She wished she had the right to speak the words out loud, but Eric wasn't ready to receive them. Perhaps he never would be.

Forcing a light tone, she answered instead, "Because I'm a woman. I know how a woman thinks."

"Yes," he said, "you are a woman, a lovely one at that, and you deserve the attentions of a whole man, not one plagued by ghosts. I apologize for my behavior. Please forgive me. I can only blame a . . . certain weakness where you're concerned."

The pain he dealt her lodged deep.

"There's nothing to apologize for," she said, her voice reedy. "Your kisses mean a great deal to me."

Eric studied the hayloft. He shoved a fist into the pocket of his trousers and ran a hand through his golden blond hair. "Don't let them, Letty. Find a man of your own, one who'll give you the love and the children you ought to have. You have so much love to give."

Let me give it to you, her heart cried, but she said nothing. She squared her shoulders. "It's best if I go home now."

"It's long past time."

While Eric hitched her two horses to the buggy, Letty studied his every move. He was a good, strong man. So noble, yet troubled and, from what he'd said, estranged from God.

It occurred to her that Eric was perhaps too noble. The sorrow of widowhood could not be denied, and neither could his love for his wife. But Martina was dead. The man who'd kissed Letty was very much alive and filled with desire—desire for her.

The thought encouraged her. If she could attract a man like Eric Wagner, why should he keep them from the gift God might be giving them? Who was to say God didn't intend for them to someday join in holy matrimony?

Wounds, no matter how deep, eventually healed. As a doctor, Letty specialized in encouraging the healing process. Could she, as a woman, encourage Eric's emotional wounds to heal?

Praying for the strength she lacked, she turned away. She did need a whole man; she needed Eric healed, heart-whole, and reconciled with God. She had to believe that with time and a healthy dose of love, he would indeed become that man. Letty wasn't ready to consign them to a flavorless existence. She knew that with God all things are possible, and she would keep her hope in Him.

Perhaps Eric thought their attraction was only "a certain weakness" on his part, but Letty remembered knuckles smoothing her cheek and a confession in a rich, male voice. *"I like you, Letty Morgan. I like you too much."*

Heartened by that memory, she took the hand Eric offered and clambered into her new, small buggy. She was glad his manners led him to escort her home. The drive to town gave her yet more time in his presence, something that could only work in favor of and enhance his growing "liking."

As he brought the horses to an easy trot, Letty glanced his way and smiled. With all her love and God's abundant mercy, Eric might soon like her far more than that lukewarm "too much."

৺

Eric stopped the horses in front of Letty's home. Irritated by the awkwardness between them, he addressed the most pressing matter.

"I'll take your rig to Amos Jimson's livery," he said. "It's only minutes west of here down Main Street. He'll board your animals for a reasonable sum."

Letty's face lost all color. Clearly, the purchase of Albert's nag had used up what money she had left, and the citizens of Hartville, although long on generosity, usually ran short of cash. The keep of one horse would be difficult for her; two could prove impossible.

"Is Mr. Jimson a fair man?" she finally asked.

"As honest as the day is long. Don't you trust me? I'd never leave you at the mercy of some unscrupulous scoundrel."

Outraged by her mistrust, Eric was torn between leaving and lecturing until she saw reason. Tempting though both options were, he knew neither would do.

"Yes, well, I trust *you*," she said, "but who's to say you haven't been swindled a time or two?"

"*I* say I haven't been taken for a fool, and I don't intend to start at this late date." Blast, but the woman was infuriating, nosy, and stubborn, and possessed of the most expressive eyes he'd ever seen.

"Your horses will be well cared for," he enunciated precisely, "and your account honestly kept. Is my word enough?"

Letty tipped up her chin, caught his gaze, and then looked down again. "Yes," she answered, so softly he had to strain to hear.

She twisted her fingers and, seconds later, dropped her reticule. At the soft plop, she grew more flustered and bent to pick it up. She rose too fast and almost lost her balance in the close quarters of the buggy. Eric ached as he watched her discomfort, well aware that his earlier attentions were its direct cause.

He said, "I'll be on my way."

"Fine," she answered, again in that hushed voice. Avoiding his gaze, she waved him to stay seated. "Thank you for the horse. Although I asked you not to buy one, I do appreciate your gesture."

Eric cringed at her stilted speech. "It was nothing," he said in his gentlest voice. "I wanted to help. Good night."

Stepping down from the buggy, she said, "Good night."

As he went toward the livery, Eric wondered how Amos had put behind the nightmares he'd endured. The former slave had been forced to watch his mother and sister raped, then killed, by enraged whites. Sensing Amos's agony, Eric had respected the man's silence and had never brought up the matter. He wondered if Amos had learned some kind of secret to surviving tragedy. Such a secret would perhaps free Eric to pursue the feelings between the pretty lady doctor and him.

He couldn't imagine any such secret existed. He couldn't envision a future with Letty. He could, however, help her.

"Where's Amos?" he asked a stable boy.

"Jus' inside, sir," answered the youth.

"Please take care of the animals, and I'll find your boss."

"Yessir," the boy answered, a smile splitting his face at the generous tip Eric gave him.

Satisfied with the care the horses would receive, Eric loped from the stable to the house, then up the front steps. He knocked and waited for Amos.

"I do declares, Mister Eric Wagner himself. An' what brings you out tonight, sir?" Amos's greeting poured out with the cadence of the deep South.

"A favor, Amos. For a very nice lady."

Amos studied Eric. "An' just who's your lucky lady?"

"Nothing of the sort, Amos. It's for Dr. Morgan."

"The one what saved the Richards's young'un?"

"The one and only. I need you to board her two horses and keep her buggy."

"*Two* horses? Cost her a purty penny, two of 'em did."

A blush worked up Eric's neck. "Well . . . uh, you see, she doesn't have much money . . ."

A frown pleated Amos's brow. He pursed his generous lips, and Eric had no trouble reading the man's suspicion. Not to mention his reluctance.

"I'm not asking you to keep two animals for nothing," Eric

said. "You're in business to feed your family. What I'd like you to do is give me her account. I'll pay for the horses' keep."

Amos's eyes twinkled. "An' what'll I tell the lady when she come to pay?"

Heat reached Eric's cheeks. "You can tell her whatever you want. Maybe that you're donating the animals' keep to help the women and children of Hartville. Many of us help cover her expenses in exchange for her expertise."

Amos chortled with glee. "An' . . . you're . . . gonna . . . pay?"

"Blast it, Amos! Don't make it so difficult."

"Nothin's difficult about it. Just plain good to see you livin' again."

Amos's slap on Eric's back spoke volumes about his opinion. Too bad he had the wrong impression altogether. Despite his best efforts to disabuse Amos of his notion, Eric couldn't convince the man he hadn't fallen in love with Letty.

Later, Eric wondered if it could possibly be true.

At five minutes to seven two days after she became the owner of two horses, Letty entered the Hartville Library, a large, book-filled hall in the back of the schoolhouse. Randy had insisted on Letty's presence at this evening's program of the literary society.

"After all," she'd said, "it isn't every day Miss Susan B. Anthony stops in Hartville and speaks to our society."

No, indeed. Letty wondered what topic Miss Anthony would choose to speak about tonight. The lady was interesting, her ideas frightfully provocative. Letty wasn't sure she agreed with, much less supported, the lady's radical views.

Inside the reading room, Letty took note of the women present. She was surprised; she'd never have thought the husbands in Hartville quite this progressive. Then again, she wondered how many of them knew the identity of tonight's speaker.

"Letty!"

Randy caught Letty's attention, and she saw her friend's colorful curls above more sedate blondes and brunettes. What was life like for a woman blessed with such height?

Letty chuckled. There was no use wishing, was there? "I promised to come, and here I am."

"Not a moment too soon," Randy said, green eyes sparkling. "Come sit next to me."

Randy led Letty to the second row. A narrow aisle divided the chairs into two sections that numbered about fifty overall. There weren't thirty women in the room, but that was a good attendance, considering Miss Anthony was speaking.

Randy sat next to a young lady and invited Letty to take her other side. Introductions were made, and snippets of polite chatter followed.

A hush descended on the room when Emmaline Whitehall, the schoolmarm and librarian, strode in, followed by a formidable-looking woman dressed in black. The redoubtable Miss Anthony, of course.

After Emmaline's brief introduction, the evening's guest spoke. Just then, Adele Stone whispered from Letty's right. "There's an empty chair."

When Letty turned to greet the late arrival, she froze. What was Eric doing here, listening to a suffragist?

The pastor's wife was matchmaking again, to Letty's unending mortification. Yes, she was in love with the man, but she didn't need such public encounters.

Seeking discretion, she scooted her chair closer to Randy's, but the chair's piercing screech momentarily drowned out Miss Anthony's voice. Eric turned to Letty.

". . . free love . . ." Miss Anthony said.

Letty blushed, and Eric's gaze snagged hers. Oh, the indignity of enduring the speaker's immoral topic while in the presence of the man with whom she'd exchanged kisses.

Sitting straighter, Letty turned back to the podium.

As Miss Anthony expounded on her topic, Letty's discomfort multiplied. The speaker based her lecture on the premise that women submitted to bondage when they married and had children. Why *that* subject? Why couldn't the noted suffragette speak about women's right to vote, or about the need to educate women, or . . . or about any other worthy topic Miss Anthony espoused? Why this? Why tonight? Why here, with Eric not four inches away from her?

Miss Anthony continued. "A woman who takes upon herself baby cares finds these quite too absorbing for careful, close, and continued intellectual effort, in addition to the entire work of her house . . ."

Letty grew angrier by the moment, her temper overcoming her former embarrassment. Yes, she agreed with the National Woman's Suffrage Association that women should vote, but she could no more accept Miss Anthony's insults on marriage than she could accept . . . well, than she could have accepted the free use of Eric's house. It was a matter of principle.

Listening to this woman speak against all Letty had given up to study medicine went against every fiber of her being. She wondered what Eric thought of Miss Anthony's diatribe against men.

Sliding to the far-left edge of her chair, she perched alarmingly close to Randy. Peeking at Eric, she saw reddened ears and the aggressive thrust of his jaw. He then extricated a small book from his breast pocket and began to take notes. He shoved the pencil over the hapless page, revealing his feelings.

Tomorrow's editorial in the *Hartville Day* would prove enlightening.

The man at her side was far more interesting than Miss Anthony's single-minded attack on Letty's fondest dreams. A surprising rush of tenderness overwhelmed her. Surprising, since Eric was so obviously angry.

She understood his anger; she even shared it. Miss Anthony's dismissal of a woman's importance to the family made Letty want to rise and challenge her, but she didn't.

A wispy veil seemed to shelter Letty's memories of the kiss in the barn, rendering them almost unreal. The episode had lasted only moments, but those moments meant so much to her that they seemed more a dream come true than true life. The passion, however, had been quite real.

Miss Anthony's words again pierced Letty's thoughts. "If I may quote Mary Wollstonecraft," she said, "one can see where monogamous marriage becomes a real impediment to the equality of women. Passionate love is transitory; it cannot serve as the basis for a lifelong association between two people. As Mary Wollstonecraft suggested, passionate attachments should only last so long as the fire blazes . . ."

A strangled sound came from Letty's right. Embarrassed by Miss Anthony's frankness, she didn't know if she dared glance at Eric. What was he thinking? Was he remembering their embrace?

Gathering her courage, Letty stole a glimpse. The taut skin over his cheekbones blazed red as his notebook slid to the floor. It went unheeded while Eric glared at the suffragist. He shifted in his seat and then, in a gesture that caught her by surprise, turned her way.

That they shared an attraction was a given, as was their opinion of Miss Anthony's claptrap, but it was the love she felt for Eric that she wanted to see reflected in his gaze. She saw something there, but she wasn't quite sure what it meant. She smiled, hoping for reassurance, but instead, Eric deliberately turned away, picked up his notebook, and began writing again.

Letty prayed for a swift end to the soirée. When it came, she slipped away after a quiet farewell to Randy, unwilling to face Eric again.

As she walked home, the slivered moon pierced the veil of her tears and the earth-scented spring night helped soothe her battered sensibilities. A cottonwood's bare, gnarled limbs hung over her, and she thought of the promise they harbored. In a short time, those branches would birth myriad leaves. The leaves would grow, give shade, shield passersby from the hot summer sun. In time, God's time, they would again wither and die.

She thought of Eric. The promise of love ran deep in him. Given time, love would be born anew. It would grow, bear fruit, be shared. When his life ended, in time, it would be after a rich and full existence.

In time.

In God's perfect time.

9

After listening to the drivel the suffragist spouted at the literary society soirée, Eric could scarcely contain his anger. How dare that . . . that *spinster* encourage women to abandon their families in favor of "passionate attachments" of short duration?

And to have the audacity to suggest children would prevent a woman from entertaining "careful, close, and continued intellectual effort." Where, pray tell, would that leave the children the women had borne? Would servants raise them?

Pain joined Eric's anger. Martina had never considered their marriage bondage. She'd treasured their closeness, and when she'd discovered her pregnancy, she'd overflowed with joy. She would have made a wonderful mother.

Had he oppressed Martina? Had he kept her from pursuing endeavors for which she might secretly have wished? Was he that sort of man?

He didn't think so. After all, he'd been most insistent on finding a woman doctor for the town. Anyone who became a physician had to develop his or her intellect to an advanced level, as Letty surely had done. Eric didn't agree with keeping women uneducated. He agreed with Miss Anthony on that matter. One need only look at Letitia Morgan to see the good a well-trained woman could do.

And that well-trained woman was bent on caring for every needy soul in town. She mothered all of Hartville while providing excellent medical care, especially for the town's women and children. Would she not succeed as wife and mother, too?

Eric laughed. Just try to tell the talented and capable Dr. Morgan she couldn't be a physician as well as a woman and all that encompassed. He pitied the poor soul who tried.

On his way to his bedroom, Eric wondered how Letty would look swollen with child. As small as the good doctor was, she'd most likely resemble a plump partridge. It took no effort to envision her nurturing a child.

A child . . .

Eric stopped. There it was. Right before him. The closed door. For the past two years, he'd let his cowardice win, but tonight he'd heard hateful sentiments about motherhood, about families. Now he craved contact with the child he'd never had the honor to know.

He extended his hand to the door latch. His fingers shook. In spite of the pain, he had to face the past.

Eric pressed down the latch. The metal grated in testimony to its disuse, and the musty smell of emptiness greeted him. Slowly he entered the room that had stood vacant for two years, two years when it should have brimmed with love and joy.

The cradle where he'd slept as an infant was still made. The linens, spread there by Martina, bore a tracery of dust. In the light of the hall lamp behind him, the shadows of a small chest of drawers and a wooden rocking horse stretched unnaturally long, mocking Eric with their enormity.

A sob caught in his throat. He made himself take another step and, extending an arm, pressed a finger to the cradle. His touch set the childless bed to swaying.

The rhythmic motion triggered the agony in his heart. Tears

burned in his eyes, only this time, instead of tamping them down, Eric let them flow. Wrenching sobs, harsh, guttural sounds that ravaged the peace in the lonely ranch house, came with the tears. They ripped through him in endless waves. Grief, honest and too long suppressed, finally found expression.

"My son," he sobbed. "Why my son?"

The next morning dragged endlessly for Letty. After dealing with her five overgrown chicks, she found little else to do. The house took scant effort, and she always kept the clinic ready for patients.

She thought of the Pattersons. She hadn't seen the scamps in days and wondered how they fared. Well aware of their father's vices, she suspected nothing had changed. Her patients' bounty filled her cupboards, and she decided to pack a basket of nourishing treats and ride out to the Patterson home.

As she put the finishing touches to the supplies, she heard a knock at the door.

"Why, Daisy!" she exclaimed. "What a surprise. How are you feeling? Is the head wound troubling you? Any episodes of dizziness?"

Daisy shot a nervous glance down the street. "N—no, miss. I'm fine. See?" She pointed to the small scar on her brow.

Letty inspected the spot and agreed with Daisy's assessment. "Please, dear, come inside. Since you don't need doctoring, I can brew us a pot of tea, and we can have a chat."

Daisy surveyed the street again. Hesitating, she rubbed a toe on the floor. She wrapped her black knit shawl closer around her. Then she met Letty's gaze. "Are you alone?"

The question threw her off guard. "Of course. Why?"

Daisy took another peek at the street behind her, and Letty wondered if she'd run away from a "client" again.

"I have a friend," Daisy whispered, furtively peering into the corners of Letty's tiny vestibule.

"And . . . ?"

"And she needs a doctor."

"I'm a doctor."

"I know."

Letty was now worried and quickly running out of patience, but she knew that by pressuring the girl, she would likely lose ground, so she prayed for endurance and waited for Daisy.

Conflicting expressions flitted over the adolescent features: fear, worry, anxiety, curiosity. Finally, the girl set her face in determined lines. "My friend needs you, but she's scared."

"I won't hurt her."

"I know," repeated Daisy. After a pause followed by a deep breath, she said, "Can . . . can she come in?"

"Of course! The clinic and I are always ready for patients. Especially for a friend of yours."

"Thank you, miss."

As the girl slipped around the corner of the house, Letty mulled over Daisy's proper language and manners. She was nowhere near as coarse as Bessie. A family—parents—had taken the care and effort to teach her at some time in the past.

When Daisy returned, Letty's shock burned away every thought of manners and speech patterns. Daisy's friend, Mim Greer, was another child. A badly beaten child.

Long brown hair covered Mim's face, which was perhaps just as well, since her eyes were blackened, her nose broken, and her lip split. A gash cut across an elegant cheekbone, and torn orange satin sagged from a girlish chest despite her every effort to hold the rent edges closed.

Daisy helped her friend limp into the examining room and, with Letty's assistance, got Mim onto the table. Letty then asked Daisy to fill a basin with warm water while she prepared a Calendula lotion to clean Mim's injuries. She again kept silent, this

126

time praying for guidance and wisdom in ministering to these two lost sheep.

Letty opened the torn bodice farther and winced at the bruises already painting Mim's ribs in reds and purples. Upon examination, she found two of the fragile bones broken. She retrieved a large roll of bandage from one of the shelves Eric had built and with a featherweight touch wrapped Mim's torso.

"He kicked her!" Daisy finally cried.

Letty studied the girls. Daisy's outburst clearly bothered Mim. Daisy looked murderous.

"If I ask who did it, will either of you tell me?"

"No!" cried Mim.

Daisy shook her head with regret.

"Well, then," Letty said, "it's just as I expected. We won't talk about who, but perhaps we should discuss why you were hit, Mim. Can you tell me that?"

Mim lowered her lashes, and a fat tear rolled down each bruised cheek. "I wouldn't do what he wanted me to do."

Letty's stomach turned. Mim was a child, younger even than Daisy, who looked to be around fifteen or sixteen years of age. What indignities had she been forced to bear?

Lord Jesus, I need your help, and she needs your healing touch.

Letty asked the girl, "What do you plan to do now?"

A shoulder rose then sank back down. "I guess I'll stay with Bessie until I'm better. Then I can go back to . . . work."

She recoiled at the very thought. If she, Letitia Morgan, had any say in the matter, and with God's bountiful mercy, this child would never go back to "work." Neither would Daisy, and nothing would force Caroline Patterson into such a life; not Caroline, not Amelia, not Suzannah.

Although she knew she treaded on touchy ground, Letty needed more answers. "Do you *want* to stay with Bessie?"

The two girls shared a telling look. In spite of it, both turned to her and nodded. Mim nodded yet again and sighed. "It's for the best, miss."

"Why would you say that?" Letty asked, knowing the answer but seeking to break through to the girls. "Have you nowhere else to go?"

Daisy shrugged. "I can go back to work. As long as I'm working, I can stay in my room. But Mim, since she can't work like this and hasn't enough to pay . . . well, she doesn't have anywhere but Bessie's."

Letty tipped up her chin, squared her shoulders, and firmed her spine. "Couldn't Mim stay with me?"

Fear filled both young faces. They glanced at each other, then Daisy turned to study the street through Letty's front window.

"We can't," she answered, finally satisfied with what she saw, or didn't see. "Please don't ask why. We just can't."

Letty could bear no more. "Girls, it's clear neither of you is happy. Neither of you is anxious to stay with Bessie, either. On the other hand, you trusted me enough to come here for help."

When neither child spoke, Letty appealed to her heavenly Father again. *Dear God, don't let me make a mistake now. It matters too much.*

"I want to help you even more," she said. "You can stay with me, Mim, until you're well, and longer still—for as long as you wish. You too, Daisy. Please, don't go back where you're in danger all the time."

Mim's violet eyes swam in tears. Rivulets coursed down her cheeks, plopping on her clasped hands. Slowly, very slowly, she nodded. Sobs broke out, and her nods became stronger, more decisive. She looked at Letty with anguished violet eyes.

"You're right. I—I don't want to go back. If . . . well, if you have work for me, I'll stay with you, but not for nothing."

Thank you, Father.

"We're agreed, then," Letty said. "I have plenty of work for a young lady like you."

A grim smile twisted Mim's lips. "I'm no lady anymore."

"Nonsense," Letty responded. True, Mim had been forced into a disastrous set of circumstances, but God could heal the child's emotional wounds, and if she trusted Him with her life, His salvation would wash away her sins. For that to happen, she had to see herself in a better way.

Letty slipped an arm around Mim's shoulders. "You work for me now, and I make it a practice to employ only ladies of great worth. God made you, and that's what you are in His eyes."

Daisy snorted. "Don't think she won't come after you, Mim."

Mim jutted her rounded chin. "You hush, Daisy Butler. You can do what you want, but I'm tired of being hungry, of dirty men, of doing things I can't bear to do anymore." Mim shuddered. "I'm staying with Dr. Morgan. You can go back to Bessie and the house."

Daisy's cheeks flushed. She lowered her head, then glowered at Mim. "She'll come for you. I know. But fine, I'll just go back on my own. Thank you so very much, Miss Lady Mim."

Letty cringed at Daisy's acrimonious tone. She didn't want to come between the two friends, but she rejoiced in the rescue of even one girl. She'd already gained a significant measure of Daisy's trust. Now, by keeping Mim under her wing, perhaps she would woo Daisy from her hideous existence as well.

"Daisy, my dear," Letty said, "you're always welcome here. I have plenty of work for two young ladies. If you don't choose to stay, you can still visit whenever you wish. And since Mim will be here, too, we'd both be happy for your company."

Daisy stood taller when Letty called her a "young lady." She straightened her marigold-and-black-striped skirt and hitched up the black lace at her décolletage. A sweet, poignant longing replaced the pride in her eyes. It was within Letty's grasp to grant Daisy's unspoken wish, but the girl had to take the first crucial step.

"I can't," Daisy said, almost as if to convince herself. "But I'll visit. I—I'm happy for you, Mim. And I'd best be going now."

"Very well," agreed Letty, aching to put her arms around Daisy and never let her leave.

Yet it was Daisy who, red faced, threw her arms around first Mim and then Letty. Letty held on as long as the girl allowed.

"Remember, Daisy," she whispered, "whenever you need me, I'll help you. Anytime, anywhere."

"I'll remember."

With her arm around Daisy's shoulders, Letty walked her to the door. She slipped her hands into the pockets of her gray flannel skirt and watched as the girl sauntered toward Main Street. Out of the corner of her eye, she saw Emmaline Whitehall standing stock-still across the street.

Agape and rigid with obvious indignation, Emmaline just stared. Moments later, she smacked her lips shut and sniffed. She deigned another look at Letty, a look rife with disdain.

Oh, no. Emmaline couldn't get away with this sort of behavior. Only God had the right to judge Letty or anyone who left her home. "Good morning, Emmaline," she called. "Do you need medical attention?"

Emmaline's jaw flapped open again. When she jerked it shut, Letty thought she heard the woman's thin lips slap together. "Not now, Dr. Morgan."

Struggling to contain her temper, Letty watched the woman turn and stalk back to Main Street. She'd lost a patient, it seemed, but she'd retained her self-respect.

She went back inside, ready to deal with the immediate need. She had a housemate. Where should she put Mim? The house was no larger than a bird's nest. When she reached the girl, she noted Mim's sleepy eyes. "Come on, dear. Let's get you to bed."

The child never argued and, moving painfully, followed

Letty to the room in the eaves. Letty slipped one of her flannel nightdresses over Mim's head and helped her into bed. Under the rose-colored quilt, the child barely ruffled the covers. Letty folded the torn orange satin dress and set it on the oak dresser. The next time she checked, the girl slept peacefully.

Again at loose ends, Letty remembered the basket she'd packed. This would be a good time to get the food to the Pattersons.

She wrote a brief note for Mim and propped it against the basin on the washstand. She ran downstairs and, grabbing the basket by the handle, went on her way.

She found Amos perched on a stool filing a horseshoe.

"An' how's Hartville's fine doctor this mornin', ma'am?"

"Very well, Mr. Jimson. How are my horses?"

"Fine, just fine, Doc. An' call me Amos. Everybody does."

She nodded. "I need Prince and the buggy. I have an errand to run."

"Goin' to birth more babies?"

"Not right now. I'm off to the Pattersons' with food for the children."

Amos frowned. "That lazy drunk ain't gonna get it, is he?"

Letty sighed. "I can't say for sure. I can only pray that the children might benefit from what I give them."

Amos rose, slapped his hands on his thighs, and headed toward the stable. "Bad," he muttered. "Them young'uns is in a bad way. Let's get you goin'."

Letty had to agree with Amos's assessment. It wasn't a wholesome place for children. When she reached the rickety house, she conquered the treacherous steps, skirted the gaping hole in the porch, and knocked, noting how the warped wood rattled against the jamb.

Caroline, with baby Willy at her shoulder, answered. "Oh, no! What did Steven do now?"

Letty suppressed a smile. "Nothing I know of, dear. I brought you some extra food my patients gave me."

"Extra . . . ? Food?"

It seemed a foreign concept to the girl. Perhaps it was in a family of five children, especially one with a father more intent on carousing than on providing for them.

"I'll trade you my basket for baby Willy," Letty offered, and they made the switch. As she cuddled the little one, she stepped farther inside and perused her surroundings. The small, dark parlor was furnished with only a torn settee. A threadbare braided rug, also torn, lay on the sagging floorboards. Heavy draperies shrouded a tall, narrow window. She thanked the Lord for the roof over the children's heads and the food for their bellies—at least in the immediate future.

"Thank ye, Dr. Miss," Caroline said. "We 'preciate it."

"Thank God for His generous provision rather than me," Letty suggested.

Caroline nodded vaguely, set the heavy basket on the floor, and wrapped her arms around her middle. She seemed unaccustomed to empty arms; each time Letty had seen the girl, she'd held Willy astride her hip. She also noted Caroline's unease. She clearly wasn't used to visitors.

Hugging Willy closer still, Letty kissed his silky, golden hair. His older sister was affording the baby basic cleanliness, although the crusty secretions on his nose did give Letty cause for concern. "Has the baby had the sniffles for a long time?"

Caroline paused to think. "Mebbe two days now, Dr. Miss."

"Has he run a fever with it? Sneezed a lot? And what about coughing? Has he done any of that?"

The girl slowly shook her head. "No, I don't think so."

Reluctant to leave, but aware of her patient back home, Letty said, "Here." She held Willy out to his sister. "I must be on my way. I have a boarder, and she's hurt. It'll soon be time for me to look in on her again."

As soon as Caroline set the baby back on her hip, he filled his fists with her hair and nuzzled her shoulder. Letty ached at the love between the two. If only . . .

"G'bye, Dr. Miss."

Despite her concern for Mim, Letty couldn't tear herself away from these two just yet. "Caroline, when did you children last have milk?"

Caroline shrugged.

"Well, then, I'll make sure that from now on you have plenty. It's important for your bones."

She nodded.

Letty took a step toward the door, then turned. "About baby Willy's nasal secretions . . . please send Steven to me. I'll have a remedy ready to clear him right up."

"Yes, ma'am."

"Good-bye, Caroline, Willy," she said, again heading for the door. As she was about to open it, a sound came from the dark stairwell in the back of the miserable room. A flash of faded red calico darted out of sight. Suzannah!

Caroline said, "That's—"

"Suzannah. Do you think she might come out and meet me?"

"Dunno," Caroline answered, frowning.

"Maybe next time?" Letty persisted.

"Mebbe."

Letty relented. She'd make no further gains today. "I really must be on my way. I'll return soon."

"Thank ye, Dr. Miss."

Caroline's quiet response followed Letty on her way home. She thought and thought, hoping to find some way to do more for the children, but beyond taking them her surplus food and meeting their medical needs, she didn't know what else she could do.

Halfway back to town, a buggy clattered past her. A very familiar black rig. Letty pulled Prince over to the side of the road, craned her head around to peer through the small cutout window in the back of her vehicle, and watched Eric head toward the Patterson home. Why would he feel it was fine for him to care for the children yet insist they were too great a burden for her to bear? The nerve of the man.

At home, she found no time to fret. Although Mim still slept, patients soon began to arrive.

Handling her consultations with her usual diligence, Letty examined her patients, asking questions to obtain a clear picture of the symptoms. When she'd gathered enough information, she prescribed the correct remedy according to the individual's constitution.

Through it all, she couldn't forget the Pattersons. Each time she treated a child with a sneeze or congested nose, Letty saw baby Willy's little face. She remembered, too, that his home lacked heat. Pneumonia could set in.

When she closed the office, she did so with unexpected relief. She ran up to her room and found Mim awake but still lying down.

"Are you hungry?" she asked her young charge.

The girl answered with a slight nod.

"Would you like me to bring you some supper?"

Mim sat up. "Oh, no, Dr. Morgan, that's too much bother. I'll come and help. Please."

Noting the girl's wince and the difficulty with which she moved, Letty shook her head. "You can't start to work until you're completely recovered, but I don't object if you'd like to join me in the kitchen."

The pot of yesterday's stew took little time to warm. Mim entered the kitchen as the rich-scented steam filled the room, and the two sat down to bowls of meat and vegetables in thick broth. A basket of biscuits and mugs of milk accompanied the hearty fare.

As Mim loaded a spoon with food, Letty stopped her. "We first give thanks for our food."

The child sent her a quizzical look, and Letty chose to show rather than tell. Bowing her head, she said, "Father in heaven, we thank You for the blessings You give us each day. Your love and salvation let us come before You washed clean of sin, and Your bounty strengthens our bodies so that we may do Your will. Bless this food, those who grew it, and those who will share it. I ask for Your healing touch on Your child, Mim, and that You guide me in all I do. In Jesus' holy name I pray. Amen."

When they'd finished eating their stew, Letty broke the silence. "I have apple pie. Would you like some?"

"It's my favorite," Mim whispered. Her eyes sparkled.

Letty reached for a rose-festooned plate she kept in the cupboard under the window and hoped Mim would soon overcome her timidity. She wanted to become the girl's friend; she wanted Mim to trust her. Then she might perhaps introduce the child to the One who would heal all her wounds.

The child's wedge of pie soon vanished. Afterward, Mim sat smiling, relaxed, chin in hand, elbow on the table. By the time Letty cleared away the dirty dishes, her patient's eyelids drooped.

"Come along, Mim. You need more rest."

"But that's all I did today," she said, her words belying the exhaustion on her battered face.

"That's all this doctor will let you do for the next few days."

The girl gave no further argument, and Letty thought she saw relief in the soft violet eyes. She wondered how long the poor mite had been making decisions for herself. Mim was a child, one who still needed the direction of an adult.

After helping Mim to bed, Letty returned to the kitchen and finished cleaning up. As she dried her hands, she heard footsteps followed by a knock.

She found Eric at her door. A very angry Eric.

Before she could invite him in, he marched into the vestibule, taking up more space than usual, seeming taller and stronger than ever.

He yanked his arms out of his coat sleeves and thrust the garment at Letty. "Why must you ignore everything I tell you?" Now unencumbered, he stormed into the waiting room and added, "You're too pigheaded for your own good."

Letty closed the door, hung the coat on the hall tree, and followed him, bracing herself against his fury. He paced the perimeter of the small room. When he turned, a muscle twitched in his jaw as it had when Miss Anthony's speech had angered him. Letty remembered her boarder, and Emmaline Whitehall's censure.

"I see Emmaline wasted no time spreading the word," she said, wiping palms damp with anxiety on her gray flannel skirt. She then slipped her hands in her pockets so Eric wouldn't notice their trembling. "Mim has only been here a few hours."

Eric stopped in front of Letty. A whiff of bay rum teased her senses. "Here?" he asked. "You have one of those women *here?*"

Letty stood her ground. "Hardly a woman, Eric Wagner. She's scarcely older than Caroline Patterson and so badly beaten I couldn't send her back to those brutes."

Eric took two steps closer. As near as he was, as infuriated as he was, Letty felt no fear. He would never hurt her or anyone else.

"Of course not," he scoffed. "You'd rather risk your livelihood for those girls. Why?"

While she appreciated Eric's interest in her welfare, something else mattered more. "Because everyone turns a blind eye to the problem. These girls need someone to love and care for them."

"Must *you* be the one to do it? Isn't it enough for you to look after your patients and the Pattersons?"

"One thing has no bearing upon the other. I can't turn my back on girls who hurt not just on the outside but also on the inside. I'm a physician and a Christian. God calls me to serve in His name."

Letty hoped Mim was a sound sleeper. "Eric, the child has broken bones. I can't send her back. She's upstairs and, I hope, still asleep. Please keep your voice down."

He frowned, and his lips disappeared under his mustache. "You're housing her, feeding her, treating her. All this for a prosti—"

"How dare you! That's a child upstairs. One who's been thrown away, abandoned, and abused by the adults in her world." She straightened to her full height. "I will not do the same."

They stood toe to toe, neither giving an inch. Letty took a deep breath, about to challenge Eric to do something good with all that anger, but before she spoke, someone else knocked on her door.

"What a night!" she exclaimed. "I usually read myself to sleep. Now I have a damaged little girl in my bed, you're steaming like a teakettle, and I might have a baby to deliver."

She flung open the door, saw Caroline, and assumed the bundle of tattered blanket in her arms hid Willy. Alarm filled her when she realized the little one wasn't at his usual perch on Caroline's hip. "Bring him into the examining room."

"Yes, Dr. Miss. He's burnin' up. An' I cain't get 'im to move. He jus' wants to sleep."

As Letty unwrapped Willy, a cough racked his chest. "Goodness gracious, Caroline. How long has he been coughing like that?"

"Pa broke the window in our room last night," she whispered. "I tried to keep Willy warm, but all's I had was 'is blanket. You saw 'is nose back at home earlier. He got the coughs jus' after you left. He got real hot a while ago, and he's been like this since."

Caroline's words sent icy fear through Letty.

🍑

Eric saw Letty blanch. He felt a corresponding shock. Willy could have died of exposure in the early spring chill.

The doctor burst into action. She checked Willy's breathing, his pulse, his skin tone. She took a stethoscope from the black leather bag, slipped the earpieces into place, and listened to the child's chest. Her teeth worried her lower lip.

Eric's rage found a new object upon which to focus: the irresponsible Horace Patterson. The children's resourcefulness impressed him in view of Slosh's neglect.

"I believe it's bronchitis, and I thank the Lord it's not pneumonia," Letty diagnosed after patting the thin chest with the bell-shaped instrument. "The deep, congested sounds in his chest and his fear while breathing tell me he's fighting thick mucus. He's also very drowsy. Antimonium Tartaricum should work wonders."

She dissolved pellets in a small amount of water and spooned drops of medicated liquid between Willy's lips. When the cool fluid touched his tongue, the child turned his head, and a dribble slipped from the corner of his mouth. Letty spooned in some more.

"Willy is fortunate," Eric murmured, watching her repeat the process. He then asked Caroline about the broken window and, from her description, figured he could make temporary repairs with some wood and nails.

When Letty couldn't coax the baby to take more remedy, she hugged him close and began to hum.

"What did you do with my coat?" Eric asked her. "There's a broken window to fix."

Letty flashed him the most radiant smile he had ever seen. "Thank you," she whispered then bent back to the baby.

"Letty," Eric said, needing to be on his way, "my coat. I must return these two to their beds."

She closed her eyes. Frown lines appeared on her brow.

"Couldn't I . . . oh, Eric, could I please keep them? Must they go back to that house?"

Eric knew regret. He'd have given her the stars if she asked, but these children weren't his to give. "They have a father, if not a good one," he said.

Letty cuddled the baby tighter. Her longing glance swept Caroline from head to toe. Silently, she swaddled Willy again and handed him to his sister. Turning her back, she went to a shelf, opened a remedy jar, and counted a number of pellets into a dark amber-glass vial, capped it, and gave it to Caroline with the necessary instructions.

Letty's concern moved Eric, and a knot tightened his throat. He coughed to clear it away. At the sound, she turned her startled gaze toward him. "Oh, yes. Of course. Your coat is on the hall tree by the door."

As he left, Eric realized just how dangerous Letty Morgan was. She had just broken through his protective wall once more.

10

While he took the Patterson children home, while he repaired the broken window, and even during the return trip to town, Eric thought only of Letty. Whether he wanted it or not, she'd found her way into his heart. He had tender feelings for Hartville's lady doctor.

That didn't mean he would act on those feelings. He'd told Letty about Martina, and in the telling his anguish had lessened. The dark misery hadn't returned since that afternoon in the barn, and he'd even found the courage to enter his dead son's room, to grieve his loss. It seemed Letty had doctored even him; his healing had begun.

Although the pain had diminished, the facts remained the same. He'd proven a terrible candidate for marriage, and Letty deserved marriage. Eric could never offer marriage to a woman again.

A woman needed a man strong enough to help her through any adversity life sent her way. Eric had lacked the strength to protect Martina when her notions threatened her life. He'd failed to live up to the vows he had once taken before God.

Martina had trusted him, and he'd betrayed that trust. "You know so much more than I about such matters," she'd often said, her blue eyes speaking her love for him, her hand patting his. She'd often admired his physical strength and always deferred to his intellect. If love had stripped him of the strength to care for such a gentle lady, how much less equipped was he to meet the needs of a woman as formidable as Dr. Letitia Morgan?

He could never be the spouse, protector, and provider she needed. Only a man who didn't let his emotions—his love—blind him to his duty could aspire to that role. Eric didn't dare accept Letty's trust. He couldn't risk betraying her at a vulnerable moment. For her sake, he had to keep his feelings from growing.

He could, however, try to protect her without her knowing. Letty didn't seem to know when to stop. She'd taken on the medical needs of Hartville, especially those of the women and children, and as the days went by, she spent more time with the Patterson children. Now, as if she didn't already bear enough of a burden, she'd decided to take in young tarts.

He admired how she stood up for her beliefs, but this time she'd gone too far. She needed help, and he'd make sure she got it. This time he wouldn't let his feelings keep him from doing his duty by a woman he cared for—he wouldn't let love make him a coward. He had to save Letty from herself. Like Martina, she was too stubborn for her own good.

Urging his horses to a faster pace, Eric soon reached Silver Creek Church. He secured the team and ran up to the manse.

"Eric!" Adele Stone ushered him inside. "How may we help you?"

He knew how the fervent matchmaker would view his request, but he couldn't avoid it. Letty needed help.

Glancing in the oak hall mirror, Eric saw that he still wore his hat. He tugged it off and twisted the brim with his fingers, wondering how best to voice his request. "I don't need help, Mrs. Stone, Le—Dr. Morgan does."

"Oh, no. Has something happened to that dear child?"

Eric squashed a curse. "I'm sorry, I'm not doing this well. No, Le—Dr. Morgan is quite well. Or at least she was when I last saw her a few hours ago, but she has gotten herself into a predicament."

Mrs. Stone tightened the belt of her wine-red robe, reminding Eric of the late hour. About to apologize for his intrusion, he saw Mrs. Stone's determined expression. He kept his peace.

She wagged a finger at him. "If it's about her consorting with pros—er . . . with soiled—you know what I mean. At any rate, I don't believe a word of it. Letitia Morgan is a fine, upstanding young lady who wouldn't have a thing to do with fallen women."

"There's the problem. Dr. Morgan has been in contact with some of them. Twice, in fact."

Mrs. Stone gasped.

He continued. "It came about because of her efforts to help the Patterson children." He then described the scene outside the brothel, the injuries the two girls had suffered at the hands of Bessie's patrons, and finally, how Letty planned to care for Mim, who had decided to leave that life.

Smoothing his mustache, Eric chose his next words with care. "Dr. Morgan has patients, she's helping the Pattersons, and now she's helping these two young tarts. She even has two roosters and three hens in her kitchen. It's too much for one woman, even though she won't agree. I fear she'll exhaust her health. That's why I need your help."

Mrs. Stone crossed her arms over her bosom, a raised eyebrow accenting her frown. She held Eric's gaze as she weighed his words.

"Of course we'll help Dr. Morgan," said Pastor Stone, who had descended the stairs unnoticed. "We'll help her and the girls. Hers is a godly mission, one to which our Lord calls us. Scripture says, 'Inasmuch as ye have done it unto one of the least of these my brethren, ye have done it unto me.' In fact, I'm ashamed it took the doctor's efforts to show me my error."

The pastor's words settled the matter for his wife, and she started up the stairs. "I'll dress quickly so that we can go to Letty's house and collect the child. The pastor and I have more room here than she does. Most likely, she's given the girl her own bed."

Eric nodded. Yes, the little fool had. Affection and his reluctant admiration now gentled his irritation with Letty's behavior.

❦

At Letty's house, they received no response to Eric's knock. He waited and then tried again, louder this time. Still no answer. Then when he tried it, the doorknob yielded, and he pushed the door ajar.

Mrs. Stone followed him to the examining room, and both came to a stop. The doctor slept curled up on her examining table, a thin sheet over her slight form.

Eric's anger boiled again.

Mrs. Stone clucked and said, "I'll fetch Mim. You can carry our good doctor to her bed once it's vacant. Surely between the two of us we can take care of these two girls."

The pastor's wife woke Mim and explained the situation, gently dispelling the girl's distrust and wariness.

"I'll still work for Dr. Morgan," Mim said at the end of the conversation.

"Of course," Mrs. Stone said. "Once you recover you can help the doctor all you want. Now, however, you'll help most by coming with me and giving Dr. Morgan her bed."

Eric admired how Adele Stone handled the situation, and he tipped his head in silent recognition. The older woman smiled and winked. He left the room to give Mim the privacy to dress, and before long, the two joined him in the examining room. He went to wake Letty, but the pastor's wife stopped him.

143

"No, son," she said. "It's best if you carry her upstairs. Just place her on the bed and cover her. She needs her rest, so for once she can sleep in her clothes."

Eric studied the inveterate matchmaker's expression, wondering if she was indeed trying to strike yet another match, but her face revealed only concern. He set his suspicions aside and, after bidding her and Mim good night, he returned to Letty's side.

With one arm under her knees and the other around her shoulders, Eric lifted Letty, surprised by how light she felt.

As he stepped toward the stairs, she stirred in his arms. A sigh escaped her lips, followed by a whisper that sounded somewhat like his name. He paused. Then, still asleep, she curled her arms around his neck. Her gesture caught him off guard, and he nearly dropped her. When she nuzzled his neck and murmured, his longing returned.

She whispered his name again.

Carrying his precious cargo to the bedroom in the eaves, his gaze caressed her pretty face, relaxed in sleep. Tenderness filled his heart. He reluctantly set her on the bed and drew up the covers. He ran a finger over an eyebrow, down her straight nose, over her cheek. She was so soft, so warm.

But he had to be strong. He was well aware that she shared the attraction, and as the more experienced of the two, he had to stay in control. He walked away.

"Eric?"

Her sleep-soft voice stopped him short of the doorway. He didn't dare face her; he doubted he could mask his yearning and need. "Yes."

"Why are you here?" She glanced around the room as if to orient herself. "Mim!" she cried. "Where's Mim?"

Blast it, she wasn't going to let him escape.

"Mim . . . well, Pastor and Mrs. Stone want to house the girl. You need your bed."

"And just how did they learn of her using my bed?"

Eric's cheeks caught fire. "I saw the dark circles under your eyes earlier this evening, and I know how great a burden you're bearing, so I fetched help on my way home from the Pattersons'."

The feisty light of indignation appeared in Letty's eyes. "I had very few patients today, and I don't see how caring for a few children is too much work at all. Besides, I'm a grown woman. I don't need a keeper, Mr. Wagner."

"Kindly stop that Mr. Wagner hogwash you start when you don't like what I do. I'm sick of your 'No, Mr. Wagner,' 'I don't like that, Mr. Wagner,' 'You did the wrong thing, Mr. Wagner.' I, too, am an adult and don't need your permission to care for you, Letitia Morgan."

❦

Letty stared, her thoughts whirling, her heart pounding. Had Eric just said what she thought she'd heard?

Mustering what dignity she could, considering a man stood in her bedroom, she rose. "I told you once before, Eric, I won't be a kept woman. You needn't concern yourself with my needs. I see to myself."

"So that's why tonight you gave your bed to a harlot?"

"That child needs your sympathy and assistance, not your condemnation. Have you no mercy?"

"Plenty." A muscle twitched in his jaw. "And I act upon it when necessary. I saw a need earlier this evening. You obviously don't know the risk you're taking, much less recognize your needs. *You* need my mercy."

Letty bit her lip. Yes, she'd ignored his advice, but she had a conscience. His attitude toward Mim and Daisy differed so greatly from his concern for the Pattersons. How could he feel such hatred without even knowing the girls?

And what did he mean by *her* needs? What had he said without coming out and voicing it? Did he really care enough about her to worry over her lost sleep? Then perhaps she *had* heard correctly.

She measured his expression but found no gentleness there, just a wagonload of determination. He was likely protecting the town's investment in a doctor.

Still, she couldn't capitulate. "Oh, Eric, there's such suffering among the Patterson children. They're starved for a woman's love." Tears filled her eyes. "I have no children and probably never will because of my career. I'm not the kind of woman a man takes for his bride. Even my mother said as much. I came to accept that to obey God's call to heal, I'd have to give up marriage and motherhood, but my heart still cries for a child. I have so much love to give."

Her eyes sought his, pleading for understanding. She stepped closer. Only the slight easing in Eric's features told her he'd heard.

She went on. "My mother devoted herself to my father's career as an army doctor and spared little time for me. Especially since I showed no ladylike tendencies. I know how these children feel. I feel the loneliness, too."

A shuddery breath quieted her impending sobs. "When I look at Daisy and Mim, I see motherless girls." She doubted the wisdom of such candor but felt compelled to confess what she harbored deep inside. "Daisy and Mim are where I fear Caroline, Amelia, and even Suzannah might end up if no one loves them enough."

Eric started as if she'd jabbed him with a hat pin, but before he could respond, Letty finished her plea. "Let me mother them. Let them be the children I'll never have. I need them, and they need me—all of them. Why should I abandon them as everyone else has?"

Her words died in a sob. She'd bared her yearnings, shared her fears, and she prayed Eric wouldn't think them inconsequential, or worse, a silly woman's ditherings.

Eric didn't betray her faith in him. He came to her side and opened his arms. Letty hesitated, then walked into the haven he offered. She laid her head on his broad shoulder, her tears flowing unchecked. The ache of her unwed, childless state poured out.

Eric nuzzled her temple. "Oh, Letty . . ." His lips found the curve of her cheekbone, where he traced a line of kisses. Down, down they went until they found her lips. His soft kiss brought tears to her eyes until she felt the texture of the caress change. It heated, deepened, making her heart race and her head spin. Eric's arms tightened around her, and all doubt about his interest in her vanished in that hungry, needy kiss.

But there was more to his touch than mere passion. His hands held her firmly yet gently, and his kiss soon matched that gentleness again. If there were ever anything like heaven on earth, Letty knew this came mighty close.

With a final gossamer touch, he released her lips.

His tenderness sent her hope soaring. She knew he desired her; he'd made that evident with his every touch, and just a brief while earlier he'd said he wanted to care for her. She knew his feelings ran deep. Yet she recognized his continued anguish over the death of his wife. Did Martina's memory remain too strong for him to love another woman?

Letty appraised his face. Affection gleamed in his dark brown eyes, a blush colored his cheeks, and the hand she held over his heart picked up the wild tempo of his pulse. She remembered the evening in the barn.

Evidently, so did he.

❦

With a rough sigh, Eric slowly moved Letty away. He fisted his hands then sent his gaze over the small room, pausing on those details uniquely hers. A stethoscope lay atop a chest of drawers. Her cape was draped over a chair by the window. The rose dimity nightdress hung from a hook on the wall by the oak washstand, and the womanly scent of violets hovered everywhere.

Now what? he asked himself, running an unsteady hand through his hair. He noted it was still dark outside. "I must go."

Letty wore the puzzled look she'd donned when he'd pushed her aside. "My rig," he explained. "The town would burn with gossip about the lady doctor who wasn't so much a lady."

"I see."

Dignity bolstered Letty's bearing, and she looked exquisite. Her trademark coiled-braid coronet had unraveled, and her dark curls cascaded over her shoulders. Her lips were dewy and inviting. Her silver eyes suggested another kiss. He resisted the temptation.

"I—" He cleared the roughness in his throat. "Tomorrow morning I'll stop by the Pattersons' and finish repairing the window in the children's room. There's no need for you to worry about it."

Letty nodded, a bemused look on her face.

He had to get away while he still could. "I'll see you again. Soon." He turned on his heel and left the room, feeling like the worst kind of fool.

☙

Eric's hands shook so hard he feared he'd drop his son. The body, still warm from its sanctuary inside Martina's womb, filled the cradle of his palms. Bruises mottled the fragile skin of tiny buttocks and back, mute testimony to the midwife's efforts to turn the infant. Miniature fists clutched at Eric's heart with their stillness.

Baby Karl's face, perfectly formed yet motionless, was an inhuman shade of purple. Tufts of golden curls covered his round head. The deep blue eyes, staring into Eric's soul, riveted him.

His son's eyes. Through the tears sluicing down his face, Eric read reproach in those eyes.

"How could you let me die?"

"No!"

Eric balled his fists into the blanket kinked around his thighs, bringing it to his chest, wishing he could stop the pain that pummeled his heart. The nightmares were so vivid, so real.

He felt the moist warmth of his son's skin; he saw accusations in the innocent eyes. He lived the reality of his child's inertness, of life that should not have been lost. If he hadn't let his love for Martina overshadow his judgment, baby Karl would by now have celebrated his second birthday, and Eric wouldn't be living in a hell of his own making.

He'd failed his wife and son. He had no right to so much as look at another woman. Not one like Letitia Morgan.

He couldn't risk loving her; he couldn't give her a child he might fail as he had his son; he dare not promise the strength he couldn't provide.

❦

"Watch your tail!"

Marmie answered with an indignant "mrrreow!"

Eric tugged off his crooked tie for the third time, his irritation growing. This maneuver normally took him seconds to complete, but today Letty's face seemed to hover between him and the mirror, making it impossible to knot the length of silk.

"Scat," he groused when Marmie rubbed against his shin.

How had he allowed himself the weakness that led to last night's passion? He knew from the outset that Letty Morgan was a most dangerous woman, and yet he'd returned to her side time and again, drawn by her compassion and her genuine goodness.

Then he'd really gone and done it. He'd kissed her with more honest hunger than he remembered ever feeling, even for his dead wife.

He simply couldn't let insanity strike again. He had to avoid Letty Morgan as if she carried the most repugnant disease.

Decision made, Eric took up his brown leather portfolio and, with his free hand, dusted off the ginger-cat fur on his trouser leg.

On the short trip to town, Eric fixed his thoughts on business matters. Ford was still looking into the activities of the swindling Swartleys but hadn't come up with the evidence to catch them. When Eric thought of those two, a chill crept up his neck. His gut told him he already had the key to the puzzle, but he couldn't quite put a finger on it. After last night, he had to wonder if his difficulty came from his preoccupation with a certain doctor.

He spouted German and slammed a fist on the buggy seat. He'd done it again. He'd let her back into his thoughts. Still, what man could forget a kiss like that?

"Good morning, Amos," he called as his horses clopped to the stable.

From his rocker on the porch, the livery owner radiated peace and contentment. "Mornin', Mr. Eric Wagner, sir."

He frowned. Last night's embrace had him so rattled, he couldn't even form a smile. That troubled him, as did his failure to keep Letty from his thoughts for more than a few minutes' time.

The horses came to a stop. He jumped down to the raked dirt and nodded to the stable boy when the youth came for the mares. Eric retrieved his portfolio and headed for his office.

"Somethin' on your mind this mornin'?" Amos asked.

Startled, Eric looked up. Heat filled his cheeks. The current state of his mind was not for anyone to know. "Work, just work."

Amos's pointed stare told Eric he hadn't fooled his friend. "Like I said, Amos, too much work, and I'd best get on with it."

"Yessir." Amos paused and then asked, "Seen the purty doc lately?"

"Oh, here and there." *Mostly everywhere, as if you were keeping track of her,* his conscience taunted. "Work is waiting. And Ford. Ford's waiting for me, too."

Amos radiated sly mirth. "Mm-hmm, work. Gotta get to it, then."

"Precisely."

Eric sped toward the privacy of his office as if to outrun an angry steer. That foxy Amos . . . he saw through everything. He even heard what hadn't been said. You couldn't fool the man, no matter what.

Slamming the door behind him, Eric winced as the shade hit the glass pane. He had to get control of himself.

"Morning, Eric," Ford offered.

"Anything on the Swartleys?"

Ford jabbed his spectacles up to his flaxen eyebrows, laying a trail of ink up the side of his nose. "Not a thing, and I've bird-dogged them. Never let them out of my sight."

On their way to his office, Eric said, "I thought about it last night."

Oh, yeah? his traitorous conscience jeered. *When? Before you embraced Letty? Or perhaps when you locked your lips on hers?*

He gritted his teeth, threw his portfolio onto the desk, then watched a mountain of paper slither over the edge. The day had become a disaster, and he still had the greater measure of it to survive.

Eric heard Ford's poorly muffled guffaw and scrambled for gravity. "As I started to say, I thought about the Swartley matter last night. We have to review everything again."

At Ford's dismay, Eric flattened his palms on the desk. "Yes, *again.* My gut tells me we have what we need in our files. We just can't see it as the key to the scheme."

Ford scratched his head. "You sure you're well today? That did and didn't make much sense."

"Enough of that. Work, we have work to do." Taking his seat, Eric opened the drawer to his left. "Here." He dropped a file labeled "Swartley" on the mess on the desk. "Let's find what we've missed."

He glanced up at Ford's sigh. The reporter's expression said, "Time to humor the boss."

Blast it, he *was* right; he felt it in his bones. His instinct for news and his pursuit of truth rarely failed him. "Please bear with me, will you? They came to town flat broke, right?"

"Sure. They started out sharing a tent with two other miners near the Hart of Silver shaft. They worked for Hart, but lazy as they are, they got fired fast, and besides, they've always spent time at Bessie's and the saloons. They're still broke."

"Not that broke. They bought the Seymours' claim, even if for a pittance."

With Ford's nod, his glasses tumbled down, and his finger trailed another ink track up his nose when he replaced them. "Then the Kurtzs' claim, and later Simpson sold out, too."

Eric tapped his fingers against the notes. He turned the facts in his mind again, but the Swartleys' game eluded illumination.

Ford cut into Eric's thoughts. "They paid them all pennies."

Clasping his hands behind his neck, Eric leaned back in his chair and crossed his ankles on the desktop. He thought and thought, counting each piece of information he knew. Before long, he began voicing his ponderings. "They only have pennies. They rarely work, then they spend their earnings at Bessie's—"

Eric's feet crashed to the floor. He bolted upright. As if someone had turned on a lamp, the answer blazed in his mind. "It's been staring at us the entire time."

Ford popped up and knocked down his chair. "If you don't mind, please explain. I haven't the slightest—"

"It's the money, Ford. Yes, they've paid only pennies, but those pennies add up. Someone is funding the Swartleys. They don't have enough money to have bought all that land, even if it was in bits and pieces."

Ford bent to set the chair upright, then sat again. The wheels in his head spun almost visibly with the new information. "I'll be hornswoggled. You're right. The question is, who's their cash cow?"

❦

When sifted sunlight kissed her face, Letty stretched in her warm bed. A fanciful smile curved her lips. Eric . . .

She didn't have the words to express what their embrace meant to her. He was Eric, and Eric was more than enough.

She, however, was a physician, and patients would soon line up for her. Still smiling, she poured water from the pottery pitcher into the fluted basin on her washstand. A splash to her face snapped her back to reality. She plied her washcloth and finished her ablutions.

Her garments seemed plainer today than yesterday, but then today she felt less plain. Today her mirror reflected excitement in the roses on her cheeks, mischief in her smile, happiness in her gaze.

Letty chided herself. "Honestly, fanciful thoughts won't heal a soul. Sick people don't care that Eric kissed you last night."

Even so, she couldn't wait to see him again.

Letty ran downstairs and poured corn into the crate that housed her growing chickens. "What am I going to do with you?" she asked as the birds fluttered their wings and pecked for kernels. "You need a proper coop and a yard to scratch up."

The thought stuck while Letty treated a steady flow of patients. It followed her when she took advantage of a lull to run to the manse and check on Mim, who basked in the light of the Stones' love. They'd insisted on keeping the child, and Letty was glad, since she had no jobs for the proud girl.

Noon found Letty back in her kitchen with nothing to do but watch her fowl jockey for position in the crate. A knock at the kitchen door made her leap at the chance to do something.

"Daisy! Come in, dear. What brings you by?"

Daisy removed the black shawl she wore over her head as a crude disguise. She glanced down the street, then stepped into Letty's kitchen. "I came to see Mim."

Letty set the teakettle on the stove. "I'm sorry, dear, she's not here. Pastor and Mrs. Stone came last night to take her home with them. They have more room than I do, and she agreed to go." Noting the alarm on Daisy's face, she hastened to reassure her. "The pastor and his wife are lovely people. Mim couldn't be in better hands."

Daisy shrugged.

"They'll be glad to have you visit her," Letty added.

Daisy snorted. "I can't visit 'lovely people,' Doc. Their flock would flee faster than mice do from cats."

"Perhaps, then, they don't belong in that flock."

She got another shrug. A fat blond curl slipped from the cascade at the back of Daisy's head and danced against the painted cheek. Letty ached at the vulnerability she saw. "How have you been?"

"Fine."

Letty bit her lip as Daisy inspected the kitchen. The girl showed no inclination to leave anytime soon, which suited her just fine, but she didn't want the visit wasted on one-syllable words.

Daisy continued her perusal, finally pausing by the typewriter. A graceful finger touched one metal key. "What is this?"

"A typewriting machine."

"A . . . writing machine?"

"Mm-hmm." Letty poured boiling water over tea leaves in the blue teapot. "Mr. Wagner's been most generous. He let me borrow the thingamabob. I don't need it, but it's quite intriguing. Want to see?"

Daisy shrugged, donning a veneer of indifference. "Sure."

I've found common ground, Letty thought. She offered, "If I show you how, will you try it?"

"Maybe."

Determined to turn that lukewarm word into burning interest, Letty showed Daisy the intricacies of the typewriter. Fascinated by keys slapping paper rolled over a metal cylinder, the girl soon fired round after round of astute questions. When she paused, Letty stood and pointed to the chair she'd just vacated. "Your turn, dear."

Alarm flickered in Daisy's eyes. Afraid the girl might leave, Letty placed her hands on her young friend's slender shoulders and guided her into the chair. Then she said, "You place your hands like so."

Daisy proved bright and capable. Her interest gave Letty an idea. Maybe this would offer the girl a way out of the world where she currently lived. Well before teacher or student called the lesson's end, however, someone cried for Letty.

Outside she found a panting, sawdust-covered youth. "Dr. Morgan, hurry, please. One of our men on Main Street—he hurts mighty bad."

Letty flung her cape over her shoulders. She grabbed her bag and returned to the kitchen. The back door closed. Daisy had fled.

Lord Jesus, please don't let this be the last time she comes.

Back with the young man, Letty said, "Let's go."

At the far end of Main Street, she found a crowd where men worked on a half-done structure. She bustled up to the onlookers. "Please move aside."

A path cleared. She set her black leather satchel on the ground near a man who twisted and turned in testimony to his pain. Holding her skirt out of the way, she knelt at his side and placed a hand on the man's sweat-beaded brow. "Where does it hurt, sir?"

"Gut," he grunted. Another paroxysm convulsed him.

Letty tried to form a picture of the man's symptoms. "The pain comes in spasms, right?"

He nodded.

She turned to her bag and opened the top. Withdrawing a vial with a dropping tube in its top, she asked, "Does it feel as if someone's wringing your insides?"

He gave another jerky assent.

"Has it happened before?"

"Not this bad."

"What did you eat last night?"

Her patient described a meal that counted bacon, eggs, biscuits with butter, and a cream-pudding pie—very rich fare. "Colocynthis, for digestive distress with cramping, is the best remedy for you," she murmured. "Help me, please. I need you to hold your head still while I place the remedy under your tongue. You should feel better after your body absorbs it."

Despite his pain, the man fought to hold still. When he opened his mouth and moved his tongue aside, Letty counted out the medicated drops and prayed for swift relief.

She looked around for a familiar face but found none. "Can someone take him home? In a buggy?"

"Yes, ma'am," answered the youth who'd fetched her. "I brought Pa's cart today for supplies. I'll take Harry."

"Thank you. Although Colocynthis works fast on troubled gallbladders, he'll be exhausted from the pain. He needs rest." She turned to Harry. "Only simple, soft foods now. Nothing heavy or highly seasoned, either, and you'll have to take to bed for the remainder of the day."

The workman nodded. Then another cramp hit, and he gritted his teeth. When it passed, he conceded, "That one weren't so bad. Thank you, ma'am."

Letty stood and shook bits of dirt from her skirt. She turned to the youth who'd fetched her. "If you'll come with me, I'll give you more pellets for him to take later on. I'm sure he'll feel better by the time you get back here, and then you can take him home."

With the young man at her side, Letty walked home. A chorus of admiring comments followed, and a satisfied smile curved her lips.

᪥

Still puzzling over the Swartleys' possible backers, Eric strode down Main Street toward the livery. Surely not someone local, was it? If so, who stood to gain? Hart had all he could manage with his mine, yet Eric knew the Swartleys had ordered mining gear—costly indeed.

They'd made their intentions clear, as clear as the cost of the proposition. Then there was the money they paid busted claim holders. True, each sum was negligible, but when he studied the entire picture, he saw a pattern of greed and wealth. Greed the Swartleys had; wealth, they lacked. So who had it?

"Eric! Eric Wagner. You wait right there, young man."

Setting aside his concerns over the Swartleys, Eric turned toward the summons. Despite a generous girth, Dr. Mortimer Henry Medford stomped toward him, his cow-handled cane rapping furiously.

Each time Eric saw the walking stick, he had to fight a chuckle. The successful surgeon spent his time away from medicine seeking new ways to pamper himself. The cane, absurd though it was, had cost a small fortune, for the cow head was of African ivory and the stick of Oriental teak.

Dr. Medford nearly bowled Eric over. "You simply *must* do something, Eric Wagner. It's all your fault."

The fury in the doctor's puffy red features took him aback. Calling on his interviewing experience, he corralled his irritation. "Since I have no idea what you say I've done, I need you to tell me what you've taken exception to."

Dr. Medford wagged the stick at Eric. "Why, that woman, of course. Who does she think she is?"

"If you would name her," he said, even though his knotted innards told him who'd angered the surgeon, "then perhaps I could tell you who she thinks she is."

"That accursed Dr. Morgan is who. And you're the one who set her loose on Hartville. Why, now she's stealing my patients."

What had Letty done? Dreading the answer, Eric spoke again. "If you'd start at the beginning, perhaps I'd understand."

Another shake of the cane threatened Eric's hat. He backed away.

"She's taken to treating men," the fleshy gent said. "It was bad enough you brought a woman doctor to town, and an archaic homeopath at that, but you insisted she'd treat women and children. Mostly, she'd deliver babies, you said. Now, the creature is dosing workmen. For free!"

Dr. Medford raised his arms as if to emphasize his outrage at Letty's dastardly behavior. Eric fought the urge to laugh.

The beefy sawbones went on. "We will *not* tolerate such a thing. You caused it, you handle it, young man. Or you'll force the men of Hartville to take action."

The surgeon stormed away.

How was Eric going to handle this development? He had yet to get Letty to look out for herself, and each time he'd tried to take care of her, to protect her, she'd invoked her adulthood. Well, he was an adult, too, and she was facing disaster. Somehow he had to stop her before she did herself permanent harm.

Across the country, physicians who opposed the simple methods and modest cost of homeopathic care had banded together and formed the American Medical Association. The rivalry was fierce, and Eric knew of cases in which homeopaths had been run out of town. With her staunch convictions, Letty had already incurred Dr. Medford's wrath.

"Evening, Mr. Wagner." The schoolmarm's pruned-up face boded ill.

Eric answered warily. "Evening, Miss Whitehall."

"I must say, sir, that's a fine sort of doctor you brought us. Why, she's mighty cozy with those . . . those floozies from Bessie Brown's horrid place. Twice, sir, twice, I've seen painted women leave her house. To think I wasted time to welcome one of her sort to town."

Eric clenched his jaw. A vicious gossip, Emmaline wouldn't stop until she'd made Letty miserable, especially with the fuel she had.

He retorted, "A medical emergency, I'm sure."

Emmaline's nose rose higher in the air, her stiff lace collar tight around her skinny neck. "Humph! If that is so, then the tart deserved it. The wages of sin, you know."

Her self-righteousness was as repulsive as the women she'd condemned. Eric's annoyance with Emmaline grew. "Anyone who needs doctoring ought to seek a physician."

Emmaline pursed her lips. "The physician needn't treat just anyone," she argued. "Our upstanding surgeon doesn't treat strumpets. Why should our lady doctor do so?"

Precisely my contention, he almost said, but he caught himself before betraying Letty. "Perhaps an overly developed sense of duty is at the root of what you saw."

The schoolmarm clutched her black handbag tighter and tapped her umbrella on the sidewalk. "Maybe, maybe not. Still, it hardly suits."

Eric couldn't stand to hear more. "Good day, Miss Whitehall." He then changed direction and set off after the indomitable Dr. Morgan.

The thought of Letty losing her patients, bearing the anger of the menfolk, or becoming the subject of Medford's greed was more than Eric could stomach. Fear filled him, manifesting itself as rage.

Letty answered his knock immediately. Without waiting for an invitation, he marched past her. "Tell me, won't you, what you're trying to do," he demanded. "I've warned you and warned you, and you've ignored me each time. Well, as I expected, the situation has worsened. I can't even walk to the livery for my mares without folks running to me with complaints about the confounded woman doctor."

"I told you to avoid the prostitutes. No one in their right mind wants their womenfolk treated by the same physician who treats strumpets. Who knows what you might pick up from them and pass on to your other patients."

Anger flashed silver in Letty's eyes, but he was determined to have his say. If she persisted, it would be in total defiance of his directive. "Vice destroys innocent people. You will not treat those women again. You can't afford to do so. The rest of the town's women and children need you. Have I made myself clear?"

Eyes flashing, lips tight, cheeks red with wrath, Letty glared back. "How dare you tell me what I can and can't do, Eric Wagner! You have no right to interfere with my work."

A blade of pain sliced through him. Her words reminded him how much he wished he had the right to make his opinion count for her.

"I'm an adult," she added, slamming both fists on her hips.

"True, but are you a wise one?"

She tipped up her chin. "Depends on whose wisdom you prefer."

"What do you mean?

She paused and closed her eyes. "I mean," she said, "I prefer God's wisdom to that of men."

Eric shook his head. "You can't count on God. I did, and see what He left me? Two graves. Yes, He's out there somewhere in heaven, but He doesn't listen to regular folks like you and me."

The tear that slid down her cheek bewildered him.

"Oh, Eric," she murmured, a look of compassion on her face. "I'm so sorry you feel that way. God listens—always—but only answers in His way and in His time, not necessarily ours. I'll pray for Him to show you that He has reasons for acting as well as for not doing a thing. We may never fully understand it, but His remains the wisdom that passes all understanding."

"His wisdom has certainly passed my understanding. I'll never understand why He didn't keep me from failing Martina and our son."

11

Although the sun shone through Letty's window the next morning, she saw only the clouds cast by Eric's rejection of God.

After he'd left, she'd closed her front door and fed the chickens. Unable to muster an appetite, she'd gone to her room and cried herself to sleep. Her damp pillow now bore testimony to a night of heartache.

What should she do? As she looked around the pink and white room, she knew discouragement for the first time in a long time.

She sat up, gathered her knees to her chest, and wrapped her arms around her legs. She felt more alone than she had the night of Mrs. Forrest's wake, but she could no more betray her convictions than she could stop loving Eric.

The Father had called her to serve, and serve she would.

Why did Eric so oppose her efforts to help Daisy and Mim? She'd made herself clear, and even though her interest in the Pattersons irritated him, Eric hadn't erupted like last night's volcano when she'd helped them.

How could she love a man who wouldn't understand her? One who discounted God and His calling on her life? How could she yearn for someone who wanted to cage her with his expectations?

She loved Eric, but she couldn't capitulate to his demands. To do so, she'd have to turn her back on the Lord. Letty simply couldn't—wouldn't—do that.

She was a physician. She'd sacrificed much to become one, and no one, not even the man she loved, was going to stop her from using her God-given gift. As a healer, she would continue to treat those who ailed, those who needed her.

She got dressed, then took care of the mundane morning chores. She ate, and as she washed the oatmeal off the bowl, she made a mental list of patients she'd visit today. Before she'd finished counting them all, Daisy burst into the kitchen.

"Morning, Doc. Can I practice typewriting for a spell?"

Satisfaction warmed Letty's heart. She couldn't give up on this girl. *Thank you, Lord. I know there's much to do, but with your help, I can do this, too. In spite of Eric.*

She hugged Daisy. "Why, certainly, dear. I was just lamenting the prospects for a dull morning. Your visit is the remedy this doctor needs."

༄

Was his weakness around lovely women congenital? Eric couldn't otherwise explain his actions of the past few weeks. How could he have felt such rage? How could he have vented it on Letty? How could he have kissed her yet again?

He didn't know how he'd face her. He'd lost all semblance of control of his temper and his desire.

She welcomed your kisses, his weak side taunted.

Still, she was an innocent. He, on the other hand, knew where his actions could lead. A man with a past like his knew better than to love a woman like Letty. He would keep her from loving him back.

A woman of principle never shared kisses as intense as theirs unless she loved the man in question. Letty was no trollop. A man could cherish her, knowing she'd never lead him to destruction like the floozies at Bessie's did. Knowing that Letty loved him made Eric want to run to her side, clasp her in his arms, and never let her go. Reason, however, told him she deserved a better man, a whole man, one without guilt.

He left for the office, barely noting the sunshine. Spring had arrived, but as far as Eric was concerned, winter could just as easily have stayed. He didn't want to breathe the fragrance of promise each day. He didn't want to hear birds woo their mates or watch them build their nests. He didn't want to see new life in flower beds or tree branches. He didn't dare feel hope in the world around him. He was a failed man, and his heart held only pain.

At the livery, he grunted at Amos. Amos returned a full-bellied laugh. Eric cast a glare at his friend and saw wisdom in his eyes as he left.

He walked faster, but when he neared Silver Creek Church at Willow and Main, his pace began to slow. His heart yearned for the woman who brought sunshine with her. A movement in the winter-nude shrubs around Letty's home caught Eric's attention, a flash of marigold and black, unusually bright for this time of year. He tucked his portfolio under his arm and went to investigate.

As he approached, he saw the young blond tart Letty had helped the night of Slosh's debacle with Bessie Brown. The girl opened Letty's back door and ran in as if she owned the place.

An oath ripped past his lips. The woman brought sunshine with her, but she also brought more trouble than a dozen women should.

Angry again, he stalked on to his office, determined to put an end to the mess. And the only way to end it was to redouble his efforts to rid Hartville of its more squalid element.

❦

Letty's progress with Daisy provided her with renewed zest, so the rest of the day flew by. No problems arose. By early afternoon, Randy Carlson was her only patient.

"You look lovely, Mama," Letty said as her friend walked in.

Randy rolled her eyes. "My skirts are too tight around the waist."

A pang of yearning struck Letty, and she had to clear her throat. "How do you feel? Any problems?"

Randy sank into the chair in front of Letty's desk. "Well, no. I came to see you because I've heard the oddest rumors, and I wanted to discuss them with you." Her green eyes dodged Letty's gaze. "Emma—"

"Emma—"

The women exchanged awkward smiles. Letty tried again. "To be fair, the bare facts are as Emmaline must be painting them. I have indeed taken two of the girls from Bessie's place under my wing."

Randy gasped, her eyes wide as the sky.

"I hope I don't offend you," Letty continued, "but I must speak frankly. Those two girls—for that's all they are—were beaten by patrons of Bessie's Barn. I couldn't in good conscience let them go untreated. I came to Hartville to treat women and children in particular. Daisy and Mim are, unfortunately, both."

Randy blanched.

"You should also know," Letty added, "that Pastor and Mrs. Stone took Mim home with them. I've been treating her injuries, and she's on the mend now. She's only thirteen years old. Could you turn your back on a misused child?"

"Thirteen?"

"Thirteen."

"Obscene."

"Indeed. So are you asking me to reject them?"

"No . . . I can't say I am." Randy paused. "How can I help you? Them?"

"Do you know what you're asking?"

Randy paused again. "Yes."

"Douglas won't be pleased," Letty warned.

"Just let him try to stop me," Randy said, narrowing her eyes. "Think of the self-righteous men who have warned their wives to stay away from you since Emmaline began spreading rumors. Many of them use the girls."

"That hasn't escaped me. If they had no patrons, the girls would find other means of support. The men perpetuate the problem."

Randy tapped her shoe against the floor, mulling over Letty's words. "I guess," she said, "but one can also argue that if the women weren't there, the men wouldn't be tempted. Does that make sense?"

Letty took a deep breath. "The Lord did promise He would never let us be tempted beyond our defenses. Rejecting the women and chasing them from town isn't the answer. Jesus never shunned prostitutes or other sinners. He came to save them. If we're to follow His example, then we must help them, too."

Randy had the grace to blush. "You're right. What do we do next?"

Glad to disembark from the same carousel of contention she'd already ridden with Eric, Letty said, "We probably should discuss this with Pastor and Mrs. Stone sometime soon. After all, they have Mim."

"That's an excellent idea. Since I'm anxious to help, I hope you'll let me go with you."

The women headed for the door, each with separate business to attend to, but both thinking of cast-off youngsters. The conversation had reminded Letty of her argument with Eric, and she decided to meet him on his own territory. Certain matters needed clarification, and she feared her cozy home might permit a recurrence of anger or passion.

"Let me come partway with you," she told Randy. "I need to stop by the newspaper." As soon as she spoke, Letty recognized her mistake.

Randy grinned mischievously. "You want to see Eric? Anything interesting to discuss?"

Letty fastened the black frog tie at the collar of her gray cape and gave Randy a reproving glare. "Certainly. I need to discuss the girls with Mr. Wagner."

"Oh."

Letty almost laughed at her friend's deflated expression. Were it not for the pain of last night's argument, she might have told Randy of her feelings for Eric. He had made it abundantly clear that he wasn't ready to love again. Letty had nothing to tell.

Soon, however, the sparkling newness of spring had her casting off her gloomy mood. On a cottonwood's branches, myriad green dots heralded the arrival of its newest garment. In a neighbor's garden, more green parted the earthy mantle that had sheltered it from winter's chill.

"Look, Randy," Letty said. "Over there, in the corner. Can those be crocuses?"

"Mine came out days ago. I love spring. It's the happiest time of year."

The sturdy blossoms that, after fighting the odds of winter, burst through in victory at the first sign of warmth brought something sweet to Letty's bruised spirit. "Hope," she whispered.

"Hope," Randy agreed.

The friends parted ways, and Letty approached Eric's office. When she was nearly there, she heard a woman's voice sing out. "Dr. Morgan! *Eine minute, bitte.*"

Letty turned and saw the first woman whose delivery she'd attended in Hartville. "I'm tickled to see you, Elsa. How's the baby?"

"Big. My mann vant know, you vant ham? Ve got goot ham this year."

"Oh, how kind of you. I have plenty of food," she said, but at Elsa's crestfallen look, she chose to alter her answer. "I have plenty of food, but your ham sounds like a splendid feast. If you're certain you and the children don't need it, I'd be honored to have it."

Elsa's bun bounced with her nod. "Ve bring it your house soon."

"And the baby, too."

"*Ja, ja.*"

The rumble of agitated male voices caught her attention, and Letty glanced in their direction. The noisy group stood at the entrance to the Hartville Day. Had Eric written another of his scorching editorials?

Letty asked Elsa if she knew the source of the men's interest. Elsa lowered her head and peered at the wooden sidewalk. She clasped and unclasped her hands in obvious discomfort. "*Nicht gut,*" she said, shaking her head. "Mr. Wagner write of bad vemen. Bessie Brown."

What had he done?

"Have you read the editorial?" Letty asked.

Elsa looked up. "Ed . . . edi-tor-yal?"

Letty regretted never learning German. "Yes, what Eric wrote. Have you read it?"

"*Nein,* my mann tell me is *nicht gut.* Bad vemen. Close houses, ja? Vemen in jail."

Letty bit her tongue. She was overcome with temptation to throttle the man who'd kissed her senseless and then undermined her efforts to improve the lot of a number of neglected children. Didn't the girls deserve a chance to change? Didn't they deserve to be loved? Shouldn't they have the opportunity to hear the gospel and learn what Jesus offered? Indeed, what could prison offer them?

Eric knew how much the girls' welfare meant to her. She'd told him how much she wanted to help. For him to decide on the course of action for all of Hartville and then use the power of his newspaper to sway popular opinion showed outrageous arrogance.

How could he caress her so tenderly and then trample her feelings, her convictions? His treachery crushed her, tarnishing her memories of their embraces.

Tears of rage filled her eyes. They had no future together. Besides, she had a first love, and that love led her to choose to serve God's children. She had a mission to fulfill.

With a swift *"Auf wiedersehen"* for Elsa and a dab at her eyes, Letty parted the male crowd and went to beard the lion in his den.

Impelled by her temper, she slammed the door behind her. Eric's reporter jumped and dropped his spectacles. For a second, Letty regretted her unladylike entrance, but she didn't let regret linger.

"I'm sorry about the door, Ford," she said. "I need to speak to him. Where is he?"

With a bemused expression on his face, Ford bobbed his head in the direction of Eric's office. He started to stand, but Letty waved him back down. "Don't bother. I know where the lion's lair is. In fact, this might be an excellent time to go and sniff out tomorrow's news. It'll likely be loud enough in here to ruin anyone's concentration."

Letty made short work of the hallway and knocked on the door to Eric's inner sanctum. She entered without waiting for an invitation. "Just what did you mean by writing such drivel?" she asked. "I can't believe a man as intelligent and well educated as you would come up with nothing better than judgmental tripe."

Fists on her hips, Letty studied Eric's reddening face. "I'll fight you on this, you know. You simply cannot jail little girls. I'll do everything I can to rescue however many I find."

Eric stood. "If we were only dealing with little girls, Dr. Morgan, then I would perhaps agree with your prescription, but brothels are full of women who prey on male needs. They also prey on your little girls and must be stopped."

Eric squared his shoulders. "Tell me," he said, "have you seen a family destroyed after the man takes a prostitute's lure? He swallows the pretty bait, but the hook ravages him, maybe kills him. I've seen it happen. Those predators must be stopped."

"Very well. Stop them. But I beg you not to just jail them, especially the young ones. They need help, and by God's grace they can be helped. I intend to help them."

Eric flinched at her mention of God. Too bad. She knew where to put her trust, and she wasn't going to hide that faith. Besides, he needed to make peace with his Father by himself.

Before she could argue further, he said, "I'm willing to compromise but only if you'll compromise, too."

"What sort of compromise do you propose?"

"I'll do what I can to keep the girls out of jail. I'll even find them help—work, even—if you stop consorting with them."

"How dare you suggest that!" Letty marched to the window, turning her back on him, fuming silently.

❦

How dare he? He dared because he cared about her and feared for her safety. What if she contracted some filthy disease while treating strumpets? What if she got caught in a brawl between a "client" and a tart? What if something happened to her? What if she ended up suffering because he'd failed her, too? He dared because he had to keep her safe.

Staring down the width of the room, he said, "Hartville needs you. We brought you to doctor our women and children . . . those who don't lead a sordid life. We can't afford to lose you."

"Oh, pshaw, Eric Wagner. Hartville's in no danger of losing me—"

"Listen to me, you spitfire! How many women and children do you think you'll see in your clinic when the men decide you've lowered yourself to an unacceptable level? They won't permit their families to seek you for treatment if they feel that's the best way to shield them from the baser elements in town."

Letty's brow furrowed. Her lips pursed as if she'd bitten into a green persimmon. She advanced and jabbed a finger in his chest.

"Now you listen to me, Eric Wagner. Those men are the ones who pay the girls to do what should only happen in the God-ordained sanctity of marriage. They're the ones you should take to task."

"That may be the case," he conceded, "but brothels have no place in a decent town. A woman's doctor does, and those men pay your fees. What will you do if they run you out of town? Did you know that after you doctored Harry yesterday, our surgeon now sees you as a threat?"

"Could it be that I threaten these men's secret pleasures?" she shot back.

Eric felt sucker-punched. "Sometimes," he said, "it's better to keep a secret if by doing so one protects decent, innocent bystanders."

Her gaze dove deep into his heart, and he felt the urge to squirm. "No," she said, "Scripture says that evil can't live in the light of God's love. What those men do in the dark of secrecy is a sin against Him."

Sweat beaded his brow. "I don't argue that one bit. Vice ruins everything it touches. I've seen a frail wife die from a stroke after learning of her husband's infidelity. When the husband's appetite for bought flesh became known and he realized he was about to lose his position, his image, and his career, he killed himself. Their son was orphaned."

Letty's gaze turned scalpel sharp. She bit her lip. "How . . . sad," she said in a compassionate voice. "But can't you see? None of that would have happened had the husband not strayed."

"He was tempted."

"He could have resisted."

"We must eliminate the temptation."

"How, Eric? By eliminating women? That's absurd. A man

can stray with any acquaintance if he so desires. The girls need help."

"The town needs to be free of that blight."

"Yes, but not by destroying the most vulnerable of God's children." Letty gathered her reticule. "I must follow my conscience. I must clothe and feed those in need as God calls me to do. Not even for you, Eric, will I go against the Lord's command."

She left more quietly than she'd arrived.

Eric admired her strength, her courage, her determination, but that didn't mean he would lessen his efforts. She had rejected his compromise. He, too, had to follow his conscience. He had to protect Hartville as well as Letty.

"Eric!" Ford called from the hallway.

"Yes," he answered absently, Letty's final words reverberating through his thoughts.

"Did you forget your interview with Dr. Medford today? He wanted to discuss his new surgical clinic."

He closed his eyes in defeat. She'd distracted him again. "Thanks for the reminder."

Cramming his hat on his head, he rattled off instructions to Ford as he left the office. He ran toward the surgeon's mansion, where the new clinic would be housed, hoping he hadn't missed him at the construction site. When he finally approached the almost-finished structure, he saw the stout man stalking away in the opposite direction. "Dr. Medford, I'm here!"

Medford planted his unique walking stick in a clump of soil. "Well! Did you think I had time to wait for you to show?"

Panting, Eric tried to appease him. "No, sir—unavoidable." He gulped a serving of spring air. "Unexpected—delay at—the office."

The peeved man tapped his cane against the support leg of the scaffold that covered the front of the mansion. "Well, get on with it, then."

Eric took notebook and pencil from his inside pocket. Letty

would be the death of him yet. He couldn't believe she'd made him forget an interview.

"Completion date is expected for . . . ?" he asked, scribbling away. He fired questions at the doctor, but Medford took his time, making sure Eric noted each lavish detail. The pompous gent beat an occasional punctuation on the scaffold with his cane, setting off an ominous rattle above. Eric didn't like the moans the structure emitted, but he dreaded saying anything that might again light the fuse to the doctor's wrath.

". . . and I've provided exceptional care for the men," he added. Then he jabbed Eric's chest with a pudgy sausage of a finger. "At least, I did until you brought that meddlesome biddy to town. Who ever heard of such an absurdity? Calling herself a doctor, and homeopath to boot!"

Medford grew more livid with each passing moment. He rapped the scaffold again. A sudden rumble roared from over-head. The framework tottered, and a wooden scream pierced the afternoon's peace.

Time stopped. The air around Eric grew thick as porridge. He couldn't make himself move. Another rending sound made him look up. Tools rained to the ground, narrowly missing him. Then he remembered Dr. Medford. The scaffold swayed, more cracks appeared in the wooden planks, and Eric lunged at the surgeon.

"Look out!" he yelled, throwing himself against the pillowy body of the town's wealthiest resident.

☙

Letty left Bergstrom's Dry Goods with a bolt of cheesecloth under her arm. She glanced down Main Street at the newest buildings and the structures now under construction. A hideous screech shocked her.

"Look out!" she yelled as the scaffold in front of Dr. Medford's mansion began to quake. Hammers, nails, and other objects hit the ground with alarming force. From her vantage point, Letty saw two men near the platform. When the taller man looked up, his hat fell off.

"Eric!"

Fear clutched Letty's heart as she started toward him, her cheesecloth a forgotten lump on the road.

The wooden planks ripped apart and came crashing down.

Beneath the boards lay the man she loved. "Lord Jesus, help him," she sobbed, running to his side. "Help me, please."

The street had gone deathly silent. A man cried, "Get a doctor!"

Letty grabbed two bystanders who stood peering at the rubble and pushed them out of her way. "I'm Dr. Morgan. Let me through."

But before she could reach the men, the collapsed structure had to be removed. Seeing that no one had yet taken control of the situation, Letty grabbed the nearest board and gave it a tug. Realizing the futility of her meager effort, she looked around the crowd.

She pointed at a pair of workmen. "You! Take this wood off them. I can't help if I can't reach them. They might die if their lungs are crushed."

Letty couldn't bear the thought of Eric seriously hurt, but she knew she had to set aside her fear and focus on her medical knowledge.

After what seemed like forever, the work crew removed the debris from the two figures in the dirt. Tears burned Letty's eyes again, and a sob tightened her throat. She gathered her skirts and sank down at Eric's side.

A tear broke through the constraints of her will and fell on a dirty cheek. "Oh, Eric . . ."

She checked the pulse at his neck with trembling fingers. Weak but steady, its thrum reassured her. As if from a great distance, she heard murmurs around her, but her attention never left him.

Soon the dry, fetid stench of dust and too many bodies tainted the otherwise fresh air.

"Move back, please. Give them room to breathe."

Feet shuffled, the oppression of bodies lessened, and Letty filled her lungs. "These men can't stay in the dirt," she went on. "I need help getting them home, in bed, where they belong. Goodness knows I'm not large enough to move either one of them."

A grizzled fellow in filthy dungarees stepped forward, then, remembering Letty's admonition, moved back again. "I can help, miss."

"So can I," said a burly carpenter, his hammer hanging from his belt.

"An' I can give Bert and Tom a hand, if I do say so myself," added a lanky blond.

"Excellent. Please get Mr. Wagner into his buggy." Another burst of fear clutched her middle. "And please . . . be careful."

Although she was reluctant to leave Eric's side, even for another patient, duty called her to check on Dr. Medford. As she reached for his thick neck, his watery blue eyes widened.

"Wha—you!" he sputtered. "Why are you here?"

Letty prayed God would spare her the humiliation she'd suffered at Mrs. Forrest's wake. "I was about to take your pulse, sir. You're injured, and I must check your vital signs. Please stay calm while I see if you've broken any bones."

"Vital signs! Broken bones! What does an uppity midwife know of broken bones?" He turned his head from side to side, creasing his fleshy neck alarmingly. His too-tight collar and necktie looked likely to throttle him. "Get me Melvin Harrison from down Rockton way. There's a fine doctor for you."

"Dr. Morgan is fine doktor," Elsa Richards asserted in her soft, accented voice. Letty smiled at her patient.

But Dr. Medford had built a good head of steam. "Woman's nothing but a midwife. Give her a fancy title, but she's still what she is, and last time I checked myself, I was no woman. Someone fetch me Melvin."

Elsa came closer, but knowing further discussion would be futile, Letty took the woman's hand as she rose. "Don't bother," she said. "He's unlikely to listen. I've known others like him."

"Ach, he is dummhead!"

Letty smiled again as some around them tittered. "Yes, he seems a bit addled in the head."

"He not polite wit' you."

She said good-bye, and by the time she reached Eric's buggy, he'd opened his eyes.

"How do you feel?" she asked.

"I've known better days." He winced when he tried to move.

"Don't," she said, a hand on his chest. "You'll be home in no time. Will Andy be there to help you inside? If not, I'll ask one of those men to come with us."

"Andy will be there."

Letty took the reins. She noticed Eric's pallor and urged the horses to a faster pace.

He moaned.

"I'm sorry," she said, "but you need to be in bed, and since I saw no broken bones, I'm going to get you home as soon as I can."

Eric's glare spoke volumes. Still, she had to get him out of the cool weather. He'd sustained a concussion and was most likely in shock. Before too long she brought the horses to a stop in front of Eric's ranch house. She hopped down from the buggy and called Andy.

As she waited, she heard a bleat come from the barn, and she turned in that direction. A white nanny goat had her beady black eyes fixed on her. The animal butted her horns in Letty's direction, then bleated again.

"Heidi!" the ranch hand yelled as he rounded the barn. "Where'd you run off to, you dumb goat?"

"Oh, Andy, I'm so relieved to see you. Mr. Wagner's hurt, and we must get him inside. I need your help."

Andy dropped his rake and ran to the carriage. "If you'll stand under his one shoulder, miss, I'll take the rest of his weight."

Letty helped Andy with Eric's transfer, which was accomplished with much muttering and moaning from the patient. Inside, she propped her portion of his weight—which seemed greater by the minute—against a wall, closed the door, and took scant note of rich wood, iron trimmings, and a mirror and table to one side. Only when she glanced at the rug did she see the blood.

"His leg," she cried. "He's losing too much blood. Here, Andy, help me get him to a sofa . . . a settee . . . something. I must stitch up that wound."

As he grew weaker, Eric stopped fighting but could no longer help. Finally they eased him onto a settee and draped his long frame on the piece of furniture.

Letty studied Eric's trousers where fabric was embedded in his wound, the spurts of blood frightening her. Then she glanced at his belt, a possible makeshift tourniquet. But the thought of touching him, the man she loved, in so intimate a place held her back. Something else would have to suffice.

Over her shoulder, she said, "I'll need scissors, Andy."

"Yes, ma'am," the anxious ranch manager answered, scurrying off in search of a pair. He returned in seconds, and Letty cut Eric's trousers to expose the wound for her examination. From the way blood spurted, she knew the large sliver of wood still in the gash had nicked an artery. There was no time to send Andy for her bag back home. With a cursory thought to decorum, she tore a long strip off the bottom of her cotton petticoat, tied the fabric above the pulsing red stream, and removed the splinter. Wadding another length of petticoat into a pad, she pressed it against the cut.

"Does he keep whiskey or other spirits?" she asked Andy. "And what about a needle and thread?"

"Eric don't drink, but I can fetch you my flask, miss. Can't say I know about needle and thread. The missus here's been dead two years."

"Martina," Eric murmured. He opened his eyes, and through the pain, Letty saw sadness. "Martina's sewing . . . in the baby's room."

Letty turned to Andy.

"Third door off the hall, miss."

"Here," she said to the wiry ranch hand. "Keep firm pressure on it. Should the bleeding slow, even though I don't think it will, fetch your flask and see that he drinks. We must dull the pain."

Letty dashed down the hall. She paused at the door to the baby's room. Dread in her heart, she pressed down on the iron latch. Inside the room, the tragedy hit her, and she knew just how deeply Eric had loved.

Dust motes danced in the stale air, lit by the weak sunlight that seeped through limp yellow gingham curtains. A cobweb draped the top of the window frame, reaching up to where the ceiling met the wall.

To the right of the window, a peg rack held a trio of smocked newborn gowns, the fabric a dull shade of not quite white. A chest of drawers, probably stuffed with blankets, hats, and nightgowns, bore a tracery of dust. Even so, she saw the love that had gone into preparing this room.

The empty cradle nearly brought Letty to her knees. A tiny, fluffy pillow waited for a fragile head. The quilted coverlet, pieced in strips of yellow and green calico, was folded back, ready for a slumbering infant.

Letty wiped her tears with the back of her wrist. Thwarted dreams lived here; it illustrated what lay in Eric's aching heart.

His dreams had died with Martina and baby Karl. Death had killed his willingness to love.

A searing pain burned away her hopes, her foolish wishes. Eric might desire her, he might even care for her, but the man who'd enshrined his dead son's room wasn't ready to love again.

He never would be until he reached out for God's healing grace.

Tears flowing unchecked, Letty buried her dreams in the remains of Eric's past.

12

Letty took a long moment to compose herself. The misery in the nursery made her weep, for the lost lives, for Eric, and for herself. She didn't think she could move, but remembering Eric's leg and the spurting blood, she forced herself to rummage through the thimbles, pincushions, and other notions in the sewing basket. When she found the spool of thread, she clutched it as if it were a lifeline.

How would it feel to be loved as Eric had loved Martina? She longed to find out, but it wasn't meant to be. This room said it all. The man she loved hadn't stopped loving his late wife, nor had he recovered from the death of their child. He wasn't ready for a new love, he might never be, and the sooner she accepted those facts, the sooner her heart would heal.

She hurried back to her patient. The biting smell of whiskey told her the bleeding must have subsided somewhat and Andy had provided Eric with a measure of oblivion. From the looks of him, he was nearly there. She loosened the tourniquet and took the flask from her patient. "In lieu of Calendula, whiskey can do the job."

Knowing she was about to inflict pain, Letty gritted her teeth and doused the raw flesh. A sound akin to that of a dying animal dug its way up from Eric's middle before he collapsed, unconscious.

Thank you, Jesus.

Eric's faint meant she could suture his wound without hurting him further. She soaked the needle and thread in the spirits, then bent to her task. Stitch by stitch, she sutured the gap, tears occasionally blinding her. By the time she tied the last knot, her temples pounded and her fingers shook.

Well, if she had to fall apart, at least her body had waited until she'd taken care of Eric. With a whoosh of skirts, she sat on the floor at his feet.

Letty had no idea how long she stayed there, sobbing. The tears, however, proved cathartic. By the time her eyes ached from weeping and her middle refused more heaving sobs, the anguish of her dying dream had dulled.

She went to find Andy. He stood deep inside the barn, shoulders slumped, staring at a hat that hung on a hook. "Eric's," he rasped out.

"I'm glad you're still here," she said, knowing her request would distract him. "I need you to fetch my medical bag. I don't dare leave him. Although he's still sleeping, I'm afraid he might toss around and reopen the sutures."

Andy's solemn gaze caught hers. "Will he . . . ?"

"I think he'll be fine, but he did lose a great deal of blood, and tonight will be crucial. I plan to stay, even though I'm praying it will be a needless precaution." She dug into her pocket. "Here. This is my key. The satchel is to the left of the front door."

"I won't be long."

☙

Letty made herself a comfortable nest in a vast leather armchair and maintained her vigil for the remainder of the evening. She made a quick meal of some bread and cheese she found in the kitchen, then returned to her post and watched over the man she loved. Eventually, she dozed, too.

Hours later, a moan pierced her sleep.

"Nooo . . ."

Aided by the moonlight flowing through a window, Letty's eyes made out Eric's shape on the settee. His fists were clenched, his features contorted, his head tossed from side to side, denying whatever visions tortured his rest. "Nooo . . ."

She placed a hand on his forehead and found it normally warm, if somewhat damp. Fever wasn't to blame for Eric's distress.

Shudders wracked him, and he bolted upright. A wordless utterance, devastating in its despair, burst from his lips.

Letty's eyes welled up. He opened his eyes, then focused on a faraway point only he could discern. His body was rigid, and sweat beaded his brow.

When the first tear dropped from his lashes, she wrapped her arms around his shoulders. Although he remained oblivious to her presence, she continued to hold him while the salty flood continued.

These tears, the tears of a strong man, fell for all he'd lost. He wept out of self-imposed guilt, and he wept for love that died before its time. As Eric grieved for his wife and son, Letty held him, also weeping, praying for God's mercy on the man she loved.

The tension in his body eventually eased. Letty lifted her tear-splashed face from his shoulder and studied his ravaged features. He blinked and shook his head. When he saw her, a hint of hope glimmered in his eyes, perhaps a lightening of his expression, but then he lowered his eyelids, stiffened in her embrace, and grasped her upper arms.

"No," he said, his voice as rough as the wood that had torn his leg. "You shouldn't be here this late. Go home, Dr. Morgan. Business hours have long been over."

Letty nearly collapsed. What had she done to receive such

a cold rejection? But thinking of the nursery, she knew she'd done nothing wrong; she was just the wrong woman. She made sure he had the medications he would need, then gathered her belongings and let herself out. Somehow she'd find the courage to treat him. She wouldn't take the coward's way out and refer him to Dr. Medford's out-of-town colleague, even if caring for him took her last ounce of strength.

❦

As Letty's footsteps faded, Eric surrendered to the pain in his body and in his heart. He'd had another nightmare. He'd relived Martina's and baby Karl's deaths. Then the scent of violets had soothed him awake, gentle arms had comforted him in grief, and he'd welcomed Letty's ample compassion.

Soon, under the influence of unaccustomed drink, pain, and loss of blood, his treacherous mind had juxtaposed scenes in which the woman dying no longer owned matted blond locks. The woman in the new vision had streamers of coffee-brown curls dampened by the striving of labor. Letty's silver gaze replaced Martina's blue eyes, and when he awoke to her tear-washed face, he knew he couldn't risk it. He had to stay away from her before his love threatened her life.

❦

One tormented week after the accident, Letty tugged on the reins, and Prince led the buggy onto the road to Eric's ranch. What a splendid day this had become! The beautiful morning had revived her optimism, and she felt, for the first time in days, the hope that always brought her through hard times. The heart that had mourned the loss of love now welcomed the dawn of the new season, and she thanked the Lord for that gift.

Although the breeze bore a nip, the sun sprinkled golden light on the fresh, new world. Around the ranch yard, scattered patches of tender grass shoots swayed in each puff of air, their green trying to brighten the hard, inhospitable soil. To the right of the porch steps, two jonquils nodded to each other as if discussing the fine turn in the weather.

Letty left her buggy and paused to admire the scene. She heard Heidi's piercing call a ways off. Underfoot, three balls of marmalade fuzz tumbled over each other in their rush to reach her skirt. Smiling, she disentangled the sharp, fragile claws of a kitten and brought the rascal eye to eye.

"You sweet thing, you," she murmured when it rasped its tiny tongue against the tip of her nose. "If I weren't so worried about your welfare around my five Sunday-dinners-that-will-never-be, I'd hide you in my bag and take you home. I wouldn't leave you to your crotchety owner."

As she set the kitten back among its siblings, it meowed its displeasure. "I agree, sweeting," she murmured. "I'd much rather play with you, but the grouch inside needs medical attention."

Although her feelings for Eric hadn't changed since the day of his accident, Letty's illusions had died. A man who enshrined his child's room two years after the death wasn't ready to give his heart again.

She'd cried bitter tears and had thought to leave Hartville, but with her faith in Christ and a busy medical practice, she'd soon put herself to rights. As long as Eric did nothing to pierce her fragile shell, she'd be fine.

With a last look at the house, a house that cried out for a woman's pride and the laughter of children, Letty dismissed its sturdy stone walls and wide porch as treasures not meant for her. She'd been called to heal.

"And heal I will," she whispered. As she let herself into the vestibule, the scent of lemon oil welcomed her. Mrs. Sauder, Eric's housekeeper, must have been by to clean recently.

Letty opened the coat closet and hung her cape on a hook. Medical bag in hand, she walked down the hall.

"Who's there?" Eric called, his tone none too welcoming.

She entered and set her bag by his bed. "It's me."

"Come to prod and push at me again?"

"Hmmm," she murmured. At the washstand, she lathered her hands with pine-scented soap. Towel in hand, she faced her patient.

His cheeks gleamed from a recent grooming, and he'd trimmed his mustache. Letty approached and removed the quilt from his injured leg. The stark white bandage struck her as an affront to his strength. She gingerly parted the edges of his torn underdrawers from the bandage. He sucked in a gusty breath.

Bracing herself against his discomfort, she lifted the dressing from the wound. Under her touch, Eric shifted. She made herself ignore him and did her work. When she finally replaced the torn pieces of gray flannel over the new bandage, he grasped her hand. "Thank you."

"I'm a doctor," she answered. "You're welcome."

"That's not what I meant. I'm very grateful that you've continued to treat me in spite of our arguments and even during my less-than-courteous behavior. Your compassion is greater than . . . than the awkwardness between us."

Letty tried to move away, but he tightened his hold on her hand. She was about to cry again, and she couldn't. She simply couldn't. "It's my duty—"

"As it is mine to protect you, make sure you're safe. I won't let anything hurt you."

Through her renewed misery, Letty heard the word *safe*. What was Eric saying? What did safety have to do with her doctoring him? Perhaps the blow had affected more than his leg.

He squeezed her hand. "I will keep you safe even from yourself."

As if doused with a bucket of icy water, Letty reared up and yanked her hand free. "What did you say?"

He blinked. "I just said I wanted to keep you safe."

"Yes, I heard that. What else did you say? After that."

Eric stared at his hands fisted in the quilt. He blushed to the roots of his gold hair.

"Well?" she prodded.

Thumb and forefinger ran over his mustache in the gesture Letty knew proclaimed his discomfort. "I said I'd protect you even from yourself."

Too stunned by the stab of pain, she prayed for control of her temper and a lessening of her grief. The man didn't know her; he didn't see the difference between her and his dead wife.

"I've told you I'm an adult," she said. "I know what I'm doing. I know it when I deliver a baby, when I help a lost child find her way out of prostitution, and, yes, even when I kiss you."

Eric shoved his fingers through his hair. Letty saw irritation, frustration, and a touch of longing in his eyes. "I . . . I care about you, Letty, and I can't let anything hurt—"

"Stop it! Just stop it, Eric. I'll only say this once, so listen carefully." She took a good look at him, dreading what she was about to do. She would hurt him, not intentionally, but because he'd left her no other alternative.

"I am not Martina. I choose to put the control of my life in the Lord's hands. I don't need you to tell me what I can do. If I place myself in danger, it's by my choice and mine alone. God holds me accountable for my actions, and I accept that responsibility." She sobbed and gasped for air, and tears fell to her blouse.

"Letty—"

"Don't. Just listen. I'm the real Letty, not the person you think I am. That woman exists only in your imagination, perhaps made up to salve your conscience or atone for your sins. Truth is, you don't know me at all, not who I really am." With the back of her hand she wiped the tears from her cheeks. "You're so consumed by your self-imposed guilt that you forget even Jesus' atonement for sin—yes, yours—on the cross."

He flinched as though she'd slapped him. Still, she had to make him understand. "I am Letitia Morgan, a physician, a mature Christian woman, fully able to live my life. I don't need you to grant me permission to do what I must do. I'm not willful, and I won't put myself in unnecessary peril."

With a last look at the man who'd destroyed her heart, she picked up her satchel.

"Good-bye, Eric."

❦

Three days after the debacle with Letty, Eric unfolded the page Ford had brought him last night. He'd said it was the only letter to the editor since the accident, and as Eric had told him to do the day after his injury, he'd included it in this morning's edition without checking with him ahead of time.

Dismay struck Eric when he saw the signature at the bottom of the message. He should have read it last night.

```
To the editor:

In the understanding of this conscientious
reader, your stance on the brothels that mar
Hartville seems rigid and biased.
   Establishments provide services. That being
the case, if demand for a service ceases, the
enterprise that provides it will also cease to
exist.
   Hartville could swiftly eliminate the
unsavory effect of houses of ill repute if
our esteemed sheriff were to jail the patrons
rather than the women who ply that trade.
For surely, where there is one wretched,
resourceful woman, another equally desperate
one can and most assuredly will take her place
once she is jailed.
   Shouldn't Hartville focus on helping these
women find other ways to earn their keep? It
has surely come to your esteemed attention
```

```
that some of them are mere girls, abandoned
and abused. Can't something be done to prepare
them for a life that doesn't rely on tawdry
carnality?
   I would challenge you and all upstanding men
in Hartville to cast out the log in your eyes
before quarreling with destitute girls over
the splinters in their young eyes.

Sincerely,

Dr. Letitia Morgan
```

Eric turned the paper over and over. He couldn't believe Ford had printed such an inflammatory letter in the morning's edition. His reporter should have told him its contents, made him read it right away, something. Provocative statements required careful handling, and these were nothing if not rabble-rousing. Life would surely get more complicated now.

True, he'd written another scathing editorial for yesterday's paper, but after Letty had fled, fear and anger had clouded what tact he'd ever had.

Each time he remembered their parting, he ached for what he'd lost. His misery was scarcely less than what he'd felt at Martina's death. Twice he'd loved, and twice he'd lost.

Surely, her words had made clear that she wanted nothing to do with him. She felt sufficient unto herself, and she rejected his protection. Well, he couldn't do as she asked. Having survived widowhood, he couldn't stand by and watch a woman he loved fly straight into danger.

Even though she wanted no part of him, he still felt compelled to eliminate the threat she faced because of her treating the young tarts.

Although Eric knew Letty would never acknowledge it, the rejection of Hartville's respectable society and her clinic's failure were not the worst things that could happen to her; not even was contracting a disease. The possibility of revenge by the seamier elements loomed over her. She was, after all, trying to close down a lucrative industry.

The memory of a struggle for a pistol between father and son made a sudden return. The father had died hours later, and the son told the sheriff it had been an accident. Since the family was above reproach, no one questioned his account. The mother died of a stroke not long after, and the boy kept the father's suicide a secret.

Eric pushed the past aside and focused on the present. He'd called a meeting of the town council in his front room. The men had agreed with him. The best option was to close the brothels and jail the women who didn't leave town in the five days the council ordered. Eric had reported those facts, no matter what Letty thought.

Discomfort struck him, especially at the thought of Regis Tolliver's self-righteousness. Everyone knew he kept Lily LaRaine, Bessie's main competitor, in business almost single-handedly. Yet he'd been among the first to stop by the newspaper and complain about Letty doctoring the girls.

How could Eric dig himself out of the hole he'd dug? First, he'd gotten close to Letty. Then when he'd started falling in love with her, he'd failed to keep her out of something so foul that now her safety wasn't certain. Finally, his fears had driven a wedge between them, and he now missed her sunny presence.

Besides, how dare she write that offending epistle on the very typewriter he'd lent her? To think she would use something that held the memory of their first kiss to defy him in a public verbal duel!

The office had another typewriter, and he could respond in kind, but he didn't want her response to it in tomorrow's issue. He didn't put it past her to charm Ford into doing just that. He had things to say that couldn't be said in public. He'd have to answer privately and hope her common sense prevailed.

Heavy footsteps alerted him to someone's arrival. He knew it wasn't Letty. "Who's there?"

"It's Ford."

"Come in, come in," said Eric, glad to see someone who could fetch him the typewriter. "What brings you back today?"

Ford's hat landed by the door. His brown coat fell a few feet farther into the room. His jacket flopped over the back of the chair that Anna Sauder, the housekeeper, had placed near the bed. Finally, Ford's ancient black tie puddled in a thin stream of tired silk at his feet.

"I heard rumblings in town today," the reporter said, rubbing the inked side of his nose. "The Swartleys seem to have another dupe."

Eric sat straighter. "Did you hear who? Maybe we can stop the swindle and even follow those swine to their source."

Ford's finger crammed his spectacles closer to his blond brows. "I hate to say anything, seeing you're hurt and can't go anywhere, and I can't be sure of what I heard, but I did hear it, and I got worried—"

"Enough. I understand you don't want to deliver bad news, but I'm not on my deathbed. Tell me. Who's their target?"

"Slosh."

"Slosh? Horace Patterson?"

The spectacles fell onto Ford's lips. Another stab of his index finger squashed his bushy eyebrows behind the glass. "I heard Slosh, and I told you Slosh."

Eric swore.

Ford flinched.

Eric apologized.

Ford scooped up his spectacles from where they had landed on top of his tie.

Eric cursed his leg and Slosh's inability to stay sober and keep his trousers shut. With the Swartleys' money, the man was sure to invest in spirits and time with one of Bessie's girls instead of in the care of his five needy children.

The one he couldn't curse, however, was the persistent doctor who would surely view this development as further evidence of male weakness and debauchery.

"Well," he finally said, "why are you still here?"

Ford bounded up. One arm of his spectacles flew off his ear and curved over his white-gold hair. He replaced it behind his ear and shoved the glass circles up his nose again. He bent to retrieve his tie and lost his spectacles altogether.

"For goodness' sake, Ford, keep track of your things, will you?" Eric rarely lost patience with his friend, but with five children about to lose their home, he couldn't tolerate wasted time.

Ford donned his coat, rammed on his hat, and stuffed his tie in his pocket. "I'm on my way," he said. At the doorway, he paused. "Just where do you want me to go? And do what?"

Eric laughed. Ford's clumsiness was legendary, and it felt good to laugh again after days of pain. "Follow Slosh. Become his best friend if need be. Just don't let him out of your sight. Don't give the Swartleys a chance."

Against his better judgment, he added, "Go tell Dr. Morgan what we suspect. She'll want to keep an eye on the children. You can also tell her the stitches in my leg should probably be removed."

As Ford left, Eric leaned back into his pillows, frowning. He'd just decided it was best not to see Letty again, yet at the first opportunity, he'd summoned her to his side. He couldn't wait until she stormed back into his life.

He wouldn't need to write that response, after all.

❦

Humming "Onward, Christian Soldiers," the hymn Mrs. Stone played at the end of Sunday's service, Letty refused to think of Eric. She meticulously swept corn kernels into a heap in the middle of the kitchen floor and decided to resolve the matter of her poultry today.

She remembered the day she'd tried to catch a chick with her strainer. A bittersweet smile curved her lips. Eric had captured the chick and handed it to her.

She sighed. Each time she tried to pretend they'd merely had a disagreement, her eyes would well up and all her attempts at normalcy would fade. It seemed she was the sort who loved once, deeply and unwisely. Eric still lived in the past, clinging to the ghosts of Martina and their son. He viewed Letty as a new version of his dead wife. She'd come to symbolize a second chance to do what he should have done back then.

While Letty would never discount Eric's love for his wife and son, she knew that if two years hadn't been enough for him to start moving toward the future, then his wounds went too deep for her love to heal. His rejection of God's love and healing power didn't bode well for his recovery, either. As a doctor, she'd learned to fight the power of pain and death, but she'd also learned that there came a point beyond which she couldn't fight on. The ghosts of Eric's past lingered at that point. They were the wound she couldn't heal. Only God could heal his heart.

Even though she brimmed with love and yearning, she could never stand in for another woman. She needed more than to be Eric's expiation.

A question hovered in her mind. Eric had told the story of a family's destruction rather coldly, but he'd stood ramrod straight, as though braced to ward off an attack. Could that be what lay behind his vehemence against the girls? Could that have been his family? Was he the youth who'd lost it all?

Surely not. She hoped . . .

And she missed him. Since their argument, Letty had spent her free time with Daisy and the typewriter, with Mim and the Stones, and with the Patterson children, hoping to lure Suzannah out of hiding. A former schoolmarm, Mrs. Stone had deemed

Mim's untutored state unacceptable and had developed a curriculum for the girl. Bright as the sun, Mim soaked up knowledge and begged for more. The girl had found a home and now flourished in the Stone's unconditional love.

Although Daisy spent an hour a day in Letty's kitchen on the typewriter, she returned to Bessie's each time. Encouraged by the girl's tenacity, Letty prayed she would soon decide to change her life.

And Randy, the dear, visited often, each time bringing clothes for the girls. Thanks to her bounty, when Daisy came to visit these days, she was modestly dressed and looked as pretty and wholesome as any other girl her age.

Letty dumped the corn kernels back into the chickens' box and washed her hands. During the noon lull, she checked the supplies in her medical bag. One never knew when a child would make its entrance into the world, and then, pity the unprepared physician.

In the examining room, she refilled a remedy pellet tube. The others she checked were full, as were the Mother Tincture vials she kept in the bag. The bandages, though, had run low, and she replaced them. As she closed the bag, she heard a yell outside.

"Dr. Morgan!" a familiar voice cried. "An accident."

Bag in hand, she rushed to the door and opened it wide. Ford, looking more disheveled than usual, was racing toward her house.

"Excellent," he cried. "You're ready. We must go to East Crawford Street."

"Ford, please, what's happened?" she asked, hurrying behind him. "I need some details."

Ford said nothing and trotted on.

Aware of his alarm, Letty fought her own fear, hoping to soothe him and learn what lay ahead. "Who's hurt?"

He slanted a glance her way, but kept up his brisk pace. His Adam's apple bobbed, and he rammed his spectacles back up to the bridge of his nose. Letty lost her patience.

"Ford, I'm a doctor! Someone needs treatment, and it must be a child, a woman, or someone Dr. Medford and his friend won't treat. Just gather your wits and tell me something, anything."

"Slosh."

Ford spoke too softly for Letty to be sure. "Who?"

"Slosh," he said, louder. "Slosh fell off a horse."

Letty pursed her lips. "Drunk again, I presume."

"Of course."

"How badly?"

"Wasn't moving."

"Breathing?"

"Didn't stop to check."

"Bleeding?"

"Puddle on the ground around his head."

Letty worried her bottom lip. It didn't sound promising. Those poor children. What would they have to face next?

"Was there a fight?" she continued. "Is anyone else hurt?"

Ford shook his head. "He'd gone celebrating and borrowed a horse. Drunk as he was, he lost his balance and slid right off. That's all I saw."

"What did Horace Patterson have to celebrate?"

Ford gulped again. "He came into some money today."

"Slosh?"

"Yes. The Swartleys swindled him. He sold his claim and shack for pocket change, then ran to Bessie's for whiskey and a harlot." He blushed right up to his white-blond hair. "Beg pardon, Dr. Morgan."

Letty waved acceptance of his apology. "The Swartleys?"

Then she remembered one of Eric's editorials. It recounted the plight of poor ranchers and miners who'd sold their property to these Swartleys, hoping to move to town and take advantage of the prosperity they hadn't achieved. They soon realized the money they'd made wouldn't buy them shelter, and jobs weren't even plentiful.

Glancing at Ford, she noticed his eyes, wider than ever behind his round lenses. She followed his gaze.

As they approached the group in the street, Letty saw garishly garbed women mixed in with the men gaping at the ground. She tried to see the object of their scrutiny but couldn't see through them all. She came closer, made her way to the center of the circle, and noticed the onlookers' silence. Bessie Brown, decked out in purple satin and black lace, stood over Slosh, her fist sealing her mouth.

Ford had told the truth. Blood turned the street dirt into a dark red halo around Slosh's head. Before Letty reached his side, she knew her haste had been in vain. The gash on Horace Patterson's head was more abuse than he could take.

Caroline, Steven, Amelia, Suzannah, and William were all alone now.

13

After she'd taken care of all the pertinent details, Letty went to the livery for her buggy, then dropped her satchel on the floor, got in, and hugged her middle. It had been one of the worst experiences of her life, but she'd done for Slosh what had to be done and what no one else would do.

Eric would more than likely kick up yet another fuss. Without conferring with him, she'd called on the undertaker, made the necessary decisions, and had the man send the bill to the newspaper.

She couldn't in good conscience have left Slosh on the street, and no one would foot the bill for a decent burial. Since Eric had such a proprietary interest in the goings-on in town, he could take care of this as well.

Letty got Prince moving. Telling the children they were now fatherless wasn't something she relished doing, but someone had to, and aside from Eric, she was the only one who cared enough to do so compassionately.

The bright spring day presented a conflicting backdrop to this latest tragedy. A man consumed by thirst for whiskey and guilty pleasures had left five innocents alone in a harsh world. Ford had said that Slosh had used the money the Swartleys paid him to clear his tab at Bessie's, then he'd spent his change buying a round of drinks for the establishment's patrons.

Now Letty fretted over how long the Swartleys might wait before claiming their purchase. What would she do with the children then?

"You can do all things through Christ who strengthens you," she said to bolster herself. Somehow she'd manage. She'd wanted those children from the start, and perhaps now she'd have the opportunity to do all she longed to do for them.

At the Pattersons', she found a shiny black carriage tied to the spindly cottonwood in the front yard. She would have thought the only Hartville residents who could afford such a luxury were Dr. Medford and the banker, and they wouldn't come here.

It seemed crime paid well indeed. Evidently, the Swartleys were offering little time for the children to find a new place. The closer Letty got, the more alarmed she grew, for in the yard she also saw the Pattersons' bedraggled settee face down in the dirt. A table lay next to it, two legs broken. Steps away, a stained feather mattress leaked its stuffing onto the ground.

Letty urged Prince to a stop by the fancy carriage.

"Please, mister," she heard Caroline beg, anger and anguish in her voice.

Letty picked her way to the defective porch. "Caroline!" she called. "Where are all of you?"

Silence reigned. Then, "Up—upstairs, Dr. Miss."

"I'm on my way." She only made it halfway up the creaky stairs before seeing the gaunt male at the top landing.

"We—ell, what we got here?" His nasal twang ruined the attempt at a drawl.

"Dr. Letitia Morgan," she said. "I came to see about the children. Who are you?"

The man's oily smile sent revulsion crawling through Letty's innards. "Egbert Swartley, at yer service."

She couldn't avoid shaking the extended hand, and its clammy feel turned her stomach yet again. She pinned Swartley in place with a glare. "I gather you bought Horace's property."

"Yes, ma'am, and I come to kick the bra—help the children move."

Letty narrowed her gaze. "No need, Mr. Swartley. I'll take over now."

"Oh, no, no, no, missy," he answered, his tone turning a tad menacing. "This here's my house and land now. You don't tell me what I can or can't do here. They're going, and they're going now."

Angry and frightened, Letty dredged up bravado. "As I said, I *will* take over the children. I'm sure," she added, "the *Hartville Day*'s reporter will be more than happy to write a piece on how you threw five orphans out on the street." Not that Egbert cared. Still, she continued. "I doubt your . . . er . . . associates would appreciate an unfavorable report, now, would they?"

Egbert swallowed hard. He pulled a handkerchief sporting a gaudy purple *S* from his pocket and mopped his brow. He shoved it in place but left the embroidered corner flapping.

"Seein' as I'm so good-hearted," he said, attempting to swagger down the stairs, "I'll give you and them kids an hour to git. I'm taking me on a ride this fine afternoon, but when I git back, you and them had best be gone. This is my place now."

"Is it, now, Mr. Swartley? I wonder in whose hand the world really is."

He slammed the door in response.

Letty went the rest of the way up the stairs. "Come on, now, Caroline. We don't want to be here when he returns. I need everyone's help."

Caroline popped her head out from a doorway off the short hall. Amelia peeped out below her chin. Steven peered around his sisters, wearing a cautious expression. In the other doorway, a sweet new face appeared. Suzannah.

If Letty made a move toward the little girl, she would most

likely scare her back, so she addressed the others. "Where's Willy?"

"Sleepin'," muttered Steven.

"Even Swartley didn' wake 'im," added Amelia, admiration in her voice.

Caroline frowned. "He's got a cough."

"Oh, dear. Again? Still?" Letty asked. "Let's let him sleep, then. It's best, since we have so much to do."

Egbert Swartley had broken the news of their father's demise to the children. Although their relative lack of sentiment didn't surprise Letty, it did sadden her.

Soon, they'd loaded the children's meager belongings onto her buggy, and she urged them inside. Steven and Amelia went gladly. Letty gathered the baby, concerned about the rattle in his chest. She'd see to that once she had them home. Caroline, however, a few feet outside the house, stared back at the place with haunted eyes.

Letty's heart broke. She had to distract the girl. "Since Suzannah doesn't know me yet," she said, "could you please bring her to the buggy, Caroline? We must leave. That dreadful man will return any moment now."

Caroline started toward the house, but before she reached the porch, Suzannah, blond pigtails swishing over her shoulders, appeared in the doorway, clutching something to her chest.

"Wait," Letty whispered. The older girl stopped. She watched her younger sister walk across the porch, down the sagging steps, and onto the dirt yard. Letty held her breath. With her free hand, Suzannah clung to a fistful of her threadbare, red-faded-to-pink calico dress.

The child climbed silently into the buggy. Caroline followed, and Letty brought up the rear. She placed Willy in Amelia's lap, Caroline scooped Suzannah onto hers, and Steven plopped down on the floor at the girls' feet. Letty took up the reins, and a whisper, no louder than the day's soft breeze, stole her breath.

"Mama," Suzannah said, extending something to Letty.

The tintype bore myriad tiny fingerprints. Through the smudges, a young woman in white cotton and ribboned lace smiled shyly. A lovely young woman, into whose image Caroline was growing. The young woman who had given life to the five children Letty had with her. The woman whose vice-riddled husband and hard life had broken her will.

Letty returned the treasure. "She's beautiful, Suzannah. I'm so glad you showed me her picture."

The tot nodded, then laid her head on Caroline's shoulder, hugging the photograph again. Alerting Prince with a tap of the reins, Letty headed back into town.

They soon arrived at her home. She tethered Prince at the post until she could take him to the livery, and the children tumbled out. As she let them in the back way, she said, "You must be hungry. I have cookies and cups of milk for everyone."

The four older children stopped in their tracks. Eight bright blue eyes studied her. "I've plenty," she added. "Have all you want."

In the small kitchen, they bumped and jostled each other, lacking even elbowroom. In their equally small space, the chickens sent up a squabble of their own.

"Chickens," whispered Suzannah. Before Letty could warn her about the sharp beaks, the little girl trotted to the box and peered over the side. She watched the scuffle, not moving a muscle, not missing a move.

Knowing the child had only ventured from her mother's bedroom for meals, Letty let Suzannah watch the birds. She made sure, though, that a fat oatmeal cookie found its way into her hand, and when that vanished, a tin cup of milk took its place.

Then a young rooster pecked a beakful of feathers from the other. The injured fellow flew the makeshift coop and knocked the milk from Suzannah's hand.

"No," she cried.

The assaulted bird skittered over the polished wood floor, seeking escape. Its claw caught on the braided rug in front of the cookstove, and the poor creature lost its balance. It flapped its wings and flew a couple of feet, landing at Steven's side.

"Hey!" he yelled, frightened to find the rooster's beak so close to susceptible body parts. He backed away and knocked over a chair.

Pandemonium broke loose. The other rooster flew from the box and chased its brother. The hens started clucking loudly, Suzannah crept to a corner and curled up into a tiny ball, and Amelia shoved a fist into her mouth. Willy began to cough.

Letty began to fret. She had nowhere to put the children. Her bedroom scarcely held her bed, small chest, and washstand. The parlor was a waiting room and the former dining room a medical clinic. She had to find more space for her five youngsters. An ample yard would be handy, since she also had five unhappy feathered friends, and a coop wouldn't hurt, either. As she enumerated her needs, an idea came to her, and she grinned. She knew just the person and the place for the children and the birds.

"Into the buggy," she cried over the commotion. Only Steven heard. He ran down the hall as fast as his short legs would go, flung open the door, and flew into the buggy. It was just as well she'd never gotten around to bringing anything inside. The children would need their belongings, what few they had, at Eric's ranch.

Letty called again. Hugging Willy, Caroline grabbed Suzannah's arm and dragged her outside. Amelia cast worried looks at the fowl but followed without comment.

Once the chickens had settled a bit, Letty scooped them up and tied their legs. She'd learned to handle the creatures. Quirking her lips in a rueful smile, she thought back on the day she hadn't been able to catch a chick with a strainer. Yet today she'd subdued two roosters and three hens and secured their lethal legs in no time.

Progress indeed.

She put the birds back in their box. "Caroline, please set Willy down for a moment. I need you, Steven, Amelia, and Suzannah to help me tie this box to the back of the buggy."

Letty and her youthful crew lifted the box onto the running board, where she anchored it to metal supports with a length of hemp rope. Chore completed, she climbed into the vehicle, gathered her charges, and headed toward the inevitable confrontation with Eric.

She hated arguing with him, especially because after the way they last parted, everything pertaining to him hurt. Her feelings, those intense sensations he'd brought to life, were too bruised to even contemplate, and she'd fought to avoid thinking of them. Still, each time she thought of him, a stab of longing pierced her.

She still couldn't face those emotions, not the shattering ones or the lovely ones. Not yet. Not until her patched-up heart grew strong enough not to tear again.

The buggy's passengers remained silent—all but the fowl. Nothing disturbed the oddly tranquil afternoon in a world where ugly things happened. Letty couldn't make herself bring up Slosh's death to the children, not in a buggy, and so the only other sound was that of Prince's hooves marking out a soothing, dirt-muffled clip-clop.

At Eric's ranch, she stopped the horse by the barn. "Andy!" she called, then warned the children to stay put while she fetched help.

"I'm in the barn, Doc."

"I've a few additions to Eric's livestock," she said with more confidence than she felt.

Andy eyed her warily as he came outside.

"Don't worry. It's only five chickens. They shouldn't be much trouble."

He snorted. "Chickens is always trouble, don't you know?"

Letty blushed. "I guess I do. Imagine them in my kitchen, if you will. Then you'll know why I brought them here."

He snickered. "Let's get 'em in the coop, then, Doc. Where are they? In the buggy?"

"No, in the crate at the back. I tied their legs so we could move them safely."

Admiration lit Andy's grin. "Good thinkin', Doc."

"Why, thank you." At least one male at the Wagner spread approved of her. "Now, I have to see your boss, but there are five children in the buggy, and one of them is ill. Could you please keep them in the kitchen so that I can confront Eric?"

Andy gaped. He stared at Letty, not a sound breaching his thin lips. Then he shrugged, nodded, and followed her to the buggy.

They ushered the youngsters to the kitchen at the back of the house, where Letty made them comfortable. She straightened her back, squared her shoulders, and, for good measure, hoisted her chin up in the air. "I'll return shortly." As a precaution, and as a delaying device, she added, "Please behave well for me."

Oh, honestly, Letitia, get on with it. What could be worse than having the man break your heart? He's already done that. She went upstairs to the lion's other den and knocked on the door.

"Come in," Eric muttered.

He didn't sound too happy. She stepped inside and saw that he'd been writing. "Hello, Eric."

He looked up from the paper before him, and his rich brown gaze seemed to touch every corner of her heart. Her pain mixed with anger, and just as she turned to seek the privacy to tend to her wounds, she saw him shake himself.

"Hello, Le—Dr. Morgan," he said, his voice raspy.

Over her shoulder, she stared at him a moment, noting the

red on his cheeks, the embarrassment in his gaze. She couldn't help but wonder . . . had his perusal been involuntary? Could she affect him as strongly as he affected her?

Before she could voice a greeting, Eric spoke. "I expected you, although not quite so soon."

"How could you have known I'd come?"

"I sent the message with Ford."

"Message? What message?"

He pushed himself higher on the pillows at his back. "Why, that your fine stitching should be removed."

"He never said a word. After today's events, I imagine he simply forgot. I didn't come to remove stitches."

Eric narrowed his gaze. "Why did you come?"

Letty spoke around the lump in her throat. "The Pattersons."

"What about the Pattersons?"

"It's Slosh. He . . . he's dead."

Eric went paper white. He clenched his fists and closed his eyes. He set his jaw, looked square at her, and said, "Their land . . . ?"

"The Swartleys bought it. Slosh used the money to celebrate his windfall, fell off a horse, and broke his skull and neck. Ford came to fetch me, but all I could do was call the undertaker."

A muscle leapt above the bony ridge of his jaw. Still, she had to confess all she'd done. "I had him bill you for his services."

"You did what?"

Attempting a nonchalance she'd never felt around him, Letty sauntered to the window. Outside, approaching dusk tinted the mountainous horizon a shade of dark rose. Streaks of purple climbed up the sky to become a rich violet, then faded into twilight blue. So much beauty out there, and such ugliness, too.

"Letty . . ." Eric's voice approached a growl.

She whirled and pointed at him. "Each time I tried to take care of the Patterson children, you fought me and said they were too much for me. Well, Mr. Wagner, this time, it's all too much for me. Who else should I hold responsible? You did want to take the burden from weak little me, didn't you?"

Letty's anger slapped Eric. The sting of her palm might have been preferable; it wouldn't have hurt as much as her words.

"Fine." He tried to control his temper, knowing she'd had to deal with the tragedy, and it couldn't have been an easy matter.

She nodded, and her chin ended up higher than where it had started. "I'm heartily thankful you feel that way, Mr. Wagner. You see, since I can't shoulder the entire 'burden,' I brought it with me. The children are in your kitchen."

Eric's head spun. How neatly she'd turned his concern for her into another bone of contention. "The children are downstairs?"

"I just said so." The gleam in her eyes made them look like pools of silver. "They're here to stay, since they no longer have a home. And that's not all. Seeing how you so kindly express concern for my well-being, not to mention my inability to bear my many burdens, I've come to agree with you on another matter."

Eric felt the promise of hope. Had she finally seen reason and decided to stay away from the harlots?

Pulling her shawl closer to her, Letty went on. "I now believe I have one liability too many. So I brought it for you as well. You're now the proud owner of five healthy chickens. Good day, sir."

❦

Later that evening, Melvin Harrison removed the last knot from the healing scar. Eric groused throughout the ordeal.

"Neat job she did here," Dr. Harrison said. "You should regain full use of the muscle soon."

Eric swore.

"She did a neat job on *me,*" he muttered. "She brought the Pattersons here and threw in her five chickens as a bonus. How am I supposed to take care of them, run a newspaper, and look after the ranch?"

Dr. Harrison patted Eric's shoulder. "You've never shirked your duties, son. Sure, and you'll manage nicely."

"I can't even bungle along yet, never mind manage nicely."

"You won't lack assistance," the doctor said, mischief in his eyes. "Hartville's unmarried ladies will be lining up to offer help."

Eric winced at the humor in the doctor's words. Blast and bother! The last thing he needed was more women taking on the cares of the world. No, sir. One was more than enough for him.

"You're right," he said, "I'll manage. I don't know how, but I will."

Dr. Harrison soon left. Since Mrs. Sauder had prepared supper after she'd cleaned house, Eric didn't worry about feeding the Pattersons. He called Caroline and gave her instructions.

A short time later, she surprised him with her efficiency. "I fetched yore supper, Mr. Wagner."

He ate heartily, glad the children would have full bellies tonight. No matter how he tried, he simply couldn't comprehend Slosh's neglect. And for what? Cheap liquor and empty pleasure with a strumpet. The trade scarcely bore consideration.

At least the children hadn't been forced to witness their father's debauchery. Slosh's death had detonated a barrage of images Eric would rather forget, and he was glad the children had been spared.

After all these years, he still saw his father in the arms of the prostitute. Why he'd had to find them, he'd never know. He was, however, thankful his mother never saw that sight.

Father and son came to blows, and hours after the fight, Eric found his father dead by his own hand. The man had betrayed his wife for years, but the thought of public shame drove him to suicide.

Although it seemed cruel, he was glad Slosh would no longer affect the children. Perhaps they would soon find someone to love them. He couldn't have them run wild on the ranch, and with his leg still on the mend, he could only hobble around. Mrs. Sauder might know someone equal to the task of herding them safely.

The next morning brought a challenge all its own. Since he now had five charges, Eric figured he should spend his day near them. When Andy came for his daily instructions, the ranch hand helped him to the settee. Only then did Eric feel equal to coping with the children.

Soon Steven discovered the joys of sliding across polished wood floors, and each time he whooshed through the front room, the furniture stood in mortal danger. It turned out that Amelia loved fire; nothing he said budged her from the hearth, where she ignited log after log with long matchsticks. The temperature in the room soon rivaled his irritation with a certain too-smart doctor.

Although too young to add to the activity, baby Willy heightened the commotion. His cries worried Eric, and he had to accept that the child needed more medical care.

Mrs. Sauder couldn't find Suzannah. When he asked Caroline about her youngest sister, she shrugged. "She's sumwhere, but I ain't seen her."

Bound to the settee by a sliced thigh and a punctured artery, Eric felt helpless. After another minute of mayhem, he roared. "That's it! I give up. Caroline, fetch Andy. Now!"

Tossing Willy's dingy blanket around him, Caroline hoisted the baby onto her hip, and before Eric could ask for him, she ran out the door.

A few minutes later Andy huffed in, scarcely taking time to scrape off his muddy boots. "Here I am. What can I do for you?"

"Get that woman back here!"

"Woman?"

Eric ran thumb and forefinger over his mustache. He hated feeling helpless; he hated being obvious even more. "Oh, go fetch Dr. Morgan. I won't shake her, even though it's what I'd like to do." As an afterthought, he added, "How are her chickens, anyway?"

Andy grinned on his way out. "Big and ornery."

"How else would her poultry be?" Eric muttered, settling back to wait and cling to sanity in a house filled with children and one disabled adult.

Later he heard horses pull a rig into the yard. Another horse trotted by. Finally, light steps sounded on the porch. Letty came in without removing her shawl.

"I concede defeat in this round," he said, not allowing her a word. "I need your help. Since you so dearly want to care for these children, and I'm unable to do much, and Andy has work outside, do help to your heart's content."

Letty's smile made something melt inside him. How easily she moved him! Even under these absurd circumstances.

She left the room, but her voice wafted back like a caress, an intangible trace just out of reach. "Caroline! I'm back, dear. Let's gather the others and begin with baths."

The good doctor soon had the five urchins scrubbed, wearing clean, threadbare garments, and eating lunch. She'd diagnosed Willy's problem as otitis media and had taken charge of the child. The exhausted boy now dozed in peace.

Blessed calm reigned once again. Eric leaned back and listened to the children's comforting murmurs in the kitchen. The house had been empty for too long. It needed young life. If only—

Letty's entrance put an end to his thoughts. "Here's lunch."

She set the tray on a low table and then helped him sit up. He thanked her and caught a flicker of sadness in her eyes. He'd hurt her the other day, but it hadn't been by design and, in the end, would likely be for the best.

"Thank you," he said.

She studied the stone wall at the rear of the room. "I'm glad I could help and that you called me, not someone else."

He hated her refusal to meet his gaze. "Letty—"

A knock at the door cut him off. Letty looked relieved and fairly flew to the entry. Eric couldn't stand their current situation, since it made her so eager to leave his side, but it *was* for the best.

"Pastor Stone," she said. "Do come in."

The reverend entered, followed by a bruised but otherwise hale Dr. Medford. Douglas Carlson brought up the rear.

"Come in, please," Eric said, wondering about the group's intentions. "Take a seat, and forgive me if I don't stand."

As his guests removed their coats, Letty slipped away.

The men had only exchanged pleasantries when another knock shook the door. Letty darted out from the kitchen and ushered in yet another set of men. This time, John White, the undertaker, followed Mayor Osgood. Hubert Tilford and Regis Tolliver brought up the rear.

Hartville's leaders sat in Eric's front room. "To what do I owe the pleasure, gentlemen? I'm sure you didn't come to ask after my injury."

Hubert Tilford stood and tugged on his lapels. "Ahem."

Had the elderly mill owner come to lecture everyone on the virtues of his toothpicks? Eric wasn't up to it.

"We hear the Patterson children are here," Tilford began in his stentorian voice. "We also know how conscientious you are about everything regarding Hartville, but we feel that this time you've taken on more than you should. Why, John here says you had him bill Horace's burial expenses to you."

"I did," Eric said, spotting the guilty party just beyond the door. He shot her a quelling glare.

"We," Tilford droned on, "feel you ought not shoulder the burden of the children as well. We will immediately place them with families in town. There are too many of them for one unmarried man."

"No."

All the males turned toward Letty. Eric smiled. This should prove fascinating. She intended to tackle the whole town.

"Dr. Morgan!" Pastor Stone said, obviously dismayed by her presence at the men's meeting.

When her chin tipped skyward, Eric fought to stifle a laugh.

"Pastor Stone, gentlemen," she said, "it's not at all in the children's best interest to separate them and farm them out like . . . a litter of kittens. I took them home yesterday, but because of my limited space, I brought them here. This large, lovely home has many empty rooms, and Mr. Wagner owns all the land children need to exercise and breathe wholesome air. I will, of course, help while he recuperates."

Dr. Medford reddened. "You're still treating Mr. Wagner?"

"As a matter of fact," Eric said before Letty could answer unwisely, "Melvin Harrison removed my stitches last night."

His answer seemed to mollify the surgeon, but it did nothing to mellow the man's glower at Letty.

The pastor weighed in. "Can you handle all this and treat your patients, too?"

"Absolutely," she stated.

Eric then heard Medford murmur, ". . . she's an unfit influence on the brats. They run wild as it is, and if the town must take them over, then we should find a responsible person to watch over them, not a hussy who mingles with tarts."

He flinched. "If you have something to say, Dr. Medford, say it so everyone might benefit from your opinion. Otherwise, please keep your thoughts to yourself."

Medford shot a venomous glare at Letty. "She's nice enough to look at," he said as he stalked to the door, "and now that she's taken up with strumpets, there's all kinds of help she'll give you."

Eric lunged, but Douglas Carlson pinned him back down. Only when the surgeon had left did Douglas lessen his hold.

Letty's face was paper white. Her eyes, dark with hurt, looked nearly black, and she'd raised her hands as though to fend off another blow.

"Letty . . ."

She shook her head and then spun on her heel. She ran for her shawl in the entryway and wrapped it around herself.

"Dr. Morgan," called the reverend.

"No," she cried and left.

"That was foul," Eric said. "If the rest of you came for a lynching, you'd best leave. I'll stomach no more abuse of a woman who's only helped folks since the day she came to town."

Hubert Tilford cleared his throat again. "You cannot deny she's consorting with fallen women, Eric."

"Helping two girls leave a sordid trade doesn't constitute 'consorting with prostitutes.'" Eric blinked. Did he really mean what he'd just said?

Good heavens, he did! Scraps of arguments dizzied him. Although her actions had angered him, her motives had been pure. Had she really changed his mind?

His mother's voice rose from the past. *You mustn't judge, Eric. Only God sees the motives in our hearts. He is our only true judge.*

He tried to ignore the words but couldn't. They rang too clearly with truth.

"Tell me, gentlemen," he continued, "what do you think will happen to the Patterson girls if they're farmed out and no one truly loves them? I can suggest one option at least two girls in our town found to be their only choice. Bessie will be happy to offer the Pattersons to those of you sick enough to lust for little girls."

Eric studied Regis Tolliver, since the man was known for his vices. He smiled when Regis squirmed.

He went on. "I would suggest that before any of you speaks against Dr. Morgan, you examine your heart. As Pastor Stone preaches, make sure you're without sin before you cast that first stone."

What had Letty done to him? She had him quoting sermons, quoting Scripture! He was even fighting for her right to help Mim and Daisy. She was as dangerous to his peace of mind—No! She was far more devastating than he'd ever suspected.

"The children stay here," he said to settle the matter. "The better choice will be the family who'll adopt all five. Only then will they leave my home. And I welcome Dr. Morgan's help.

"In case you care, one of the children is ill. Dr. Morgan has treated him free of charge since she arrived in town. She's also fed all five from the food she's received for her services. She doesn't deserve Medford's rancor. Or yours. Good day, gentlemen."

As the men left, Douglas smiled at Eric, sympathy in his gaze.

Pastor Stone waited until the door closed. "Don't for one moment think I harbor such thoughts about Letitia," he said. "I know her too well. I am, however, concerned. About you, Letitia, and the children. I came hoping matters wouldn't get out of hand, but my presence today mattered little."

"Nothing matters to Medford save what things will cost him," Eric spat out, "or how they might further gild his reputation. Please help me up, Pastor."

"Son, I don't think you should strain your leg."

"Perhaps, sir, but I must find Letty."

14

Eric finally realized how obstinate he'd been and how right Letty had been. He regretted that it took Slosh Patterson dying and orphaning the three girls for him to recognize what Letty had feared from the start. He'd heard her arguments all along, but he hadn't wanted to accept the truth. He'd wanted to see himself and the pillars of Hartville society in a kind light, one that shed no blame on them.

He hadn't wanted to revisit his father's guilt, either. He'd kept hidden the dirty secret behind his parents' deaths. It had been easier to focus on the lessons of truth and light his father had taught him at an earlier time than to acknowledge the man's hypocrisy.

"Evil can't flourish in the light of truth," the elder Wagner had often said. The truth, however, was the dark double life he'd led, the life Eric accidentally uncovered.

In any case, the virtues his father taught had served Eric well. He'd led an unimpeachable life. He'd fought against the brothels but had, as Letty said, blamed only the women and let the men's offenses slide. He'd thought himself virtuous; he'd been self-righteous.

Where had the upright folks of Hartville been when Mim

and Daisy needed help and guidance? Mining silver, building mansions, buying rare walking sticks, running the town's politics, minding their own business. Bessie, with her eye on profits, had seen the opportunity, and the girls had suffered.

He now knew how, if left with no alternative, sweet, responsible Caroline might become desperate enough to be lured by Bessie to support her siblings by selling herself. She had no education or training, and Eric would rather die than let that become her fate.

The strength of his conviction amazed him. He'd told himself he was helping the Pattersons because as a prominent person he bore a responsibility to the less fortunate, yet that had been a lie. True, charity and the urge to atone for his failures had started it, but since then his feelings had changed. He cared what happened to those five scamps, and he would not let more tragedy touch them.

He slowly left the porch, leaning on the cane Dr. Harrison had brought him last night, and headed for the barn to look for Andy. Letty's buggy, still in the yard, caught him by surprise.

She hadn't left.

Disgusted with his weak leg and resenting the need for the walking stick, he picked up his pace. He had to find her, and when he did, he would swallow his pride and accept her help.

He stood well inside the dark cavern when he heard a sound in the far right corner. What he saw stole his breath.

A beam of light entered through the loft window. Where it belled into a puddle of spring gold, Suzannah sat surrounded by orange and brown balls of fluff, giggling as she played. Sprigs of hay stuck out from her blond braids, and the sunlight turned her faded calico dress a rich shade of rose. Beside the child, tears washing her cheeks, sat Letty, a hand on Suzannah's shoulder. She leaned forward to whisper in the youngster's ear. The little girl turned and smiled in response.

A woman, a child, a ranch, everything Eric had wanted, everything death had taken away. Yet here, in another time, with another woman and another child, Eric saw what might still be. If he dared.

Emotion suddenly choked him. When had he begun to feel so much? And how dare he when he couldn't trust himself to protect them?

He'd failed his wife and child. He'd failed to prevent Slosh's death and the loss of the children's home. He'd even failed to protect Letty from the town's scorn. How could he hope, even for the thinnest slice of time, to share their lives?

It hurt to face his weakness, to forgo a future that promised more joy than even his brightest dreams. His feelings for Letty were different from those he had felt for Martina. Whereas he'd loved his wife with sweetness and gentle emotions, Letty evoked in him something rare and rich and tumultuous. Their tenderness was spiced with desire, their friendship heated with passion born of their differences, and he did love her despite those differences.

Then, too, the Pattersons needed what he ached to offer, but he was flawed, and his was a mortal flaw. After all they'd suffered, those children deserved better than another failed father.

He took in the fresh fragrance of hay underscored by the musk of healthy animals, and he remembered the afternoon he and Letty kissed in the shadowed shelter of the barn. Her words returned to haunt him. *"You bear no blame in Martina's death. She made the choice. . . . I'd rather have love such as you gave her than all the medical training in the world. . . ."*

His memory became his enemy. It taunted him with what he wanted most. Letty was too innocent to see the danger she'd risk if she depended on a man like him.

Eric yearned to join them, yet he backed away, denying himself the chance to make his dreams come true. There was no atonement for him. Were he a different man, were there not a cloud

215

over him, then perhaps he could have gone to their side. Instead, wisdom forced him to leave.

He left his heart with them.

❦

As Letty's last patient left, Randy called a greeting from the kitchen.

"I'll be there in a moment," she answered. "I'm tidying the examining room."

The impulsive Randy joined her instead. Noting the redhead's expanding girth, Letty reached out and patted her middle. "Growing well, wouldn't you say, Mama?"

"I couldn't be happier." Then her smile crumpled. "Oh, I do so wish you and Eric—"

"Hush."

Letty turned to avoid her friend's gaze. After yesterday's confrontation with Hartville's men, she'd finally accepted Eric's rejection. She shuddered and again asked God to heal her heart. Then, digging deep for strength, she blinked hard, refusing to spend another minute nursing her wounds. She'd started the morning with Scripture and refreshed faith in Christ. He promised and she believed that He would see her through. Besides, she had a visitor.

"How may I help you?" she asked Randy.

"I didn't come for help. Douglas told me what happened at Eric's ranch. How could they just ignore civility and treat you like that?"

She shrugged. "As you said, Douglas was there, too. Won't he be scandalized to learn you're here with me?"

"On the contrary. He urged me to come see how you were."

Letty arched an eyebrow.

"Really. He went with the others because he's a lawyer. The mayor has asked him to help with the children's adoption."

"He didn't say a word the whole time."

216

"What did you want him to do? Turn the scene into a brawl? From what he said, he kept Eric from pounding Dr. Medford into a pulp."

"What about the hypocrites who fight me and talk about closing the houses but haven't done so yet? Did you know they make use of the attractions at the brothels?"

Randy sniffed. "I'll have you know Douglas would never frequent those places, and if he even entertained the notion, I'd incapacitate him. Permanently."

"Oh, dear heart," Letty said on a sigh. "I wasn't condemning your husband. Not all men indulge in those vices, but I can't excuse the ones who keep Bessie in business. The bordellos' clients don't want their playgrounds closed or the girls otherwise employed."

Randy shrugged.

"What happened, happened. I'll keep caring for my patients and helping any child who needs me. Especially the Pattersons, Daisy, and Mim. My morals can withstand what scrutiny the town gives them. I won't stop doing what God's put in my heart to do."

"I don't expect you to, and knowing what I know now, I want to do more," Randy said, surprising Letty. "We need to see if there are more girls like Mim and Daisy in those houses. Then we'll need a scheme to get them away."

The back door opened. "I wouldn't call it a scheme," Adele Stone said, entering. "Strategy is the better term."

Letty took Mrs. Stone's wrap. "You're ready to help me even after yesterday's confrontation?"

"I'm not simply going to help, I'm determined we will succeed. As Randy just said, we must find any additional children who might be in the brothels, and we must free Daisy from Bessie's control."

Letty's eyes teared. "Although I have everything I need in

Christ, I still felt alone through the night. I felt I'd let down those who brought me here."

Mrs. Stone laid an arm around Letty's shoulders. "My sweet, as the pastor always says, when one goes about God's work, Satan sets up great barriers, but if one abides by the Father, He will draw together like-minded brethren. Silver Creek Church stands with you."

Letty released a relieved sigh that was part laugh, part sob, part hiccup. "Even if you lose your parishioners?"

"Are they truly in the Father's flock with their hardened, judgmental hearts? We must not fret but commend them to the Holy Spirit. We must speak with my husband, plan our strategy, and work diligently for our Savior."

Letty and her visitors stepped outside. Randy and Adele were truly staunch friends who made up for those fair-weather companions who had abandoned her when she challenged the masculine bastion of medicine back in Philadelphia. Perhaps, despite her heartbreak and the scandal sparked by her convictions, God had really brought her home.

Here she'd found the friends she'd longed for.

In Hartville, God had gifted her with love.

❦

"Randy Carlson, I can't condone the murder of pregnant ladies. When Douglas learns what you're doing, murder will be his first response."

"Oh, hush," Randy shot back.

"Look," Letty said, "we didn't come to argue. But I do wonder if I'm not too gullible. I don't know how you persuaded me to come haunt East Crawford Street's back alleys."

"Of course you know. We can't send Douglas, Eric, or Pastor Stone to ask an establishment if it offers children unlawfully and then have the men gather up the youngsters and bring them home."

Letty tightened her shawl. "You're right, but I don't like this part of our strategy, especially since neither Pastor nor Mrs. Stone knows what we're doing."

The shrub in the alley behind the targeted emporia offered dubious camouflage. Letty hoped no one happened by while they were there. Then she heard an argument coming from one of the upstairs windows in Bessie's Barn. A familiar voice demanded, "Bessie, how could you?"

"Daisy," Letty whispered in dismay.

The madam answered, "Business, kid, and I do the business here."

"It's a rotten business, Bess," the girl countered. "Those little kids have nowhere to go, and you didn't even need the money."

The crack of a slap elicited Daisy's cry. Letty took steps toward the brothel. Randy held her back.

Bessie went on. "Don't tell me what I need or don't. You jus' keep doin' what you gets paid to."

Letty cringed at Bessie's crudeness. She tugged against Randy's restraint, ready to drag Daisy away no matter what the girl had to say about the matter.

But Daisy fought back, her voice defiant. "Still, Bess, it's wrong. You and that . . . that man . . . of yours, you have so much money, I don't see what you want with more. The kiddies have nothing, not even a father anymore."

Letty tipped up her chin. She was not leaving without Daisy. A glance showed her Randy's equal determination. She nodded; Randy nodded back. They marched up to the back door, but the sound of a scuffle upstairs stopped them cold.

"Who're you tellin' what's right and what ain't? I'll teach ya to talk back at me. Who fed ya when you was so hungry you was eatin' garbage? Who gave ya work to keep on eatin'? Just who gives you a place to live? Remember that, Daisy, and get back to work. Itchy miners don't hold to no hours. Go on, I said. Get back to work."

Wood crashed against wood. Daisy cried out again.

"I won't," she sobbed. "Not anymore, Bessie. I can't do it again. I'd rather eat garbage than face another client. I'm leaving. You and your man can beat me till I die, because I'd rather be dead than be like you."

Bessie roared her rage. Letty turned to Randy. "I'll go out front. You stay here. We can't let Daisy run away."

Randy stepped closer to the door, and Letty ran around the building. Realizing how she must look, she slowed her pace and prayed she wasn't too late. As she reached the street in front of the bordello, she saw Ford walking toward her. Not wanting to be detected, she ducked behind a bush at the corner of the building. A moment later, a disheveled Daisy burst from the brothel's swinging doors and plowed into Ford.

The silver-framed spectacles flew off the reporter's face. His decrepit hat toppled to the ground, gaining a grubby new look. A pen slipped from somewhere and landed at their feet. Daisy lifted her tear-stained face. She blushed as the dumbstruck Ford stared at her. "Excuse me, miss, but are you all right?"

Daisy's blush deepened. "I'm so sorry, sir. I was . . . distraught. It's all my fault."

"Nonsense," the reporter answered, clearly enchanted by the pretty girl in his arms. "I should have paid more attention where I was going."

"You're too kind."

"And you're in need of assistance. Where shall I escort you?"

Daisy eased out of Ford's embrace. She looked around and then examined her companion's earnest expression. Letty recognized the look dawning on the girl's face. It looked much the way she felt in Eric's presence. Could Ford hold the key to Daisy's restoration?

"I . . . I don't rightly know. Oh! Perhaps . . ." Her voice trailed off. Then she straightened. "Yes. I'm on my way to Dr. Morgan's home. I'd be delighted if you would escort me there."

Letty hurried home, thanksgiving for God's answer to her prayer singing in her heart.

☙

Five days after Daisy escaped from Bessie, Letty treated another controversial patient. She followed her conscience and put her medical training to good use.

"That'll do, Mr. Abrams," she said, securing a bandage on the workman's lacerated arm. Another accident, another patient—another male patient—and she'd been the nearest doctor.

"Thank you, Doc Morgan. I know yore mostly a wimen's doctor, but I knows you fixed up Eric Wagner's leg real good. I was bleedin' like a pig, and I figgered you was closest."

Gathering her scissors and bandage scraps, Letty smiled. "I can sew a cut on a man, woman, or child. I'll treat anyone who needs my help."

The burly carpenter slipped his injured arm in his jacket sleeve. "Pride's too costly, ma'am, and yore a right fine doctor. How much I owe you?"

Letty named a sum, Mr. Abrams paid her, and she walked him out. "If you see any red streaking or if the flesh around the wound becomes hot, come back right away. Otherwise, just use common sense."

"Common sense tells me some's not gonna be happy with a right good lady doctor in town. No, ma'am, and one as charges fair at that. Thank you kindly, miss."

Letty mulled over her patient's parting comment. The town was up in arms about her crusade to rescue the young soiled doves, but what had Mr. Abrams meant about her charging people fairly? Had someone accused her of bilking patients? Had she done something else to cause trouble? Surely not.

"Share them with me," Eric said, startling Letty with his sudden arrival.

"I beg your pardon?"

"Your thoughts. They seem to have you in thrall."

Letty waved in a helpless gesture. "It's just that . . . well, I stitched up a nasty cut on a carpenter's arm, and before he left, he made some odd remarks."

Eric stood straighter. "Did he offend you?"

"No, no. Quite the opposite. He paid me a compliment, but then he mentioned those who resent a woman doctor and added that I charge fairly for my services."

Eric shifted more weight onto his cane.

"Oh, dear," Letty said. "Do come in. I've kept you standing out here too long. Come, take a seat in the waiting room."

She followed Eric, keeping a close eye on his limp. Satisfied by his progress, she didn't question the wisdom of his being out.

In the parlor-cum-waiting room, she made certain to keep the length of the room between them.

"I'm afraid your patient's right," Eric said, propping the walking stick on his good thigh. "News travels fast in Hartville. On my way here, I heard from three interested parties that you had treated another man. Two of the newsbearers were pleasant, if not thrilled by your actions. The third, however, was irate."

"What should I do, Eric? Turn away an injured person?"

Eric raised his arms in surrender. "I've warned you plenty, so I won't tell you what to do. You'll have to act on your conscience."

Letty clasped her hands in her lap and then cocked her head. "Very well," she said, "warn me again. What mustn't I do? And why?"

"I'll answer your last question first. Dr. Medford—he is why. He has taken your actions personally, not only your efforts on the girls' behalf but also your treating men."

"Why would helping two girls bother him? And I've only treated the man with gall troubles and Mr. Abrams today."

"And me."

A flush painted Letty's cheeks. She looked appealing, feminine. "I still don't see—"

"You're taking business from him, and he charges dearly for his services. How do you think he can afford the life he leads? Surely you've noticed his penchant for the costly and exotic."

"The mansion and the peculiar walking stick."

"Precisely. In addition, you're a homeopath. He's an allopath. You know the difference in cost between the types of treatment and the antipathy of allopaths for homeopaths."

"I do indeed." She began to pace. "Medicated pellets and tinctures cost a fraction of what their invasive treatments cost."

Still pacing, she fell silent, deep in thought. Eric respected her need to consider the situation, despite his urge to run out and make things right for her. How could he make things right? He didn't know, but that didn't change how he felt.

Suddenly she stopped. "Losing three patients and my work with Daisy and Mim shouldn't cause such an uproar. There's something else here. Does Dr. Medford go . . . that is, does he patronize Bessie's Barn?"

This time, Eric blushed. "I'm afraid so, and you could be right. He might have an ulterior motive for his attacks. Still, I wouldn't hang the man on supposition."

Her eyes sparked silver with anger, her cheeks went red, her shoulders heaved with her gulped breaths, and Eric knew he'd never seen a more fascinating woman.

She advanced on him. "I see you're defending another man. It's so very like you, like all men. That surgeon can say atrocities about me, and yet I'm wrong to hate his lust for bought flesh?"

"He's not the brothels' only patron."

A steely stare hit him square on, and Eric knew he'd said the wrong thing. But she didn't let him speak.

"Am I to learn now that the esteemed publisher of the *Hartville Day* is yet another of Bessie's clients? That the disingenuous denial of your patronage the day I arrived in town was nothing but a bald-faced lie?"

Fascinating was one thing, but enough was enough. "You needn't question my character, Letty. I don't buy harlots. I prefer the intimacy of one man and one woman within the sanctity of marriage. And you know it."

Silence crackled between them.

Eric continued. "This story isn't pretty, but you need to hear it as much as I need to share it with you. The boy I told you about, the one who found his father with a harlot, was me."

Letty's gaze turned sympathetic.

"I threw myself at him," he said. "I wanted to fight away the ugliness, take away the pistol he had, but I couldn't. Even though he stored it in his desk before I left and promised not to use it, I found him dead later that day. He'd taken his own life. My mother, who'd been bedridden for a year, overheard our argument. Her heart failed, and I lost my entire world."

He narrowed his gaze. "I would never buy a woman."

❦

The room closed in on Letty. Truth, raw and real, burned in Eric. Yes, he'd spoken true when he denied frequenting brothels, and his anger now was justified, but below the anger, below his righteous indignation, Letty found something that stole her breath. It paralyzed her, leaving her open, vulnerable, completely bared to its intensity.

Eric's emotions shone clear in his eyes. They brought back everything she'd felt when they'd embraced, kissed. They told her she was indeed the only woman he needed, and if she dared believe, they said she still held his interest. Perhaps even a place in his heart.

Her pulse kicked up its rhythm. Her heart pounded in her chest. Excitement fizzed up her back, sparked in her veins, made her dizzy, giddy, and dazed.

Eric reached out and touched the fists at her sides. One by one, he unfolded her curled fingers and wove them through his. The heat from his palms sent shocks up her arms, to her head, to her heart. Such longing, and only for him.

"Eric . . ."

He slowly pulled away, and a glance showed Letty the feelings weren't one-sided. But he'd still backed off.

"Go," she said. She remembered too well the enshrined room. "You're still haunted by the past. I am the present."

Eric nodded and retrieved his cane.

Letty turned her back to him. She heard him step away, his walking stick thudding on the floor. He paused.

"I've no right to interfere," he said, "but my conscience insists I warn you. You've gained a powerful adversary. I argued on your behalf at my house the other day, but I can't promise your safety if you won't listen to me."

"I can take care of myself."

"So you've said, but please hear me out. You've accused me of seeing you as I saw Martina. I could never do that. No two women could be more different than the two of you. I watched Martina die because of her stubbornness. I don't know that I could stand to see you suffer after rejecting my help."

Letty heard Eric's anguish and saw his shoulders slump. On his way out, he added, "I couldn't live with myself if I failed you, too."

She could almost touch his torment, and she would have given almost anything to follow him, but she couldn't fight his ghosts for him.

Instead, she sought God's comfort in her room.

15

"This is remarkable," Letty told Daisy. "Only two mistakes on the entire page. I'm proud of you."

Daisy chuckled. "Me, too."

In the two weeks since the girl had left Bessie's Barn, Letty had watched her undergo a transformation. The colorful wardrobe Randy had provided was modest enough to please the most critical eye, and since Daisy was also staying with the Stones, no garish paint sullied her pretty face.

When the Stones gave the girl free rein of their modest library, she surprised everyone with an affinity for the written word. Her tenacity at the typewriter was also reaping results.

"You, Daisy girl," Letty said, "are ready for new employment. We must find somewhere for you to put your superb skills to use."

The girl's joy vanished like the sun behind a storm cloud. "Who'd hire a—"

"Don't defeat yourself before you launch the battle. That attitude will bring more trouble than all the mistakes you've made."

"No, Doc, I don't think so. You see, I . . . 'took care' of most of the men around here at one time or another. They sneaked off to me when they should have been with their wives." Daisy fisted her hands. "Do you think they want me near their businesses? They're afraid of what I might say about them. None of them will give me a job."

"Look at me," Letty said, thumbing her chest. "I'm a doctor, a woman in a man's world. I know how much they fear women. I don't always win my battles, but as God's servant, I must go where He leads."

"You only threaten their pockets, Doc. I threaten their pride."

"Pride is another sin. You can't—"

Heavy footsteps clattered up her porch, putting paid to Letty's effort. She wouldn't let Daisy give up. Still, she couldn't wage war against the girl's fears with someone else around.

"Dr. Morgan? Daisy?" Ford called.

"In the kitchen," Letty answered. Daisy's cheeks colored nicely. Perhaps, as she'd thought that afternoon two weeks ago, God would use Ford in Daisy's restoration.

The reporter slapped his crushed hat against his thigh. "Good afternoon, ladies."

Letty bit her lip to hide a smile. As usual, Ford looked like the innards of someone's ragbag. Every garment on his wiry frame had more wrinkles than an average octogenarian. His tie hung askew, and a pencil rode over one ear. The perpetual smear of ink clung to the side of his nose, and for the first time since they'd met, she noticed what a well-shaped nose it was. Clear blue eyes peered with intelligence and curiosity from behind his spectacles. White-gold hair curled over his forehead, giving him a youthful look. It suddenly dawned on her that Ford was close to her own age.

She'd never looked closely at Eric's reporter, since Eric had always captured all of her attention. In view of what was happening in her kitchen, however, she now realized how attractive Ford really was.

And Daisy, because of what she'd been forced to experience,

was not so much the girl she should otherwise be at sixteen. Vibrant, blond Daisy was as lovely as the summer flower whose name she shared, somewhat soiled by tragedy, but a delightful young woman who needed a chance.

"Ford," Letty started, "as a reporter, you know just about everything that happens in Hartville, right?"

The young man slung his jacket over a kitchen chair, wadded his shirtsleeves to his elbows, then met her gaze. "Usually."

She prayed for gumption. "Would you know of any business that needs an excellent typist?"

Ford's spectacles slid down his nose. "You, Dr. Morgan?"

"No," she said, eyeing Daisy, whose pale curls flew from side to side. *Too bad, my dear girl.* "Not me. Her."

Ford turned to Daisy, an appreciative gleam in his eyes. "Perhaps I do know of something. How well does she use the machine?"

Letty waved Daisy's paper before his nose. "Only two mistakes on the whole page, and her fingers plumb dance over those keys."

Smiling, Ford looked up at Letty then back at Daisy. "Would you ladies care to visit the office with me? We might be able to arrange something."

At the newspaper, the trio removed their coats, and Daisy sat at Ford's desk. Ford lost his spectacles the moment her long, graceful fingers touched the keys, but he didn't seem to notice. He watched her type and, from what Letty could tell, also took in how fetching the girl looked in her apple-green shirtwaist and forest-green skirt.

When she reached the end of the piece, Daisy folded her hands in her lap.

"I believe, ladies," Ford announced, "that I'm looking at the newest employee of the *Hartville Day.*"

"And who might that be?" asked Eric from the doorway, startling Letty. She'd been so charmed by the scene before her that she hadn't noticed his arrival. Her heart began to pound.

"Daisy Butler, of course," answered Ford.

Letty risked a look at Eric and, as she'd expected, saw the thunder-clouds blow into his fine features. His forehead creased, his eyes narrowed, and his mustache twitched, mirroring the muscle in his cheek. "May we speak in private, Dr. Morgan?"

"Why, certainly, Mr. Wagner," she answered, meeting his mutinous gaze. She turned to Ford. "Please show Daisy the office."

Letty squared her shoulders and followed him. Despite his need for the cane, he quickened his pace down the hallway. He flung open the office door and stalked to the far side of the room. Letty couldn't help but note how well he maneuvered despite his recent injury, and thought perhaps the thump of the cane lent added emphasis to his temper.

"I see nothing humorous in this situation, Dr. Morgan."

"And what situation would that be?"

"For starters, charming my reporter into hiring that . . . that—"

"That *girl*. One who wants an opportunity to earn a decent living. Just how, Mr. Self-righteous Newspaperman, is she to do that when men like you deny her the right?"

Noting Eric's scramble for a response, Letty took advantage of the rare lapse. "Actually, in view of something Daisy said, asking you to hire her is my way of paying you a compliment."

Eric's stunned look gave way to one rife with skepticism and curiosity. "How so?"

"You've made clear your strict avoidance of brothels, right?"

He nodded.

"Daisy said earlier that no one in town would hire her because they would fear she might expose them and their manly foibles. Since you're utterly honorable, you have nothing to hide or lose by employing Daisy."

Triumph tasted sweet when Eric gaped.

He raised his arms in surrender. "I don't know why I try to reason with you. You have the most convoluted sense of logic of anyone I know."

❦

Eric couldn't refute the truth in Letty's contention. Unlike his father, who'd cloaked his vice in secrecy, he had nothing personal to lose by hiring a fallen woman. He did, however, have a business to run, and it would surely suffer once others learned the identity of his latest employee.

On the other hand, might his gesture bring about other acts of compassion? Could his action turn the tide for the abused girls and strike a blow to the cathouse trade? Was it a surge of hope like this that drove Letty to fight for what she believed?

He sought her gaze and caught his breath. Lamplight fell on her braided crown, catching the strands of gold among the richer brown hair and giving her a regal bearing. Her eyes blazed, and her cheeks bloomed the same shade of rose as her lips. And she was furious.

Why did he anger her so much? And why did he lose his temper with her? Was the attraction between them to blame? Or did his fear for her come out as rage, just as his fear for Steven had the day they nearly ran him down? Honesty nudged him with the truth. He didn't want to face it.

Yet he must. While he admired Letty's fiery response each time they argued, ever since she'd accused him of casting her in the same light as Martina, he'd used their arguments as an excuse. He wanted to push her away, and their differences provided him with fragile but effective protection against her appeal.

He had to maintain that barrier. Especially if all it took was keeping his opinions to himself.

"I challenge you," she said, breaking into his thoughts, "to give Daisy a chance to prove herself. If your newspaper suffers

230

from her presence, I'll make restitution for your loss. Since you know how few means I have, you'll also know that I'm confident she'll please you with her work."

"Enough, Letty. Go home. Take the girl with you. Ford will let you know our decision."

She measured his words and his expression. Whatever she found there must have reassured her. On her way out, she added, "You won't regret hiring her. I guarantee it."

The scent of violets remained in the room after she'd left. Eric breathed in, enjoying its freshness. Everything about Letty pleased him. Well, not her mulishness, but certainly everything else.

And he couldn't pursue such pleasures.

"Ford!" he yelled.

When the reporter appeared, he wore a besotted expression.

"Dare I request an explanation?"

Ford's glasses flew off again. He dropped to his knees, crept under the desk, and retrieved the eyepiece. A grunt escaped his lips when he hit his head on the chair.

"Of course," he finally said, setting his spectacles on his nose. "I told you last week. We need more help, someone who can type and is organized. You agreed and even ordered another machine. Daisy is perfect."

Eric cocked an eyebrow. "Are you aware of her former trade?"

A harsh look appeared on Ford's youthful features. "I am, and like you, I hate it. I hate everything about it, but I like her."

"Enough to behave foolishly because of her?"

"Yes."

"Enough to risk your reputation?"

"Yes."

"Enough to fall in love?"

Ford faced him, uncommon gravity in his expression. "Afraid so, Eric. The Lord does call us to show compassion."

Eric recognized his reporter's maturity. "What power women wield to make fools of us men."

"And we help them, but God—"

"How goes it with the Swartleys?" he asked, turning away.

Ford sighed. "Everyone knows Slosh sold out to them and died making merry. Beyond that, you and I appear to be the only ones who suspect they have outside backing."

"So there's nothing new."

"Nothing."

"We just need something, anything, with which to pin them."

"What we need, Eric, is help."

"Yes, of course, but whose?"

As Ford visibly struggled to contain a response, Eric returned to his desk. "You'll have to cover the upcoming Silver Celebration. The workmen are already building the dais for the speakers on Main Street. This leg won't let me do much." Turning to his calendar, he added, "Plans are for the second week in June."

Ford glanced at the notes. "Everyone is pitching in, and the town means to have itself one bang-up party."

"And the *Hartville Day* will cover every minute of it."

♋

On the sidewalk outside the newspaper, Letty didn't know whether to rail against Eric's stubbornness or to give thanks for Ford's infatuation with Daisy. The girl now stood a chance of supporting herself by decent means.

Letty turned to Daisy. "Why don't you return Prince to the livery? I have some thinking to do, and on a sunny day like today, I'd rather walk."

Fearful of meeting Hartville's folks under normal circumstances, Daisy hadn't strayed from the shelter of the parsonage and Letty's house. Knowing the girl had to make a place for herself, Letty refused to let her put off a first step.

"Well . . . I . . . oh, Doc, you have that look about you. Nothing I say will change your mind, will it?"

Surprised that Daisy had so easily read her, Letty said, "No."

"I don't have a choice, do I?"

Letty shook her head.

After climbing into the buggy, Daisy tugged on Prince's reins. "If I have any trouble, you'll hear all about it."

Letty agreed, glad for Daisy's spark of bravado. The girl seemed well on her way to healing, head held high, shoulders straight and proud. *Father,* she prayed, *give me the words, the chance to introduce her to You.*

God had worked a miracle in Daisy's life. Now, if He would just help Letty heal her tattered heart. How would she care for the Patterson children now that they lived at Eric's ranch? How would she deal with the chance of meeting him anywhere she went? She was strong, but this, this was too much.

Oh, the irony of it. After being told most of her life that she would never attract a man because of her unwomanly career, she had attracted a man despite the career, only to lose him because of her womanly need to mother children he viewed differently than she did.

Yet matters were more complicated than that. Their differences were a symptom of a deeper malady. Haunted by undue guilt over his wife's death, Eric wanted to assume responsibility for Letty. He believed her actions jeopardized her just as Martina's refusal to avail herself of medical care had endangered her. Until he recognized Martina's responsibility in her death and Letty's responsibility for her actions, there was little she could do. She couldn't overcome something Eric had to master himself.

More important still, until Eric accepted God's forgiveness and forgave himself, they had no future.

As she neared the church, someone called her name.

"Mrs. Tilford!" she exclaimed. "What a pleasure."

In a costume of purple tweed, the gray-haired lady bustled up and clasped Letty's hand. "How have you been?"

"Busy."

"More likely *too* busy," Hubert Tilford reproved. He then grasped his wife's elbow and tugged. "Come now, Agatha, this is unseemly."

The bewildered Mrs. Tilford looked at her husband. When comprehension struck, her mouth formed a perfect *O*. She dropped her black bag on the wooden sidewalk and then looked down as if wondering what to do.

Letty solved the dilemma by gathering the purse and handing it to its owner. When she sought Mrs. Tilford's gaze, the lady averted her face. "G—good day, Dr. Morgan," she stammered and hurried after her spouse.

Letty felt the blood drain from her face. She'd lived through similar scenes in Philadelphia, but this time was worse. The people of Hartville had welcomed her with open arms until her career and her faith had demanded actions that offended their sensibilities.

They'd rejected her as a doctor. They'd disdained her as a potential mother, too. Yet Eric's betrayal hurt most. At his side she'd truly felt feminine, wanted, a whole woman at last, but one he wouldn't love.

She wondered how soon her practice would dwindle to nothing. Would she be left destitute because of her convictions? Would she have to uproot and move elsewhere? Would leaving be easier than seeing Eric everywhere she went?

What about the girls? her conscience asked. *What about the Pattersons?*

She looked up at the sky, knowing God had heard her, even if He hadn't answered yet. "I will not run away, Eric Wagner. Children depend on me. And the hypocrites can continue to entertain sin!"

More determined than ever, she walked into her house, where Daisy had already arrived.

"I'll be out for a bit longer," she told the girl. "Would you like to stay and practice some more?"

Daisy gave the water glass in her hand a final swipe with a dish towel. "Could I, Doc?"

"Of course. I must look in on the Pattersons."

Daisy's gaze skittered away, as it did each time Letty mentioned the children. She sensed Daisy knew something about them, but she didn't know how to ask without scaring the girl away.

Setting her speculations aside, she retrieved her medical bag. "One never knows when those scamps might need treatment."

"You love them, don't you?"

Sweet sensations unfurled in Letty's heart. "Yes, I do. I wish . . ."

Wisdom showed in Daisy's eyes. "You wish they were yours, don't you? That you could keep them?"

"If this were a perfect world, then indeed those five would be mine. And you would as well."

Daisy's cheeks colored. "Really?"

"Really," Letty answered, tears misting her eyes. Seeing Daisy's uncertainty, she opened her arms wide.

The girl rushed to claim the love Letty offered. "Oh, Doc."

They held each other. Then, like a child, Daisy sniffled and backhanded her tears. Letty smiled. Helping this child out of the mess her life had become was one of the finest things she'd ever done. Scripture never failed. When it said, "Inasmuch as ye have done it unto one of the least of these my brethren, ye have done it unto me," it spoke God's truth. Her actions had blessed her as much as they had Daisy.

"I must be on my way now," Letty said, giving the girl one final hug. "Otherwise I'll be late getting back home. Will you still be here? Or are you due at the manse soon?"

As if the sentiment they'd shared abashed her, Daisy hesitantly said, "I'll be here . . . if you'll have me."

"Couldn't be better, my dear. Not one bit better for me."

On her way to the livery, Letty sang her praise to the Lord until a strident female voice cut through her joy.

"Bold as brass and walking down Main Street with not a care in the world," Emmaline Whitehall proclaimed.

Letty squared her shoulders and waited for Emmaline's further assault.

Emmaline obliged. "Fraternizing with tarts! Such disgrace you've brought upon yourself. Not to mention the smirch your scandalous behavior has brought down on Eric Wagner."

"Enough, Miss Whitehall," Letty said. "Consider that there, but for the grace of God, go you. If you hadn't had a family to love and protect you, you might have been forced to resort to questionable means to support yourself."

Emmaline turned puce. "Jezebel! And to think I helped prepare for your arrival. I've never regretted anything so much. My poor cousin must be spinning in her grave, seeing how you've besotted her husband with your loose ways."

Letty's curiosity curbed her anger. "Your cousin?"

"Martina would never have lowered herself to the level where you wallow, madam. She was a lady, and Eric worshiped her. Don't think I haven't seen you gawp at him, all cow-eyed and simpering. I know you covet him, but you'll never win his heart. You're only fit for the same as your floozy friends."

Although she should have been immune to such an accusation, Letty couldn't hold at bay the misery that cut through her. She felt ill wondering if Eric agreed with Emmaline. Did he see her as a temptation that could destroy him, like the woman he believed had ruined his father?

At least she now understood how Emmaline, the one who had hosted a suffragist who spoke of free love, could oppose a doctor who treated adolescent soiled doves. Emmaline feared Letty would usurp her cousin's rightful place, and she fell far short of the standards Martina had established.

Emmaline's hate-filled stare made Letty wince. "I regret your cousin's untimely death," she said sincerely, "but I have no aspirations to the position of Mr. Wagner's wife. I'm not the woman to marry Er—Mr. Wagner."

Letty clenched her hands, unnerved by her near slip. Emmaline would have pounced and made the most of it. "You needn't fear me," she added. "I'm a doctor and in Hartville for that purpose, not to displace Martina in Eric's affections."

Too late she realized she'd said his name. Emmaline's eyes narrowed. She sniffed and stalked down the street. "A likely story," she muttered.

Letty stood frozen to the spot, unable to do more than gasp for air. She made herself put foot before foot and pace the distance to the livery. Thoughts, snatches of conversations, darted through her mind. Her mother's criticisms, Mr. Forrest's rejection, Emmaline's indictment, even Eric's warnings coalesced into a jigsaw picture of her, Dr. Letitia Morgan. Physician, healer, woman. The wrong woman for the man she loved.

She was glad she'd decided to call on the Pattersons today. It gave her something to do, something productive to prove she hadn't erred by following her conscience. She hadn't been the proper daughter Mother wanted, nor was she the delicate creature Martina had been. It would seem she'd done well to train as a physician.

She clambered into her buggy and forced all thought of Eric, Martina, Mother, and her failings from her mind. Instead, she thought of all she'd accomplished during her time in Hartville.

Prince's clip-clopping hooves marked time as she traveled to Eric's place. The closer she came, the less possible it became to keep him from her thoughts. She wondered if he'd be there when she arrived. Had he stayed at the office to keep working? Or was he resting the leg? Would he reverse the progress he'd made by pushing himself too soon?

Oh well, the man was just that: a man. A grown man. And she had no right to hover over him.

As usual, she stopped Prince by the barn. Steven spotted her first. "Hey, Doc! Watch me."

When Letty realized what he was up to, her innards tangled in knots. The scamp hung by his knees in the air, swinging from the limb of a gnarled cottonwood tree.

"Oh, Steven, even I can't put you back together if you fall from up there. Please come down, and be careful, now."

Steven wrinkled his nose but obeyed. Each time he responded so readily, Letty wondered what he might have been like if normal discipline had been present in his life. He was thriving in the atmosphere of routine and attention.

He wiped his hands against the seat of his trousers and said, "'M really good at it, ain't I, Doc?"

"That you are, Steven, but that's the only head you have. Understood?"

"Yes, ma'am."

"Where are the girls?"

"Caroline an' 'Melia are inside. Suzannah's in the barn."

Suzannah had blossomed through her love for animals. The chickens had been the first to catch her attention. Then Marmie's kittens had stolen her heart. Even the ornery Heidi made her giggle. Life on the ranch had done wonders for the love-starved child.

"Here," Letty said, handing Steven her satchel. "Please take this inside for me. I'll find Suzannah and bring her with me."

With a two-fingered salute, Steven grabbed the bag and ran to the house. His gesture reminded Letty of the day she'd arrived in Hartville when Eric's mares had narrowly missed trampling the boy. She shuddered to think what might have happened.

She went after Suzannah. At the barn door, Eric's words brought her up short. "You put your hands like so, Suzie."

"Mm-hmm."

Letty tiptoed in, unwilling to disturb them but dying of curiosity. Eric sat on a stool next to the goat, and Suzannah watched as he taught her the mechanics of milking. "You wrap your fingers around Heidi's teat. See?"

"Mm-hmm."

"Now comes the hard part. When you hold tight, you have to pull and squeeze all at the same time. Watch."

The stream of milk hit the tin pail Eric held with his feet, and Suzannah chortled with pure pleasure. "Me now?" she asked.

"Watch me again."

"Mm-hmm."

Another trickle hit the bucket, and Suzannah's laughter brightened the barn. Emotions swelled in Letty's heart when Eric stood and knelt behind his stool.

"Sit here," he said. "I'll hold you so you don't fall off. This is hard work, you know."

"Mm-hmm." Nodding her blond braids, Suzannah sat in the shelter of Eric's arms. She reached her hands out to Heidi's udder and wrapped her little fingers around the teats. She turned to Eric and whispered, "Like so?"

"Just so," he answered, pressing his cheek to her head.

The tears that had been so close to the surface all day poured down Letty's cheeks. This meant the world to her. Here was everything she'd ever wanted: that man, that child, and the four in the kitchen.

Lord Jesus, have I asked for too much? Am I selfish to love Eric and the children and want them to be mine? To love and cherish and coddle and train them? Her heart urged her forward; her love brought her to Eric's side.

Unable to resist, she touched his shoulder. He turned and met her gaze. The love in his eyes stole what reason she had left. She pressed the muscle under her hand, enjoying its strength.

Brown eyes clung to gray. Unspoken messages came and

went as their lonely hearts spoke as if with the same voice. Letty smiled.

Eric turned to the little girl in his arms. She'd stolen his heart, just as the woman behind him had.

He prayed silently, *Father in heaven, what should I do about it?*

16

Letty entered the house quietly. She almost regretted inviting Daisy to stay, since she needed time to collect herself.

She would never forget those last few moments in the barn. What she had seen in Eric's eyes moved her more than any gesture could have. There'd been longing and resignation in the depths, something so sad she refused to think what it might mean.

She went to the kitchen but stopped at the threshold. Caught up in a kiss, Daisy and Ford held each other tightly near the back door.

When the young man lifted his head, Letty saw Daisy's tears, and her protective instincts awoke.

"I understand," Ford murmured as he stroked silky blond curls from Daisy's brow. "I know how frightened you were, but now that you don't depend on her, you can tell me what you know. He must be stopped, and I'm going to help you."

Daisy rubbed her cheek against Ford's shoulder. "I know he must be stopped," she whispered. "I'm afraid of what he might do to you."

Ford gazed into Daisy's eyes, and Letty witnessed another kiss. She debated interrupting, but intuition told her she would learn more if she remained unnoticed.

When Ford regained his composure, he whispered against Daisy's lips, "You are sweet. But you needn't fear for me. I can take care of myself. And now I can care for you as well."

Daisy blushed. Letty found it hard to believe this was the same girl who had "taken care of" many men in town. The child had clearly been forced to submit. Ford's tenderness seemed to salve the soul-deep wounds the others had inflicted.

"He's awfully powerful," Daisy said.

"So is the newspaper," Ford countered.

"Bessie will come after me. She knows I know what's going on."

"That's why you wouldn't leave when Dr. Morgan first doctored you, isn't it?"

"Bessie swore they'd kill me if I left or told."

"Don't worry. Plenty will happen but none of it to you."

Daisy shuddered. "Bessie's horrible. She's purely evil."

"He's worse," Ford retorted, making Letty want to shake him by the ears. Who were they discussing? And what had "he" done?

"He hit me, you know. With that cow stick of his."

Medford! Letty knew only one such obscenity, and the surgeon owned it. Now, if the two in the kitchen would just blurt out what Medford and Bessie were up to—

No. A chill shot down her spine. It couldn't be. Dread sank into Letty's stomach and filled her heart. Daisy and Bessie's argument had been about the Patterson children. Now the girl had told Ford something about Medford and Bessie, something dangerous.

Letty thought back to the day Slosh died. Matters began to grow clearer. Bessie and Medford had something to do with Slosh's death, and she meant to find out what.

She would need Eric's help, but in order to put a stop to Bessie and Medford's crimes, he would have to confront the vice that had destroyed his family. Considering what she'd be asking of him, she hesitated.

"Father God," she whispered, "please sustain me. Give me the words and soften Eric's heart to receive them." She paused and shivered. "Lord, he needs You. Please draw him back to Your loving arms, and please, please, don't let me be a stumbling block to him. He needs to truly understand that Your Son already paid the price for his sins if he'll only accept that ultimate sacrifice on his behalf."

Opting for a noisy entrance, she marched into the kitchen, making Ford and Daisy blush and jump apart. "I'm sorry to interrupt," she said, "but you both know how important this is. Daisy, tell me every last detail. Ford, please fetch Eric."

Four eyes focused on Letty. "Come, now," she urged. "We must get to work."

Like knitting at the mercy of a cat's claws, the story unraveled before Letty. Dr. Medford had set Bessie in "business" shortly after his arrival in town. Two years later, he had an exclusive claim on her attentions, while his wife languished at home.

When Hart hit the new, rich silver vein last year, the surgeon tried to buy into the boom. Achieving no results through legitimate means, he'd sought out the shady element he'd met at Bessie's, allying himself with the Swartleys. The three men had agreed on a plan: Medford wanted silver but didn't care to soil his hands with the work required to extract it. The brothers wanted money to sustain their vices and had no trouble carrying out his dirty work, that of the mining operation as well as the swindling of unfortunate folks.

As Eric had suspected, power and money backed the Swartleys —Dr. Medford's power and money.

As soon as Ford and Eric arrived, they set their plan in motion. Daisy shared details of Bessie's and Medford's routines, and Eric and Ford, with Daisy in tow, soon went for the newspaper's camera. Then they headed to the brothel.

"I may not be able to end prostitution altogether," Eric said, "but I can and will stop this criminal wave."

Before leaving, Eric admonished Letty to stay safely at home.

His words only served to reinforce her determination. Once they left, Letty ran to the alley behind Bessie's Barn. Again seeking the cover of the shrub, she came right up to the house and was glad for the open windows on the second floor.

Inside, she heard footsteps followed by a knock.

"Yeah?" Bessie called.

"Can I come back to work?" Daisy asked.

"No more high'n mighty lady doctor for ya, eh?"

"I need the money."

"Ya gonna sass me again?"

"I have to work for you, don't I?"

Bessie laughed. "Yeah, and ya know now better'n to go spoutin' off at me."

"I understand."

"'Spose ya brought a man with ya."

"He's waiting for me."

"Git goin', then."

"Mm-hmm."

The door closed, footsteps crossed the width of the building, and another door opened. "He's with her," Daisy said. "Smirking and drinking—"

The closing door cut off Daisy's words, but Letty didn't have long to wait. Her heart sped up, and she bit her lip.

She ran to the front, determined to miss nothing. And she heard plenty: Medford howled, Bessie wailed, Eric yelled, and Ford answered in kind.

After what felt like hours but could only have been ten or fifteen minutes at most, Daisy parted the swinging doors to the sordid emporium. Bessie followed, hands tied with red and black suspenders, Ford prodding her on. She wore a magenta peignoir trimmed in exotic white feathers that quivered with her every step. Her brassy hair stood on end, giving her the oddest look of lunacy.

Behind her came Medford, missing his suspenders. The surgeon's hands were also tied, but, lacking his suspenders, he had to clutch the waist of his trousers so as not to parade in yet more scandalous attire.

"What are you doing here?!" Eric roared the moment he saw Letty.

She lifted her chin. "I have every right to help bring these two to justice." Not to mention satisfy her curiosity.

Shame had brought on Medford's confession, and after Medford implicated her in the scheme, Bessie crumbled, admitting her complicity. With his hold tight on Medford's upper arm, Eric led the strange company to the sherrif's office, pausing every so often to give the surgeon the chance to hitch up his pants. Bessie's ludicrous feathers fluttered in the breeze, but at least she was covered. With an arm around Daisy's waist, Ford kept the madam in line, and Letty brought up the rear of the parade.

She was glad to have played a part—no matter how small—in exposing the culprits.

After the sheriff took their statements, Eric and Letty returned to Eric's office. In the lamplight, she noted the strain on his face. He must have relived every moment of his parents' tragedies.

"You have all my respect and admiration," she said. "I don't know if I could have faced what you did tonight."

His jaw tightened and his mustache twitched. "I had no choice, did I?"

"Of course you did. You could have said no."

"I had to take care of this matter, especially since you seemed intent on doing so yourself." The corners of his mustache danced. "Didn't do so well there, did I?"

Letty had the grace to blush. "You know me well enough. Did you really think you could keep me away?"

"I can always hope for change in your mule-headed ways."

"Me? Mule headed? How about you?"

A weary smile lightened his demeanor. "Merely determined, Dr. Morgan."

"Pshaw! Stubborn and ornery." Letty paused. "I meant what I said. I admire your courage and your strength of character. You confronted your ghosts head on."

She hoped he'd leaned on God for that strength, but she doubted he had.

"Oh, I don't know, but I thank you for the kind words." He blew out the lamps and held the door for her. "May I see you home?"

"Of course."

❦

In the following days, Hartville went into shock followed by a voracious uproar. The outcry against the bordellos reached fever pitch. Although Medford's swindles no longer posed a threat, Letty's insistence in helping the youngsters in the cathouses became, if possible, less popular than before. Dr. Medford's vehemence had done its damage before his downfall, and her presence outside Bessie's place at the time of his comeuppance had done her no good.

Eric had been right. Her brush with the squalid side of Hartville was having a dreadful effect on her life. Even though Letty's motives were pure, her career was now in shambles.

While Eric became the town's hero, Letty went down to four patients: Mrs. Stone, who was in excellent health; Mim, who'd recovered and needed no medical care; Daisy, who, now that her romance with Ford was in full bloom, insisted that when the time came someday, she wanted Letty at her birthings; and Randy, who, with her robust health and ever-increasing middle, remained loyal.

Letty began to wander through her clinic, cleaning surfaces that already gleamed, folding linens creased to perfection, scrubbing each glass she used for a drink of water. She even missed her chickens.

Although she longed for the busyness of her medical practice, that didn't compare to the aching emptiness in her heart. She missed Eric. She missed seeing his mustache quirk up on one side before a smile bowed the entire hairy fringe. She missed his warm touch, his tender kisses.

She sat at the kitchen table and thought back on her life. As her mother had predicted, Letty was alone. Eric and the Pattersons were at the ranch, Douglas still hoping to find a family who would adopt all five. Letty had nothing to show besides a second failed medical practice and a broken heart.

She tried to help with the preparations for Hartville's Silver Celebration, but the women at the fellowship hall snubbed her, and after several determined attempts, their rejection won out. Letty stopped offering her help in order to spare Adele Stone further embarrassment.

So she sat at home alone, with a heart so empty, so torn, that even Dr. Morgan didn't know how to mend her own wounds. A tear fell on the tabletop.

"Lord God, will I ever erase the memories?" she whispered.

How could Eric turn his back on all they might have? Was a ghost more satisfying than her love?

She gave in to the tears she'd fought so hard. Rivers flowed down her face. Cries breached her throat, burning it with sadness.

"Father, was I so wrong to want to help those who needed help? To love a man?"

The silence held no answers, so she asked the question she most feared. "Jesus, are you asking me to surrender everything? Everything?"

Would she lose all she'd once had?

An acrid laugh escaped her lips. Was she deluding herself in thinking she'd had Eric's feelings to lose? How could she know?

The silence grew deafening.

She clenched her fists, anger joining her anguish. She had to know. Somehow she had to learn if for a fraction of time God had given her the desires of her heart.

The emptiness continued. God again withheld His response.

Well, then, she knew just how to find the answers to her questions. She knew where to find Eric.

Her preparations were brief. Soon she arrived at Randy's elegant brick home, needing a favor she was sure her friend would grant. Moments after voicing her request, the two women climbed into Letty's buggy and headed for Eric's spread. As Randy chattered with what seemed forced brightness, Letty wondered what her friend thought of her boldness.

Then she decided it didn't matter what Randy or anyone else thought. She had to know what Eric felt for her, if her imagination had conjured the images of . . . love. Yes, love.

At the ranch, Letty helped Randy cautiously exit the conveyance. The expectant mother went to find the children as Letty went to find the man who'd captured her heart.

She found him in the barn, wearing ancient brown trousers and a worn flannel shirt, pitching forkfuls of hay into a stall. His back muscles played under his shirt, maintaining the smooth rhythm of his work.

The sight of him strengthened her resolve. She longed to wrap her arms around his waist, to lay her head on his chest, and she needed to know if she'd ever have that right.

"Very busy today?" she asked.

He stopped. "Not especially. I'm sick of lying around, and my leg needs exercise. I can't afford to let the muscle freeze up."

Letty nodded and twisted her hands at her waist. This barn bore so many memories. It was quite fitting to find Eric here today.

"I wondered," she began, butterflies flitting in her middle, "if you aren't too busy, that is, if you would care to share my picnic? To celebrate the end of Dr. Medford, Bessie, and the Swartleys' misdeeds."

Eric studied her, his face unreadable. "That would be a pleasure," he finally said, "especially on a warm spring day like today."

Letty blushed, remembering her plans. "That's what I thought. I heard of a spot—"

"I know just the place. Trust me."

Eric hung the pitchfork from a hook on the wall. He strode to a tin bucket in the far corner and scrubbed his hands with the yellow soap by the pail. After drying his hands on a red and white piece of towel, he shook the rag and hung it on another hook. He then gestured for Letty to follow him.

"Wait!" she cried. "The basket. We mustn't forget our food."

Eric's chuckle encouraged her. "So true," he said, picking up the hamper Amelia had once purloined.

They left in companionable silence. Every so often Eric pointed out something of interest, items unnoticed by Letty with her thoughts so intent on her secret purpose.

After a short while, they came to a willow at the edge of Silver Creek. A few feet away, a group of shrubs, silvery in color, followed the water's trace. The willow beckoned, offering shade in contrast to the brilliant sunlight.

"It's lovely," Letty murmured.

Eric flashed her a smile.

She spread a quilt inside the bower of the willow and set out their feast. A bowl of golden-brown chicken fragranced the breeze. Sliced-potato salad, pickles, and deviled eggs followed. Finally, after uncovering a quartet of biscuits, she withdrew a rare treat: her last jar of strawberry preserves.

"Wonderful," Eric murmured.

"Mm-hmm," Letty responded, uncovering the berries. "These are lovely. I brought three jars when I came out west—"

Eric's expression dried up her words. He glanced from the berries to her mouth, to the berries again, and finally rested his gaze on her lips. Two steps brought him to her side. With one hand he removed the jar from her trembling fingers; the other slipped around her waist.

His kiss was hungry, different from the other kisses they'd shared. It went on as time vanished, rushing wildness to Letty's heart. And then its flavor changed. It mellowed, gentled, and she felt cherished and loved in a way she'd never known before. Joy and gladness soared through her, and she even thought she heard bells.

Too soon, or so it seemed, Eric pressed a soft touch on her lips and let her go. He smiled tentatively, unusual in the usually forceful man. He sat on the quilt and helped himself to the food.

For the first time since they'd met, he seemed at ease. His brow was smooth, his lips curved in the slightest smile. The creases at the corners weren't as pronounced, and his breathing sounded even and deep. If nothing else, Letty had just given him the gift of a peaceful time.

But she needed more.

"Eric," she said when they'd finished their meal.

He lifted his head.

"I need to speak with you. I mean, we have matters to discuss."

He went through a metamorphosis. He frowned and clenched his jaw, and even his eyes seemed to darken.

Her determination refused to tremble. "This is difficult for me, you understand." Not daring to meet his gaze, she stared at her fidgety hands. "Our situation can't continue as it is. I care deeply for you, and I need to know—I need more."

Eric sighed.

Letty studied a weed next to her foot. She pulled on its stem, and it bobbled precariously. She knew just how that tough little fellow felt. Here she sat, wobbling on the edge of expectation; one word from Eric, and surely she would topple.

"Please stop," he finally said. "I know what you mean, and I take full responsibility."

From beneath lowered lashes, Letty saw him stand. A tingle of awareness coursed through her, a rush of remembered feelings she had no business remembering just then. She looked him in the face and flinched. Eric was in pain. When he spoke, his voice matched his expression.

"I'm a flawed man, yet knowing I should stay away, I let my . . . affection for you defeat my common sense. You deserve a whole man. One who can care for you the way every woman needs."

Letty stood. "But—"

He held up a hand. "Hear me out, please. I've told you my many failures." He leaned against the willow's trunk, his arm supporting his forehead in a posture of extreme exhaustion.

His voice came out rough. "After we spoke in the barn that day, I reconsidered the events that led to their deaths. Because of some things you said, I realized Martina was more responsible than I for her death. I began to think perhaps I'd been too hard on myself, and I tried to prove I wasn't the failure I saw."

He turned, rested his back against the tree trunk, and closed his eyes, his shoulders sagging. "Then matters went badly for you, and I failed to protect you from the venom of the town. You're now virtually destitute—"

"No, Eric." At his look, she bit her bottom lip, determined to hear him out.

A grimace twisted his mustache. "That's not all. When Mrs. Patterson died and Slosh lost control, I took care of the children. I provided their basic needs. I thought I'd protect them where I'd failed to protect my son. And where did that lead? It led them straight to the loss of their father and their land. I failed them, too."

Eric moved from the tree, his steps deliberate and heavy. He stopped just beyond its shadow, where a sunbeam kissed his hair with gold. Letty had never loved him more. She also knew he'd never been less hers.

"I can't offer more than the kisses we've shared," he said, his voice tight, harsh. "Everything in me pushes me to you, but I can't take a wedding vow again. I can't promise to love, cherish, and protect. Not you nor any child we might have, and without that certainty, we can have nothing more."

A vise tightened on Letty's heart as Eric spoke. She'd lost. She'd taken a reckless gamble and had lost it all. Fleeting images of moments shared, of words spoken, of kisses exchanged went through her head in a vertiginous whirl.

Desperate to contain the tears that rushed to her eyes, she gathered her plates, bowls, and quilt. She wanted as much distance between her and Eric as possible.

He kept quiet; so did she. They had nothing more to say.

He again sought the shelter of the willow.

She walked away, his words ringing in her mind. *"I can't offer more than the kisses we've shared. Without that certainty—"*

Certainty.

Assurance.

Blessed assurance.

"Eric," she murmured, "no one can offer perfect assurance. Only God can. Only God is in control."

The sob caught in her throat made it hard to draw breath. Soon she had to stop to force air into her aching, empty lungs.

Empty. Yes, she was empty. Empty of hope, of dreams, of joy. She'd given them all to Eric, and he'd been unable to receive them.

She turned around one last time and studied the raw beauty of the land. A breeze rustled the silver shrubs, and the willow danced to the song of Silver Creek. No dancing or singing could touch Letty's heart right then.

She gathered her courage and stole a last look at Eric. Although he remained within the circle of shade, he no longer stood but knelt at the foot of the weeping willow, holding his head in his hands.

She'd gambled, and it seemed they both had lost.

17

The rollicking tempo of a Viennese piece waltzed out of the entrance to Hartville's Grand Hotel. As she approached the lobby, Letty experienced another nudge of nerves, and she asked herself yet again how she'd let Randy talk her into attending a ball.

She smiled. Randy had had formidable help once Mrs. Stone and Daisy joined in the gentle bullying.

But then, they weren't the only guilty ones. She'd let vanity override her sensible side, and she'd had a gown made for the occasion. The dress hadn't cost much. Randy had offered some "leftover" royal-blue brocade that "just happened" to match a remnant of silk she'd "fortuitously located." "Coincidentally," Mrs. Stone remembered "storing" a length of blue velvet no more than a shade darker than Randy's offerings and promptly presented it to Letty. Of course, it made the perfect trim. In addition, Daisy found she had "extra" lace after making her gown from materials paid for by her wages from the newspaper.

Despite Letty's every effort to refuse the bounty, her friends had maintained a united front, and she'd eventually succumbed to the tempting yards of exquisite fabric.

Amos's wife, Mattie, an outstanding seamstress, had then cajoled Letty into trusting the dress to her gifted hands. The most exquisite gown soon took shape, and tonight, with no one in particular for whom to wear such a garment, Letty looked better than she ever had.

Another gay piece began as the waltz came to an end. *Oh, honestly, Letitia. You can't just stand here listening to the music and feeling sorry for yourself.* With a final tug to the bretelles that billowed at her shoulders and a determined swish to her blue silk train, Letty lifted her chin and sailed into the salon.

Dr. Letitia Morgan would bid Hartville a stylish farewell.

౿

The relentless three-four beat of the orchestra's waltz made Eric's temples throb. The Silver Celebration had taken a feverish grip on the town that, he hoped, tonight's culminating ball and fireworks display would finally break. Then the town could, perhaps, settle back to normal, and he could resume mourning a second lost love.

After Letty had run away the afternoon of their ill-fated picnic, Eric had stayed under the tree and let the bitter tears flow. Twice he'd loved, and twice he'd failed the women he loved.

Feeling emptier than he'd thought possible, he eventually returned home. His mind set, he began to withdraw from the Pattersons. After all, Douglas was seeking adoptive parents. Eric had to protect himself from their wrenching final farewell.

He'd thrown himself into the preparations for the Celebration. He'd volunteered for any chore that needed doing, regardless of how tedious or undesirable it might be, no matter how sore his leg grew. He'd do anything to avoid thinking of his loss of Letty.

The frantic pace he kept, however, didn't distract him for more than minutes at a stretch. It seemed his heart had made a perfect nest for a silver dove.

He'd heard a rumor that Letty would soon leave town. Nobody knew where or when she planned to go, but everyone felt it would be soon. It was for the best, they all said.

His foolish heart refused to agree. He had to admit he wanted Letty close enough to watch her walk down Main Street, to see her focus on Pastor Stone's sermons, to hear her drive her buggy to another birth.

A flash of royal blue at the entrance to the ballroom caught his eye. He turned. Letty had arrived. Not the Dr. Morgan Letty he knew, not even the fellowship-dinner-and-charades Letty he remembered, stood under the glow of candlelight. This Letty was breathtaking.

From the top of her upswept hair to the end of her small train, she radiated femininity. Her cheeks glowed deep rose, and the blue dress made her skin resemble rich cream. The gown's square neckline underlined her collarbone, modestly framing her lovely face.

He took two steps toward her, then stopped. No matter how beautiful she was, no matter how much he wished to stand by her side, no matter how much she meant to him, one truth remained: He didn't deserve Letitia Morgan.

❦

She should never have come. She should have fought her determined, well-meaning friends and stayed home. Feeling more out of place than she ever had before, she skirted the edge of the room, avoiding the dance floor. Since no chair could be found, she continued circling the room.

A potted palm next to a tall window provided her a somewhat private niche. Although she still lacked a chair, the secluded corner suited her just fine. She turned her back on the festivities and studied her reflection in the window.

She saw a woman utterly different from the one she faced each morning in the washstand mirror. Her cheeks were red from her discomfort, and her hair, for once, obeyed her commands. The fabulous gown gave the illusion of a perfect hourglass figure, while its train rippled with her every move.

Even to her own eyes she looked lovely. And alone. Behind the woman in the window, merrymakers waltzed two by two.

The crystals of the chandelier above the dance floor reflected the flicker of candlelight. Women in jewel-toned finery clung to dashing partners whose black coats set off the rose, heliotrope, purple, and emerald silk, satin, and lace. The scent of varied perfumes blended into the aroma of a flower garden, and Viennese waltzes played counterpoint to the evening's gaiety.

"Letty!" called Randy.

She smothered a groan. The last thing she wanted was to force a mimicry of cheer. "Hello, Randy."

Bedecked in emerald moiré that spanned her sizable belly, Randy exuded pure joy. She took Letty's hand, turned her in a pirouette, and exclaimed, "You put us all to shame, you're so beautiful."

Randy turned to beckon someone Letty couldn't see from behind her palm.

Resplendent in plum silk and pearls, Adele Stone approached.

"No one could outdo either of you," Letty said, envying her friends' happiness.

Randy waved across the room. "There's Douglas. I lost him the moment we arrived. Perhaps when he gets here, we can have a dance or two. That is, if my doctor allows it."

"There's no reason you can't," Letty said, "as long as you don't overexert yourself. And if you feel up to dancing, I certainly need not worry about your general health."

"I feel wonderful now that—"

When Randy stopped midsentence, Letty followed her gaze. She gasped, and the floor seemed to drop from under her. She wanted to run but had no escape.

Douglas Carlson approached, deep in conversation with Eric. Letty shivered. He'd always affected her. The letter he'd written to the college had led her to admire the man who'd composed it, and her first glimpse of him on the station platform had quickened her interest. Still, she'd never seen a more imposing man than Eric Wagner in evening attire. Well groomed as always, his golden hair shone in the lamplight. His formal white shirt and bow tie set off his skin, which already wore a deeper hue from his work outdoors. A single-breasted vest hugged his torso, and his black garb lent his long lines an elegance few men could achieve.

The lines at the corners of his eyes had deepened, and he looked tired. Letty longed to comfort him.

"I've a splendid idea," Mrs. Stone said. "Although the pastor and I don't dance, why don't you young people enjoy this next piece?"

"Wha—what?"

"Yes, dear, the four of you should dance." The pastor's wife turned to the men. "Douglas, Randy is dying for a whirl on the dance floor. Do indulge her, dear. And you, Eric Wagner, this is a ball, not a funeral. Spare us that undertaker look and take the loveliest woman here onto the floor. Please make yourself have a good time. Pastor Stone always says that the joy of the Lord is our strength."

After her outrageous speech, Mrs. Stone took Letty's hand and dragged her to Eric's side. The determined woman took Eric's hand and placed Letty's fingers on his callused palm. Unable to gracefully demur, Letty looked up into chocolate-colored eyes.

"May I?" Eric asked, his voice husky.

Unable to talk past the lump in her throat, she nodded.

Hand in hand, they took up the graceful steps of another Strauss piece. The room faded around them as the music swept them to another place and time, somewhere far, far away, the Danube perhaps. Through the mists of distance, the waltz echoed the beat of Letty's heart.

She looked up at the man she loved. She'd probably never see him after tonight, and never again experience his embrace.

The waltz gathered speed, swirling around them in romantic, lighthearted fashion. Eric's hand on her back inched her closer, and Letty reveled in his scent. The wool of his suit, the spice of bay rum, the clean, masculine musk of man. That very essence of him was imprinted in her memory, in her heart.

A tear rolled down her cheek. Another soon followed, despite the pleasure of his presence and the gaiety of the music. A sob rose up, and she failed to smother it. She couldn't fall apart here, not before the entire town, in Eric's arms.

"No," she whispered and tore herself away.

Blinded by tears, she ran from the ballroom and kept running until she reached Main Street. She pushed her way through the crowd intent on celebrating the town's good fortune.

"Excuse me," she said when she bumped into a lady.

"Pardon me," she begged a man.

Shouldering a path, she kept running, afraid to stop. She gasped, scarcely able to draw air. Under the glowing summer moon, she paused to gulp a breath and press a hand to her pounding heart. Lanterns hanging from poles up and down both sides of the street blazed and illuminated the town. In the moonlight, under the radiance of the lamps, Letty knew only gray.

"Letty!" Eric called.

Turning, she saw him in the hotel's doorway, silhouetted in the light from the elegant lobby. He ran out to the street and peered in both directions. A moment later, through a gap in the throng of humanity clogging the road, he spotted her.

❦

Backlit by lamplight, illuminated by the moon's silver gleam, Letty's royal-blue dress became the beacon that showed Eric the way.

"No!" she cried and ran again.

Eric picked up his pace. Why was he so intent on catching her? Logic told him it was foolish, and yet when she'd pulled away in the ballroom, something inside him had died, something precious and bright. He needed her to bring it back to life. The darkness he'd seen in those few moments had struck terror in his heart. He needed her. He needed her brightness. After years of gloom, she'd brought light back to his heart.

"Letty," he called again, running, weaving between the revelers. In seconds, he reached her. In less time, she was in his arms, the lamps overhead lighting up the night. He brought his lips to hers.

The noise disappeared; the crowd ceased to exist. But the passion, the tenderness, the love still remained. He pulled Letty closer and lost himself in their kiss. Her lips felt like velvet, and her violet scent surrounded him.

He could no longer deny the love inside him, growing every day, binding him to this woman with every beat of his heart. Love, the kind that made a man foolish, made him hope and dream again. She quivered in his arms. How could he let her leave? He tightened his embrace, and she looped her arms around his neck.

A sudden scream rent the night. "Help! It's a child! It's Steven Patterson!"

Eric dragged himself from the kiss and looked around. Passersby stared at one of the lantern poles, but the lantern no longer hung there. At the base, a woman on her knees wailed and pawed at flames on the ground.

What had Steven done? "Dear God!" Eric cried instinctively, seeking the help he'd shunned for years, the help he'd learned, as a child, was always there if he sought it.

At his side, Letty moaned. Eyes wide and wild, she held a fist to her mouth. A shudder shook the fabric on her shoulders, and her cheeks bleached to marble. She stumbled forward. "No," she murmured, holding a hand to hold Eric back. She nearly fell with her next step.

"Don't!" Eric ordered. "You might hurt yourself."

Letty was overwrought.

"Wait here."

Eric elbowed his way to where the woman still fought the flames that devoured Steven's clothing. He pushed her aside, muttered a vague "Sorry," and rolled the boy over in the dirt. Over and over again he turned the thin body, fighting time and fire for Steven's life.

The ground, which had been sprinkled to keep the dust of the crowd to a minimum, steamed each time a flame touched down. After what seemed like hours but could have been only seconds, the last spark died. In spots, Steven's clothes still smoked, and to keep them from igniting again, Eric stripped off the remains of cloth and then wrapped the boy in his evening coat.

Portions of the boy's body were charred. His arms bore the largest burns, and raw welts striped his chest. Bringing Steven close, the stench of seared skin assaulted Eric's nostrils. He gagged. *Merciful God, don't let this one die, too.*

Letty walked to his side. "Is he . . . ?"

"We'll soon find out. Let's get him to your clinic."

Main Street had never seemed longer. When they finally gained the corner of Willow and Main, both heaved sighs of relief.

"He's breathing," Eric said in response to the question in Letty's haunted eyes.

She led the way inside and into the examining room. He counted each of Steven's shallow breaths a triumph, each thready heartbeat a victory.

"Please lay him on the table. I'm ready."

Eric wondered if guilt had birthed Letty's strange expression and toneless voice. Knowing her, the momentary failure to respond at the scene of the accident would weigh heavily on her conscience. She held herself to a higher standard than most, and fear had paralyzed her. He knew that anguish well.

He longed to comfort her, to tell her he'd helped, that together they were giving Steven his only chance, but the closed look on her face put an end to the notion. Eric did as she asked.

She bathed the child's blackened flesh with wads of cotton soaked in Calendula lotion. She checked every inch of Steven's body, clearing away ashes and burnt scraps of cloth. Over and over she soaked the seared chest and arms, never once uttering a word.

After a time, a knock pulled Eric from the woman and child. He prayed no one had gone into labor. His breath gusted out in relief when he found Mayor Osgood and Pastor Stone at the door. Mrs. Stone sat in the carriage tied at the hitching post.

"We came to inquire after the boy," the mayor said.

"He's bad," Eric answered, his voice low and rough. "But Le—Dr. Morgan is working on him. I don't know."

As the men followed him inside, he heard Mrs. Stone get out of the carriage. He gestured the men toward the waiting room, then held the door for the pastor's wife.

"How is he?" she asked.

He shrugged. "Only God knows. Letty's fighting for him with everything she has."

The mayor spoke. "May we see him or speak to her?"

Eric shook his head, but then he remembered that despite her preoccupation with Steven, Letty wouldn't appreciate his overstepping his bounds. "Let me ask."

After a whispered consultation, Letty left the examining room, glancing back at the unconscious child with every step. Tiny vertical lines marred the smoothness of her forehead just above her nose, and she'd pressed her lips tight, the pressure turning the edges white.

"How is he, my dear?" Pastor Stone asked, giving Letty a fatherly hug.

She trembled. "I can't say for certain. So much of him is burnt that he should by all rights be dead. If he makes it through the night, it'll only be by the grace of our Lord."

"Well, then," the reverend answered, "we should head home and pray for just that." He turned. "Come along, Mrs. Stone.

We'll do more good on our knees than filling Letitia's waiting room."

On their way out, Mrs. Stone glanced at the small body on the table. She gasped, averting her eyes, tears wetting her face. The last Eric saw of her, she stumbled down the walkway, shaking her head.

Mayor Osgood turned to Eric, accusation in his gaze. "What led to this, Mr. Wagner? Did you leave those imps unattended while you waltzed?"

Eric gritted his teeth. "I don't know what led to the accident. I felt it more important to bring the boy here so he could receive the best care possible than to ask questions. As far as your second question goes, I hired Anna Sauder to watch them this evening. She was to bring them to town for the fireworks display. I would never leave children unattended. I'll learn what happened, though. You can count on that."

The mayor tugged on his lapels and shot Eric another fierce glare. "I don't see why we can't dispatch them to the Shakers in Cleveland and get on with our lives. Hartville can't be responsible for those brats."

"They are not brats!" Letty's vehemence stunned both men. "And as for sending them away, you just try it, gentlemen. I'd rather die than see them shipped out like raw ore or cattle."

Eric smiled. "I second the doctor's sentiments, Your Honor. Now, due to Steven's precarious condition, I urge you to return to your duties so that Dr. Morgan and I can carry out ours."

The mayor turned scarlet. He opened his mouth, but before anything came out, Caroline called from outside. "Dr. Miss! Is Steven with ya?"

"Come in, dear," Letty said. "I'm afraid he is. What happened tonight?"

"Miz Sauder took us to see the show. By'n by, the crowd pushed in, and Steven weren't no longer there. We been looking and looking, but there ain't no sign of him nowheres."

Eric gritted his teeth. Visitors by the trainload had bloated Hartville for the Silver Celebration, too many for the town to handle. The change in fortune had first brought sordid success to East Crawford Street, and now it could claim an innocent life.

"Too much too soon, Mayor, wouldn't you agree?" he asked.

"Don't start in on me again, Eric Wagner. I know what you think of Hartville's progress, but this is a separate matter altogether. You can't deny the benefits of the boom. The town nearly died sixteen years ago when yours and a few other families couldn't do more than scrabble a tough living with your stock. Tonight's accident is a separate matter altogether."

"I don't see how anyone can be so blind to the effects of greed." Eric congratulated himself on his even tone of voice.

The mayor now turned purple. "We can discuss this at a later time. As you said, I must return to my duties. Besides, as Dr. Morgan said, the kid probably won't make it through the night. It's just as well, too, I—"

"Aaah . . . !" Caroline flew at the mayor.

Eric silently praised her as he disengaged her fists from Osgood's gray hair, and if he read the look on Letty's face right, she agreed.

Letty went to the front and opened the door. "Kindly remove yourself from my home, Mayor Osgood. I'll consider it an honor and a privilege to help your opponent in the next election."

The mayor straightened his coat on his way out.

Caroline burst into tears, her sobs filling the air. Eric reached her first. He wrapped his arms around her and began to rock the two of them. "Come, come, *liebchen*," he said, patting the girl's heaving back. "You shouldn't listen to him."

Caroline's blue eyes met his. She muttered an oath.

"Caroline!" Letty cried. "Don't ever lower yourself to his filthy level. Why don't you go home with Mr. Wagner, dear? I'll take care of Steven. Believe me, I'll do everything possible for him through the night."

Eric took note of Letty's cautious words and recognized the gravity of the situation. "Where are the others?" he asked the girl.

"Miz Sauder took 'em home. She said I's to find Steven."

"Let's go, then." Eric turned to Letty and read fear in her gaze. "I'll come right back."

"No need," she said.

With a nod, he left, taking Caroline's cold hand in his, and headed toward Amos's livery.

"What's the matter, Mr. Wagner, sir?" Amos asked when he answered the knock.

Eric sent Caroline with the stable boy to fetch the rig, and as soon as she was out of earshot, he turned to his friend. "It seems I've done it again. I failed one more soul who depended on me."

Amos shook his head. "Don't tell me that, Eric. Yo're the most dependable man I seen in my days."

Bitter laughter roughened Eric's throat. "I fake it well, Amos."

"Cain't much fake honor an' decency. I seen enough of the other to know."

Eric's grip on his temper slid into oblivion. "You know I killed my wife and unborn child as if I'd used my own hands. I failed them when they needed me most." He ran his hands through his hair, then smoothed his mustache with his thumb and forefinger. "Then when I brought a lady doctor to town, I failed to protect her, too."

In his frustration, Eric walked away and gripped the porch balustrade. "Now the Pattersons. I tried to take care of them after their mother died." He shot his friend a glare. "See how well I did? They lost everything and became orphans in the bargain."

Shoving his hands into his trouser pockets, Eric stared down the street. All he saw were the condemning lanterns mocking him with the fire that had burned Steven.

"I left the children with Anna Sauder tonight, thinking she

could bring them to the fireworks. The streets grew crowded, Steven became separated from the others, someone pushed him into a lantern pole, and now he's hanging on to life by mere hope."

"Son," Amos said in his rich voice, "you gotta learn yourself somethin'. Somethin' I learned durin' the war. When I was made to watch them white men rape and kill my mother and sister, I cried. I told myself I was worthless. I done nothin' to stop them animals."

Eric recognized Amos's pain, but he had no words, no comfort for the man.

"Yessir, Eric, I couldn't do nothin'. See, I was tied to a tree while another of them whupped me." A lone drop glistened silver against Amos's earth-brown cheek. He stared at Eric, unashamed of his tears. "You listen here, son. Pastor Stone done told me this, and he told it good. The good Lord forgives, and so you gotta do it, too. 'Forgive, and y'all be forgiven,' the Good Book says. Forgive yourself. If you don't, Pastor says you as good as call God a liar. I ain't no fool, man. I don't call Him nothin' but Master."

Eric smiled at Amos's humble delivery of Scripture. "I'll think on it, Amos."

"Do that. And get yourself back to that purty lady doctor. That's where you belongs."

Eric waved at Amos, unwilling to respond, as he wasn't certain he could accept what the former slave had said. But on the way to the ranch, as Caroline dozed, his mind gnawed on Amos's words.

He remembered Pastor Stone's many sermons on forgiveness. And he knew the basis of the gospel of Christ. But was it really so? Could it be so simple as to accept Jesus' passion and death on the cross as atonement for his own sin? For the weakness that had led to two deaths?

Ever since Letty came to town, Eric had witnessed her strength and envied it. He'd admired her decisiveness, her certainty in her convictions. Now he wondered. Had she been strong, decisive, certain of herself or, rather, of the One she served?

After all, each time they'd argued, she'd made clear her actions came as a response to God's call on her life.

Just what had God called him to do? And had he been too mired in his guilt and self-recrimination to hear that call? Might he not be the failure he felt himself to be? Was there really hope even for him?

Could he still claim the hope he'd once learned was in Christ?

Once home, he dropped off his charge and asked Mrs. Sauder to elaborate on the events that had led to Steven's accident. Eric learned nothing more than what he already knew. Steven had been pushed away from her side by a large group of visitors. The crowd had apparently carried him along, and the boy had inadvertently been pushed into the lantern's post. The lantern fell, and he'd seen the results.

Minutes after arriving home with Caroline, Eric was back on his way to Letty's home. Again his mind returned to what Amos had said. Could it be as simple as that? Could he take God at His word and accept Jesus' atonement in his stead? Could God forgive him? Could he forgive himself and then get on with his life?

But how did a man truly forgive himself for repeated failure?

Looking up, he realized he'd arrived. Despite his gloomy thoughts, a pull deep inside drove him forward. Eric knew that once in Letty's presence, his pain would feel less sharp. He ran up the walk and onto her front stoop as if a throng of demons were behind him.

"Eric?" Letty called when he opened the door without knocking.

"Of course."

She emerged from the examining room, wiping her hands on a white towel. "I told you there was no need for you to return."

"I know. I heard you. There was a need. There's no reason for you to go through this alone. I want to be here with you."

"For Steven's sake."

About to correct her, he thought better of it. "For Steven's sake."

Letty returned to her patient's side, not sparing so much as another look in Eric's direction. Fine. He didn't need her to chat with him. He just needed to be here for her, for himself. Perhaps it was time he spoke with God again.

He strode into the waiting room, picked up a chair, and brought it into the clinic. There he stopped her objection with a glower. "Not a word. I'm here, and here I'm staying."

He made himself as comfortable as possible, considering his long frame and the nature of the discarded dining-suite chair. He propped his left ankle on his right knee, set to watch the good doctor work.

After a bit, she said, "Since you're still there, could you please hand me the jar of Cantharis? I must dose Steven again."

He obliged then sat back as she dissolved three medicated balls and spooned the liquid into Steven's slack mouth.

Each of her gestures was as familiar as her sweet face. The way she cocked her head to consider something, her movements light and very much like those of a bird. The way she used her hands, skillfully, economically. The straight line of her spine lent a spare quality to her steps. This woman wasted no time on mincing steps or swaying hips. No, Letitia Morgan was innately feminine and always straightforward.

Despite the trouble brought down upon her by the more ignorant residents of the town, Letty was a success unto herself. Whereas he—

No, he wouldn't go into that again. Not when he had other matters to contemplate. Like the curls that escaped her elegant coiffure to trail at the nape of her slender neck. And the way the blue of her gown showed off the cream of her skin.

He smiled at the irony. He'd finally realized how desperately he needed her, and at nearly the same moment, an oversight on his part had led to Steven's accident. He should never have gone to the ball. He should have stayed with the children and Mrs. Sauder, bringing them to the fireworks himself.

Again, because he'd failed to act as he should, a child could lose his life. A child he'd come to love. If only he had the right—

"I want to thank you for what you did tonight," Letty said, breaking into his thoughts. "You were magnificent."

Eric looked up without a clue as to what he'd done.

"You may have saved his life. Fear held me back, and Steven might have died waiting for me to remember that God's love casts out all fear. Even if I'd reached him, I was so shaken that I might have done him more harm than good. And probably injured myself at the same time. What you did was heroic."

Fighting his urge to refute her words, Eric nodded, accepting her gratitude. But . . . heroic?

He watched her straight back as she checked Steven's pulse, the child still tenacious in his grip on life.

"No change," she murmured for his benefit.

Closing his eyes, he leaned his head back. He hadn't been heroic. He'd simply done what needed to be done. He'd put out the fire burning Steven's garments and kept Letty from hurting herself. Was practicality heroic?

He opened his eyes and caught the gleam of the lamp near the examining table. It burned steadily, comfortably, giving off its clear light, illuminating the room. It could burn and savage, too.

The lamplight seemed to Eric very much like love. It gave light but could just as easily char everything to stark darkness. Such was love; love gave life and just as easily crushed the life it gave. At least his did.

He'd loved Martina, but his love for her had nearly crushed the life out of him. He'd also borne the guilt for her death, but if what Letty, Amos, Pastor Stone, and God's Word itself had said were true, then perhaps he needn't shoulder that burden.

Perhaps he wasn't responsible for what had happened. He had tried to provide his wife with the best care possible. Martina had refused to let Melvin Harrison see her. He'd done everything in his power, everything he could control. His wife had rejected the medical care he'd tried to provide, and he hadn't wanted to force it on her against her will. An honorable man never forced his will upon another, just as God gave His children the gift of choice, the right to sin or not.

Perhaps he hadn't been quite so despicable when he'd held back his insistence, when he'd realized how weak arguing made Martina, leaving her ever more distraught.

Thinking through all the layers of blame he'd heaped upon himself, Eric realized he'd tried to assume others' accountability. He couldn't have forced Horace Patterson to change his ways; Slosh had made his own destructive decisions. He couldn't have forced the townspeople to accept Letty's actions any more than he could have kept her from following her conscience. And he couldn't have controlled the crowd tonight. Even if he'd been at the boy's side, he still could have been helpless to prevent the accident.

In the dark hours before dawn, Eric saw himself as Letty did. It was as if someone had turned the key on the lamp in his heart. No, not someone. Something. Love now lit his heart.

He, Eric Karl Wagner, had indeed jumped in and protected both Steven and Letty. The light inside him grew brighter. His thoughts turned back to when he'd held her for the duration of a magical waltz. He remembered his feelings when she'd pulled out of his arms. Had he not attended the ball, he might never have realized the depth of his love for her.

Now he knew what Scripture meant when it said that perfect love casts out all fear. Puny and imperfect though his was in comparison to the Almighty's, his love had made him act. He'd saved Steven and protected Letty without a thought to his fears, without a thought to his past. How much stronger, more decisive, more courageous might he be if he accepted Jesus' sacrifice, God's precious forgiveness? If he forgave himself for being a mere man?

Now he understood what Amos had meant. Forgiving himself would be a matter of constantly remembering Jesus' love for him, the Lord's willingness to suffer on that cross so that he, Eric Karl Wagner, might be reconciled to the Father in heaven. He wasn't perfect. He couldn't fix or even control the world around him. His guilt lay in his efforts to do just that.

In the stark hours of dawn, in Letty's little clinic, Eric turned from the lamp and sought the woman who'd led him back to the one true Light of his heart. Feeling freer than he had in years, he allowed a smile to curve his lips.

His love for Letty had taught him to hope again, and that hope had led him to renewed life in Jesus Christ.

18

After Steven's accident two weeks earlier, Eric's behavior began to change. Suddenly, it seemed as if he was always . . . there. No matter where Letty went or what she did, Eric was nearby, his intense, dark eyes upon her.

She had no idea what his constant presence meant. Perhaps he didn't trust her to take proper care of Steven. She'd seen ample evidence of the love between Eric and all the Patterson scamps. But if that German blockhead thought for one moment that she'd let anything preventable happen to those children, then . . . well, then he was duller than a butter knife's edge. She loved them as much as he did.

"We shall see what he says when he sees how much Steven's wounds have improved," she muttered, closing a container of Calendula ointment. The boy's recovery had progressed so well that she was taking him and a supply of remedies back to Eric's home. Steven would fare well in the homey cheer that now filled the large ranch house.

Earlier that day, she'd brought her buggy from Amos's place and had left Prince tethered to the post out front. After closing her satchel, she took it to the vehicle and then made a pallet for Steven on the floor.

Back inside, she helped her patient prepare for his journey. "Glad to be going home, aren't you?"

"Yes, ma'am," answered Steven, enthusiasm in his blue eyes. Letty smiled, thankful he'd been most severely burned on the more discreet parts of his body. His face had been spared serious scarring.

After settling the boy in his temporary bed, Letty took up the reins and set Prince to a fast trot. Occasional glances at Steven told her he wanted to get there quickly. She couldn't blame him; she was taking him to Eric's home, to everything she herself held dear. If only—

Oh, stop it! She'd begun to seek a position in towns without medical care. The chapter of her life reserved for Hartville had almost ended. It hurt plenty to leave behind the love of her life; to also leave the Pattersons would take all her willpower. The children had stolen her heart from the moment she'd set eyes on Steven. Leaving them hurt nearly as much as losing Eric. At least she could take comfort in knowing she wouldn't leave them alone. Eric meant to keep them together and at his side, at least until a family for all five was found. They would be fine. She ought not torture herself with "if onlys" and "what ifs" any longer.

As she pulled up to the barn, Letty didn't indulge in the bittersweet pleasure of admiring the ranch house. Steven's welcoming committee set up an instant clamor, offering her a welcome diversion. She laughed for the first time in a long, long while.

🍂

Eric found Letty surrounded by children, laughing, and if he were granted the honor, he would make sure she remained like that for the rest of her life.

He approached the buggy. "The wounded warrior returns in a blaze of glory, I see. May I have the honor of escorting him to his quarters?"

Letty turned, and in that first instant, Eric thought he saw love and longing in her gaze, but he blinked, and by then she'd shuttered her eyes. He didn't at all like that, and he made up his mind never to let it happen again. He planned instead to make joy and laughter permanent in the life of the woman who, with her heart-healing love, had shown him the way out of the depths of his pain.

". . . just don't press against the large burn on his right side," she said, and Eric realized she'd answered his question while he'd envisioned their future.

He would have to take care of Steven before he could claim Letty's full attention, and he was selfish enough to want the woman he loved to concentrate on him, and him alone, when he asked her to become his wife.

"Of course I'll be careful, Letty. Aren't I careful, children?"

"Yes, Mr. Eric." The voices sounded as one, but the giggles that followed ruined the charming effect.

He reached into the buggy and gathered Steven to his chest. For a moment, he just held the boy, relishing his even breaths, his steady heartbeat, his renewed life. He was glad he would never again live through the night when Steven nearly died.

"I'm so glad you're healing, son," he said. "So very glad."

As he went back to Steven's room, Eric felt Letty follow him with her gaze. He didn't pause to look at her. He knew that if he did, he might lose sight of Steven's need for bed rest and leave the boy to manage on the front room settee. Then he'd sweep the pretty doctor straight to Silver Creek Church.

❦

Letty paused on the porch before entering Eric's home. The memories of her last visit here were, at the very least, daunting. She squared her shoulders and stepped up to the threshold, but before she went any farther, the arrival of a horse and buggy caught her attention.

Dismay made Letty's already wobbly composure falter. Emmaline Whitehall descended from the conveyance with a brown paper–wrapped parcel in hand. "Dr. Morgan! A moment of your time, if you please."

Letty hoisted her chin upward. "Of course."

"I heard about the boy. How you saved his life." A patch of red stained each of Emmaline's hollow cheeks. "Here," she said, thrusting the package at Letty. "I thought you might give him this to pass the time. You likely have all you can do to keep the lad in bed, and I hoped to help."

Letty caressed the rough wrapping, her gaze on the schoolmarm's flustered features. Emmaline had brought more than a gift for Steven; her white flag of peace had come wrapped in brown paper. "Thank you so much. I can use all the help anyone cares to offer."

The older woman took a step back from Letty and then studied the ranch house. A suspicious shine glossed her eyes, and she nodded. "You'll do," she said. Then she hurried to her buggy without acknowledging Letty's good-bye.

Letty's eyelids prickled with emotion, and she hugged Steven's gift to her heart. One more person had acknowledged her adequacy. Randy, the Stones, Elsa Richards and her brood, and now Emmaline had accepted her. It wasn't enough to change her mind about her future, but their acceptance offered comfort she would carry with her to her new home. Wherever that chanced to be.

Buoyed by her personal triumph, Letty followed Eric and Steven. She found them in the boy's room, preparing the patient for a much-needed rest. Caroline, Amelia, Suzannah, and baby Willy were justifiably reluctant to leave their brother's side.

"Here," she said, giving Steven Emmaline's gift. "Miss Whitehall brought this for you. She thought you might enjoy it."

The boy ripped off the covering and found an illustrated copy of *Hans Christian Andersen's Fairy Tales.* "An appropriate gift from a librarian, wouldn't you say?" Letty asked as she put away the sickroom supplies she'd brought.

ॐ

While the children studied the pictures in Steven's new book, Eric admired Letty's movements. Efficient as always, she soon had the room arranged to her purposes. She smoothed the boy's hair off his brow, plumped up a pillow behind him, and asked how he felt.

"'M burnin', Dr. Miss. Feels like ants is crawlin' on my burns. Hurts more'n I can tell."

"Yes, well, Steven, I understand," she said. "But it's best if you say that you feel *as though* ants *are* crawling on your burns." She caught Eric's smile and added, "Don't you dare laugh. Something must be done about their language."

"Yes, ma'am," he said, solemn as an undertaker.

With dignity, she returned to her patient. "Since you're right by it," she said to Eric as she helped Steven sip fresh water, "please take the vial of Hypericum from my bag. The injured nerves are causing him pain, and he needs relief to rest."

Eric obeyed, glad to have her in his home again. She dropped three pellets under Steven's tongue, made him comfortable, and shooed the others off to play. She took the baby from Caroline and, crooning, carried him to his bed. After changing the little one's diapers, she settled him in for a nap.

Eric saw his opportunity. "I need to speak with you," he said. "Privately, so I waited until you'd seen to the children. Please come with me to the front room."

Apprehension filled her eyes. She squared her shoulders and shot her chin up. "Of course," she said in a wobbly voice.

Eric led her to the settee, yet he remained standing. Questions flew from her eyes, and the moment was his. He tried to remember what he'd planned to say, but nothing eloquent came to him.

"You were right," he finally burst out, and he cringed at his clumsiness.

"How so?"

He sat at her side and took her hand. "This isn't easy, Letty. Please bear with me. When we spoke about Martina, you said I bore no guilt in her death, and in the strictest sense, you were right. After my family fell apart, I tried to control the world around me to try to make the outcome of any event sure. But I couldn't force a doctor on Martina, just as I couldn't force Slosh to be the father the children needed. I couldn't even close the brothels and clean up the town."

In her eyes he read sadness, sadness he'd caused. "I realize now that I could no more force you to betray your conscience than I could force the town to accept your commitment to helping the girls. Folks have to find the merit in your actions on their own. Just as I did."

Their nearness turned into a torture of the sweetest sort. Eric longed to hold her, kiss her, make her promise she'd marry him, but he had more to say, none of it easy. A maddening whiff of violets teased him, and he rubbed his thumb across her palm. Letty's shiver gave him the courage he needed to go on.

"All this became clear when I tried to take the blame for Steven's accident simply because I'd gone to the ball. The mayor came second in accusing me of negligence, but then you called me a hero, and negligence isn't heroic. The more I thought, the more I saw how I'd tried to control my world, to control even you. I was wrong."

Letty dropped his hand and curved her palm around his jaw. "Oh, Eric, don't paint me so honorably," she said. "When I saw Steven burning on the ground, I froze and my prided self-sufficiency vanished. God used that moment to show me my headstrong ways. Instead of depending on Him, I'd often say I did but then ran off to act as I pleased without waiting for His guidance."

She stood and began to pace. "It's no wonder I felt lonely for so long. The Father would grant me the help I'd asked for, but if it came in a form I didn't particularly like, why, then I rejected it as an attempt to thwart my obedience to His calling."

"But—"

"Please let me finish. This isn't easy for me, either."

She stopped wearing a path on Eric's rug, but she kept her back to him. He stood, needing to bridge the distance, but her words brought him up short.

"You were quite right in warning me," she said, and he knew how much the admission had to cost her. "Although my intentions were good, my actions often placed me at the center of a storm. I never considered that the Lord might have been using you to speak to me, to caution me against my tendency to follow my will or my emotions instead of accepting wise counsel."

She looked over her shoulder. "Yes, from even you."

Her rueful smile beckoned him, and he went to her side.

She hadn't finished, however, but wrung her hands and took a deep breath. "Now," she said, "the very folk I came to care for, the expectant mothers, their children, the poor in town, the most vulnerable of all, are either forbidden or unwilling to come see me. I have indeed endangered their well-being."

Eric took hold of her fidgety hands. "I remember you telling me once that I judged myself too harshly," he said. "I've learned I did exactly that, and also blinded myself to God's precious forgiveness. Now I try to remember Jesus' sacrifice each time the darkness returns. I can't bear to see you suffer the same way I did."

Letty shook her head. "The difference, Eric, is that I am guilty. I'm as headstrong as you said I was. Whenever I decided to follow my heart, I'd put on blinders. I shouldn't have taken on the entire town like that. All I did was put myself out of work and risk the lives of others."

Eric slipped his arm around her shoulders and pulled her close. At first she resisted, then with a sigh, she allowed the intimacy.

"Don't change, Letitia Morgan," he whispered into the hair at her temple. "People like you, those who listen to their hearts, who hear God's call upon them, are the ones who bring about change."

The contact must have moved her as much as it did him, for another tremor ran through her. "Come," he said. "There's something I want to show you. Something you must see."

༜

Letty wondered what he was up to now, but his expression gave nothing away. He led her down the hall and stopped at the first door. Baby Karl's room.

"Eric, no. You don't have to—"

He placed a finger on her lips. The contact was sweet, yet it sent heat through her veins.

"Hush," he said, nudging her into the room. She closed her eyes but stumbled over her feet in her reluctance to again experience the anguish inside.

He walked around from behind her and chuckled. Letty kept her eyes closed tight. With a finger at her chin, he lifted her face. "Open your eyes, little bird. I brought you here so you could see something, not so you could shut out what I'm trying to say."

Letty cracked her lids a tiny bit. Then her eyes flew open. The last time she'd seen the room, the shutters had been latched, allowing scant light to filter through the curtains.

She turned her head one way then the other. She couldn't stop a surprised "Oh!"

The windows were open, and crisp, white curtains wafted in and out on the spring breeze. Where dust had covered the furniture, today the wood boasted a liberal application of lemon oil. And where a sad cradle, an unused dresser, and a lonely rocking horse had once stood, the room now held shelf upon shelf of medical texts, a cabinet stocked with amber remedy jars, and an enormous desk with myriad cubbyholes beckoning her to fill them with her notes.

"Do you like it?" Eric asked, urgency in his voice. "Could you work in an office like this?"

Letty nodded, keeping the slightest hint of hope from swelling inside her.

Eric took her hands and brought them to his lips. He kissed her palms and then folded her fingers over them. Pulling her closer, he tucked her hands against his heart. His tenderness brought tears to her eyes and hope to her heart.

"Are you willing to take on a crotchety, widowed newspaperman?" he asked. "For life? I love you, you know."

She gasped. Tears spilled onto her cheeks. "Eric . . . ?"

"Yes, *liebling,* will you marry me?"

More tears careened down her face. She nodded, then said, "No."

"What? You won't marry me? Why not?"

"Oh, Eric," she cried. "It's not that I don't want to, because I do. It's just that I—I can't. Not while I'm in the shadow of scandal. I hate what that could do to you, your newspaper, your standing in the town you love so much."

He ran his hands through his hair, then smoothed his mustache. "Scandal means nothing to me," he said. "The newspaper can deal with controversy, and if this town doesn't like the woman I marry, well, then, that's just too bad. They're not the ones who'll take you into their home. It's me, and that's where you belong—in my home and in my heart."

"Perhaps, but not while I can cause you trouble."

Determination burned in his eyes. "Fine. If that's the way you must have it, then fine. But you can say yes to my proposal."

When she didn't answer, he persisted. "It's a matter of solving a problem, not that you won't marry me. Right?"

In that one final word, Letty learned the depth of Eric's vulnerability, the power of his need, and she couldn't find it in herself to deny him further. "I love you, Eric."

"As the Lord in heaven is my witness, Letty, I love you, too."

Strong arms swept around her. The tears of moments ago returned, only this time they came with joy. Eric pulled away to look at her, and as she met his gaze, she saw matching dampness on his lashes. So much loneliness had been banished by such few, precious words. Such a future opened up before them by the power of those words.

He brought his lips to hers and, with infinite gentleness, kissed her. His mouth pressed against hers, touching, warming, loving her with a new sense of rightness, a sense of belonging such as Letty had never known. A sigh escaped at the exquisite feelings Eric sent through her. He loved her.

She pulled her lips from him. "You honestly want to marry an unwomanly woman? A female physician?"

Eric laughed. "Letty, if you were any more woman, I might not be able to handle you. How in the world did you form such an absurd image of yourself?"

"My mother always said I was a sorry excuse for a woman. I didn't see the point to delicate embroidery, nor did I possess the tact she thought so valuable in dealing with society. It struck me more like hypocrisy. I was a trial to her, an inconvenience. So you see, Eric, a man in your position should consider the social liability in marrying what many see as an unnatural woman, certainly one who speaks her mind regardless of how others might view her opinion."

Eric's laughter roared. "If that's your way of scaring me off, you've failed. I've dealt with all that since the day I launched my campaign to bring a female doctor to town. You're no inconvenience to me. Remember who built your shelves. I love who you are—you, the talented, courageous, and forthright Dr. Letitia Morgan."

When he again reached for her, Letty flew into his embrace. With her head against his chest, she felt the rumble of his words.

"It's that honesty of yours that broke through my shell of self-pity. Don't change—or only your name. Please become Mrs. Wagner. Don't take away the light you brought back to my heart."

Letty smiled through her tears, then lifted her chin. "Yes, Eric, I'll become Mrs. Wagner. As soon as the scandal is past."

"Blast the scandal with dynamite—"

"No, Eric. I now accept that my mother was right. The perception of those around us matters. She did say that due to my unladylike behavior, men would see me as good for meeting only certain . . . needs. In fact, a while back a man in Philadelphia began to show interest in me, interest that I returned. But Mother must have been right, since when I continued my studies, he stopped coming around. Less than a year ago he married a pristine debutante."

෭

At Letty's mention of a former suitor, Eric felt indignation fly up from his gut. How dare the fool judge her inadequate? Then he smiled in triumph. It was just as well that the man had. Letty was meant for him, for Eric Wagner, and for no one else.

Her sad, sweet voice went on. "Here in Hartville, my stubbornness made matters worse. I don't regret fighting for the girls, but my curiosity made me ignore your advice, and I followed you to Bessie's Barn that night. It's no wonder many lump me with Bessie's girls. No lady would be present at that moment. Mother predicted my future quite accurately."

"And blast them, too—"

"Hush, Eric. Listen to me, please. You're a wonderful man, very influential, too. You need a lady, a woman who can share your prominent position. Why, Mother gave up having me join her and Father when company came for supper. My conversation wasn't suitable for proper guests. I'd rather die than embarrass you any more."

"Hogwash! Your mother was wrong. Most likely your intelligence surpassed hers, and she couldn't appreciate your talents. That was her loss, not a failing on your part.

"As far as a man is concerned," he added, grasping her determined chin, "a woman as strong as you is quite exciting, and a mature man relishes the challenge you pose. At least, I do."

His finger against her lips stopped her response. Her eyes widened at his impassioned words.

"Your mother and all the others are mistaken. You're more woman than those silly chits who know nothing more than curling their hair or the latest style of bustle. I admire you, respect you, and want you in every way a man wants a woman. I want you for my wife, the mother of my children, and the lover in my bed. Your mother's bias belongs to the past. You and I have a future to share."

Tears of joy filled Letty's eyes, tears that Eric felt honor-bound to kiss away. Those kisses led to others, delicious caresses that momentarily made him forget they had a house full of children. He asked her to set a date. She refused.

"When the gossip dies," she argued. "When scandal doesn't taint me."

❦

No matter what he said or did, Letty wouldn't budge. He scheduled his days so he could spend as much time as possible pressing his suit. To no avail.

Days turned into weeks. Letty remained unmoved.

Many in town had noted her tenacious care of Steven. Pastor Stone sang her praises from the pulpit, and patients began trickling back. No one disputed her medical talents; Letitia Morgan's worth shone through despite the hypocrisy of certain residents of the town.

Eric didn't know how to make Letty see the change. He couldn't take her from house to house for personal apologies. And he was fast losing patience. He wanted her for a wife, and he wanted her now.

A month after he'd proposed, Eric sat at his desk at the newspaper office, gnawing on the wood casing of a pencil and pondering his predicament. All that time wasted and they still stood at an impasse. He couldn't sleep for seeking a solution, and work failed to hold his interest. A paper range had grown on his desk, nearly burying his hapless typewriter.

The typewriter! Perhaps it would help him reach Dr. Letitia Morgan-soon-to-be-Wagner.

Now that Mortimer Medford was awaiting trial, Eric knew he could take on Hartville's outmoded attitudes, and now he could win. He swept the papers out of his way, sending loose sheets through the air. With his hands poised over the keys, he thought for a moment. Once his ideas came together, his fingers rapped out a furious rhythm.

SELFLESS CARING, GIFTED HEALING
Dr. Letitia Morgan Battles Death for Child

The morning's editorial soon took shape, followed by the one for Sunday's edition.

PUBLISHER ADMITS ERROR
Children in Brothels: A Town's Lack of Love

A satisfied publisher closed the *Hartville Day*'s offices that Friday afternoon. Eric felt that his persuasive description of Letty's fight for Steven's life would make even the hardest-hearted in town give her another chance. His public admission of error regarding the youngest soiled doves would play music to Letty's heart.

Debating whether to stop by her home and visit, Eric paused at the corner of Willow and Main. He remembered the day he saw Daisy run in to visit Letty. She'd even been right about the girl. Daisy was hardworking, efficient, and clever with words. She'd become vital to the office, and now Eric lived in dread of the day Ford would marry her. Not that Ford had said anything about marriage, but from the looks they sent each other, it was only a matter of time before Eric lost his best employee to his best reporter.

He decided to put off his visit until the morning paper came out.

Whistling, he stopped at the livery, collected his mares, and headed home. As he pulled in, he paused to count his blessings. The ranch, although small, was thriving. From the looks of the smudges of dirt on Amelia's face as she dashed behind a heavily laden rosebush, the Patterson brood was blooming, too. Making certain Steven rested sufficiently had become a daily battle. Eric couldn't wait until Letty joined them and became the one to run herd and wipe the grime off those mischievous faces.

Each time he thought of the children, a pang struck his gut. What if Douglas found a family to adopt them? What if he lost them?

"Mister Eric! Yo're home!" He looked at Suzannah's sweet face, and his heart turned a somersault. Why did he have to lose them?

He vaulted from the carriage, threw the reins on the seat, and tossed the little girl through the air. "And how is my *liebchen?*"

Her blue eyes sparkled as she giggled. *"Sehr gut,"* she answered, thrilling him with her newest language skill.

He set her down, and she grabbed his hand, tugging him toward the barn. *"Kommen Sie mit mir,"* she said, insisting he accompany her. When they reached Heidi's corner, she showed Eric where she'd set out the stool and pail. She smiled. "I'm ready."

"Go on, then."

Suzannah had taken to starting his evenings with the ritual of milking Heidi, and the otherwise ornery nanny goat seemed to bask in the child's attention. Suzie's little fingers fought to extract thin streams of the rich milk. She soon turned, beamed her bright smile at him, and, following their standard pattern, announced, "Yore turn."

She bounced off the stool, and once Eric sat down, she slipped in between his knees to lay her head back against his shoulder and watch. He reached for Heidi's udder and began to milk the goat in earnest. When he was done, Suzie turned around and threw her arms around his neck. "I love you," she whispered.

Eric's heart swelled with emotion. "I love you, too, Suzie." He kissed her, pressing his cheek against her silky hair.

"If you love me and I love you, can you be my papa?"

Could he? Had he really let the Lord free him from his bondage to the past? Was he finally free to marry Letty and live the life he so wanted? Was he the father Suzie and the others needed?

Wanting and wondering, a sudden flash of clarity showed him the flaw in his final set of fears. He realized that with baby Karl, he couldn't have done a thing to keep his son. The unborn child's life had been in Martina's control. This time, the fate of Caroline, Steven, Amelia, Suzie, and Willy lay in his hands. Only he could decide if he would be, as Suzie had just asked, their father.

The decision was his, and the almighty Father's. Could that be the joy God held for him at the end of his long night of sorrow? Peace suffused him with a richness and certainty he'd never felt. He closed his eyes.

"Thank you, Father," he whispered. He cupped Suzie's chin. "I am, *liebchen*. I already am your papa."

After cleaning the milking equipment and storing Heidi's contribution for the day, Eric set off to satisfy the desires of at least two of the most important females in his life. Suzie held his heart in the palm of her grubby hand. Her softly voiced question sent him running to Douglas Carlson's house after hours.

In all honesty, Eric had to admit to an additional reason for his haste. Another softly voiced question required his response. Another feminine voice, one with the power to bring to him either happiness or sadness, had posed a similar question once before. His heart told him that if he failed to correctly answer Letty's and Suzie's questions, seven lives would be filled with sadness.

"Couldn't I keep them?" she'd asked. At that time, Eric had been forced to speak of the children's father. This time, he had the power to grant her heart's desire.

After a hurried ride into town, Eric leaped from his rig and pounded the Carlsons' brass door knocker. When Douglas responded, Eric strode in, his steps strong with determination. "I'm keeping them," he said. "All five of them."

"The Pattersons? Do you know what you're doing?"

"Never more," he answered, certainty warming his heart. "Has another family tried to adopt them?"

Douglas shook his head. "You know the answer to that. No one is willing to take five half-grown delinquents."

"Watch your words, counselor. Those are my children."

"You really are serious."

"As a parson."

Douglas removed his spectacles from the bridge of his nose and rubbed the slight indentation there. An owlish look to him, he studied Eric. Eric didn't care how long his friend stared at him. He was willing to stand under close scrutiny until those five imps became his. His and Letty's.

His expression must have satisfied Douglas, who nodded and smiled wanly. "Here I thought I was brave with one on the way. You're taking on a full regiment! Come on, let's start the paperwork."

Over cups of steaming coffee, attorney and client accomplished the best thing that ever happened to those five neglected children.

By the time he left the Carlson residence, with Randy's vow not to breathe a word of his surprise to Letty, Eric felt certain he would soon be a married man. As he drove past the corner of Willow and Main, he knew he was unable to see Letty and not tell her about the adoption. So he went home to spend another night dreaming of the day when she'd be at his side when morning came.

When he awoke, he knew that tomorrow he'd see Letty and reveal his plans. He spent the day working around the ranch and playing with the children, enjoying them even more than before. He especially relished hearing Suzie call him Papa.

When Ford came to relate the town's favorable response to his piece on Letty, Eric sent her a message. He would stop by in the morning so they could all attend Sunday worship together. Once she saw the town's renewed acceptance at church, he would break the news about the children.

As usual, he helped Caroline put the younger ones to bed. The joy in Suzie's candy-sweet kiss would stay with him the rest of his life. Amelia no longer scuttled away when he came near, and Steven asked if he, too, could call him Papa.

"I am your papa now." Joy brought tears to his eyes. "And soon Dr. Morgan will become your mother. What do you think of that, son?"

Steven's eyes grew large, and he let a whoop rip from his lips. His approval brought the two older girls running into his room. Eric reassured them and then asked them the same question. In their unique ways, each answered similarly.

When the house teemed with the night's peace, Eric sat on the settee, missing Letty more than ever. His Bible in hand, he noticed how the lamplight brightened everything in the room, seeming to illuminate it from inside. Just as Letty glowed with the love in her heart. Just as his heart now guided him with the light of God's love.

He set the Bible on the lodgepole table next to his armchair and leaned his head back on the leather upholstery. Life had begun to feel quite good, indeed. All he needed for complete contentment was the silver-eyed dove at his side.

The clopping of horse hooves broke the haze created by his pleasant fantasy. He found Ford coming up the porch steps.

"What brings you out at this time?" he asked, worried that something might have happened to Letty.

Ford's spectacles slid to his upper lip. He shoved them back, further smearing the mess of ink on his nose. "I thought you might want to see the first copy of tomorrow morning's edition."

Eric searched his mind for possible problems that might have cropped up. He found none. "Let me see the thing. Here I was finally settling down to a well-earned rest . . ."

His words trailed off as he opened the paper. His editorial confessing to his wrong response to Letty's mission took up half the page. That didn't steal his voice, but next to his piece, in bold print, Ford had published a most outrageous letter.

```
To the editor:

After much careful consideration, this mule-
headed doctor capitulates. You were right,
sir. It is a mere matter of solving a problem.
One we can best tackle together.

Therefore, with due respect and honor, I
accept your proposal of marriage.

Yours,

Dr. Letitia Morgan
```

☙

The torrent of German outside her door announced her betrothed's arrival. Smiling with mischief, Letty opened the door.

In he stalked, waving his arms. "You contrary woman, you. You're likely to be the death of me one day."

He stormed into the waiting room and paced its short length. "I never loaned you that blasted typewriter for you to make public every last bit of correspondence we exchange. Why didn't you come to the ranch to tell me you'd finally stopped being stubborn?"

Lifting a shoulder, Letty smiled even more.

"Furthermore, how dare you pry newspaper information from my employees? They never should have revealed the contents of my editorial. There is such a thing as journalistic privilege and protection for a source."

Eric was growing pompous again. Perching on the least uncomfortable of the six chairs in the waiting room, Letty suppressed a laugh, although her smile never faltered. "I felt that since I'll soon be your wife, I should take greater interest in your business."

Her soon-to-be-husband glared in response. She had gone a bit far, but it had been worth it. He'd been so noble confessing his errors in public that with Daisy's and Ford's help, she'd matched his gesture. Now, the poor man didn't know how to contain his irritation.

Letty knew just what to do. She stood and reached up to stroke his golden hair. His pacing stopped.

"Eric," she said. "Let's not quibble. We have a lifetime of happiness to plan."

She watched the thrilling transformation. The chocolate brown of his irises gave way to the deepest darkness.

"Is the waiting finally over?"

"Yes, it's over."

"Why?"

She stood on tiptoe and placed a featherlight kiss on his lips. "Because, my darling man, when you stripped yourself of all pride and wrote that article for my sake, I realized that nothing mattered so much but that God had brought us together, and nothing else should keep us apart. Not the town's opinions, not a scandal, nothing. He will be faithful to help us overcome all those. I was wrong to place such significance on those matters."

"I'm hardly that noble," he said. "My selfishness inspired that editorial. I'm ready to do whatever it takes to have you as my wife."

As he spoke, Eric remembered saying similar words earlier—to Douglas. He'd best tell Letty she was about to become the mother of five wild urchins, before she imagined their married life a paradise for two. "Ah . . . Letty?"

"Yes?"

"There's one other thing you should know."

"And that is . . . ?"

"Well, I just couldn't let anything happen to them, and since I know how much you care for them, and because I love them myself . . ." Eric ran his hand through his hair, thinking over what he'd said. "Blast, but I sound like Ford!"

"I noticed."

"Well, they're ours. All of them. And you'd better like it, because I refuse to quibble about it."

She reached a finger to his mustache, then feathered her touch onto his lips. "I know," she said.

"You know? How could you? They promised not to tell."

Letty's finger followed the angle of his cheekbone. "I don't know who promised what, but I've known all along that the man I love would never let anything harm those children. You love our five rapscallions too much to leave them unprotected in this fallen world. I presume you've spoken to Douglas about the adoption."

Her trust stole his ability to speak, to think. He could only feel, and he felt humbled. Letty loved him. She trusted him to be the man he wanted to be, the man she needed. With her at his side, her faith behind him, he could be just that—a family man, a man of God.

For a moment he treasured the emotion in his heart. Then he saw the lamp in the corner of the room. Its flame glowed, steady and clear, illuminating their surroundings. For the first time ever, he recognized the corresponding glow within his heart. Tears of joy welled in his eyes, tears of love.

"I'm yours," he whispered into Letty's violet-scented hair. "You led me back to God, and He gave me life again. Now I'm His . . . and yours."

"As am I, my love."

"That you are, light of my heart."

Ginny Aiken, a former newspaper reporter, lives in Pennsylvania with her engineer husband and their four sons. Born in Havana, Cuba, and raised in Valencia and Caracas, Venezuela, she discovered books at an early age. She wrote her first novel at age fifteen during downtime from the Ballets de Caracas, later to become the Venezuelan National Ballet. She is now the author of fifteen published works.

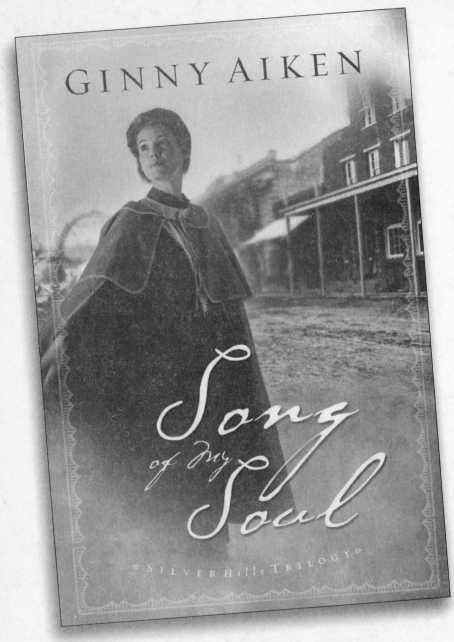

GINNY AIKEN

Song of My Soul

SILVER HILLS TRILOGY

Coming in June 2004

Excerpt from

Song of My Soul

Adrian Gamble wasn't his name, but it was the one he was willing to use.

He led his horse down Hartville's main street, taking note of the sights and sounds it offered. On either side, solid buildings had replaced the ramshackle structures he'd expected to find in the mining town. Evidently, the residents had found a good enough living here and decided to stay. They'd established permanent homes and businesses and looked to be thriving.

He hoped he'd live long enough to do the same.

As had become his habit, he glanced over his shoulder and to either side, checking to see if any familiar face followed in his wake. He prayed every minute of every day for the Lord to keep him safe from his pursuers.

He hoped out-of-the-way Hartville and its established mining company would provide a measure of anonymity.

A wooden sign in the window of a plain, whitewashed storefront on the right side of the street told him he'd reached his second-to-last destination for the day. Douglas Carlson, attorney-at-law, did business within.

"Good afternoon," he said to the bespectacled and serious man he found shuffling papers just inside the door. "I'm looking for Mr. Carlson."

"You've found him. And you are . . . ?"

He bit his tongue to keep the dangerous name from popping forth. "Gamble," he said. "I'm Adrian Gamble, and I'm here to finalize my purchase of the Hart of Silver Mining Company."

A flicker of interest showed from behind the glass lenses as the lawyer extended his hand. "Pleased to make your acquaintance. I've been looking forward to this day."

"So have I," Adrian answered, returning the firm clasp. *But for very different reasons,* his conscience taunted. He ignored the irritating taskmaster, well aware that subterfuge was his only hope at present.

"Please, follow me." Carlson gestured toward the open doorway at the left side of the room. "My secretary, who's gone to Denver for a family funeral, prepared all the documents you need to sign. I have them at my desk."

The attorney closed the door to the simple but attractive office. "Do take a seat," he added, pointing to the comfortable-looking leather armchair in front of his neat desk.

"Ah," Adrian said as he sank into it. "It's a pleasure to sit in something other than a saddle after riding a ways."

Carlson grinned. "There's a reason trains are such popular means of travel from practically any part of the country."

Adrian didn't take the bait. He had no intention of revealing his departure point or explaining his reasons for avoiding crowds. "So you say everything is in order."

Carlson's eyes again gleamed, this time to broadcast that little escaped his notice. Adrian would have to remember that in the future and guard his tongue.

"Everything from the deed to the property to the general store and its inventory, as well as the Harts' former home and all its furnishing. You only need to sign and assume the reins."

Adrian allowed himself a satisfied smile. "I'll also need to gather the two boxes I shipped ahead in care of the company. Would they still be at the train station?"

The lawyer pushed a pen-and-inkwell stand toward Adrian and handed him a sheaf of papers. "No. I decided it made more sense if everything was delivered to the General Store, since the porters know to take all mine company supplies there."

With conscious effort, Adrian avoided signing the wrong name on the deed. His man in Virginia had assured him he would be the owner of the mine and all the other company property despite signing as the stranger, Adrian Gamble. The man he once was no longer existed.

"There," he said, laying down the pen. "What's next?"

Carlson stood. "As I said, all you need is to move right in—to your new home and business. Both are ready."

The man's efficiency impressed Adrian. "You did indeed take care of everything. I'm much obliged."

The lawyer shrugged and reached for a brown overcoat hanging from a hook on the frame of a tall mirror near the door. "If you don't object, I'd like to show you around."

"First I must find a livery."

"Of course. Amos's Stables are right around the corner, and you won't find a better man or better place to keep your animal."

Nodding, Adrian followed his guide. He'd achieved a major goal and wanted to celebrate, but the wariness that had replaced his formerly easygoing nature prevented him from even the slightest lowering of his guard. His life depended on his vigilance.

The stables proved as clean and well tended as any Adrian had ever seen. But the owner? Amos was another matter altogether.

"Where you hail from, son?" asked the large black man in a kind voice.

"Oh, from just about everywhere," Adrian answered, giving the reply that had served him well for a while.

Amos's brown eyes narrowed. "From just about everywhere, you say. An' precisely whereabouts *is* everywhere?"

Canny smarts lay behind the slow, molasses-rich southern words.

"Back East," he answered, hoping he wouldn't have to outright lie.

Amos nodded slowly. "I see. Back East." The livery owner's perusal turned to scrutiny, and Adrian began to chafe under its intensity. Then the older man added, "An' just what brings you to Hartville?"

"Give the man a chance to catch his breath, Amos." Carlson evidently knew the livery owner well. "He's just ridden into town, and from the looks of him and his horse, he's been on the road for a fair spell. This is Adrian Gamble, the mine's new owner."

Still more interest lit the older man's smile. "Mm-hmm. Looks like we'll have us plenty time to get us better acquainted, won't we, Mistah Gamble? I don't figger you'll be travelin' *everywheres* for a spell. Runnin' the Heart of Silver takes a toll on a man's time."

Adrian squared his shoulders. "I'm not afraid of work—never have been. I know I've taken on a large responsibility, but I trust the Lord will make me equal to it."

Again the wise brown eyes narrowed. Adrian felt as though his drawers were flapping open in the brisk Colorado wind. "Glad to see you're a God-fearin' man, Mistah Gamble. Always good to know another brother on the straight an' narrow road to heaven."

Adrian squirmed. He hadn't fooled Amos for a second. And he wouldn't be taking him up on his roundabout invitation to get better acquainted, either. "Pleasure meeting you, Amos, but I must be on my way."

Amos laughed. "Is it now? Well, we'll soon see, son, how much pleasure you do find in Hartville. At least you'll know for the next while where you hail from, now, won't you."

Adrian spun on his heel and headed out the wide entry to the stables. Carlson took several loping steps and caught up with him seconds later.

"I'm sorry about that," he said, gasping. "Amos is incorrigible. He survived the hell on earth of slavery, and he figures he's entitled to say whatever's on his mind. Sometimes he goes a mite far."

"He has a right to speak as he wishes." Adrian slanted a glance at his companion. "And to keep his counsel, too."

Without missing a step, Carlson met his gaze, acknowledging Adrian's meaning. "He certainly does." The lawyer then waved toward the substantial structure they'd reached. "And the General Store's a good place to be mindful of that. Not much that happens or is said here stays within these four walls."

Adrian paused on the steps to the store's porch. "Surely you're not saying I've a gossiping busybody in my employ."

"Heavens, no," Carlson said with contrition. "Phoebe Williams is a hardworking woman, not given to excesses of any sort. And as a pastor's widow, she's the soul of discretion."

Adrian forced his shoulders to relax. "I'm glad to hear that. I can certainly use an efficient and sensible manager at the store."

This time it was the counselor who slanted Adrian a sharp look. "Excellent. The whole town has worried about Mrs. Williams's future. No one knew your intentions for the store, and she depends on her wages."

"I hope no one's thought I'd come to turn folks out on the street. I don't intend to make many changes—if any—to what seems to be a well-managed operation."

"Well," Carlson said, an odd note to the word. "There is something you might want to consider. You've a sizable number of Chinamen working the mine, and the situation might be growing troublesome. You'll have to watch for—"

"Oh! Dear me, Douglas," exclaimed the tiny, gray-garbed dynamo who barreled into the attorney. "I had no idea you were out here. Did I hurt you?"

The woman's question brought a smile to Adrian's lips.

Carlson laughed. "Letty, you're no bigger than a minute. Of course you didn't hurt me. And if you had, what then? Why, I'm sure you'd patch me right quick." He turned to Adrian. "Allow me to introduce our intrepid physician, Dr. Letitia Morgan."

Adrian arched a brow and extended his hand. "A most progressive town, Hartville."

The doctor's chin rose as she took his fingers in a firm clasp. "As they all should be, Mr. Gamble."

Her use of his recently acquired name gave him pause.

She noticed. "I'm afraid your fame precedes you, sir." At his alarm, she chuckled and waved. "Nothing to worry about, though. It's merely a matter of small town reality. Everyone knows most everyone here. You see, before she left, Mrs. Hart gave us enough particulars regarding the sale of her late husband's holdings to satisfy the rampant curiosity, and your name was one of those particulars."

"I see." As his heart beat wildly, Adrian renewed his determination to guard his privacy.

With a bob of her head, the doctor smiled, patted Carlson's hand in a friendly way, and started down the boardwalk in the direction from which he and the lawyer had just come.

She paused and said over her shoulder. "I'll run along now. But do keep in mind, Mr. Gamble, that my clinic is on Willow Street, just a few houses down from the church—in case you're in need of my services, of course."

"Of course," he echoed, wondering if the good doctor was someone of concern.

"Letty is the most generous and caring woman in town," Carlson said, holding the store's door open for Adrian. "Besides my dear wife, you understand."

Adrian grinned. "Ever given thought to politics, counselor?"

The lawyer laughed as they stepped inside. "Call me Douglas, and no. I just favor living longer. My Randy happens to be Letty's closest crony, and I have a healthy respect for those two. Alone they're impressive, but together they're nothing short of formidable."

"Perhaps there's a good reason for a man to remain a bachelor," Adrian commented, blinking at the contrast in lighting.

Carlson shook his head. "Life would be too dull if I had to live it alone. Randy and our new little Emma Letitia—after the good doctor, you see—are God's greatest gifts to me."

Pain stabbed Adrian in the deepest part of his heart. He'd said farewell to his family forever. He'd had to do so to ensure their safety. The hole left by the knowledge that he'd never again see Mother, his brother Steven, sweet Priscilla, the youngest of the three, and Aunt Sally was a deep, ever-aching wound.

"Hello, Douglas," a woman said, her voice melodic and sweet.

"Good afternoon, Phoebe," the attorney responded. "I've someone here I'm sure you're anxious to meet. This is Adrian Gamble, your new employer."

Although Adrian's eyes hadn't yet adjusted to the darkness, he didn't need perfect vision to recognize fear. The woman's sharply indrawn breath said it all.

As the darkness around him cleared, brightened by a gas lamp, Adrian made out a feminine form next to a long counter. Tall and well proportioned, Phoebe Williams seemed stunned by his presence in the store. He'd never thought himself fright inducing, but one never knew when one might strike another as such.

"I'm pleased to meet you," he said in his kindest voice. He remembered Carlson's concern for the widow's livelihood. "I've heard excellent things about your skills. I hope you'll do me the honor of continuing in my employ."

Evidently, he'd said the right thing. The tight line of shoulder and neck eased just enough to let her nod. "I'd be much obliged, Mr. Gamble. I hope everything is to your approval, but if it's not, please let me know, and I'll take care of those changes you wish to make."

To his delight, his eyes finally cooperated. Although pale, Phoebe Williams looked quite unlike what he'd expected. From Carlson's description, he'd thought the preacher's widow would be much more timeworn and gray. Instead, Mrs. Williams looked scarcely older than twenty, with soft blue eyes and honey-colored hair pulled up into a soft knot on her crown. Her simple cotton blouse buttoned up to her throat, and a small cameo brooch held it closed. Her hands, clasped at her waist, looked more like those of a musician than those of a shopkeeper. Although not beautiful in the classical sense, Phoebe Williams was attractive and undoubtedly the most feminine creature Adrian had ever seen.

He was intrigued.

Realizing Carlson and Mrs. Williams stood awaiting his response, he went on to say, "I'm not one to make hasty or unwise changes, so I won't disrupt what works. The documents I've seen say the store is in good working order. I'm certain its success is in no small measure due to your excellent influence."

He turned to Adrian. "Lead the way to the house, counselor. I'm afraid the road has got the best of me. I'm looking forward to washing away the road dust and crawling into a bed."

Carlson nodded and headed for the door. In Adrian's last glimpse of Phoebe, he noted the heightened peach tint in her cheeks. "I look forward to working closely with you here at the store, Mrs. Williams."

Something he said must have flustered her, because she blushed a deeper shade of apricot and nodded, her knuckles whitening as she tightened her clasped hands. Then she smiled, and Adrian felt as though the sun had just come over the eastern horizon for the second time that day. Her smile made him think beauty inconsequential as it illuminated her features from within, bringing them a certain softness and a warmth that reached him where he'd been too cold for a long time.

She glowed with something he lacked, something his words had just given her.

Hope.

It glowed from the lovely widow's face, and Adrian knew he had to watch himself. Phoebe held the future in her graceful hands, while his future had died on a train nearly a year ago. Without his identity and with killers on his trail, he had no hope, nothing to offer, no future in sight. He certainly had nothing for the too-appealing Phoebe Williams, nor even for himself.

His life came to an end on the day he killed another man.